P9-AGI-145

Reason to Breathe

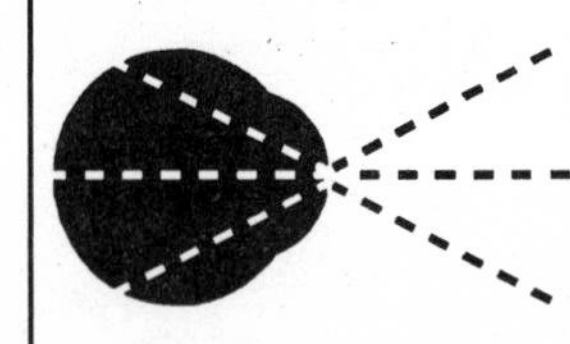

This Large Print Book carries the Seal of Approval of N.A.V.H.

A CHANDLER SISTERS NOVEL

REASON TO BREATHE

DEBORAH RANEY

THORNDIKE PRESS
A part of Gale, a Cengage Company

Farmington Hills, Mich • San Francisco • New York • Waterville, Maine
Meriden, Conn • Mason, Ohio • Chicago

Thorndike Press, a part of Gale, a Cengage Company.

Thorndike Press® Large Print Christian Fiction.
The text of this Large Print edition is unabridged.
Other aspects of the book may vary from the original edition.
Set in 16 pt. Plantin.

LIBRARY OF CONGRESS CIP DATA ON FILE.
CATALOGUING IN PUBLICATION FOR THIS BOOK
IS AVAILABLE FROM THE LIBRARY OF CONGRESS

ISBN-13: 978-1-4328-6160-5 (hardcover)

Published in 2019 by arrangement with Gilead Publishing

Printed in the United States of America
1 2 3 4 5 6 7 23 22 21 20 19

To my sweet sisters,
who were my first friends
and remain my very dearest friends.

Above all, love each other deeply, because love covers over a multitude of sins. Offer hospitality to one another without grumbling. Each of you should use whatever gift you have received to serve others, as faithful stewards of God's grace in its various forms. If anyone speaks, they should do so as one who speaks the very words of God. If anyone serves, they should do so with the strength God provides, so that in all things God may be praised through Jesus Christ. To him be the glory and the power for ever and ever. Amen.

1 Peter 4:8–11 NIV

Chapter 1

January

A beam of late-afternoon sun canted through the mullioned windows of the breakfast room in her parents' house — *Dad's* house now — casting a checkered shadow across the tile. Phylicia Chandler picked up the last addressed envelope from a stack that'd been nearly a foot high when she and her sisters started writing thank-you notes yesterday afternoon. She pushed up the sleeves of her sweater and licked the flap of a pale pink envelope, then pressed the seal with the palm of her hand and passed it to her youngest sister. Britt put the envelope in the "finished" box awaiting a trip to the post office.

"Well, that's done." *Finally.* She hated that it had taken them two months to get these thank-you notes written and mailed. But Dad had been uncharacteristically indecisive, and they were all scrambling to catch up with work and everything else in their lives.

She looked past her sisters into the living room where the Christmas tree still sat — at the end of January — its white lights twinkling even now, thanks to the automatic timer. Dad wouldn't have put up a tree at all if she and her sisters hadn't insisted. But now Phee regretted pushing him, and the tree seemed to mock them, a garish reminder of their first Christmas without Mom.

It wasn't like Dad to leave things undone. Turner Chandler had always prided himself on being a get-'er-done kind of guy, even if it meant delegating. But Dad hadn't been himself for a long time.

Phee blew out a weary sigh.

Britt gave her a questioning look. "You okay, Phee?"

Her "baby" sister had asked her that at least twice in the space of an hour, and Phylicia still wasn't sure of the answer. She took a long swig from her iced-tea glass, the last unbroken piece from a set that had been a wedding gift to their parents more than thirty years ago. "I'm fine. Just . . . tired." Her words came out muddled, her tongue thick with the residue of envelope glue.

"So, what do you guys think we should do

with the memorial money?" Britt swiveled and put her stockinged feet on the seat of the chair beside her. "Dad said something about planting trees at the Langhorne City Park, but last time I checked they were taking trees *out* of that park."

"Not to mention we have over four thousand dollars." Joanna frowned and placed a hand on the stack of sympathy cards they'd been sorting through for two days now. "That's a lot of trees."

"Do we have to decide right now?" Britt asked. "I think Dad should be in on the decision."

"Britt, if we were waiting on Dad, these thank-you notes still wouldn't be written." Phee went to the other side of the kitchen island and placed the kettle on the burner. A swift *click-click-click* of the gas, and the burner flickered to life. She didn't even like hot tea, but it had become a habit, making tea for her parents each evening. Now, the kitchen felt foreign without Mom in it — despite the fact that Mom hadn't set foot in this room since last October, too weak by then to get out of bed. "I'm wiped out."

Joanna gave her a wan smile. "It'll be okay, sis. We're all weary. Things will look better tomorrow."

Would they? Joanna, although she was

three years younger than Phylicia, had always played the mother hen, and even more so after Mom became ill. The eternal optimist, Joanna had told them the same thing that night two months ago when their mother had taken her last breath after three long years of battling pancreatic cancer.

Phee centered the pot on the burner. While she appreciated Joanna's outlook, and while she *had* felt relief knowing that Mom's struggle was over, that she was finally free from the agonizing pain that had marked her final weeks on earth, Phee still couldn't truthfully say things were better.

Not with Dad off in Florida as of two days ago, leaving the three of them to figure out what the next chapter of their lives would look like. They'd all put their lives on hold to usher Mom into heaven. And Phee had expected they'd spend the next few months dealing with the aftermath of Mom's illness. And with helping their father grieve. Helping Dad figure out what was next for him.

But it was starting to look as if he already knew what was next — as if he were the only one of them who *did* know what was next. Not that he'd shared that information with them. Dad had been vague about . . . well, *everything.* About why he had to go out of town and what, exactly, he was doing in Orlando. And about when he would return.

She glanced up at the array of empty vases on the counter that, until she'd taken it upon herself to clean them out yesterday, had held funeral flowers. So many arrangements had been sent to the house after Mom's passing that they'd overwhelmed the air with their cloying scent. One bright turquoise-colored vase caught her eye. Ironically, Phee had chosen the pretty vase herself and arranged the flowers at her job at Langhorne Blooms. None of the other hospice workers had sent flowers, and Phee had thought it a bit too . . . *personal* at the time. Especially the way the young nurse, Karleen Tramberly, had signed the card with "My heart and soul go out to you." *Soul?* That seemed a little over the top. But then, Phee had been surprised by how overly sensitive she'd become since losing Mom.

Still, Phee couldn't shake the suspicion that *she* was with Dad. A woman she and her sisters had met only a handful of times during those last weeks, but who'd seemed on awfully close terms with Dad. Karleen actually lived in Orlando but was originally from Cape Girardeau and was filling in for the director of the hospice organization in Cape. Karleen had been nothing but helpful and warm, even attending Mom's funeral service, which had surprised Phee.

And maybe that was all the woman was to Dad — a kind nurse who'd taken good care of his beloved wife. But looking back, something had struck Phee as . . . *off* from the very beginning. She hadn't dared voice her concerns to her sisters yet. And she wouldn't. Not unless there turned out to be something to her hunch.

But hospice nurse or not, *something* was going on with Dad. And it wasn't good. Not only had he met with Karleen Tramberly twice — that she knew of — in the two months since the funeral, but what man left his daughters to tie up all the loose ends so soon after his beloved wife's funeral?

She and her sisters had written every last thank-you note, yet he'd left them hanging about what to do with the memorial money, and as far as she knew, he'd done nothing about ordering Mom's headstone. Dad had dropped the ball big-time.

On Thursday, Phee had taken yet another day off from the flower shop to drive Dad to St. Louis to catch a flight to Orlando. With so many things still undone. And even though he'd said the trip was for business, Dad had seemed almost . . . *excited* to leave town. The construction company he contracted for had sent him to Florida a few times over the years, so maybe the trip was legit. But according to Dad's own complaints, with all the work he'd missed while Mom was dying, he was so far behind on projects here in Missouri that he had no business leaving town.

Joanna scraped her chair back on the Italian tile and carried her coffee cup and Phee's iced-tea glass to the sink. "No, we don't have to decide right now."

"About what?" Britt looked confused.

"The memorial," Phee said. "Isn't that what we were talking about? Dad is leaving it up to us what to do with the money."

"We can talk more tomorrow." Joanna tamped down an already neat stack of thank-you notes. "Are you guys staying here again tonight?"

"Like I have a choice," Britt said. "Please don't leave me here alone, you guys."

After Dad flew out on Thursday, the three of them had spent the last two nights here in Langhorne, in the house where they'd grown up, in the bedroom they'd shared, with its three twin beds lined up like with Goldilocks's three bears.

Britt had left college in the middle of the semester and moved home to Langhorne when Mom could no longer take care of the house. And although Phee and Joanna had apartments in Cape Girardeau, more often than not the past few months, they'd all spent their nights here too. Phee had thought she'd find it comforting to be here with her sisters after the funeral, but instead — probably because Dad *wasn't* here — the house had just seemed sad . . . and a little creepy.

Phee ran a hand through the tangles in her hair — hair that was a shade darker than its usual tawny brown because it was in desperate need of shampooing. "I really need to go home tonight. My plants haven't been watered in eons and I . . . I just have stuff I need to do."

Joanna riffled the stack of thank-you notes. "You want to come home with me, Britt? I really need to go back to my apartment too. And I think Ginger is out of town this weekend. You can have her bed."

Joanna's suggestion made Phee feel guilty she hadn't offered first. Unlike Joanna, Phee didn't have a roommate to inconvenience.

"I guess I will." Britt shrugged, moving the box of stamped envelopes off the table. "I'm sure not staying here by myself."

"You're not scared, are you?" Phee did not want Britt moving in with her. Her studio apartment was a one-woman setup, and Britt wasn't exactly the easiest houseguest to entertain. At least not for an introvert like Phee.

"Not scared," her sister said. "Just not crazy about being here alone right now."

"I don't blame you. This house seems a lot bigger without . . . them." Joanna looked around the room as if seeing it for the first time. "I still do *not* get why Dad had to go to Florida so soon after —"

Phee's phone trilled Dad's ringtone. "Speak of the devil . . ." She touched Accept. "Hey, Dad. How's it going?"

"It's going. How about there? Everything all right?" His voice didn't reveal his mood the way it usually did.

"I guess. We just finished the thank-you notes." She hoped he felt at least a little guilt for leaving the job to them.

"So, the girls are there?"

"Right here. Let me put you on speakerphone." She punched the speaker icon and laid the phone on the edge of the table.

"Hi, Dad," Joanna said.

"Hi, Daddy," Britt chimed, coming to huddle around the phone with them.

"Hey, girlies. I was hoping I'd catch you all together."

Melvin, Mom's fat black-and-white tuxedo cat, chose that moment to hop up on the table and purr into the phone.

The sisters laughed, and Melvin put his tail in the air and performed a pirouette on the polished stage, eating up their attention.

"Melvin! You know you're not supposed to be on the table." Phee lifted the sixteen-pound cat and returned him to the floor.

"How's ol' Melvin doing?" Dad's voice filled the room.

"He's good. I think he misses you." Phee stroked the cat with her stockinged foot.

"When are you coming back?" Britt pouted.

"Yeah, Dad. I'm getting a drama queen for a roommate until you get back, so any speed at all would be appreciated." Joanna gave Britt the stink-eye.

"Britt," Dad scolded. "Don't tell me you're still scared to stay there by yourself."

"Okay, I won't tell you." Britt elbowed Joanna, jockeying for a spot closer to the phone. "Don't worry . . . I'll come by every day to feed Melvin. He'll be well taken care of."

Dad laughed. "That ol' boy could probably afford to miss a few days of kibble."

"When *are* you coming back, Dad?" Phee sensed he was dodging their question.

After an overlong pause, Dad cleared his throat. "You, um . . . you girls might want to sit down."

The three of them exchanged curious looks.

"We *are* sitting down. What's going on, Dad?" Phee tried to keep her voice upbeat, but she braced her elbows on the table.

"Actually, I'm going to be staying here in Florida —"

"Staying? How much longer, Daddy?" Britt had put on that infernal smile she always wore when she talked to her "daddy."

This time the silence on Dad's end went on so long, Phee thought they'd lost the connection. But finally, he spoke. "Girls, I'm going to stay . . . a while. Indefinitely actually. I've taken an apartment here."

"Taken? You mean like *rented*?" Phee scooted her chair closer to the table, as if by accosting the phone, she could change his mind. "Dad? What is going on?"

"I can't explain everything right now." His voice sounded odd. "I'm still fleshing out some details. You girls don't know this, but . . . I've been working on a deal down here for a while."

"A deal? What is the nature of this deal exactly?" Joanna kicked into lawyer mode. She worked as an administrative assistant for an attorney in town, but she'd actually just started law school in Columbia when

Mom was diagnosed. Like Britt, Jo had quit school and moved back to Cape at the end of her first semester. Her career might have been temporarily derailed, but that didn't stop her from speaking like a full-blown attorney.

"I'm going to be putting the house on the market."

Dad's announcement brought them all to their feet. "What?"

"This house? *Our* house?" Britt's voice went squeaky. "When were you going to tell me this? What am *I* supposed to do?"

"Now, Britt, calm down. All of you just take a breath and let me explain."

Again, the three exchanged looks, but this time it was worry Phee saw reflected in her sisters' blue eyes. Eyes that matched her own. Like Mom's. Phee went to the sink, retrieved her iced-tea glass, and took a sip. The liquid was lukewarm and diluted.

"First of all, I want you girls to know that you'll be taken care of. The house is paid off, so once it's sold — even after the hospital and funeral expenses — we'll — *I'll* be fine. Mom barely touched her inheritance from Grandma Clayton, and she wanted you girls to have it. You'll each have a share deposited in the bank. It should be there by the middle of February, if not before. Britt, it'll be enough for you to rent a nice apartment until you find a job — unless one of your sisters wants a roommate."

Joanna shot Phee a scowl that said, *Over my dead body.* Phee returned the look. They loved their baby sister, but Britt was high maintenance and a little spoiled — a truth even Britt herself didn't dispute, demonstrated by the fact that two months after Mom's death, she still hadn't started looking for a job. Yes, she kept house and cooked for Dad . . . well, if Dad sold the house, Britt wouldn't have even that excuse any longer.

"What about your house, Dad?" Phee picked up the phone and spoke directly into it, as if that might change his mind. "Why would you sell this house? What will you do when you come back?"

He cleared his throat loudly. "You girls *are* sitting down?"

They exchanged glances again, and Britt slid back into her chair.

"Dad? What's this all about? When *are* you coming back?" Phee was starting to get a bad feeling about this. She glanced over to the hutch where a framed photograph of Mom and Dad perched — a picture from happier days, before cancer devastated all their lives.

Dad's sigh filled the room. "I'm not sure I'll *be* coming back, girls. Not to stay. And even if I did, I don't want to rattle around in that house. There are too many memories there. Too much history."

"Exactly. *Our* history." Joanna put her hands on her hips, looking defiant. Except for the tears brimming in her eyes.

"Can you all hear me?"

Something about Dad's tone caused Phee to grab her sisters' hands. She and Joanna took their seats again, straining toward the phone.

"What is going on?" Phee asked again.

"If you girls want to use Mom's inheritance money to buy the house together, there would be enough that your payment — divided by three — would be as cheap as any apartment. And I'd cut you a nice deal." His laughter sounded forced.

"That's not even funny, Dad." Phee's voice came out in a squeak.

He ignored her and continued. "Seriously though, I hope you'll think that through carefully. Owning the house together could be a bit of a mess once you all start getting married. And you know the house is old. It has some issues that might be pretty pricey to fix down the road. I don't think it would be the wisest plan to try to keep the house.

But I'll pay you girls to get it ready to list. Quinn can handle the details."

Quinn Mitchell had worked for their dad for as long as Phee could remember. He was a nice man, and she trusted him. But that didn't mean she liked Dad's plan any better than she had five minutes ago.

"Are you still there?" Dad raised his voice as if they had a bad connection. "Quinn should be getting in touch with you in a day or two, Phee, and he can walk you girls through everything."

"He already knows about you selling?" The hurt in Joanna's voice was thick.

Phee suspected it was because Dad had made Phee — the eldest daughter — the contact person for Quinn instead of *law student* Joanna.

"How long have you known you were going to sell out from under us?" Britt asked.

Phee shared her sisters' irritation — shock, really. And yet she couldn't help but be a little relieved that the house was all it was. Still, she had a feeling there was something Dad wasn't telling them. In all the times he'd traveled to Florida for work, he'd never once mentioned relocating there. Certainly not since Mom had gotten sick.

"You girls take whatever you want from the house . . . except I'm having my desk and the den furniture shipped down here, and I'd like the Sandzen paintings. You girls will get them when I'm gone, of course, but I'd like to have them in the new place."

"Place?" Britt's voice turned breathy. "You already have a *place* there?"

"I told you I've rented an apartment."

"How long have you been planning this, Dad? And why are we just now finding out about it?" Joanna spoke in a whisper, but she threw a look at Britt and Phee that said she was wondering if she was the last to know.

But they shook their heads and shrugged, equally clueless. It was so unlike Dad to up and do something like this without a word to them.

Phee reached for her glass and took a sip of watered-down tea before speaking woodenly into the phone. "Can't you at least come home long enough to help with the house? What . . . what's going on in Florida that's keeping you there?"

The three of them sat like statues, bent over the phone, waiting for him to reply.

After what seemed like an eternity, Dad finally spoke. "I really didn't intend on you finding out this way. I . . . I was going to break the news in person next time I came back, but I suppose this is as good a time as any." He sucked in a breath that was audible over the miles. "I'm getting married, girls."

The glass — Mom and Dad's last wedding glass — slipped from Phee's grip and shattered on the tile floor.

Chapter 2

Phee ran to take the kettle off the burner. But she'd lost her appetite for tea.

"Married? Very funny, Daddy." Britt's voice trembled.

"It's not a joke, sweetie. I —"

"Dad? Who?" Joanna's voice trembled.

Phee put a hand on Jo's back. It was damp with perspiration — not at all like the cool, calm Joanna who usually had her world and everyone else's organized. "It's okay, sis . . ."

But it *wasn't* okay. It wasn't okay at all. How had their father had time to fall in love? *Unless it had happened while Mom was still living.* The thought made her blood run cold.

Phee could understand that Dad had already grieved losing Mom. They'd run out of treatment options the first year after Mom's diagnosis, and they'd all had a full two years of knowing they were losing her. The three sisters had talked about the stages of grief until they were sick of the topic. But *they'd* lost their mother, not their life partner. Not their lover and soul mate. Was Dad so desperate not to be alone that he would grab onto the first woman he met? Before Mom was barely cold in her grave?

But that was just it. It had to have started before Mom died. And that nurse . . . she'd always been just a little too attentive to Dad. Bordering on flirtatious, yet in a way that could have been simply part of her playful nature.

"*Who* are you marrying?" Britt moaned and turned to her sisters. "How did he even have time to *meet* someone? This is insane!" She seemed unaware of the phone — set to Speaker — that they were huddled around.

Phee nodded, but her momentary relief was gone. She knew *who.*

"Wait . . . let him answer." Jo jumped to Dad's defense. "Before you convict him."

Britt, despite always having been somewhat of a daddy's girl, glared at her sister. But she kept silent.

"Is everybody still there?" Dad's voice had lost some of its bravado.

"We're here, Dad." Phee moved the phone two inches to the left on the table, as if that might influence the answer he would give.

"Well, like I said, I'm getting married. We

haven't set a date or anything, but . . ." He cleared his throat. "I know this must come as a shock, and I don't expect you girls to understand. But I want you to know it's all going to work out. Everything will be fine and —"

"It's *not* fine! How can you even say that?" Britt covered her face with her hands, her shoulders shaking.

Joanna looked stunned. "Are you going to tell us who it is, Dad? Is it someone we know?"

And how did you get to know her? Phee wondered. Dad had been at Mom's bedside practically every minute the last six months of her life. If he'd been a murder suspect, he would have had an alibi with any one of them for that period of time. He couldn't have been running around. He just couldn't.

"Actually, you've all met her. It's Karleen, from the —"

"Karleen?" Phee clenched her fists, and her jaw tensed. "Karleen, as in the hospice nurse?" She wasn't sure why she was pretending to be surprised. It was a good thing Dad hadn't waited to tell them in person, because right now she wanted to strangle him.

"Hospice nurse?" Realization lit Joanna's pale-blue eyes. "Are you *kidding* me? She's *my* age!"

"No, she's not, Jo. She's . . ." Dad hesitated. "She's older. Older than Phee."

"What, *thirty*?" Phee hated the sarcasm in her voice, but she could not believe they were even having this conversation.

"Listen, girls . . . I'm going to hang up now. I'll explain everything. I'll answer any questions you have, but I can see you need some time to let this sink in."

"This will *never* sink in," Phee said between gritted teeth. "Never."

She jabbed at the phone until the End button appeared, then clicked off before their father could hang up on them.

She slumped into a chair at the table. Her sisters did the same.

"Oh my gosh, you guys. What just happened?" Britt's eyes glazed over. "Did you know about this?" She looked accusingly at Phee.

"I didn't *know.* But I was starting to be suspicious." Phee shrugged. "You guys know who Karleen is, right?"

Britt nodded, still looking dazed. "Of course I know. That blond nurse that came on duty toward the end. She was . . . really nice. At least I thought so. She was Mom's favorite. But . . . she's *really* young."

"Exactly."

Joanna raised her hands in a defensive mode. "Guys, Dad's fifty-two. It's not like he's an old geezer."

"Dad said she's older than me. Ha, I bet she's all of thirty-three."

"Phee, you don't know that," Britt said.

"And it's barely been two months since Mom . . . Do you think they were having . . . an *affair*? Right under Mom's nose?" Phee's voice scaled the octave.

Britt shook her head. "I don't know how else it could have escalated to . . . *marriage* —"

"Hang on . . . let's give him the benefit of the doubt." Joanna straightened in her chair. "This doesn't sound like Dad. Let's not accuse him before we know all the facts. He has a right to be innocent until proven guilty."

Phee gave a little growl. "Don't go all Judge Judy on us, Jo. What else could it be? He sure in blazes didn't have time to fall in love with her in the two months *since* Mom died. The months he was supposedly devastated at losing her."

The more she thought about it, the more her blood boiled. But it was more than anger. Her dad was her hero. Always had been. It was maybe one of the reasons she'd never dated anyone for more than a few months. Because Dad had always been her measuring stick. And nobody ever measured up. *Oh, how the mighty have fallen.*

She remembered how the hospice nurse — Karleen — had touched Dad's sleeve at the memorial service. It had seemed innocent enough, and yet, even that day, a warning light had flickered. Now, that light was flashing neon red.

"There has to be an explanation." Britt shook her head, not looking convinced. "Something we don't know about or —"

"So what are we supposed to do now?" Phee shoved her chair back and paced the length of the breakfast room.

"Dad said he was sending that guy from the office" — Britt's brow knit — "Quinn? . . . to talk about getting the house on the market. How can he do that without even talking to us? Without even asking what *we* want to do. Where am *I* supposed to live?"

"Well, it *is* his house," Joanna conceded. "I guess he has the right to sell it if he wants to. But he could have at least asked us what we thought." She reached to put a hand over Britt's. "And don't worry, honey, we won't let you be homeless."

Joanna shot Phee a look over Britt's head. They'd been sisters long enough they could almost read each other's minds, and this look said, *She is not staying at* my *apartment.*

"Dad said Mom left her inheritance from Grandma to us." Britt's eyes welled with tears.

"I wonder how much it is." Phee cringed inwardly. Now that the words were out, it seemed like a tacky thing to say. But she truly was thinking of Britt. This whole turn of events was a shock to all of them, but Britt was the one whose life would be most turned upside down, especially if Dad sold the house. "Dad said it'd be enough for you to get an apartment, Britt." A wave of guilt swept over her. "But you can stay with me until you find a place."

Their "baby" sister had never been out on her own. She'd lived at home while she worked for a couple of years to save money for college, and then after less than a year in the dorms, she'd moved back home to help their father with Mom and the house. They had all put their lives on hold to help with Mom, but Britt had borne the brunt of it.

"It's okay, Phee." Joanna gave her a long-suffering look. "My place is bigger than yours, and besides, most of her stuff is already there."

"I don't have that much stuff." Britt frowned. "So sorry to be such a burden on everybody."

Phee and Joanna chose to ignore her sarcastic appeal for sympathy, and Joanna looked thoughtful. "I don't know how much is in Mom's account, but remember when the Lamberts's house came up for sale? I heard Mom tell Dad that she was tempted to buy it."

"She surely wasn't serious. She loved this house."

"No, I don't think she was serious. I think Mom just meant she *could* have bought it, and that little house was selling for almost two hundred grand at the time."

"Wow. You really think Grandma left her that much?" Britt's pout disappeared, replaced by raised eyebrows. "How come she never spent any of it?"

"She spent a little. Remember?" Phee said. "That's how she redid the sitting room and collected the paintings."

"Back when Sandzen's stuff was reasonable," Joanna added. "You were probably too little to remember, Britt."

Phee must have been about twelve when Mom had received the inheritance from her mother's estate. She vaguely remembered that Mom and Dad had argued over how she would spend the money. They rarely argued. Apparently, Mom got her way, for soon after, the rarely used sitting room off the kitchen had been painted and the carpet pulled up. Over the years, the walls gradually filled with an eclectic gallery of paintings that Mom picked up whenever she traveled with Dad.

The two Sandzen originals had actually been an estate sale purchase, bought in Cape Girardeau. Mom paid several hundred dollars for the two small pieces, and the purchase had been a bone of contention between their parents — until the paintings appraised for over five thousand dollars a few years later.

Mom had gloated for the rest of her life about her great eye, and Dad good-naturedly let her. Phee had always liked the paintings — the whole gallery. And the room's decor had stood the test of time with its hardwood floors, grayed teal walls, and a worn-to-perfection Persian carpet. Dad rarely spent time in the room, and when they were younger, the girls had been forbidden to play there unless they were reading or listening to music with Mom. Maybe that was why Phee loved the room so much. She knew it was where she'd come by her love of classical music. She sometimes dreamed of recreating this room in her own home someday. It was still the place in this house where she felt closest to her mother.

Yes, Dad had been under tremendous pressure with Mom having been sick for so long. But they'd all supported him . . . practically moved in with him and Mom. Britt had officially done just that. They'd all pitched in, cooking and cleaning, shopping and nursing. Panic clawed at Phee's throat. They'd made things as easy as possible for Dad. And she thought he'd handled it well. But this?

This *was* insane.

CHAPTER 3

Quinn Mitchell hung up the phone and raked a hand through his hair. He wasn't sure what was up with Turner Chandler, but it struck him as very odd that the man who'd lost his beloved wife mere weeks ago had suddenly up and moved to Florida. Especially when all three of his daughters still lived here in Langhorne. This was the third time his boss had called him in as many days, each call about Turner's daughters. This was *not* part of his job description. And besides, Turner knew Quinn was putting every extra hour into finishing his own house. He didn't have time to be worrying about his boss's house. Or the man's daughters.

He buzzed the office assistant he and Turner shared at the construction company — or at least *had* shared before his boss's transfer to Florida. Though he often referred to Turner as his boss, it wasn't what people envisioned when they heard the title. Technically Turner *was* his supervisor, but the two of them had worked together so long — and so well — that the man felt more like a friend. At least until he'd started taking advantage of Quinn's generosity.

Megan appeared in his doorway a split second after her perfume announced her approach.

"Hi, Meg. Do you have phone numbers for Mr. Chandler's daughters? He said you would."

"Sure. Shall I email them to you?"

"Actually, would you call and set up a meeting, please?"

"With all three of them? Is everything okay? I heard a rumor Mr. Chandler was staying in Florida . . ." She waited, obviously hoping for all the juicy details.

"I'm not sure how long he'll be there." That, at least, was true. "Everything is fine. And on second thought, yes, just email me Phylicia's phone number." He wouldn't have filled Meg in even if he *knew* all the juicy details. Megan Spidle was good at her job, but if she had a character flaw, it lay in the arena of nosiness and indiscretion. And for now at least, this issue would require a great deal of discretion.

She left the room, and a few minutes later

the phone number appeared in his inbox. He picked up the office phone. *May as well get this over with.* Which was an odd thought for a man who, not that many years ago, had jumped at any excuse to be wherever Phylicia Chandler was.

Phylicia wasn't even the prettiest of the three blue-eyed, tawny-haired sisters. The middle daughter, Joanna, probably claimed that distinction. But it was Phylicia who always drew his eye, and who could make him smile without even seeming to try. She could drop by the office for five minutes to see her dad, and the rest of Quinn's day was somehow better.

If circumstances had been different, he would have asked her out long ago. But given that the girl was his boss's daughter — but more importantly, his *friend's* daughter — he wasn't about to go there. No doubt the "off limits" tag he'd bestowed upon her had more to do with the fact that she'd still been in high school when he first came to work under Turner at Langhorne Construction.

And then there was the age difference. He'd practically watched Phylicia grow up, and she'd only become more attractive and interesting to him with every year. But their age difference didn't seem as stark as it had back when she was sixteen and he was twenty-eight.

Of course, she had been out of college by the time he and Heather started dating, and Phylicia kind of fell off his radar.

Heather was history now. And Quinn could clearly see that she'd been all wrong for him, but that didn't make what had happened hurt any less. He'd wasted too much time coming to terms with it. And he considered it a victory of sorts that he could actually feel glad for Heather, who was living her dream now, married to a miracle man, with an infant daughter and a big new house in Austin, Texas.

And now that Phylicia was — if memory and math served correctly — probably close to thirty, it didn't seem so absurd to think of her the same way he had BH: *Before Heather.* Still, Phylicia's age didn't change the fact that he was twelve years older than she was, and it sure didn't change the fact that she was his boss's daughter. Quinn liked his job and wasn't looking to leave Langhorne anytime soon.

Of course, if Turner ended up staying in Florida, he would no longer be Quinn's supervisor. Turner had never said he was transferring for good, but Langhorne Construction's interests in Florida were expanding, so it made sense he could have a permanent position there if he wanted it.

Quinn frowned. If Turner relocated permanently to Florida, Quinn might never have a good excuse to see Phylicia again. A forty-two-year-old man shouldn't need an excuse to call and ask a woman for a date, but he was more than a little gun-shy after everything that had happened with Heather.

He dialed the number from Meg's email, not sure if it was a work phone or her cell. Last he'd known, Phylicia worked for Langhorne Blooms, the flower shop downtown. But according to Turner, all three of his daughters had taken some time off to help during their mom's last days, and he didn't know if she'd gone back to work or not.

She answered on the second ring. "Hello, this is Phylicia."

"Hi there. Phylicia? . . . This is Quinn Mitchell. I hope I'm not catching you at a bad time."

"No. Not really." She sounded a little cool. Not the friendly girl he remembered from a few years ago.

"Did your dad mention that I'd be calling?"

"He did."

He waited for more but didn't get it. And the silence grew awkward. "I don't know if you and your sisters have had a chance to visit about everything yet, but I assume your dad told you he asked me to help out with the sale of the house?" Quinn became aware of an irritating tapping noise. Then realized *he* was the culprit. He placed his pencil back on the desk.

"Yes, he mentioned it when he called on Saturday." A sigh filled the connection. "Can I ask you something?"

"Sure." He braced himself.

"I know you and my dad talk a lot. Or at least you used to. Do you know how long Dad has been . . . *seeing* this Karleen?"

Whoa. Turner was seeing someone? He hadn't seen that coming. "I . . . don't know who that is. Did I miss something?"

"I assume Dad told you he's getting married."

Quinn squinted at the phone. Surely he'd misheard her. "Married? No. He didn't say anything about that. Is . . . that what he told you?"

"Yes. Karleen was one of my mom's hospice nurses."

"I think maybe your dad introduced me to a hospice nurse at the . . . at your mom's funeral. But I didn't know she was anyone . . . special." He cringed at his poor choice of words. Besides, that couldn't have been her. The woman he'd met was closer to his own age.

"Well, apparently she *was* . . . special."

Turner had been understandably scarce at work, staying home the last few weeks before Myra's death. Then he'd gone to Florida to work on a project with their Orlando affiliate. As far as Quinn was aware, there was no other reason for his boss's transfer. But then he and Turner hadn't talked as often, or as personally, since Myra's death. Quinn had chalked it up to grief. But now he wondered.

He struggled to process the news. It had to have happened practically overnight. But he had a hard time believing it had happened before Myra died. Turner was not the kind of man who would cheat on his wife, no matter the circumstances. The man had never had anything but praise for his wife, and he'd been devastated when Myra was first diagnosed with cancer. Quinn could understand why. Except for his own mother, he'd never known a more selfless and charming woman.

Myra Chandler had taken Quinn under her wing that first year he couldn't go home to Asheville for Thanksgiving, insisting he join the Chandler family at their holiday table. He'd loved Myra like a favorite aunt ever since, and though he doubted anyone else would understand why — he wasn't sure he fully understood himself — he'd taken her death hard.

Phylicia cleared her throat politely on the other end of the line, and he realized she was waiting for a response.

"I'm sorry . . . I truly didn't know anything about this. Except for meeting her at the funeral . . . assuming that was her. Did your dad say *when* he's getting married?"

"No, but even if it's next year, that doesn't change the fact that he got engaged two months after Mom passed away."

"I didn't know." He grasped for something that might comfort her, but it was an effort when his own suspicions began to seep in. "Phylicia, your dad never spoke to me about anyone but your mom. And that was always in glowing terms. Right up to the end. I'm sure you know this, but your dad loved your mom very much." Every word was the truth as far as he knew, but how hollow those words would ring if he was defending a guilty man.

She stuttered, started to say something, then breathed out a sigh that tugged at his heart. Turner getting married. He still couldn't fathom it. Couldn't picture his boss with anyone but Myra. If this was hard for *him,* how must Turner's daughters feel? It was difficult enough that they'd lost their mother, but they must feel as if they were losing their dad now too.

And now the man had left Quinn with the task of helping the sisters sell the home they'd grown up in? It was a dirty trick. Until this moment, hearing the bitterness in Phylicia's voice, it hadn't occurred to him that they might resent *him* for being involved in what must seem to them to be a forced sale.

"I've never questioned that my dad loved Mom. But I'm really struggling with . . . what he's doing now. Two months? What is he thinking?" She seemed to be talking to herself as much as to him.

"I'm sorry, Phylicia. I really am." The words sounded trite. He grappled for something better, but finally just went with honesty. "I wish I could say something to help, but frankly, I'm still trying to digest the news myself."

"Well, don't tell Dad I told you. I don't think he said not to tell anyone, but we were all so shocked, I may not have heard him. I just don't get it." She took a shaky breath.

"No, I don't understand it myself."

"Well, that makes two of us . . . four if you count my sisters."

How he wished he knew the words that would remove the pain from her voice. Thinking about the whole situation now, he had to admit that Turner had seemed different after Myra became ill. Guarded, and a little cynical at times. And while his boss's outspoken faith had never seemed to waver, his joy had. Understandably so.

Quinn had prayed fervently over the years while Myra was battling cancer. He'd prayed boldly for healing, and his prayers had been full of hope till the very end. Because hope had been rewarded in his own brother's fight against cancer — a fight Markus had won in the most miraculous of ways. Even Markus's doctors had called it a miracle. A miracle that — ironic as it seemed now — had planted the first seed in Quinn's journey of faith.

When Myra died, Quinn's faith was more mature, and it hadn't faltered, but he had suffered surprisingly deep . . . *disappointment* with God. Myra's death had dredged up his confusion about so many things. The whole fiasco with Heather. And then losing his own parents. Two funerals barely a year apart. He still questioned why God chose to answer equally fervent prayers so differently. Why had God healed Markus, who didn't even claim to believe in Him, but taken

Myra who'd honored Him with her life — and who had three daughters that still so obviously needed her. And Turner too.

Quinn prayed he would never be in Turner's shoes. It was a selfish prayer — not that he had a wife to lose, but he hoped to one day — and he'd always taken an honesty-is-the-best-policy stance when it came to God. Now that he was talking to Phylicia, he wondered if maybe it wasn't such a great idea to apply that same honesty with people. But how else would he broach the subject with her?

He sighed. "Do you and your sisters *want* to sell the house? Your dad seemed to think that was a given, but . . . maybe not?"

Phylicia cleared her throat. "It's not that we want to. We don't really have a choice. We're each getting some money from my mom's estate, but we'd have to pool our money — all three of us — to buy the house, and it's not like we all want to live in our childhood home forever. Especially not together."

He curbed a grin. "I understand. Your dad said something about Brittany still living there now though."

"Britt, you mean?"

"Oh, sorry. I thought it was short for Brittany."

"No. Just Britt. And yes, she left college and moved back home once Mom . . . was bedridden. She'll probably go back to school at some point, but I doubt she'll want to live in the dorms. She'll have to find an apartment and —" Her voice broke.

"I'm so sorry." He spoke softly. "I'll be glad to help however I can. Your dad thought it might be easier if someone else handled the details of getting the house listed." He was tiptoeing around, but Turner had warned him to ease into the other proposition.

"Could I talk to my sisters first and get back to you? I don't think we know what we want. It's all still kind of a shock. Maybe we could come down to the office to meet with you tomorrow after we've had a chance to talk."

"Of course. That works for me. And . . . I'm so sorry. This can't be easy." He sighed, wishing he knew the right thing to say in light of everything they'd been through, everything they'd lost.

"No. It's not easy."

"I just think he's . . . trying to help. Your dad, I mean. Trying to patch things up. For needing to sell your house. And for leaving town at such a bad time."

She huffed. "You don't patch things up by

sending your —"

He wasn't sure what she'd started to say, but it was obvious she'd caught herself.

"What I was going to say —" Her voice softened. "You don't — or shouldn't — send your employee to do your dirty work. But that's not your fault. We're grateful for your help."

He couldn't quell a smile, thankful she couldn't see it. But he chose not to acknowledge her little rant. "Would you be willing to meet me at your dad's house? We could take a look at what all needs to be done before we list it. In the meantime, I'll check on some rental options for your sister . . . for Britt." He committed the names to memory in order: Phylicia, Joanna, and Britt. Not that he'd ever forget Phylicia's name. But Turner usually just lumped the sisters together as "my girls" when he spoke of them. And the younger two had still been in school last he'd seen them.

"Could you meet us there tomorrow evening? Jo and I are going over then anyway. I could probably get off a little early and meet you at, say four thirty, so you can see the house in the daylight. Will that work?"

So much for finishing the tile in his kitchen. "I'll make it work. See you at four thirty then." He wasn't sure how he would accomplish it, but he wanted to help Phylicia and her sisters out of a tough spot if he possibly could.

And frankly, right now, he wanted to read Turner Chandler the riot act for not being there for his daughters when they needed him most. And for not mentioning the rather significant detail that part of his reason for transferring to Florida was to get *married.*

CHAPTER 4

Phee handed off the winter floral arrangement she'd been designing to a coworker and left the flower shop a few minutes after four, hoping to freshen up a little before Quinn Mitchell arrived. But when she pulled into the driveway at her parents' house, he was already there, standing at the curb beside a navy-blue SUV, blowing on his gloved hands and stamping his feet in the thin dusting of snow on the street. She wondered why Britt hadn't let him in, but maybe he'd only just arrived.

Joanna's car wasn't in the driveway, but then, she was notoriously late. Dad had always teased her that she'd never make it as a lawyer because she'd never get to court on time.

Phee parked in front of the garage, and by the time she turned off the ignition and quickly slicked on some lip gloss, Quinn was beside her car.

He opened her door. "Good afternoon."

"You too. Thanks for coming."

"No problem." He looked up toward the house. "I wish it wasn't closing in on sunset. The house looks great with snow on the eaves like that. For the listing photos."

"You weren't going to shoot photos tonight, were you? It doesn't seem like January is a very good time to try to sell a house." No time was a good time to sell *this* house. *Their* house.

"It's not the best. Not for photos for sure, but this would make a nice shot." Tucking the manila folder he was carrying under one arm, he held up his hands, thumbs together, framing the shot like a movie director. "The snow kind of makes up for what's missing in flowers and greenery. The light is good for indoor shoots this time of year though."

"Well, come on inside."

He followed her up the walk. "I hope it wasn't a problem to get off work."

"No. Things are kind of slow at the store right now."

"You still work downtown?"

"At the flower shop, yes. We're doing flowers for a wedding this weekend, and things will pick up in a couple of months."

"Ah. That's good."

She hadn't seen him since Mom's funeral,

and that day was such a blur in her memory that she wouldn't have sworn for certain he was there. But she remembered addressing an envelope to him and writing a thank-you note for Mom's memorial. Quinn's donation had been notably generous.

"I think Britt is here already." She unlocked the front door, calling out to her sister. "Joanna is never on time. But come on in. You can take a look around the house before it gets dark." She hadn't thought to ask Britt to have the house cleaned up, but she had no doubt it would be in good shape. Britt was a bit of a neat freak anyway, and one of the things the three sisters had done together during the long vigil with their mom was deep-clean the house. They'd thought they were doing it for Dad's sake — not staging their childhood home to sell.

Over the last few months of her life, when she'd still been mobile, Mom had distributed many of her belongings to her daughters and her closest friends — yet another gift she'd left them, since it meant they'd had very few personal items to go through after the funeral.

Sometime during those final days, after Mom had slipped into a coma, Dad had packed up the last of her clothes and toiletries and disposed of them. All except her favorite blue dress that she was to be buried in. At the time, Phee thought it was because it hurt too much to see Mom's things in the house — that the purging was part of the grieving process for him. And it shouldn't have bothered her so much. After all, Mom had doled out her jewelry and other personal items to Phee and her sisters months ago. All that had been left when Mom died were the colorful scarves she'd worn to cover her bald head. And none of them had wanted those reminders of the indignities their mom had endured.

Joanna contended Dad was just being his practical self in taking care of things even before Mom was gone. Now, Phee wondered if it had all — everything — been about *Karleen.*

"Sis? Britt, are you here?" She started back to the kitchen. "Come on back, Quinn."

He followed her, his boot heels echoing on the hardwood floors. Britt appeared from the hall, far more dressed up than Phee had seen her in a while. "Quinn, you remember my sister Britt."

"The *baby* sister, right?" He reached to shake her hand.

Britt laughed. "I probably *was* a baby when we first met."

"You were all babies when I first met you."

Phee straightened. "I'll have you know I was a young woman of sixteen."

"Really? You remember?"

Her cheeks prickled with heat. "I do. Only because our mother was so taken with you." That was true enough, but Phee had also developed a schoolgirl crush on her father's handsome coworker the first time Dad brought him home. As she matured, she realized how ridiculous it was, given how much older Quinn Mitchell was.

"The feeling was mutual, I assure you. Your mother was quite a woman."

It warmed Phee to know that he remembered Mom that way. "Let's sit at the kitchen table." She led the way.

Melvin greeted them in the dining room, tail aloft, quickly choosing Quinn as his shedding post. Phee gently shooed him away. "Sorry. This is Melvin. Not in the market for a cat, are you? He's an equal-opportunity shedder."

"Excuse me?"

Phee laughed. "Whether you're wearing black or white, he's got fur to contrast with your outfit."

The tuxedo cat looked up, tipped his head, and gave Quinn one of his heartbreaker stares.

Apparently unmoved, Quinn sidestepped the cat as if it were a skunk. "No thanks. I already own a cat-eating dog."

"Seriously?" Britt looked worried.

Quinn laughed. "Mabel has never actually eaten a cat. At least to my knowledge. But she would make this one wish he'd never met her. No offense to your cat."

"Melvin," Phee supplied, feeling suddenly defensive of Mom's cat. "His name is Melvin."

"Melvin, my man." Quinn tipped an imaginary hat and took another step in the opposite direction.

"Why don't you sit there." Phee pointed to the head of the table where Dad usually sat.

Quinn started to sit down, then straightened again as the front door opened and Joanna breezed in.

"Sorry I'm late."

Quinn extended a hand. "I don't know if you remember . . . I'm Quinn."

"Of course I remember."

His gaze swept the room, encompassing the three of them. "Your mother was very kind to me. I'll always remember that about her."

"Thank you." Phee swallowed back the unexpected lump in her throat. The house suddenly felt hollow and empty without Mom here. Or Dad. Maybe it would be a good thing to get untangled from this place that held so many memories, both sweet and painful.

As if she sensed Phee's emotion, Joanna motioned for Quinn to sit. "Or would you rather look at the house first?"

"Let's talk first." It sounded as if he had a plan. Good. Somebody needed to.

They all took seats around the table and Phee offered drinks.

Quinn waved her off and her sisters declined too. Her mouth felt like cotton, so she quickly poured herself a glass of water and set it on the table.

Melvin headed for Quinn again, the swish of his tail saying his goal was Quinn's lap. Britt intercepted him and settled the cat on her own lap.

"I guess, first, I should make sure you're all on the same page about selling the house."

The sisters exchanged glances, and Britt bit her bottom lip. "We kind of don't have a choice."

"None of us can afford to buy the house alone," Phee explained.

"And we sure don't want to live here together," Joanna joked.

"Right. We had enough of that growing up." Britt's voice wavered even though her eyes said she was teasing. "But I do need a place to live. I moved out of the dorm when Mom . . ." Her voice trailed off and her bottom lip quivered.

"Yes, Phylicia mentioned that," Quinn said. "Unfortunately, decent apartments are pretty scarce, even in Cape. Until school's out in the spring."

"Yes, and most of them charge a fortune if you have pets." Britt's pout was back.

"So, you're the one taking Melvin? I didn't realize there was a cat involved when I started checking places. But actually" — he opened the folder he'd brought — "one option I wanted to show you would solve that problem. Not that Melvin's a problem . . ." He slid the faded silk-flower centerpiece to one side and scooted the open folder closer to them.

As one, the sisters bent their heads over the papers.

"What is this?" Phee looked at what appeared to be a real estate listing. "Jo and I have apartments. And I don't think Britt's in the market for a house . . . are you, sis?"

"No, I think an apartment would be better. Something close to campus in case I can start back next fall."

Quinn tapped the folder. "This is actually three houses. And not *too* far from campus." He looked dubious.

Phee shook her head, wanting to dismiss him quickly. "Why would we want three houses?"

"Let me explain." He turned to the second page of the listing sheet and creased the corner where it was stapled.

Maybe he was getting a commission if he could sell them on this property or something, but either way, this was a waste of his time and theirs. Besides, if the photos were any indication, these houses appeared to be way beyond fixer-uppers.

Tearer-downers was more like it.

Quinn took a fortifying breath. This was going to be a harder sell than Turner had implied. But Quinn had promised his boss he'd at least make the presentation. He held up a hand. "Hear me out, okay? And then if you're not interested, I promise I won't mention it again. And — full disclosure number one — I've already talked this over with your dad, and the idea has his strong approval." He looked from one to the other around the table, trying to gauge their enthusiasm. A strong zero. Maybe minus two.

But they waited politely, so he continued. "Here's the deal: This property has been on the market for over a year. To be honest, our company considered buying it at one point for a company retreat, but they ultimately decided we were spread too thin as it was. And with the layoffs last summer, it didn't seem wise to be talking about retreats."

He studied the three sisters. He still had their attention, so he plowed ahead. "Anyway, that's how your dad first became aware of it. But, like I said, it's been over a year and the owner is getting antsy. He recently lowered the price pretty significantly. It's a beautiful piece of property. The address is Poplar Brook" — he scratched his head — "*Road,* I think . . . I forget the number."

"Poplar Brook Road?" Phylicia shook her head. "I don't think I know where that is."

"It's on the north edge of town just inside the city limits. There are only a couple of other homes with that street address. At one time, years ago, this place was listed as a waterfront property, since it's technically on a small tributary of the Mississippi."

Britt's forehead wrinkled. "So, what changed the waterfront part?"

"Apparently, in recent years the tributary has become more of a mud hole. It's not reliable year to year for fishing or canoeing or kayaking. All the things that would have people snapping it up. That, and the fact that it's a little too close to town for most people looking for that kind of property. Hence, the drop in price. Even so, the place is wooded with hundred-year-old trees shading the site, and there's a gravel drive." He gave a little laugh. "I'll be honest, if this had been on the market when I was looking for a place to build my house, I would have snapped it up."

"So you finally built that house you used to talk about?"

He was pleased Phylicia remembered. "I did. Well, correction: I'm in the process of building. For about four years now."

Britt's eyes grew wide. "Wow, it must be a big house."

He laughed, then cringed. "Actually, it's on the small side. But I'm doing all the interior work myself. It's slow-going when I only have evenings and weekends to work on it."

"At least you'll know it's done right," Joanna offered, sounding so much like her dad, Quinn couldn't help but smile.

"Well, you'd hope so. The jury's still out." He held up the listing papers. "Back to *your* property though . . . The grounds are a little overgrown, but nothing a Bush Hog couldn't make short work of and —"

"Wait . . . But you would have built there?" Joanna's expression said her interest was piqued — or at least her curiosity. "I thought there were houses still on the property."

According to Turner, Joanna was the one who'd have the legal mind for the deal. He trained his gaze on her. "There are. Three small cottages. Sorry it's taking me so long to get to the point, but I want you to have all the details."

"No problem," Joanna and Britt said in unison.

Phylicia took a sip from her water glass but remained silent, so he aimed his pitch at the two younger sisters — even though he was pretty sure it would take all three of them investing to make this work.

"What I meant to say is that the houses are still there. Your dad and I looked all three of them over for another client last summer, and — at least as of a year ago — the houses were in fairly sound condition. Good condition even. They're stone cottages that were built probably in the thirties or forties, so they're built solid. They don't make houses like these anymore."

"But they're old too," Phylicia countered.

"True. Now, the largest one has had some remodeling done in recent years" — he chuckled — "probably not to your taste, I admit, but it's livable. And the last inspection said electric and plumbing are up to code in all three units, so everything in the two smaller homes is cosmetic. But . . . it is *everything* — flooring, paint, some pretty hideous wallpaper that probably needs to be stripped —"

He stopped. All three women were shaking their heads. Frowning. He'd lost them. On wallpaper?

He forced a laugh but felt deflated. "Okay, I get it. Not your thing. I had to try."

Phylicia tilted her head. "We really do appreciate the thought, but I don't know what we'd do with three fixer-uppers. You must have misunderstood Dad."

He took a deep breath and held up a handful of fingers. "Can you give me five more minutes to make my case?" He had to be able to tell Turner that he'd given it his best shot. Not that he was conning the girls. It *was* a good deal, a good opportunity — for the right party. Turner had thought it might be right for his daughters. Quinn had been skeptical. Not about the property. He'd been skeptical the sisters were the right party. And rightfully so, it appeared.

He'd be sure to thank Turner for making him look like an idiot next time he talked to the man. "Just five minutes, and then I promise I'll drop it."

Phylicia smiled, but she checked the time on her phone. "Five minutes. You're on the clock." He couldn't tell whether she was kidding.

"Okay, full disclosure number two: your dad and I have run some numbers, and even if you three went in at full price — given the new reduced asking price — there would still be enough money left for our company to come in and do the work. It's not really contracting work . . . well, unless you decide to do some major remodeling. But we're in a position right now to take on some smaller jobs, so we could get a crew in to do the flooring, paint, change out the appliances, whatever else you want to do."

Phylicia's brow furrowed. "I don't understand. Dad talked to you about us buying this property? Are you — and Dad — suggesting we buy these three houses to live in ourselves?"

"Well, you could do that. It would still be a good investment of the money you're getting from your mom." He cringed inwardly. He was pretty sure Turner had told the girls about Myra's inheritance, but his boss may not have intended Quinn to reveal that he himself knew about it. "I hope you don't mind that your dad shared that information with me."

Tentative nods from all three, so he continued. "Anyway, you'd own the homes free and clear, including the renovation — unless you do some really extensive upgrades. So you'd never pay rent or a mortgage payment. Your only real expense would be the property taxes and eventual upkeep. And if you ever decided to sell, you'd easily make your money back. Or, if only one of you moves, the others could either buy you out, or at the very least, you'd have the luxury of choosing your neighbors."

Joanna gave her younger sister a playful shove. "Could you live all alone in one of those houses, Britt? If *we* were your next-door neighbors?" Her question seemed tongue-in-cheek, and the sisters laughed at some joke Quinn didn't get.

"It depends." Britt narrowed her eyes and turned to him. "How far out in the country did you say this property is?"

"It's practically on the Langhorne city-limits line. But that's the beauty of it. There's already a well on the place, so your water bill will be next to nothing. Yet, you'd be five minutes from anything in town, and still less than fifteen minutes to Cape Girardeau. And that's important for the next thing I want to propose." He glanced at Phylicia. "How am I doing on time?"

She smiled, her crystal blue eyes twinkling. "You still have a couple minutes left."

Her smile reminded him of how dangerous this whole plan could turn out to be. A danger Turner Chandler knew nothing about, and one Quinn dared not think about until he'd pled his case with Turner's daughters.

"Okay. You guys are familiar with VRBO — vacation rental by owner — and Airbnb?"

Britt frowned. "You mean where people rent out their homes, kind of like a bed and breakfast?"

"Exactly. There's a huge need in this area for something like that. I was talking to Link Whitman the other day — he manages the Chicory Inn just outside of Langhorne — and he said they are booked solid most of the year, especially around the holidays. And people book a year or more in advance for college graduation. You can't find a vacancy in Cape Girardeau during big events like that, so people are always looking to stay nearby in Jackson or here in Langhorne."

"So you're proposing we open a bed and breakfast?" Phylicia sounded incredulous.

"Where did Dad get that crazy idea?"

Quinn bit the inside of his cheek. "Uh, from me, actually."

"I don't know . . . Sounds like a *lot* of work."

"I'm not saying it wouldn't be. But I think it would solve a lot of your problems." He *had* promised to shut up if they weren't interested after hearing the proposal. In a last-ditch effort, he counted off on his fingers. "First, it's a great opportunity. This property is kind of a best-kept secret. I think if you saw it, you'd understand. Second, it would be a sound investment of your money. Not only will it give you all a place to live rent-free, but the value is sure to appreciate once —"

"But if it's sure to appreciate, then why is it still on the market after a year?" Joanna's expression had turned doubtful.

"That's a good question. Personally, I think it's been purely a failure of marketing. The property itself is small, only about eight acres. And who wants to buy three houses at once? Unless someone planned to tear down all the homes and build new, it really didn't make sense. And frankly, I think the houses are too nice to tear down. In addition, the owner was originally asking almost twice what the price is now." He paused. "I truly don't want you to feel like I'm pressuring you, but I think that place will get snapped right up once people realize how much he's come down on his price."

Phylicia frowned. "So not only do you want us to quit our jobs, buy *three* fixer-uppers, and open a B&B, but now you're saying if we don't hurry, the opportunity will be lost?"

He laughed. "I know it sounds a little on the crazy side. But hear me out . . . Back to my list." He tapped his third finger. "Third of all, I never said you'd have to quit your jobs. In fact, I wouldn't advise it. Not right away at least. Not until you see what kind of income this generates."

Phylicia's frown deepened. "I don't get how it will generate income. If we're renting it out, we'd have to keep our apartments, right? I mean, if the place is going to be 'booked solid' like you said." She chalked quote marks in the air with pink-manicured fingers. But at least now she was smiling.

"Well, there are several ways you could do it. Some people only rent out a bedroom or a suite — a room with a private bath. Of course, you can charge more for a whole-house rental. But there's a whole culture of people who love this kind of experience. And they're not expecting hotel-perfection."

Britt giggled. "That's a good thing."

"Yeah, Britt . . ." Joanna made a goofy face. "Your job will be cleaning the bathrooms."

More giggling and another joke that went over Quinn's head. He'd grown up with a brother, and he supposed he and Markus had once had their own private jokes stemming from childhood, but these three were practically communicating telepathically.

He chose to ignore them and got to the punch. "What I'd propose you do is live in the larger house while you renovate the other two. I'd guess — if you're willing to do some of the work yourselves — we could . . . *you* could have one house ready to let within five or six weeks. Well, at least ready to decorate. It might take a few weeks beyond that to be booking-ready."

Joanna glanced past Phylicia to the dining and living rooms, looking thoughtful. "Dad said we could have any of the furniture he's not taking, which is most of it. I bet there's enough here to furnish three houses . . ."

"Joanna Chandler?" Phylicia's eyes went wide. "You're not actually considering this, are you?" She turned to Quinn. "Dad always said you were persuasive, but this is just . . . a little crazy. And a lot out of the blue."

"Think about it, Phee." Joanna's voice took on a cajoling quality. "It really would be a good investment. Something that could make us all some extra money and save us having to pay rent."

"You've always said you couldn't wait to decorate your own house, Phee." Britt shot Quinn a conspiratorial look. "Here's your chance."

"Britt! Not you too!"

He risked getting one last score with the youngest Chandler. "And don't forget, this would solve your problem about what to do with Marvin."

Britt laughed. "Melvin, you mean? But you're right. I wouldn't have to worry about finding an apartment that allows pets if we did this."

Phee turned to Quinn, an apologetic smile on her shapely lips. "Could you give us a minute, Quinn? In private? We sisters need to discuss — before I have a mutiny on my hands."

"Aye, aye, captain. I need to take a look around the yard for your dad's listing anyway." Trying to look appropriately sheepish, he started for the front door. "I'll be outside if you have any questions."

Phylicia might be a holdout. But he had a

feeling he'd made some serious inroads with two out of the three.

Chapter 5

Phee looked out the kitchen window to the backyard where Quinn was measuring the patio, jotting notes on a small pad. She turned to her sisters. "Are you two actually entertaining this idea?" But Phee could tell, before her sisters even opened their mouths, that they *were* considering it. Seriously.

And she had to admit she saw the appeal. Yet with serious misgivings. "You guys, we haven't even seen the place yet. For all we know, it's a total money pit. *Three* money pits!"

Joanna shrugged. "If it's a dump, we walk away. But what can it hurt just to look? Quinn seems to think the property has potential. And Dad apparently does too."

"But, Jo, this isn't something we've ever, in our wildest dreams, even talked about. I don't get why Dad would encourage this. And you heard Quinn. We'd have to live together in the same house for a while. I love you guys, but I don't know that I want you for roommates." She forced a grin.

"It'd just be for a while. How's that any different than what we've been doing these last few days?" Britt looked so hopeful — like a kid on Christmas morning — that Phee caught a glimpse of why Mom and Dad had always had so much trouble saying no to their youngest.

Phee frowned. "But if we each move into our own house, what are we supposed to rent out?"

"There are two bedrooms in each cottage, possibly three in the bigger one." Joanna counted on her fingers. "That's the beauty of the Airbnb rentals. You can rent out the whole place or just a room. And it's not like we'd have people staying every night. When we do have guests, we can all pile in at each other's places."

"And what if it's a rip-roaring success and we book every room every night?"

"That would be great, but probably unlikely. Cape Girardeau isn't Waco." Joanna kicked into lawyer mode. "See, *we* choose how many rooms and how many nights. Total freedom to make it work with *our* schedules. And even if we rent just one eighty-dollar room a night, that would add up. Two rooms a night, and one of us could retire."

Britt raised a hand. "I volunteer!"

Phee cast a sideways glance at her little sister. "Um, excuse me, but you can't retire if you're already unemployed."

"Hey!" Britt affected a pout. "That hurts."

Phee did some quick math, and she had to admit the numbers were encouraging, especially since they wouldn't have a mortgage on the property. Or apartment rent to pay. And it wasn't like they'd have to quit their jobs to run the place.

Joanna eyed Phee, no doubt sensing a chink in her armor. "Let's just go take a look. It can't hurt anything. I'll review the realty company's listing material."

Still, Phee hesitated. "Except it could well be a waste of Quinn's time and maybe keep him from selling the property to someone else who would hire the company to do the work . . . like he wants us to do. *That's* what's in it for him, you know."

"But Phee, this is what *Dad* wants us to do too. And Quinn said that up front. It's not like he's trying to con us." Britt had turned on her little-girl charm — and she had plenty to turn on.

"If Dad was so fired up about us doing this, then why didn't *he* tell us about it?

Why did he leave it to one of his employees?"

Joanna rolled her eyes. "Probably because he figured we'd be too mad at him to listen to anything he had to say."

"Well, he was right about that." Phee's blood simmered again just thinking about it.

"Let's just go look." Joanna rose and went to stand at the window. "We don't have to consider it until we've seen if it's even viable. But I've got to say . . . think about it, Phee. We'd be really good at this. I can handle all the paperwork and legal stuff, you're great at decorating and design — even for the ads and website and stuff like that, you'd be perfect. And Britt is the hostess with the mostess. We really would make a great team for something like this. It'd be a lot of fun."

"And a lot of work." Phee wasn't convinced by a long shot. But Joanna was right. Their talents were diverse, and they would each bring something different to the table. She had to admit it felt good to be in this together with her sisters. And maybe there was something to the idea. Even if she wasn't very happy with her father right now, she did trust his business sense and that he had *their* best interests at heart. "I guess we can go look."

Britt and Joanna cheered and hugged her, which made her laugh. Until she thought about the crow she'd have to eat when she told Quinn Mitchell that they would take a look. If he gloated, she just might have to change her mind.

She found him in the backyard measuring the patio. "For Dad's listing?"

Nodding absently, he uncapped a ball-point pen and quickly jotted some numbers on the edge of the listing sheet in his manila folder. He tucked the papers back in the folder and turned his full attention to her. "Sorry, I wanted to get that down before I forgot. The house looks to be in good shape. I don't think your dad will have any trouble getting his asking price. You're sure you and your sisters don't want to buy it?"

She looked askance at him. "I thought you were all about us buying these three houses on the river."

He eyed her. "Oh? The vibe I was getting didn't sound like you were very interested."

She shrugged. "We decided we should at least go look at the property."

His face brightened, but she got the impression he was trying hard not to look too pleased. Smart man. "I can take you out there tomorrow, but I'd really prefer for you to see it in daylight. Is there any way you could get off work early again? Maybe try to get out there by four?" He looked apologetic.

"That should work. Britt's not back to work yet, so I think she's good. I'm not sure about Joanna. We've all missed quite a bit of work these last few months, and Jo's boss isn't too happy with her. But I'll talk to her and let you know if it doesn't work."

"Sounds good. I'll just pick up whoever can go right here. Let's say a little before four, if that's all right. And I'll treat you all to supper afterwards."

She hesitated. If they decided the property was a dump, a meal together might not be a very pleasant affair. "Let's play supper by ear, okay?"

"Sure. Of course." He capped his pen and secured it in the pocket of his button-down shirt. "Okay if I do a quick walkthrough inside?"

"Sure. I'll show you around."

His expression gave away nothing.

So why did she have the feeling that inside that handsome head of his, he was celebrating some kind of victory?

CHAPTER 6

February

"The driveway is just ahead." Quinn expertly steered his SUV up a canopied drive. "This really is a hidden wonder of Langhorne."

Phee frowned. *Driveway* was being generous. This was more like a mountain trail. Though she had to admit it was a pretty spot. Especially with the remnants of this afternoon's rain glistening on the branches, the tree limbs making a tracery of brown and white against the blue-gray sky on this first day of February.

Quinn slowed the vehicle and wound through a path that wasn't discernible except for the fact that it was the only space a vehicle would fit between the dense woodland.

"How far back does this go?" Joanna asked from the backseat where she and Britt still gripped their armrests from the bumpy ride up the drive from Poplar Brook Road.

"Well, it's just under eight acres, but it's a long, narrow plot. And there won't really be any upkeep on seven and three quarters of an acre. Unfortunately, according to this" — he tapped the same manila folder he'd had with him yesterday — "the timber was harvested a few years ago, probably sooner than it should have been, which may be one reason the property has sat so long."

"Oh, I think I see something . . ." Phee pointed through the windshield. "Is that a roof?"

Quinn peered over the steering wheel. At that moment, a tan doe leapt across the path in front of the SUV, its distinctive white tail held high. And on the doe's heels, a huge buck followed, still sporting an impressive set of antlers.

They all gasped as the vehicle jerked to a halt.

"Good grief!" Phee exhaled.

"How cool is that!" Jo breathed.

In awed silence, they watched the animals disappear into the forest.

After a minute, Quinn turned in his seat. "Did I mention they come with the property?"

Phee eyed him, then saw the tiniest smile tip his mouth.

"But seriously," he continued. "That's something you'll have to watch for, especially in the evening."

Phee looked in the direction the doe and buck had disappeared. Deer were thick in this part of the county, and it was unusual to drive anywhere and not see half a dozen of the majestic animals in the fields and ditches on either side of the winding roads. But thinking about them on property *she* owned gave her a strange feeling of pride.

If she didn't know better, she'd have sworn Quinn had personally arranged their little wildlife encounter. What else could he have up his sleeve?

She'd tried to reach Dad several times last night without success. And he hadn't returned her messages, even though she'd asked him to call back as soon as possible. Jo said she'd tried to call him too, with the same result. It was starting to feel as if Dad's new life in Florida didn't have room for daughters in it. For the first time, Phee wondered if Karleen had children.

Looking out the passenger-side window, she tried to ignore the pang of jealousy that sliced through her.

They drove in silence for another minute before Quinn pointed. "There's your rooftop. That's not the main house though. The biggest one sits back the farthest. But they're all a stone's throw from each other."

"Oh, I see them." Joanna pointed in the same direction Quinn had. "See, Britt. Look up there."

Quinn rounded a corner and the houses appeared, three of them arranged in a semicircle, as if they were huddled around a campfire. A crumbling rock wall separated the cottages from the water's edge — or what would have been the water's edge if the riverbed wasn't almost dry. There appeared to be a narrow rocky beach below the wall.

Faded shutters hung haphazardly from the two smaller cottages, and it was hard to tell what color the original trim had been. Gray, Phee guessed. Which was partly why they'd been almost upon the clearing before they spotted the buildings. The shake shingles were gray as well. But the stone siding gave the buildings a certain charm. Something that made her think of them as cottages rather than houses. Of course, their diminutive size was partly responsible for that.

Quinn pulled up in front of the larger house and turned off the ignition. He fished in his pocket and produced a tattered keychain. "This key is supposed to get us into all of the houses. We . . . *you* will probably want to change all the locks so each house has its own keys. For sure if you decide to rent the cabins."

Despite a scene that any sane person would label "ramshackle" — or at least, "overgrown and neglected" — a strange sense of excitement welled up in Phee. She couldn't deny the unexpected eagerness building inside her. Still, she tried not to show it, and even silently chided herself. She needed to remain dispassionate and realistic, because judging by the looks on her sisters' faces, Joanna and Britt were already mentally painting walls and arranging furniture.

Quinn swiveled in his seat, looking at each of them in turn. "Well? Let's go take a look, shall we?"

Joanna and Britt all but bolted from the SUV. Phee followed behind them as Quinn led the way.

He picked a path along the leaf-strewn trail leading to the largest cottage. "Oh! See that?" He stopped and pointed.

A bunny hopped across the trail, pausing to cock its head at them before disappearing into the tall grasses. Phee wondered what other wildlife lived in these woods. Rabbits and raccoons and deer she would love spotting. Coyotes and badgers and opossums, not so much. A little shiver crept through her.

A screened-in porch ran the length of the front. The porch's screen door was unlocked, and Quinn held it open for them.

"Oooh, this is cute!" Britt peered through the arched opening in the stone wall that formed one end of the porch.

"I love the view!" Joanna looked out the matching archway opposite their youngest sister. "You're practically in town, but all you can see is acres of woods. I could get used to this!"

Phee turned to look out the front toward where they'd parked. The porch screens sagged in their frames, and the porch floor was in sore need of a coat of deck paint, but she could just imagine little globe lights strung across the beadboard ceiling and a lineup of comfy chairs and ottomans for sitting on summer evenings, sipping iced tea. *Knock it off.* If her sisters were going to go nuts over the place before they were even inside, someone had to stay rational.

Quinn unlocked the door to the house and stepped aside, motioning for them to proceed. Phee inhaled, waiting for her eyes to adjust to the dim light inside. The place had a musty smell about it, like Grandma Clayton's cellar. "How long did you say it's been since anyone lived here?"

Quinn checked the real estate flyer. "It's been on the market a little over a year, but I don't know when the last residents moved out. I don't think the other two cottages have been lived in for a while."

Britt wrinkled her nose. "It does smell a little stuffy."

"That's only because it's been closed up for so long." Quinn crossed the room and tried to crack a window — one that appeared to be painted shut. He quickly gave up his efforts and turned to face them. "A good airing and it'll be fine."

The front door opened directly into a large living room with a dining room beyond, separated by bookcase colonnades. Phee pointed. "Do you guys remember Grandmother Chandler's house? It had the bookcase dividers just like this."

Joanna shook her head. "I sort of remember the kitchen in that house, and the back stairway, but that's all."

Phee worked to keep any trace of sentimentality from her voice. "It was a lot like this house . . . on a bigger scale."

"Some new paint would help a lot." Britt walked over to a light switch and flipped it on.

Quinn nodded. "Some white — or that

pale gray everyone's using — would really brighten things up. And I'm sure these windows let in a lot more sun at midday. You might want to clear a few trees away from the house to let in more light. That way you'd have some wood for the fireplace too."

The brick fireplace surround was dark with soot, but the long mantel would be perfect for Christmas decorations — greenery and twinkle lights, and candles in the high windows on either side of the mantel. "Does the fireplace work?" Phee bent to peer inside the firebox.

He tapped the papers. "Says here that it does. But you'll want to have the chimney inspected and cleaned out before you use it."

She frowned. "Now it's starting to sound like a lot of work. And *this* is the move-in ready cottage?"

He held up a hand. "Now wait . . . I don't think I ever used that phrase. I said it was *livable.*"

Phee raised her eyebrows. "Big difference. Well, let's see the rest of it."

He pointed behind her. "Through those doors is what was probably originally a bedroom, but it looks as if they might've used it as an office."

She turned to see pretty glass-paned French doors that led to a large room beyond. It would make a great office space or music room.

"Wouldn't this make a great library?" Britt's eyes grew large as she panned the room. "I wonder if Dad plans to take the bookcases out of his office."

"They would look great in here. But you don't think they're too tall?" Phee quickly caught herself again. She had to quit dreaming and be realistic.

"Well, we'd have to put the lower ones under that window, but look at all this wall space." Joanna crossed the room, her boot heels clicking across the floors. "We could get all of the bookcases from Dad's office in here with room to spare. Add a library table in the middle and all this room would need to make it absolutely perfect is a fresh coat of paint."

"A little paint would work wonders on the whole house. Inside and out." Quinn looked as if he wanted to move in himself. "But the floors are all in surprisingly good shape, and the woodwork just needs a good polishing."

Phee frowned. "Well, let's look at the kitchen before we start polishing woodwork. It's usually the kitchen and baths that are the deal-breakers in these older homes."

"There's only one bath." Quinn tapped the real estate listing sticking out of his jacket pocket. "Each of the houses are two beds, one bath. Unless you decide to make that 'library' into a bedroom again. That would give you a third."

"But no closet."

"If it's for a rental like VRBO, you wouldn't really need a closet." He seemed determined to challenge her at every turn. "But you could always buy an armoire or chifforobe."

Phee narrowed her eyes. "You're sure you aren't getting a cut on the sale of this place."

"I promise you, I'm not. And quite honestly, now that I've seen it, if you don't buy it, I just might." He gave her a half grin that she ignored. But his tactic — if that's what it was — had worked. If he was so impressed with the place, maybe it was worth the elbow grease they'd have to put into it.

Walking back through the French doors, she caught a new view of the living room with the fireplace as the focal point. She'd always loved a room with a fireplace. It'd probably be easiest to just paint the bricks or maybe whitewash them. That would brighten up the whole room and really make the fireplace the star.

It would take some work, but it was doable. Might even be fun. She already had decorating ideas dancing through her head. Mom wouldn't have batted an eye at fixing up a place like this.

A wave of grief rolled over her unexpectedly and she swallowed back tears. But even as she did, she caught a glimmer of how much it would honor their mom if she and her sisters actually went through with this. Maybe if they did turn this into a little bed-and-breakfast-type place, they could even name it after Mom. *Myra's Maisons* or *Myra's Moorings.* She smiled wryly to herself. They'd have to get some water in the creek before they could have moorings.

What are you doing, *Chandler?* So much for being dispassionate.

Shaking away the thoughts, she headed back to the kitchen beyond the dining room at the back of the house. Britt scurried behind her, and Joanna disappeared into the hallway off the dining room.

"Hey, it's not bad." Quinn was already in the kitchen, having apparently circled through the hallway into the back kitchen entrance. He was tapping on a wall that jutted out as if it might cover a chimney. "We could expose brick here too, I bet."

"Move-in ready, huh?" She shot him a skeptical look.

"Livable." He wagged a finger at her. "I said *livable.* And it is."

"It's *very* livable." Joanna popped into the kitchen. "Wait till you see the bedrooms, Phee. This place is adorable. Straight out of *Fixer Upper.*"

"Before or after?"

"Well, I don't think we'll be knocking out any walls or laying new hardwoods, so I'd say after."

"After," Britt chimed in. "After Chip's demo day, but before Joanna Gaines has put her signature touches on it."

"Well, *this* Joanna would love to put *her* signature touches on it." Joanna opened a cupboard door and stuck her head inside. "Plenty of storage here."

The cabinets had all been painted white at some point, but they were dingy and the paint was peeling in places. Still, it wouldn't take much to touch them up. The floor was an old vinyl pattern that looked dated, but it had a Bohemian vibe that Phee kind of liked.

Half an hour later, they followed Quinn out to the other two cottages. These were twins that sat down closer to the water's edge — although the tributary here was more like a muddy creek. Each cottage had a low stone wall around it. But the crumbling state of the walls made them look more like the piles of sandbags people surrounded their homes with during the spring flood season.

Phee turned to Quinn. "Do we need to worry about flooding? There's not much water now, but if we got a downpour, it seems like these would be pretty close to the water's edge."

"That may be why the walls were built at some point." Again, Quinn consulted the real estate listing. "It doesn't say anything about flood issues here, but we can do some checking to find out if there's any history of problems. From what the real estate agent told us — your dad and me — it's more of a problem that the creek has been dry for so long. It would be selling for a lot more if it was a true waterfront property." He unlocked the first cottage and held open the door.

Phee led the way inside and groped for a light switch.

"I don't think the electricity is on for the two smaller cabins." Quinn pulled his phone from his pocket and shined its flashlight into the room.

The sun was low in the sky now, and all the window shades were drawn. Phee waited for her eyes to adjust, but Britt crossed the room and raised a shade.

At the same moment, something skittered across the floor.

All three sisters screamed like little girls. Phee would have scrambled up onto a chair or table if there'd been a stick of furniture in the room.

Quinn threw his head back and laughed. "You might need to set some mousetraps until we get things sealed up here."

Her pulse still pounding, Phee felt a measure of her earlier excitement drain away. She'd let herself grow hopeful about this property, and Quinn's nonchalant sales tactic had almost worked. But as they wandered through the rooms, it was apparent this cottage needed extensive work, and she assumed the other one would be the same, if not worse.

In the dining room and bedrooms, layers of cabbage-rose wallpaper peeled, the floors were covered in dingy ancient carpet, and cobwebs festooned everything. The exterior of the cottages had seemed in surprisingly good shape, but even they needed new paint on the trim and doors. And who knew what kind of mold, rot, and termites lurked beneath the surface. Phee grew weary just thinking about where they would start with the smaller cottages. Especially when there was plenty to do in the larger one.

And with only two bedrooms in the main cottage, if they were to take advantage of being "rent free," they'd all need to live there — together — until one of the smaller homes was finished. The whole project suddenly felt overwhelming.

They hurried through the last cottage, which appeared to be a mirror image of the other small one, but the electricity was off here too, and by now it was too dark to see much. Phee could make out the same floral wallpaper pattern and the same worn carpeting.

Quinn locked up the last cottage and turned to the sisters. "So, what do you think?"

"I say let's do it!" Britt bounced on her heels like a five-year-old at Christmas.

Phee shook her head. "Britt, there's no way this —"

"I *love* this place." Joanna put her arms behind her and looked up at the trees towering over them. "It's like being on vacation, except we're fifteen minutes from work and church and —"

"And *everything.*" Britt beamed.

Phee looked back and forth between her sisters. "Are you guys serious?" She dared to look at Quinn, who wore a cat-that-ate-the-canary grin. "I don't think you guys realize how much work it would take to get this place livable. Even one of the cottages."

"It's all cosmetic, Phylicia." Quinn sounded frustratingly calm. "With a crew of three or four guys, we could completely redo a cottage in a month's time."

Ignoring him, she reasoned with her sisters. "You guys! There were mice!"

"You just need to move Melvin out here," Quinn offered, his tone far too confident. "Those mice won't stick around long if he's here."

"We'll need three Melvins then." Phee shook her head. How had this man won her sisters over so easily?

"If there were mice in the main house, you would have seen signs," he said. "You saw what good shape it's in. A little paint and maybe have the brick cleaned on the fireplace, and you could move right in. Once you get your furniture in, hang some pictures — that covers a multitude of sins. And you wouldn't have to do *anything* to that house right away. You could concentrate your efforts — and your funds — on the smaller houses. Get them ready to rent, and then while the income flows from that, you can do whatever you want to the main house. Before long, you'll each have your own place and you can decide how you want the rentals to work . . ." He took a breath and eyed her, as if to determine whether she was still with him.

Phee sighed. "I think you're all crazy." But even as she spoke, she knew why — at least partially — she hesitated to give in to them. And maybe she was being overly dramatic. But if they bought this property, it would feel as if she were admitting — even accepting — that she'd be single for the rest of her life. Well, at least for the foreseeable future.

Quinn held up a hand. "I promise this is not a bribe, but how about I take you all out to supper. We'll talk it over, crunch some numbers, and see if I can dispel your concerns. Because I really do think this is doable. Not just doable, but a no-brainer."

"Oh, so now you're calling me stupid if I don't go along?" Phee had meant it in jest, but it came out sounding overly harsh. She gave him a smile meant to soften her words.

"That's not what I said." He returned her smile and pulled his car keys out of his pants pocket. "I'm hungry. Let's talk this out over a good supper. My treat."

Joanna checked the time on her phone. "I wish I could, but I need to be back to work in fifteen minutes."

Britt shrugged. "Sorry, I can't either. Book club tonight."

Quinn's shoulders slumped. "Phylicia? Since you're the one who actually needs convincing, what do you say? I'm buying." He waited, eyebrows raised.

"Talk some sense into her, Quinn." Joanna checked her phone again and looked back toward Quinn's vehicle. "I really do need to get back."

"Oh . . . sure. Hop in." He trotted to the SUV, and Phee's sisters scrambled for the backseat spots. Phee went around and climbed into the passenger seat beside him. They were all assuming she would take Quinn up on his offer. *Fine.* She *was* hungry, and it would be a good chance to ask him some questions. But not about the property.

About her father.

CHAPTER 7

"You sure you want McAlister's? It's my treat, and I'd be happy to take you to Bella Italia, or we could drive over to Gordonville." He knew the Gordonville Grill was one of Turner's favorite places. Maybe it was hers too. And the twenty-minute drive would give them a little more time to talk.

"McAlister's is fine."

Phylicia's mood was decidedly cool. Quinn sneaked a look beside him in the SUV. Her focus was straight ahead. Not even a blink. He decided not to push it and mentally slipped on his kid gloves.

He took a parking spot close to the deli's entrance, and she was out of the car and halfway to the door before he could even come around to open the passenger door for her. So much for being a gentleman.

The aroma of simmering chili and yeasty bread wafted over them as they pushed through the restaurant's entryway. His stomach rumbled in response.

At the counter, Phylicia studied the menu for only a few seconds before ordering a bowl of vegetable soup.

"Anything to drink?" the girl behind the counter asked.

"Just water, please."

He touched her elbow lightly. "Don't you want a sandwich with that?"

"No thanks. I'm fine. I'm not really hungry."

"Suit yourself." He ordered a club sandwich and a Coke, paid with cash, and took the number the cashier handed him.

"Booth okay?" He usually ran into someone he knew here. Hopefully a booth would afford them a little privacy.

"That's fine."

Everything was fine with her tonight. He wove his way through the maze of tables, claiming the corner seat with a view of the entrance. He lopped his jacket over the back of the seat and waited until Phylicia was settled in across from him.

She shivered and pulled her coat tighter around herself.

"Do you want my jacket? I can get you a cup of coffee."

"I'm fine."

He stared at her, then let his smile come

slowly. "So I gathered."

She squinted. "Huh?"

"Never mind."

"I don't get it."

He leaned back in the booth. "Everything's been *fine* tonight. McAlister's? Fine. No sandwich? Fine. Booth? Fine. Cold? No, you're fine."

"Well, excuse me for being fine." A glimmer of a smile touched her lips.

"Except I get the feeling you're not . . . *fine.*"

She gave a soft huff. "What do you want me to say? I feel as if I'm being ramrodded, Quinn."

Even if he didn't like what she said, he liked the familiar way his name tripped off her lips. Not formal, the way it had sounded yesterday when he'd met the sisters at Turner's house. "I promise it's not my intention to ramrod you. I'm only doing what —"

"I know —" She held up a hand. "You're my dad's spokesperson."

He shrugged. He couldn't really deny it. "You say that like it's a bad thing. But . . . I happen to agree with your dad."

"Of course you do."

"What's that supposed to mean?"

"Never mind." She folded a paper napkin

into thirds, then twisted it into a rope, seeming hesitant to meet his eyes. But when she did, he felt the weight of her stare. "So, do you think my father just set this all up so he wouldn't have to feel guilty about running off with some woman when my mom is barely cold in the grave?"

Quinn stared, knowing he needed to choose his words carefully. His first instinct was to defend Turner Chandler, although he wasn't sure the man deserved it. "Phylicia, I can't know your dad's motives, but I do know that in all the years I've known him and worked for him, he's shown nothing but love and respect — passion, even — for your mom. And for his 'girlies' as he always calls you. Much to the amusement of a certain crowd at the office who has a slightly different definition of *girlies.*"

Phee smiled, and he hoped she was warming to him a little.

But her smile faded too quickly. "I feel a *however* coming on."

"Excuse me?"

"It just seems like you're struggling to understand what my Dad is doing too — moving away so suddenly, and everything that's happened with Karleen . . ."

He didn't dare deny it. This woman had an uncanny way of reading his thoughts.

A server headed their way with a tray of drinks, and he waited until the girl left. "I guess you're right about that. I don't understand what he's doing. The move, I mean . . . and the woman. I *do* understand him arranging the deal with the property with his daughters in mind. It's a good deal, Phylicia, and apparently your dad felt like it would be something you and your sisters would be interested in — and up to handling. Maybe I don't know you well enough to make a judgment, but from everything I *do* know — and everything your dad has said about you guys — it seems like a no-brainer."

"Well, you sure have my sisters convinced."

His shoulders were going to be sore from all the shrugging he'd done tonight. But he didn't know how else to respond. "I hope you believe me when I say that I don't have a stake in the deal. You can hire someone else to do the work if you want. I'd be happy to give you some names."

While that was true, it wasn't the whole truth. He didn't give a hoot about the job. The company would make minimal profit, and personally, he wouldn't gain anything. Not financially anyway. But if he was honest with himself, he had to admit to ulterior motives. Being around Phylicia Chandler these last few hours had done nothing to diminish the attraction he'd once felt for her. Quite the opposite.

"It's just so sudden." She looked at the table, then at the twisted napkin in her hand. "Not just the opportunity, but the change with Dad. I feel like I'm . . . grieving all over again. And why isn't *he* here talking to us? Why did he pawn the job off on you?"

Silence — and fresh grief — settled between them.

"I don't know," he finally said, unfolding the napkin in front of him and placing it in his lap. "Have you asked him?"

She shook her head. "No. We were all too much in shock, I guess."

"Why don't you call him?"

The server headed their way again. Quinn waited while the girl set their food in front of them. When she was out of earshot, he gave Phylicia a questioning glance.

She ignored him and bowed her head over her food. He did the same, but looked up quickly, not wanting to let her change the subject. She blew on her steaming soup. Something about the gesture made her look so vulnerable, and his heart went out to her. She was barely thirty and had lost her mother . . . and now it must feel as if she'd lost her father too.

"Look . . ." He risked putting a hand over hers across the table. But only briefly. "I know this must be really scary . . . and confusing. Not just with your dad, but with the decision about the property and where your sister will go —"

"Go?"

"Where will she live? From what your dad said, I think that was one reason he thought of the property."

Phylicia rolled her eyes. "Renting an apartment would be a lot simpler. If she can find a place that will take Melvin."

"I think your dad was thinking about an investment."

"That sounds like him."

"So, Melvin was your mom's cat?"

She nodded over a spoonful of soup. "Britt's pretty attached to him. He's definitely not negotiable. *Especially* because he was Mom's."

"Of course. And he *would* take care of the mice problem."

She set her spoon down. "Fine. I'll buy three houses on eight acres for the sake of a cat."

He laughed. "Those weren't my words."

"That's about what it amounts to though."

"Well, that and a place for your sister to live and a great way to invest your money."

"Whatever. Anyway, I said I'd consider it. I'll talk to my sisters, and we'll call Dad tomorrow and try to get something worked out."

"You're sure?" He couldn't help the excitement that rose up in him. "And you don't think your sisters will change their minds?"

"If I'm on board, they will be too."

He worked to keep his voice even. "You won't be sorry, Phylicia."

"You can call me Phee."

He frowned. "But . . . Phylicia's such a pretty name." Her given name rolled off the tongue so beautifully. *Phylicia.* Besides, he'd rather think of her as a perk or a bonus, rather than some *fee* needing to be paid. He was pretty sure the woman had no clue how attracted he was to her. But given that she was already hurting over her father's involvement with a woman many years his junior, she probably would not take kindly to the advances of an "older man."

Still, when tears sprang to those blue, blue eyes, his reaction was instinctive. He put a hand on her arm. "Are you all right?"

She shrank from his touch and pushed away her bowl of soup. "Excuse me. I . . .

I'll be back." She slid from the booth and all but ran to the restroom.

Quinn stared after her, replaying their conversation, hoping he hadn't said something thoughtless. But he didn't think he had. He sat for a moment, reminded that grief was still fresh for Phylicia. Her mother had been so young, and Turner's engagement couldn't have come at a worse time for his daughters, especially when it came on the heels of his move to Florida.

Almost ten minutes passed, and Phylicia still hadn't returned to the table. He started to get up to go see about her when the restroom door opened and she appeared. Her honey-brown hair slightly disheveled. Red-eyed. And completely beautiful.

She looked his way, angling her head toward the exit. "Can we go?" she mouthed.

He rose quickly, grabbed his jacket off the back of his chair, and hurried toward the door where she stood.

Without a word, she pushed the door open with both hands and made a beeline for his SUV.

Silent and somber-faced, Quinn backed his vehicle out of the McAlister's parking lot.

Phee took a deep breath, trying to collect herself. "I'm so sorry. Did you even get to finish your sandwich?"

He waved her off. "I'm not hungry. It's fine."

She felt awful for rushing him out like that, but she couldn't help the smile that came. "Now you sound like me."

He didn't return her humor. "It's obviously *not* fine, Phylicia. What's going on? I didn't mean to make you . . . *cry.*"

"It's not you." She shook her head, his sober expression influencing her own. "It's just . . . everything. Mom, Dad, this decision."

"See, it *is* me. I'm the one who's forcing you to make a decision."

"No, it's not you. It's Dad. I know how he can be."

"You mean caring and helpful and generous?"

She studied him, not sure if he was serious or teasing. "You really think he's doing this out of concern for us?"

His eyes said he was dead serious. "Phylicia . . . why else would it be?"

"Maybe he feels guilty. And he's just trying to get us set up so he can sell the house and be rid of us."

"You don't really believe that."

"Sometimes I do. I can't even get him to answer my phone calls." She shook her head. "I don't know what to believe anymore, Quinn. This just all seems so sudden. And so unlike my dad."

It felt odd, confiding in him this way. Yes, she'd hoped he could shed some light on her dad's strange behavior. And she'd hoped to convince herself it would be a mistake to buy the property. But look how *that* was working out. She'd been blindsided by her sisters suddenly being so gung-ho about the prospect of owning property. And Quinn *was* persuasive.

"I think you need to talk to your dad. It's not fair to accuse him when you haven't heard his side of things and —" He stopped short, apparently thinking better about whatever it was he'd been going to say.

But she could almost read his thoughts. He was afraid she'd start crying again. She shouldn't care so much what he thought, but none of this was his fault, and she didn't want him to feel responsible. He was only doing what he'd been directed to do by his boss. Yet another reason she wanted to throttle her father.

She hadn't been fair to Quinn, lashing out at him, when all he'd done was try to help. Doing the things her father should have been doing. She rubbed her arm absently, remembering the tenderness of Quinn's touch, her surprise at how the warmth of his hand had comforted her.

"Are you okay?"

His voice intruded on her thoughts, and she tucked them away to explore later.

She looked up at him, sighing. "Okay, I'll call my dad tonight. Maybe I can get to the bottom of this." She checked her phone. "It's an hour later in Orlando. Would you mind taking me back to my car so I can get home and call him before it gets too late?"

"Of course." The relief in his voice was anything but subtle. "I really think you'll feel better after you talk to him."

She wasn't so sure. She wrapped her coat tighter around her. But at least she'd be getting the talk with Dad out of the way.

Quinn drove her back to Dad's house in silence, which she appreciated. As soon as they pulled up, she noticed Joanna's car was gone. "Oh . . . Britt must have gone back to Jo's apartment."

"Is that a problem?"

"No. Sorry . . . I'm just thinking out loud. Britt doesn't like to stay by herself, so she's probably staying at Jo's again tonight." She opened her car door and slid out, careful not to slip on the snow that crusted the driveway.

Quinn opened his door. "I'll walk you to

the door."

"You don't need to do that." She'd intended just to get in her car and drive back to her apartment. But she probably should check on the house. And make sure Melvin had been fed.

"I don't mind." He came around and met her in front of his vehicle, offering his arm.

She accepted and they started up the walk together.

"So, Britt's scared to stay alone?"

She nodded. "Of what, I don't know. It's not as if the big city of Langhorne is teeming with criminals."

"You think that's why she's so excited about the property?"

"Not having to live alone?" Phee considered the possibility. "I'm sure that's one reason. She'll need to find a place of her own — if we don't buy the property."

They climbed the stoop and Quinn waited while Phee found her keys. "You don't think your sister will be scared living out on the edge of town?"

"Not if our houses are that close together." Shoot! Now he had her thinking about the property again. "Either way, Britt is just going to have to grow up and get over it. She's twenty-four years old! It's about time she learned how to spend a night by herself, don't you think?"

He shrugged, obviously not wanting to take sides in this sisterly spat.

Feeling guilty for her unkind words, she stamped snow off her shoes and inserted the key into the lock. Britt had been braver than all of them when it came to taking care of Mom — and it had gotten pretty ugly at times. Times when Phee had found excuses to disappear and let her sisters take the brunt of Mom's pain. *Forgive me, Lord.*

"Well, thanks for the ride." She gave a little wave, then opened the door. "And for supper. Such as it was."

"You're welcome." He started to say something, then closed his mouth and turned away. But quickly turned back. "Not to hound you or anything, but if you could let me know in the next few days — one way or another — about the property. I don't think it'll last long in this current market."

"I'll let you know." She knew he was only doing what Dad would expect of him. Which only served to rankle her further.

She waited until Quinn's SUV was out of sight before entering the house. Melvin met her in the hallway, and she bent to stroke him. "Hey, buddy. Did they abandon you?" He meowed in reply and trotted toward the basement where his food and water dishes were.

Phee followed him and checked to be sure Britt had fed him, then did a quick walk through the house. Passing by the door to the guest room, memories overwhelmed her. The hospital bed had been returned, replaced by an antique bed Mom had inherited from her grandmother. But all Phee saw was that clinical, sterile room where Mom had lived out the last days of her life. She could almost smell the pungent tang of Betadine and disinfectant that hospice had used to mask the smell of death.

Sloughing off the memories, she hurried through the house to the front door. Her cramped, boring apartment in Cape sounded welcoming compared to this empty shell of a house.

And besides, she wanted to get the call to Dad over with.

CHAPTER 8

Her apartment was freezing, since she'd turned down the heat before leaving for work this morning. Phee tapped the thermostat up to seventy-four and went to change into a sweatshirt and pajama bottoms.

She made a cup of Earl Grey tea and tuned Pandora to a classical music station, knowing full well she was stalling. But she couldn't stall forever. Like she'd told Quinn, it was an hour later in Florida, and it would not be conducive to a good conversation if she woke Dad up.

She carried her tea into the living room, curled up on the sofa, and brought up her dad's number on speed dial. While she waited for him to answer, she looked around the sparsely decorated room. As much as she loved decorating and "nesting," she hadn't done much with this apartment because . . . well, because it had never really been home to her. Or more accurately, she hadn't wanted to turn it into a home because that would be admitting that she was settled. And alone. That no one had showed up to share her life. Not in college. Not even after she'd graduated and entered the working world. Never mind that working in a flower shop meant the only men she ever met were buying flowers for their wives and sweethearts. Not exactly conducive to meeting the love of your life.

"Hey, Phee! How's my girl?" Dad's overly cheery voice interrupted her dreary thoughts.

"Hi, Dad. How's it going?"

"Good! It's going well. How about you? Everything going okay there?" Her father's voice took on a false tone. The way it sometimes did when she showed up at his office unannounced . . . as if he were putting on a show for everyone. Not that her dad was a fake, but he was concerned about appearances. Always had been. It was part of his job, she supposed. And maybe the reason it bugged her so much was because she was too much like him in that regard.

"Yeah, Dad. Everything's —" If she didn't broach the subject now, it would never happen. She inhaled, feeling as though she were breathing through a wet dishrag. "No. Actually, everything is *not* okay. Everything *stinks.* We need you, Dad. We need you *here.* You picked the worst possible time to move, and I'm sorry, but I don't understand why you would do that!" She took another breath, not wanting him to get the chance to try to reason with her. But she'd run out of words.

"Phee. Don't do this. I feel bad enough as it is."

"Well, maybe you should feel bad." In all the years Mom had been sick, there hadn't been a harsh word between her and her father. He'd been a wonderful dad and a caring husband — at least she'd thought so. But maybe that had only been for appearances too. She didn't know what to believe now.

"Phee, I know this is hard. But you girls have each other. This is a good time for you all to pull together and figure out what's next. Don't think I'm not aware of how much each of you sacrificed for your mom —"

"And for you, Dad! We didn't do it just for her. We did it for you too. And this is how you thank us?"

"Phee. Stop. You don't know all the circumstances. Now don't say something you'll regret."

"Then *tell* me. Tell me the circumstances

so I can understand." She held out her right hand and tried to steady her trembling fingers.

"It's not that simple. If I told you, I doubt you'd understand. I'm still . . . to be honest, I'm still figuring things out myself. But I need time to do that. I think it'll all make sense eventually. To you girls, I mean. But right now, you're too close to your mom's death. Grief is making you see things differently than they really are. That's normal. It's happened to me too. But please just trust me. I need to be here — in Florida — right now."

"With her?"

"Karleen, you mean?"

"Who else would I mean?" It was too late to soften the anger in her voice.

"Phylicia. Don't do this, honey. This isn't like you." His voice went soft, and he once again sounded like the loving daddy she could scarcely remember. And she knew he was right about one thing — grief was distorting everything until she felt they hardly knew each other anymore.

The lump in her throat wouldn't let her speak for a minute. Finally, she managed to mutter an apology. She wanted to throw herself into her father's arms and weep.

But he was in Florida. With *her.*

And Phee honestly didn't know if she could trust him anymore. *That* hurt more than anything.

"Phee? Are you there?"

"I'm here." She forced herself to speak calmly. "I mostly called because Quinn Mitchell showed us that property and said you thought we should buy it."

"Ah, good. He's talked to you about it then."

"You really think that's what we should do?"

"I'm not going to tell you what to do. You girls are all adults. It ultimately has to be your decision. But I do think it would be a good deal . . . a good investment for you girls. And Quinn had some good ideas about how you could maximize the investment."

She struggled off the couch and went to turn down the music while Dad gave her pretty much the same spiel Quinn had given them. "Okay then. We'll talk about it, Dad. I think Jo and Britt are already onboard."

"Good. I'm glad." He sounded distracted. "Well, honey . . . I need to run. Tell the girls hello. I love you all."

That was it? He wasn't going to let her talk? He wasn't going to answer the questions she'd asked or explain why he'd left them to deal with all of this on their own?

Anger threatened to spill again. But her dad knew her too well, and she said goodbye before she said something she'd regret.

As soon as she laid her phone down, the anger dissolved into tears. When they'd buried her mom, she never dreamed they were losing Dad too — as surely as if he'd been buried there beside her. It hurt too much to think about.

She picked up her phone and texted Joanna. *Is Britt with you?*

No, I'm in Cape. At my apartment. Believe it or not, she stayed at the house tonight.

She wasn't there when Quinn dropped me off at my car.

She just left my place a few minutes ago.

Seriously? She's getting brave. Because of Melvin?

Melvin is at Mom and Dad's.

Her breath caught. They all did it — called the house Mom and Dad's. And she wasn't sure how she would ever drive down that street again once someone else was living there. But then, it couldn't be any worse than having no one living there, could it?

She tapped out a reply to Joanna. *I KNOW where Melvin is. I meant, is that why Britt stayed?*

Your guess is as good as mine. She didn't say.

OK. Talk to you tomorrow.

Wait . . . What are your thoughts about the property?

Still mulling. I'll call you tomorrow.

No fair.

Phee giggled. She "hearted" her sister's message and clicked off her phone. She could just picture Joanna's frustrated growl. Jo was probably texting Britt right now, hypothesizing about whether Quinn Mitchell had swayed Phee to their side.

The sad thing was, maybe he had. Between Quinn's enthusiasm and what little Dad had said, it was probably a done deal. But her sisters didn't need to know that yet. Let them sleep on it a night. Let them lie awake thinking of the thousand things *she'd* thought of that could go wrong.

She just wanted Dad to tell them what to do. To walk them through this, to *be* there for them the way he always had. She did not understand what was going on with him, and as much as she loved him and grieved to have him so far away, she wasn't sure she could ever forgive him.

Most of all, she just wanted everything to go back to the way it had been before Mom got sick. But that wasn't going to happen. Not ever.

The jangle of her cell phone on the nightstand startled Phee from a sound sleep. Justin Bieber. *Baby, baby, baby, oh . . .* Her baby sister's ringtone. Britt had chosen it herself, and the song made Phee smile every time. Except —

Propping herself on one elbow, she squinted at the clock and gave a little gasp. It was after one a.m. "Britt? What's wrong?"

"Oh, Phee. Can you come? I did something really stupid." Her sister sounded out of breath.

"Britt? What happened?"

Silence.

"What is going on, sis? Where are you?"

"I'm home . . . at Mom and Dad's. The . . . the police are here, Phee."

"What?" She threw off the covers and hurried to her closet to look for a pair of shoes and a jacket she could throw over her pajamas. "Why are the police there?"

"I'll explain everything, but can you please come?"

Heart pounding, Phee threw her coat on and headed for her car, keeping Britt on the phone as she ran. "I'm on my way. I'll be there in fifteen minutes. Are you okay?"

"I'm fine. Just . . . please don't be mad." The phone went dead.

What in the world? Without bothering to buckle up, she backed out of her parking space and drove too fast through streets that were, thankfully, empty.

But almost the minute she turned down Cape Street, the strobe of police lights lit the night sky, and her heart rate ratchetted up another notch. *What could have happened?*

Chapter 9

Two police cruisers were parked in front of the house, and neighbors dressed like Phee — jackets hastily thrown over pajamas — milled in the front yard or stood shivering on their front porches.

Phee parked in the street as close as she could get to the house and ran up the driveway, casting about wildly, looking for Britt. Halfway up the drive, she spotted her, huddled on the front steps talking to an officer. When Britt saw Phee, she ducked under the officer's outstretched arm and hurried toward her.

"I'm so sorry, Phee," she said again and again. "I jumped the gun. I shouldn't have called the police."

"What happened? Britt? Why are the police here?"

The officer approached her. "Are you the sister?"

"One of them. I'm Phylicia. What happened?"

"Everything's okay. Just a misunderstanding." He pointed back toward the house where two officers stood on the porch. "We're just checking everything out to be sure."

"Sure about what? Britt? What happened?"

Britt put her head in her hands. "I'm so sorry, officer. I feel so stupid!"

"It was an honest mistake, ma'am. Could have happened to anyone."

Phee let out a breath. "Would someone please tell me what is going on?"

"It's Melvin's fault," Britt said. "He knocked a vase off the counter. I heard glass shattering and I thought someone was breaking in, so I . . . called the police."

"I told her better safe than sorry." The young officer gave an understanding nod. "We'll get out of your hair now and let everyone get back to bed."

"Thank you, sir." Phee put a hand on Britt's back, suddenly feeling somehow responsible for what had happened. She knew Britt was skittish. If she hadn't been so selfish, she would have stayed here with her.

"Once I figured out it was only Melvin, I called 911 back and told them not to come, but they were already pulling onto our street by the time I hung up."

"Come on, Britt. I'll help you clean up. Where's Melvin?"

"He's inside. I shut him in the basement so he wouldn't escape while everybody was coming and going."

"Okay." She turned to the policeman. "Thanks again . . . for everything. We're all right now."

"No problem, ma'am. Okay if we let the neighbors know what happened? Give everybody a better night's sleep if they know it was a false alarm."

"Of course. Thank you."

"Oh, and . . . hang on a second." The officer disappeared around the corner of the house and returned with a red plastic bag marked *Biohazard.* "Don't let the bag scare you. I'm afraid the vase might be beyond repair, but in case it had sentimental value, I saved the pieces."

He opened the bag, and Phee peered inside to see shards of bright turquoise — the vase Karleen Tramberly had sent. "Thank you, but you can take it away. We don't want to repair it." She swallowed against the bitterness in the back of her throat.

The second cruiser had already backed

out of the drive by now, and neighbors were starting to disperse. Phee nudged Britt, who was shivering and still muttering under her breath about how stupid she was. "Come on. Let's go in."

All the lights in the house were on, and they could hear Melvin yowling from the basement.

"I'll go let him out. You get a broom, in case there are any slivers left." Phee started for the basement door.

"No, I already cleaned up the mess. That cop helped me, actually."

"Seriously? Well, that was nice."

"Are you mad at me?"

"No, I'm not mad." She tucked a wayward strand of hair off her sister's pretty face. "But why did you suddenly decide to stay here by yourself? It's kind of unbelievable that the first night you stay by yourself, *this* happens."

Britt gave a little laugh. "Tell me about it."

"So, what's the deal? You just decided to go for it?" Phee had a feeling something else was at play, but she couldn't guess what.

"Promise you won't get mad if I tell you?"

Phee frowned. "You make it sound as if I'm some ogre you have to be scared of. I'm not going to get mad."

Britt looked at the floor. "I just didn't want you making a decision about the property on the basis of me being too chicken to stay here by myself."

"Why would you think I'd do that?"

"I could just tell. You were worried about me. I just wanted to prove that I can stay by myself if I have to." She gave a humorless laugh. "I guess I blew that, huh?"

"It's okay, sis. I probably would have done the same thing. And I'm sorry you had such a scare."

Britt rolled her eyes. "It's funny. Now that I lived through that, it really wasn't so bad. I can't believe how fast the police got here!"

Phee had to smile. "Well, it *would* have been bad if it had been a real break-in! Don't let this be the little boy who cried wolf."

"I didn't cry wolf! I really thought someone was breaking in —"

"No, no . . ." She put a hand on Britt's arm. "That's not what I mean at all. I meant, don't let this make you think it's just Melvin next time you hear a noise."

Britt's forehead knit with worry, and Phee suppressed a groan. *Oh, great.* Now she'd have her sister focused on what *could* have happened. Would she ever learn to control her big fat mouth? "I have to work tomorrow, sis. You okay if I go home? Or do you want to stay with me tonight?"

"No, I'm fine. I'll be fine. Sorry I woke you up. I'm not sure why I called you, really."

"Because I'm your big sister. What else are sisters for if not to come and rescue you when your house is surrounded by handsome policemen?"

Britt giggled. "Oh, yeah, now I remember."

Phee wrapped an arm around her, emotion thick in her throat. It should have been Mom and Dad here, comforting Britt. Phee felt as if she'd been thrust, most unwillingly, into the role of matriarch — and she didn't like it one bit.

The alarm on Phee's cell phone went off far too early, and Phee stumbled to the bathroom to get ready for work. She avoided checking her phone for fear there'd be texts from her sisters pressuring her to let them know her decision about the property.

She probably should call to check on Britt after what had happened last night. But she didn't really have time. She felt bad that her younger sister had seemed scared to open up to her about her fear of staying alone. And yet — Phee squeezed a line of toothpaste onto her toothbrush — she was almost flattered that Britt thought Phee might make her decision purely out of love and concern for her baby sister.

Phee glanced at herself in the mirror. If only she were that selfless.

But somebody had to be practical. Someone would need to keep Mom and Dad's house ready to show and staged for the open house. Not that there was any rush about that. She'd checked this morning, and the money from Mom's inheritance hadn't been deposited yet, so even if they did sell the house, it wasn't as if they could make an offer on the other property until the funds were there. Part of her was inclined to take her sweet time. And if the place was still for sale when they had the cash, then she'd take it as a sign they were supposed to buy it.

She'd never been one for putting out fleeces, but she didn't know how else to make a huge decision like this. Not without Dad to guide the way.

A short while later, she arrived at the flower shop to find half a dozen cars crowding the parking lot. By the time she'd hurried in through the back door, a queue had already formed at the counter.

Mary Feldman, the owner, finished ringing up a bouquet of carnations, then hollered over her shoulder, "Phee! Thank goodness you're here."

Phee glanced at the clock over the checkout counter. "I'm not late, am I?" She'd already decided she wouldn't mention the excitement of last night. Small-town gossip could turn a simple call to the police into an international incident. But she felt bad making Mary stress out. Her boss had been down off and on with some kind of bug for at least a month now, and Phee didn't like the pallor of her complexion today.

"No, you're not late." Mary waved a hand. "But we're swamped. Apparently some speaker told the men's group at First Christian last night that flowers were the way to a woman's heart."

Phylicia laughed. "And how much did you have to pay the speaker to say that?"

"Hey, if I'd paid, I would have specified roses and orchids." Mary rolled her eyes and ran a hand through her salt-and-pepper hair. "We've had a huge run on daisies and carnations."

"I bet you won't hear the wives complaining."

"True. And business is business. I'm *not* complaining."

"For a minute I thought it was Valentine's Day already." Phee grabbed an apron off the hook, looped it over her neck, and tied a loose bow at her waist. "You want me at the register or in the back?"

"Back, if you don't mind. Burgess isn't coming in until one to deliver, but we have some orders that need to go out over the lunch hour. From that church group, I assume."

"Man, that must have been some speaker."

Mary shot her a droll grin. "Do you mind arranging those . . . and maybe delivering them too?"

"I don't mind." That wasn't exactly true. If anything hammered home her still-single status, it was delivering flowers to somebody's sweetheart. Still, it beat delivering funeral flowers — just barely.

As she beelined for the back room, two customers stopped her along the way. She quickly answered their questions and then continued on to the back, where she looked over the orders. Except for the few "Please deliver over the lunch hour" requests, nothing unusual popped up. She could listen to music and get lost in her work. Besides the flowers themselves, that was her favorite thing about this job. A job she'd had since graduating from Southeast Missouri State — with a teaching degree. She'd been offered the job at Langhorne Blooms her first summer after graduation, and when the teaching offer finally came, it was for a halftime kindergarten job — the one grade she'd adamantly *not* wanted to teach. She'd chosen to stay on with Mary just for the school year, even though the money was nowhere near as good.

Six years later, here she still was. Mary had been generous with raises each year, and Phee had never even put in an application for another job. If she were honest with herself, she had no desire to teach now. It was kind of the default degree at Southeast, and she'd come out of four and a half years of classes with no clearer idea of what she wanted to be when she grew up than she'd had the day she started school.

And she liked the flower-shop job a lot — liked making people happy with the bouquets and arrangements she created. Liked working with the amazing colors of God's creation, choosing unique containers for her bouquets, and experimenting with unusual combinations of flowers and greenery. Oh, the job had its downsides, but what job didn't?

She put together half a dozen little bouquets she thought would be just what the men's group was looking for — sweet pastel posies tied with ribbon or twine. When she finished, she carried them to the front and arranged them on the little flower cart by the checkout. Mary had created a sign for the top of the cart that read, "Buy a Bunch of Happy. Or Two!"

Phee thought it a little cheesy when she first saw it, but the little posies sold like hotcakes and proved to be a perfect way to use up the blooms left over from wedding and funeral flowers and the more formal, arranged bouquets.

By eleven, the crowd had thinned considerably, but as she turned to go back to the workroom, the bells on the front door jangled, and she turned to see a familiar figure walk through.

Quinn saw her before she could make her escape to the back, so she approached him with her best retailer smile. "Good morning. How can I help you?"

"Oh . . ." He glanced from her name tag to the hem of her apron and back, looking uncomfortable. "I was kind of hoping you wouldn't be working this morning."

"I've been working here for seven years, Quinn. Why would I not be here this morning?"

"My bad." He held up a hand. "Well, this is awkward."

"Excuse me?"

His grin turned sheepish. "I was going to have flowers sent to you. You and your sisters, of course. Not just you —"

"Flowers?" The man was acting as if he'd just robbed a bank or something. "Why would you send *us* flowers?" And which one of their apartments did he plan to have them delivered to?

He shuffled his feet and stuffed his hands into his pockets. "I heard about what happened last night."

"What? With Britt?"

He nodded.

"Seriously? How on earth did you hear? It just happened a few hours ago!"

He shrugged. "Gotta love small-town gossip."

She made a face. "So, who told you?"

"I'm friends with a couple of the guys at the station."

"The police station?" She narrowed her eyes. "Aren't they supposed to keep this stuff confidential?"

"They didn't mention any names."

"Then how'd you know it was Britt?"

His expression turned sheepish. "Promise you won't get mad?"

Britt had said the same thing to her last night. Did everyone think she was a cranky old witch? "Why would I get mad? Just tell me."

"One of the guys — a cop — who was on the call mentioned . . . it was two hot chicks. In pajamas."

Hiding a smile, she put a hand on one hip and tried to act annoyed. "What? So you're telling me he said 'two hot chicks in PJs,' and you just immediately deduced it was Britt and me?"

"He might have mentioned the street it happened on." He poked one cheek out with his tongue. "Oh . . . and that a cat named Marvin might have been involved."

She glared at him. "It's *Melvin.*"

"Sorry. Melvin."

She closed her eyes. "Great. Just great. Way to protect our confidentiality, policemen of the world."

"Hey, I don't think you need to throw all policemen everywhere under the bus. This was a good buddy. He knew I wouldn't say anything."

"Did he know you'd come to the flower shop — where I just happen to work — to buy flowers for the victims?"

"Victims? The way I heard it, the *cops* were the victims."

She sputtered a few nonsensical syllables before she found her voice. "Tell you what . . .” She put a hand on his elbow and steered him toward the front door. It took great effort to keep a straight face. “You can just save yourself forty dollars and go right back to your car. You *are* aware it was flowers that started this whole mess in the first place? Or maybe your friend left out a detail or two.”

He didn’t even try not to laugh. And she had to admit it was kind of funny. But not funny enough that she was going to encourage him. She was still . . . *confused* about why he would want to buy them flowers.

“Hey, I just thought some flowers might cheer you up.” He shrugged one shoulder. “Excuse me for being thoughtful.”

“It was a sweet thought, Quinn. It really was. But if I want flowers, I can get them with my employee discount. Thanks for coming in.” Barely curbing her laughter, she took his arm and escorted him through the door.

She closed the door behind him. But even with his back to her, she could see his shoulders shaking. If her sisters managed to talk her into this little business venture Quinn was suggesting, she would need to search for some tasty recipes for preparing crow.

CHAPTER 10

Hiding behind the huge Langhorne Blooms logo etched on the plate-glass window, Phee watched Quinn drive away, waiting until his SUV was out of sight. She turned back to the checkout desk.

Head tilted to one side, Mary stared at her. "What's so funny?"

Phee quickly wiped the smile from her face. "Oh, nothing."

"Wasn't that Quinn Mitchell?"

"Yes. You know him?"

"He was the contractor when we remodeled the store."

"Oh, I kind of remember Dad saying something about that. That was before I came to work here."

"He's a great guy. Want me to put in a good word for you?"

"A good word for what?"

A smirk tipped the older woman's mouth. "Don't play dumb. I saw the way you were looking at him. And vice versa, I might add."

She cringed, looking around the shop to see who might have overheard her boss's comment. "How old do you think I *am,* anyway?"

"Are you an adult?"

"Yes. Just barely." She grinned, hoping her boss would drop the subject.

"I happen to have access to your most private information, which clearly says you're almost thirty."

"Hey! Isn't that supposed to be kept strictly confidential?"

Mary ignored her teasing and tipped her head. "How old do you think *Quinn* is?"

"Too old for me."

"Dear girl, there's no such thing as too old when you're as old as you are."

"Now that's hitting below the belt." She knew Mary was teasing her, but the comment stung a little. "So, how old do *you* think Quinn is?"

"Ah, so you *are* interested."

"He's a nice guy, but he must be . . . at least forty."

"So? Forty is just getting good. Most men aren't ready to settle down until they hit forty. I say grab the man while you can."

"Stop. You make me sound desperate." Phee didn't know how old Quinn was, but she'd always thought of him as a whole generation ahead of her. Closer to Dad's age than hers. That had never kept her from thinking he was a fine specimen of a man, but to be talking like this with Mary was a whole different thing. Still, if Mary didn't think it was awkward for her to think of Quinn that way, maybe —

The bells on the door made them both turn — and offered a blessed interruption.

Burgess, the retiree who did their flower deliveries, came through, shrugging out of his jacket before he even stepped over the threshold. "Got to strip down for this hot-house."

Mary laughed. "Maybe you should work back in the cooler and let Kelli do the deliveries today."

"Oh, no . . ." Burgess chuckled and shook his head. "You don't want me arranging flowers . . . any more than you want Kelli driving the truck."

That cracked Phee and Mary up. Kelli Parsons had gotten her third traffic citation last week — this one for going the wrong way on a one-way street.

When their laughter died down, Phee blew out a sigh of relief, thankful that Mary seemed to have dropped the subject of Quinn Mitchell. With a wave to Burgess, she escaped to the back room.

But she couldn't quit thinking about what her boss had said. She wondered what Mary had seen on her face. How, exactly, did she think Phee was looking at Quinn? Worse, did Quinn see the same thing in her expression? Her cheeks heated to think that her feelings were that transparent.

But Quinn was her father's coworker. Sure, he was handsome . . . and turning out to be a pretty decent person too. She'd often wondered why he wasn't married. But what if Mary was right and he was only forty? That wasn't such a big deal —

Instantly, she thought of her father and Karleen. *That* was a big deal. An almost creepy deal. But that was different. For one thing, Dad was probably close to twenty years older than Karleen. And he'd just lost his wife. That was the real issue.

The anger she'd been harboring toward him roiled.

She worked on bouquets for the flower cart for the next hour, then relieved Mary at the cash register so she could get some lunch. Phee was just about to take her own lunch break when Joanna's ringtone sounded from her purse in the break room. The shop was empty, so she fished out her phone and plopped down at a table near a window overlooking the alley.

She pressed Accept. "Hey, sis —"

"Why didn't you call me?"

"Well, hi to you too, Jo. My day's going great, thanks for asking. How about you?"

"Me? Not so great. It would have been nice not to find out from someone else that the police made a middle-of-the-night run to our house."

"Someone *else*? Who?"

"Quinn Mitchell called me. Why didn't you tell me?"

"Seriously? You heard from Quinn? What, did he try to send you flowers?"

"Huh?"

"Never mind. So Quinn told you about Britt's run-in?"

"Yes, and right after I talked to him, my boss asked me about it."

"Are you kidding me? Is that the most exciting thing people in this town have to talk about?"

"What happened, Phee? Why didn't you guys call me?"

"What did Quinn tell you?" She wondered if he'd talked to Joanna first, or after he left the flower shop. An emotion she couldn't quite identify niggled at her. It felt oddly like . . . jealousy.

"Quinn said it was a false alarm. But there

were three police cars there? Why would they send that many cops for a false alarm?"

"There were *two* police cars. Langhorne doesn't even *have* three police cars, do they? Good grief. It'll probably be on the front page of the *Missourian* tonight too, and blown all out of proportion! What is wrong with people?"

"Is Britt okay? She's not answering her phone."

"She's probably embarrassed. But yes, she's fine. Or she was when I left there last night. It was just Melvin. You heard that, right? He knocked a stupid vase over."

"Yes, that's what Quinn said."

"I'm actually proud of Britt for staying by herself."

"She stayed even after the police came?"

"She did. Said it actually made her feel good to know the police could get there so quickly."

"Well, that's rich." Joanna sighed. "But that's good, I guess. Okay, I'd better get back to work. But . . . I don't mean to nag you, Phee, but I just wondered if you'd thought any more about the property."

Her hackles went up, and she scooted back from the table. "How could I think about anything else? Between you and Britt and then Quinn and Dad, that's all I *can* think about."

"You talked to Dad about it?"

She hadn't told her sisters about calling him last night. Another thing she resented Dad for. She and her sisters had become so close during Mom's illness. But it seemed as if they'd been at odds more often than not these last few weeks. She blamed her father.

But maybe that was as much her own fault as his. She shot up a prayer for a quick attitude adjustment. "I called him the other night, but we didn't talk long. He seemed in a big hurry to get off the phone. He thinks the property is a good idea for us. And it sounded like he did ask Quinn to approach us about it. I guess that makes me feel a little better."

"Would you be willing to go look at it again tonight?"

"Tonight?"

"Well, I guess it doesn't have to be today. But we don't want to wait too long. I think Quinn's right that once people realize they've come down on the price, it might sell quickly."

"And you think we should buy it?"

"Britt and I have talked about it a lot, Phee. I'm excited about it. I really am. But we couldn't do it without you and — sorry,

I didn't mean that to sound like a threat or anything. But Britt and I were talking and . . . well, if you're not interested, we might even see if we can find a third partner to go in with us. Maybe Quinn."

Phee's jaw dropped. "He wants in on it himself?" Is that what this was all about? But Dad had been behind the idea.

"No, no . . ." Jo sighed. "We haven't even talked to Quinn. We're hoping *you'll* go in with us. You're our first choice. But Britt and I want to do it. No matter what."

Phee felt immediately guilty for having accused Quinn, even in her mind. "Wow. I just don't get how you both are suddenly so full-steam-ahead on this."

"We just got to talking, and the more we talked, the more we got excited. If the three of us went in on this, we'd all have more freedom. No mortgage, an investment, income from the rentals. Britt and I could go back to school and —"

"Fine. I'll go. Just to look."

"Oh good! Thanks, Phee. Any night this week would work for me, and probably for Britt. I might talk to Quinn about it too. He sounded as if he might be interested in the property himself, so maybe he'd want to go in with us if you decided not to."

"Wait . . . Don't say anything to him yet. I

want a chance to look at the place again. To be honest, I wasn't really looking at it with the idea of making an offer the first time." She'd just been humoring Quinn. But wow. They were really serious about this.

"Don't worry." Phee could almost hear the smirk in Joanna's words. "We won't offer him a partnership or anything until you're sure you don't want in on this. But I'd feel better if we had Quinn to help negotiate with the real estate agent. After that, I can find my way around the legal stuff."

"Okay."

"And Quinn doesn't necessarily have to come with us to look at the property, but I'd feel better if he did."

"I can talk to him if you want me to." She wasn't sure where that had come from, but she felt oddly grateful for an excuse to call him.

"Oh, that'd be great, sis! I'm so glad!"

Phee knew that barely controlled pitch in her sister's voice. "I haven't said yes, Jo."

"I know. I know . . . I'm not rushing you. But . . . I am excited. Britt will be too."

Despite her prayer of a minute ago, Phee didn't dare tell her sisters that she was starting to get a little excited about the whole idea herself.

The more she thought about Quinn coming in to buy them flowers, the more she regretted not letting him do just that. It was the kind of thing Dad would do . . . at least he would have before he went nuts and moved to Florida.

Her phone rang almost as soon as she disconnected from talking to Jo. She checked the screen.

"Hi, Dad." No doubt he'd heard about the whole police fiasco. "How's it going?" Hearing the tentativeness in her own voice, she knew Dad would pick up on it too. They hadn't exactly ended on a happy note last night.

"Hi, honey. I know you're at work, so I'll make this quick."

"It's okay. I'm on my lunch break. How are you?"

"Oh, I'm fine. I'm just calling to let you know that your mom's money has been deposited in all you girls' accounts. You should be able to access it now."

Something in his voice — was it *finality*? — made her want to cry. "Oh. Thank you, Dad. Wow . . . that was quick."

"Not really. But I got it in there as soon as I could. Have you made any decisions about the property?" Now he was pressuring her too? She wondered if Jo had put him up to this.

"I'm going to go look at it again with Jo and Britt tonight."

"That's good. Well, there shouldn't be anything keeping you from jumping on the deal now. So, you girls all like the idea? The property?"

"Jo and Britt are sold, that's for sure. I'm still kind of on the fence, but we're —" The flower shop phone rang from both the front desk and the wall phone behind her.

"Sounds like you need to go. No worries. I just wanted to let you know about the deposits."

"Wait! Dad, can you hang on for just a sec?"

"It's okay. I know you're at work. We can talk later."

"Wait, Dad . . ." But the line was already dead. What was his deal? Something just wasn't right, and she didn't know what to do about it.

Chapter 11

It had all happened so fast. One minute, she didn't even know if she wanted to take a second look at the property, and now, here she stood, barely two weeks later with the keys to not one, but *three* houses in hand. Three stone cottages on Poplar Brook Road that she and her sisters now owned free and clear. It seemed a bit surreal.

But a little thrill went through her. Chased by a shard of sheer terror. *What had they gotten themselves into?*

"Congratulations. And happy Valentine's Day, ladies." Quinn grinned as if he'd won some huge wager. "Every Valentine's Day, you'll remember the day you closed on your first homes."

"Maybe," Joanna said, "but you know who we're calling the first time something falls apart."

"Or the first time we have another mouse incident." Phee shivered at the memory.

He laughed. "There is absolutely nothing to worry about. The exterminators have done their thing, and once Melvin moves in, you likely won't see another mouse within a two-mile radius." He looked from Phee to her sisters. "When do you think you'll move in?"

"We want to get this cottage painted and cleaned first. We're hoping to get in this weekend and get started."

"Do you have somebody coming, or are you doing the work yourself?" He scraped a trail in the dusting of snow on the porch with the toe of his boot. "I know a guy. Good painter. And he's cheap."

"Really?" Phee didn't want to spend a fortune on this cottage. The two smaller cottages would take most of their leftover cash, and those were the ones that stood to make them some income. At least she hoped so. "Can you give me his number?"

"If you're game, I'll just have him show up Saturday ready to paint."

"How do you know he's available on such short notice?"

"I'm pretty sure he is. But I'll let you know right away if not."

She shrugged. "Sure. That'd be great. We'll have the paint and supplies here and be ready to go. Say eight o'clock?"

"Sounds good."

She had a feeling she knew just what *guy* was going to be showing up to paint Saturday. And even though she still felt a little bit as if they'd been hoodwinked into this deal, Quinn had held their hands all the way. The whole process had gone as smoothly as she could imagine such a thing going — not that she'd ever bought a house before. Let alone three of them. And they had Quinn to thank for so much.

They hadn't even told Dad about the closing yet, although she had a feeling Quinn had been in touch with him all along. Dad had emailed her and her sisters the bank deposit slips. Another reminder that Mom was gone and was never coming back. Maybe Dad too. Her throat tightened and tears threatened.

She still struggled with the whole thing. Dad up and moving away. And supposedly getting married? She couldn't let herself dwell on it. Thankfully, the process of buying the property had occupied her thoughts in recent days. Still, in those moments just before sleep overtook her each night, her heart broke to think she'd lost both of her parents. Never mind that she was almost thirty. She didn't think there ever came a time when it didn't break your heart to lose loving parents.

And to have her life change so drastically — even if, ultimately, those changes turned out for the best — seemed like the worst possible timing. If ever she and her sisters needed stability, it was now.

"Okay, well, I think I'm going to take off." Quinn put on his newsie cap, then tipped it in their direction. "You girls celebrate! You made a very good investment. You won't regret this decision."

Joanna gave him a spontaneous hug. "Thank you for everything, Quinn."

Phee felt unaccountably shy. "Yes. Thank you. I'm not sure we could have done it without you." She couldn't bring herself to hug Quinn, even though Britt had gotten in line behind Jo to thank him with a bear hug.

"Of course you could have," he said. "You just needed someone to give you a little push."

"More like a shove off a steep cliff." She sort of meant it, yet she was glad when Quinn shot her a quick wink.

"Whatever it takes." Grinning, he turned and walked toward his car.

She had to admit, she was going to miss seeing Quinn Mitchell almost daily as they had these last few weeks. Her father's friend and employee had, in many ways, stepped in and done the things Dad *should* have been here doing.

After Quinn's SUV disappeared onto the highway, Phee turned to her sisters, determined not to ruin the celebratory mood. "We did it, guys!"

"I know." Joanna had a deer-in-the-headlights look in her eyes. "I hope we know what we're doing."

"Of course we don't." Britt grinned. "That's what makes it so exciting."

"Fine. If it's excitement you're looking for" — Jo threw Phee a wink — "we'll let you sleep in one of the old cottages."

"Nice try. But I'll be happy to take the smallest bedroom — until we get one of the other cottages livable."

Phee yawned. "I need to get home. It's been a long week."

"I bet." Jo nodded. "What were you thinking trying to close on the property right smack in the middle of the flower shop's busiest week of the year?"

"I have no clue. I apparently *wasn't* thinking."

"Well, it's done now," Joanna crowed. "We're homeowners, sisters!"

"And speaking of which, back here on Saturday to paint?" Phee hated to be a party pooper, but all she could see was the work that needed to be done before they could actually move in. "Can you both make it?"

"I'm in." Britt practically beamed.

"I'll be here." Jo seemed more sober.

"Hey . . ." Phee touched Jo's sleeve. "You're not having buyer's remorse are you?"

"No. Not yet, anyway. I might change my tune after Saturday though. Anybody want me to pick up coffee on my way out?"

"Let me just bring a coffee maker. We'll want one out here anyway." And it would save them a chunk of change. They were going to have to start living frugally until they knew what it would take to get the cottages livable.

"Okay." Jo squinted in skepticism. "Just don't forget."

Phee laughed. Jo loved her coffee more than most.

"Don't worry, I won't forget your precious coffee. And I might come out here after work tomorrow too. Just to do some cleaning. Anybody else want to come?"

"I'm so sorry, you guys, but I have to work late." Joanna's wrinkled brow said she was more worried than she let on. "I'm a little nervous they're going to ask me to work Saturday too. We're working a pretty big case."

"I can help you, Phee," Britt offered. "I'll bring some cleaning supplies from Mom and Dad's house."

Phee checked the calendar on her phone. "Okay. Will five thirty work?"

"Sure. That'll give us almost an hour of daylight too."

"I promise I'll make it up to you." Joanna looked genuinely disappointed. "And don't do anything too fun without me."

"Don't worry, Jo, we'll save the cleaning of the toilets just for you." Phee grinned, but she wished she felt as enthusiastic as her sisters.

Phee turned a three-sixty on one heel in the middle of the living room, surveying their cottage. The smell of coffee brewing mingled with the clean scents of Windex, Clorox, and a host of other cleaning products, making her forget the musty smell the house had worn the day they'd first looked at it. She and Britt had accomplished so much the last few nights, cleaning the kitchen and bathroom and wiping down the cupboards. Last night, when Joanna had joined them, they'd washed all the walls and cleaned the windows inside and out in preparation for painting.

She ran a hand along the spotless windowsill. It was hard to believe what a difference simply washing windows made. With the film of grime gone, sun streamed through the divided panes, casting a charming grid-work of shadows on the wood floors. They'd discovered that the old hardwood floors were in surprisingly good shape and would probably just need a good polishing for now.

She wished Mom could see what Grandma Clayton's inheritance had bought. Phee thought her mother would be pleased. Dad too. The familiar ache radiated from the vicinity of her heart. *If Dad even cared anymore.* She couldn't let herself think about him right now. It was too painful, too confusing.

She checked her phone. Almost eight o'clock. Quinn had texted earlier that "the paint guy" would be there by eight. Jo and Britt weren't coming until nine, so Phee had volunteered to come early and let the guy in. She'd be surprised if it was anyone but Quinn Mitchell himself.

She stepped out the back kitchen door and looked up into the woods that cradled the cottages. Quinn had walked the property, and she and her sisters had viewed it via satellite maps and photographs, but it was too cold right now to actually go exploring. She couldn't wait until the weather became warmer so she could see for herself what was back there.

Their property was only eight acres, but they had only one neighbor, and that house couldn't be seen from anywhere on the property — even with all the tree branches leafless — thanks to the dense woods and a nice slope on the lot.

Spring here promised to be glorious. She hoped they'd get some rain, so the "waterfront" property might boast some actual water. As long as it wasn't too much. Despite Quinn's reassurance, the stone walls around the two small cottages made her a little nervous, as if they'd been built of necessity to keep the water out of the yards. In their current state, she feared they'd be more like giant sieves.

She heard tires on the gravel on the other side of the house and went around to greet the painter. Sure enough, Quinn's SUV was coming up the lane. Smiling, she stood in the side yard and watched until he got out of the vehicle. He wore blue jeans, a sweatshirt, and a ball cap. It was a good look on him. She didn't think she'd ever seen him in anything but dressy khakis or a suit and tie. He went around to open the back hatch and extracted a folding ladder and what looked like pieces of scaffolding.

She didn't think he'd spotted her yet, so she ducked into the shadows, went back around to the kitchen door, and walked through the house to the front porch, trying in vain to come up with a witty comment about his attire.

He looked up when the front screen door slammed. "Good morning." He gave a nod, his arms full of painting equipment.

"What's going on?" She feigned innocence. "Did your guy back out on us?"

His grin turned sheepish. "Nope. He's here right on time."

"So *you're* the guy?"

"One and the same."

"Quinn . . . Why didn't you say something?"

"Because I figured you'd argue and tell me not to come."

"Well, you're right about that." She sighed and tilted her head. "So are you as cheap as this 'other' guy?"

"Even cheaper."

"Then quit standing around and get to work."

His laughter followed her into the house. And for some crazy reason, the sound of it made this place feel like home.

CHAPTER 12

Quinn laid his paint roller carefully in the pan and stepped back to admire their handiwork. They'd only been working on it a little over an hour, but Britt and Phylicia already had all of the woodwork taped off, except for in the wallpapered bedrooms. He had trimmed and rolled one whole wall in the living room, and the transformation was amazing.

He could tell Phylicia felt it too. She kept stepping away from the wall, tilting her head and squinting, as if imagining what the finished house would look like. And judging by that smile, she was pleased with what she envisioned.

They had the doors open to ventilate the paint fumes, and though the temperature outside was in the forties, the winter sun warmed the room and splashed dappled patches of yellow across the wood floors.

Joanna appeared in the front doorway.

"Looking good, you guys. Wow!"

Britt blew a strand of hair from her eyes. "Glad you could finally make it."

Phylicia didn't say anything, but Quinn sensed tension in the set of her jaw. He'd seen that expression before when Joanna was late for something — which seemed to be most of the time. He made a note to steer clear of the topic. The last thing he needed was to get in the middle of a sister fight.

Joanna and Britt started on the dining room and kitchen, while he and Phylicia finished painting the living room. He breathed a sigh of relief when the last touch-up was done, and he stood back to take in the results. "Looks pretty good, if I do say so myself."

Phylicia nodded. "Better than I expected." But her eyes said she was more than happy with the way it had turned out.

Even if the two smaller houses turned out to be closer to tearer-downers than fixer-uppers, this cottage was going to be one stunning place. Already, it made him think of Turner and Myra's house, which had always exuded a kind of warmth owed to the decor, but to something more than that. He thought Phee had inherited her mother's gift for making a house become a home.

A while later, he glanced at the clock. "You hungry?"

Phylicia laid her brush down. "Famished!"

"I'll go grab us something to eat." He went to the kitchen to take Joanna and Britt's orders.

Half an hour later, when he returned with sandwiches from Panera, Phylicia was doing some kind of paint treatment on the fireplace. He'd never been a fan of painting over brick, but this method let a lot of the natural brick show through, while considerably lightening up the overall look. He watched as she dabbed and brushed with confidence. "Have you done this . . . *technique* before?"

A corner of her mouth quirked. "Nope. But I've watched every episode of *Fixer Upper* ever aired and about a hundred how-to videos."

He laughed. "God bless YouTube. I've watched my share trying to finish my house."

She stopped, paintbrush aloft, and turned to him. "How's that coming along?"

"Slow. Very slow." He held out a short stack of Panera boxes, not wanting to reveal that his after-hours work here at the cottages was partly why progress on his own house had come to a screeching halt. "Can you take a break and eat something?"

"Mmm, definitely. But first . . . I need to stretch." She groaned as she rose from her haunches. "I forgot what hard work this is. Chip and Joanna make it look way too easy."

"Yes, but look at the results." His gaze swept the space. "What a difference."

"It's looking really good, isn't it? I can't wait to start bringing in furniture." She held up a hand in warning before hollering at her sisters in the next room. "Lunch is here!"

A paint-splattered Joanna and Britt appeared in the arched doorway to the kitchen.

Joanna's gaze fell on the half-finished fireplace. "Wow! That's looking really good, sis. Keep doing what you're doing."

"Thanks." Phylicia brushed her hands off on her jeans. "And hey, can you two come to Mom and Dad's house tomorrow and help sort through furniture?"

They both nodded, eagerly took the boxes Quinn offered, and disappeared back into the kitchen.

"I haven't seen the house since it was listed." Quinn unwrapped his sandwich. "Do you know if your dad has had any bites?"

Phylicia frowned. "One showing. And no offer."

"Don't worry. It's still early. Is your dad coming for the open house?" It looked as if she was the one carrying the burden of the deal.

Shrugging, she took her wrapped panini from the box. "I don't know. I . . . haven't talked to him." She dropped the sandwich, still in its wrapper, back in the box. "Let me go wash my hands and get us something to drink."

Quinn wanted to throttle Turner Chandler for placing this extra burden on his daughters. They were already reeling from too many difficult changes and the stress of a purchase they hadn't really sought. Quinn felt somewhat responsible, since he'd let Turner "bully" him into influencing the sisters, though he still thought they'd made a wise decision.

He hadn't spoken to Turner since his boss had called to inform Quinn that the money from Myra's inheritance had been deposited into their daughters' accounts. And Turner had been in a big hurry to get off the phone. Quinn had barely had time to congratulate him on his engagement. In fact, thinking back on it, Quinn couldn't remember having a decent conversation with his boss since he'd left for Florida. Quite the contrary. He had recurring fantasies about calling the man and letting him have it. Maybe he still would, especially now that the property had been safely transferred to the daughters' ownership. It probably wasn't any of his business, but he'd come to love these women like sisters.

The thought scarcely took shape before honesty blew it to smithereens.

He glanced over at Phylicia who was attempting to fix her ponytail in the dim mirror over the mantel. His gaze swept her silhouette, wanting to linger longer but resisting the temptation. Even dressed in ratty jeans and an oversized sweatshirt, she drew a man's eye. And no way did *this* man see Phylicia Chandler as a sister.

Far from it. And it was getting worse every hour he spent with her.

Phee gave up on making her hair look decent and wadded it into a messy knot on top of her head. If she'd been certain that Quinn was "the paint guy," she would not have rolled out of bed at the last minute and showed up with no makeup and unwashed hair. But she didn't want to be too obvious either. The thought stopped her short.

What did she care how she looked for Quinn Mitchell? She'd caught herself having similar thoughts far too often recently.

She glanced up at the bouquet of wilting roses on the mantel. Britt's flowers. Dad had sent all three of them roses for Valentine's Day, and Britt had been so thrilled she'd toted the vase out to the property with her. Not that getting flowers from Dad was surprising.

Phee couldn't remember a Valentine's Day they *hadn't* received roses from him, even when they were still living at home. Pink ones for the girls and yellow for Mom. After she started working at Langhorne Blooms, Dad continued to order from there, but Mary was sworn to secrecy.

Still, Phee hadn't expected roses from Dad this year. Not when he'd made himself so distant. And not when he had someone *new* to buy flowers for now. At least he hadn't forgotten his daughters. They'd each gone home from the closing meeting to find a delivery attempt had been made, and later that evening, roses were delivered to each of them at their respective addresses. They'd texted each other photos, comparing notes. He'd signed the card the same to each of them: *Love, Dad.* That was all. She wondered what he'd written on Karleen's card.

Phee had been almost relieved — and then felt guilty at her relief — when her roses wilted the fourth day. She'd thrown them in the Dumpster outside her apartment building before leaving this morning. Mary would have insisted on replacing the flowers if she'd known they hadn't lasted a week, but Phee wasn't about to tell her. Besides, she hadn't exactly taken good care of her bouquet. As if that might prove something to Dad.

Shaking off the unsettling thoughts, she picked up the sandwich box Quinn had left for her on the mantel and turned toward the kitchen.

He hooked a thumb over his shoulder. "It's close to fifty degrees out there already. You want to get some fresh air and try out the front porch?"

She shrugged. "Sure. Hang on a sec . . ." She crossed to the kitchen doorway and called to her sisters. "We're going to eat on the front porch. Want to join us?"

From her perch at the top of a low ladder, Britt pointed at two empty Panera boxes on the kitchen counter. "Thanks, but we already ate."

"Besides, we're about to whip this baby out." Joanna towered above both of them, standing on a countertop, touching up painted cupboards that reached all the way to the ten-foot ceilings.

"It's looking great in here." Phee felt bad she hadn't commented before. "I can't believe how much we've gotten done in a few hours."

"Many hands make light work."

"Thanks, Mom." Phee tried to keep her voice light, but it was Mom's favorite quote, and Britt sounded just like her.

Britt beamed at the compliment.

Phee quickly changed the subject. "Okay. We're taking a quick break, then I'll be back to help you finish up."

Quinn was still waiting by the front door, sandwich in hand. He followed her outside, then leaned against the porch railing with the sun at his back. "Now this is what I'm talking about. Feels like spring."

She hopped up to sit on the railing a few feet from him. "I wish it was. There's so much I want to do out here." She looked up at the cobweb-strewn ceiling. "Paint this ceiling, for one. Blue."

"Haint blue? Like all good Southern porches?"

"Haint?"

"That's what the color is called — haint blue. I think it means ghost."

"Huh-uh. There will be no talk of ghosts in *this* house." Shaking her head, she leaned to peer into the house through the open front door. "Especially not in earshot of Britt."

"Why? Is she afraid of ghosts?"

"Not ghosts. At least I don't think so. But" — she rolled her eyes — "as the whole town now knows, she's chicken to stay alone. Even in town at Mom and Dad's. And if she hears even a hint about ghosts — or bats or mice, for that matter — we'll never get her to stay out here."

He pinched his thumb and forefinger together and "zipped" his lips. "Then you did not hear that thing about ghosts from me."

"Let's just call it aqua, shall we?"

"Huh?"

"The color for the porch ceilings."

"Ah. Aqua it is. Aqua all the way." He took a man-sized bite of his sandwich. "And gray for the floor?"

She rubbed her toe across the peeling paint underfoot. It had originally been a traditional soft gray color. "We'll have to scrape it first."

"That won't take long. So, when do you want to start painting out here?"

"Let's finish the inside first. Will you be around next Saturday?"

"I'll be around any night this week — if you want."

"Really? That'd be great." She took a long swig from her water bottle. "The three of us will probably come out here every night. Except I don't think Jo can come tomorrow night."

"With three or four of us, we can probably knock out a bedroom a night. We'd be ready to paint that porch by Saturday . . . top to bottom."

"Wow. We could be moving in by next week." It almost didn't seem possible.

"You really could."

"Yes, but this was the easy one." She frowned. "The other two cottages aren't going to be done in a week."

"Rome wasn't built in a day."

"Or a month, for that matter."

"True." He grinned at her and took a step closer, smoothing a thumb over her cheek.

His hands were warm and his touch surprisingly soft, but she grabbed the rail and reared back, startled.

"Sorry." He pulled his hand away and took a step back, looking embarrassed. "You had a spot . . . of paint . . . on your cheek." He touched his own cheek in the same spot.

She rubbed at the place he'd touched, feeling her face warm. What was *wrong* with her? It had been a totally innocent gesture. It wasn't as if he was putting the moves on her or something. "Did I get it?"

"Almost."

She jumped down from the railing, desperate to escape. "I . . . need a mirror."

She sought refuge in the house and hurried back to the bathroom. The room was dark and the mirror dingy, but the door afforded her some privacy to calm down. She was acting like an adolescent. Quinn must think she was a total fruitcake.

She washed the remaining paint off her cheek, redid her messy bun, and took a deep breath before opening the bathroom door.

When she entered the living room again, Quinn was already back at work, pulling tape up from the woodwork.

"Is it dry?" She tried to affect a nonchalant tone.

"Dry enough." He kept working, not turning to face her. "I wouldn't touch it or hang anything until morning, but we can pull up the tape and clean up the mess. See what it's going to look like before it gets too dark."

She helped him wad up the tape and fold the drop cloths. When they were finished, she quickly vacuumed up the dust, then put the vacuum away in the tiny hall closet. She stood in the hallway and looked through to the living room and what little of the dining room she could see into. "Big improvement."

"That's an understatement."

"Jo? Britt? Come in here."

Her sisters appeared in the doorway.

"Looks awesome," Britt said.

"Huge improvement," Joanna agreed. "Give us twenty minutes and we'll reveal the kitchen."

"Can't wait."

Quinn motioned to her. "Help me carry this stuff out to the porch, and then I have something I want to show you."

Her curiosity won over her nervousness at being so close to him.

Chapter 13

Quinn tossed the bag of trash he'd gathered into the back of his SUV and surreptitiously checked his reflection in the rear windshield, making sure he didn't have paint on his own face.

He wished he could rewind the clock by an hour and undo his hasty actions. He shouldn't have touched her. It was too forward. She'd put distance between them more than once. Maybe he just needed to take a hint. And in truth, he hadn't meant his action to be so intimate. The problem was, he'd touched her so often in his imagination, in his dreams, that it felt like the most natural thing in the world to reach up and brush his palm across the softness of her cheek.

But if they were going to be working together here for any length of time, he needed to cool it with her. She obviously wasn't interested.

"You wanted to show me something?"

He hadn't heard her approach and turned to face her, immediately feeling guilty at his ruse. He did want to share something with her, but it had really just been an excuse to apologize — out of her sisters' hearing.

"Yeah. Follow me." He started up the hill into the wooded area behind the main cottage.

After a minute, he realized he didn't hear her behind him. He turned to see her standing at the bottom of the hill. "You coming?"

"Where are we going?" Suspicion tinged her tone.

He truly was an idiot. Poor girl probably thought he was dragging her into the woods to accost her. "Sorry. I should have explained." He went halfway down the hill, careful to leave some distance between them.

"Explained?"

"What I wanted to show you. When the inspector was here, we walked a ways into the woods. Found something kind of cool up here. It needs some work, but I think you guys will use it."

"What is it?" Still suspicious.

So much for surprising her. "There's a stairway built into the hill."

"A stairway? Leading to what?"

"It's hard to tell. It looks like maybe they had campfires up there. There's kind of a clearing at the top."

"That sounds cool. Jo and Britt will want to see this. Hang on . . ." She turned and started down the hill.

"Hey, Phylicia . . . Wait a sec."

She turned back, looking up at him.

He came as close as he dared, wanting to put her at ease. "I wanted to talk to you — in private — first. If you don't mind."

She narrowed her eyes. "About what?"

"I'm sorry about . . . well, back there." He motioned toward the porch. "I didn't mean to . . . make you uncomfortable. With the paint." He swiped at his own cheek again.

"Oh. No problem." She pawed at a stick with the toe of her paint-splattered tennis shoe. "Is . . . that it?"

He shrugged. "I shouldn't have done that. I just . . . saw the paint and didn't think. I tend to have that problem."

"Not thinking?" The hint of a grin came, then disappeared just as quickly. "It's no big deal. Really."

She sounded sincere, and relief washed over him. He'd dodged a bullet and he was grateful. "Okay. Thanks. Just wanted to make sure."

"Can I get my sisters now?"

"Sure. The stairway is just at the top of that rise. You can almost see it from here if you know what you're looking for."

She shaded her eyes and squinted in the direction he was pointing, but shook her head. "Be right back." She jogged down to the cottage and disappeared inside.

A few minutes later she was back with Joanna and Britt in tow.

"What'd you find? A secret stairway?" Britt looked intrigued.

"I don't know about the secret part, but yes, there are steps up there." Quinn nodded toward the hill before them.

"Are you sure they're on our property?" Joanna had learned to look at everything from a legal angle first.

"According to the inspector, they are. The clearing beyond — what I was telling you about, Phylicia — is right at the boundary line. Come on, I'll show you."

They trudged after him, the sisters chattering until the stairway came into view.

"Hey, that's cool." Britt scooted ahead of her sisters.

They followed him up the wide board-stairway. The wood had been painted a dark brown at one point, presumably to blend in with the wooded hillside, but the paint was mostly worn off and the wood weathered to gray. Even though a few of the steps were starting to rot out, they felt sturdy, built tight into the side of the hill as they were.

"Look how wide they are." The suspicion was gone from Phylicia's tone now, replaced by awe. She gave a couple of bounces on the first step. "They seem like they're in pretty good shape."

"The steps are. The clearing they lead to is pretty overgrown. I'm talking might-take-a-Bush-Hog overgrown. But I think it could be a really neat place. Potential." He quickened his pace and beat them to the top, then held out a hand, smiling. "Ta-dah!"

Their reaction did not disappoint.

"This is *incredible*!" Joanna lifted her head, scanning the natural canopy of leafless branches.

"Just think what it'll be like this summer. I bet when all the trees are leafed out, it's twenty degrees cooler up here than out in the sun."

Britt giggled like a little girl and went to sit on one of two low log benches someone had erected at one edge of the space. "This is amazing! Like our own little amphitheater. We could have concerts up here."

"Well, you'd be a little limited. Keep in mind there's no electricity up here." Quinn hated to burst their bubble, but somebody had to be realistic.

"Weddings . . ." Joanna strode to the end of the clearing opposite the staircase. "You guys, we could do *weddings* up here. Think what a grand entrance a bride could make coming up those steps after the guests are already seated." She paced off imaginary seating and an aisle, muttering to herself. "Do you *know* how much wedding venues make these days?"

"Uh . . . can't say I've priced one recently," Phylicia drawled. "But Quinn makes a good point about electricity. Don't start booking the venue yet, Jo. We might want to finish at least one of the houses first."

Quinn shot her a look. "Don't be such a party pooper."

"Hey, I'm not the one who went all Eeyore about the electricity."

He laughed. "Touché."

"Seriously, though," — Phylicia looked sheepish — "what *would* it take to get electricity up here?"

He looked down the slope at the bucolic scene the cottages made below. The sisters followed his gaze — and gasped in unison.

"What a view." Phylicia's whisper held awe.

Which made Quinn feel undeservedly proud.

"*This* is your property, ladies." Quinn beamed and looked sideways at Phylicia. "Any regrets?"

"No way." Joanna almost sounded as if she might cry.

"And we have you to thank for it, Quinn." Britt's smile held genuine gratitude.

He held up a hand. "No. Don't forget your dad was the one who first spotted the property and thought of you guys."

"Yeah, while you did all the work." The lines in Phylicia's forehead appeared again. And he made it a personal goal to rid her permanently of that furrow.

"Seriously, guys. I only did what your dad asked me to. He's the one you should be thanking." What he'd told them was true, but he did still wonder about Turner's motives and why he'd left the sisters to handle everything without him. It didn't make sense, and it sure didn't fit with the man he'd known most of his adult life.

Phylicia walked to the far side of the clearing and looked down on the nearly dry riverbed below. He noticed she always seemed to find an escape when the subject of her father came up. He went to stand beside her. She craned her neck to peer over the ridge and Quinn did the same. A trickle of water flashed in the channel, but nothing that could be called a creek, let alone a river or tributary.

"It's awfully pretty up here." He let the words linger on the crisp winter air and took a step away from her, lest she fear he was going to touch her again. Or maybe it was more for his own sake that he put some space between them.

"It is pretty. I'm really glad we bought the place. Thank you, Quinn."

"Like I said, I didn't —"

"Stop. I'm just saying thanks for what you *did* do. You were there when Dad wasn't. I honestly don't know what we would have done without you."

Her tone made him want to just shut up and take any credit she was willing to dole out. But his conscience wouldn't let him. "You would have done just fine without me. And if I wasn't here, your dad wouldn't have let you make a mistake."

"Are you sure about that?"

He looked askance at her. "What do you mean?"

"Do you know what's going on with my dad?"

He shook his head, not sure why she was asking him this since he'd already told her everything he knew. "I don't know any more than I did last time we talked about him. I didn't even know he was getting married until you said something."

She bit her bottom lip.

"Is he married already?" he asked softly. Maybe that was what had her so down.

"I wouldn't know. He hasn't called once since we told him you'd talked us into . . . since we bought this place," she amended. She glanced over her shoulder to where Joanna and Britt were gathering pinecones and lowered her voice. "Well, unless he's called my sisters and they're holding out on me."

"Why would they do that?"

"I don't know. I guess they wouldn't. We haven't really talked about Dad much. Joanna seems to let it roll off her back, and Britt just gets defensive."

"Defensive? Why?"

"I guess because she knew Karleen — the hospice nurse Dad ran off with — better than Jo and I did. Britt liked her."

"I wish you'd quit saying 'ran off.' It's not as if your dad ran *out* on your mom. Right?"

Her jaw tensed. "I don't really want to talk about it."

"Okay. Listen, if I knew anything, I'd tell you. Okay? The only thing I've talked to him about is this property."

He bent down to pick up a small pile of

brush that had collected in the crook of a large maple. He tossed the mass over the ridge and turned away from the dust that billowed up from the debris. "I wish I had my work gloves." He gathered up another pile of brush.

"Let's worry about the cottages first. We can work on the outdoors later this spring."

"Good point." He dropped the debris back in the spot where he'd found it and brushed the dust off his clothes.

"Thanks for showing us this spot. It's really cool."

"It is. I knew you'd like it. All of you," he added quickly.

But for once, she didn't seem uneasy at his comment. She wiped her hands on her jeans and started toward the stairs. "We'd better get back to painting if we're going to finish before dark."

He checked his phone. "We've still got a good four hours. We can do it."

"Come on, sisters. Back to work." And just like that, she was back to her cheery self.

CHAPTER 14

"Thank you. Come back and see us." Phee handed the customer her receipt and forced cheerfulness into her voice. She couldn't remember a day that had dragged on the way this Monday had. So much for February being a short month.

The shop was empty and since it was President's Day, there wasn't even any mail to sort, so she went to the workroom to finish an arrangement of sunflowers. Usually she loved working at the flower shop in winter. The colors and smells of the blooms and greenery was a little shot of spring that carried her through Missouri's dreary winter months. But these days, all she wanted to do was work on the cottage. They'd finished painting the main rooms on Saturday, and she and Britt had gone back Sunday afternoon to clean the floors and pull up carpet in the bedrooms.

They'd found hardwood underneath, but

it was in bad shape and needed refinishing — which she didn't know the first thing about. Quinn probably "knew a guy," but she hated to say anything to him, lest the guy was *him* again. He'd assured them he'd send a bill for his time, but knowing him, it would be half of what he should charge them. She didn't want to take advantage, even though the discount would be a huge help.

And she had to admit, she liked having him around.

She, Jo, and Britt had managed to each put three thousand dollars into a renovation fund after closing on the property, but they'd already spent almost a thousand of that. And it was the smaller cottages that were going to break the bank. Plus, they hadn't moved into the cottage yet, so she and Jo still had rent to pay for their apartments. They'd talked about moving in together, but in the end decided it would be too much time and hassle to move twice just to save eight hundred dollars.

According to Jo, Britt had been staying at Mom and Dad's house by herself most nights, but judging by the dark circles under her little sister's eyes, Britt wasn't sleeping very well. At least there'd been no more visits from the police. Phee looked forward to meeting Britt at the house after work to haul some of the furniture out to the cottage.

She was in the middle of wiring a gerbera daisy stem when the shopkeeper's bell on the door announced a customer. She dried her hands and hurried to the front. "May I help y—"

She instantly recognized the slender young blond standing at the counter. But several seconds ticked past before recognition cleared the fog from Karleen Tramberly's wide blue eyes.

"H-hello." Karleen's voice was tentative. "You're . . . Turner's daughter."

It wasn't a question.

"Yes." She nodded. *And Myra's daughter too.* "How may I help you?" The Chandler sisters had all been taught that politeness was next to godliness. But Phee tried — and failed — to inject a warmth she didn't feel into her tone. Mom would have been disappointed in her.

"I'd like to have a plant sent to Murfurd's Funeral Home. For the Jensen family."

Phee's mind went blank for a second. "What . . . price range were you thinking?" Avoiding Karleen's eyes, she grabbed a pencil and order pad.

"I'd like a specific plant if you have it. But

I'm not sure it's in season. Do you have any cyclamen?" She glanced back toward the display window. "I didn't see anything . . ."

"Yes, we have a few nice ones. But I'll have to check whether or not they're in bloom yet. I'll be back in a moment." She sneaked a glance at Karleen's left hand. No ring. Not that that meant anything. Mom had rarely worn her wedding ring, insisting she was too afraid of losing it. But sometimes, when they were little, she'd let Phee and her sisters take the diamond out of her jewelry box and try it on just for fun.

She started for the stockroom, then turned. "Were you wanting a certain color? I think we have pink or white. I'm not sure . . ."

"Pink would be nice."

Phee escaped to the back, surprised to find her hands were trembling. She found a pink cyclamen in bloom, popped it into a foil sleeve, then carried it to the front. "You want this delivered to the funeral home, correct?"

"Yes, if you don't mind. That's a pretty one. Mrs. Jensen was partial to cyclamens."

They'd done a few other flowers for the Jensen funeral, but Phee didn't know the family well. Only that the woman had been about her mother's age. She wondered if

Karleen had flirted with Mr. Jenson too. Glad the woman couldn't read her thoughts, she took the credit card Karleen handed her across the cashier's desk. "We'll get it delivered first thing in the morning, if not tonight."

"Either one will be fine. Thank you."

Phee ran the card and returned it, avoiding Karleen's eyes.

"You're . . . Phylicia — the oldest, right?"

Again, Phee stared, amazed — and honestly a bit taken aback — at the woman's boldness. "That's right. I am."

Karleen cleared her throat. "So . . . How is your father doing? If you don't mind my asking . . ."

Phee frowned. And noticed for the first time how Karleen was fidgeting with the zipper on her purse. "You would know better than I do."

"Excuse me?" Confusion glazed the young woman's eyes, then alarm. "Wait . . . has something happened? Is your dad all right?"

Phee held up a hand. "What I mean is . . . I thought you were *with* him. In Florida."

"Oh . . . No." Karleen shook her head. "Not for a couple of weeks now. He didn't tell you?"

"I — haven't spoken with Dad recently."

"Then you thought we were still —"

"Listen . . ." Phee held up her hands. "I don't really want to talk about this with you. It's between you and my — you and him."

Karleen reached to place her hand briefly over Phee's. The action did not endear her to Phee. "Please, Phylicia, call your dad. I don't know what he's told you, but he at least owes you an explanation."

Pretending she didn't hear, Phee pulled her hand away and straightened a stack of flyers on the counter. "We'll get your order delivered by tomorrow at the latest."

Karleen leveled her gaze, but not in anger. Which surprised Phee even more.

"Phylicia? Is everything okay? I've thought so much about you and your sisters these last few months. I hope you're all doing okay."

Oh, I'll bet you have. "We're fine, thank you." She didn't wish to be out-and-out rude, but she did not want to have this conversation. Even though her curiosity was nearly killing her.

"Your mom was one of the sweetest women I've ever had the privilege of caring for. I want you to know that."

Paralyzed, Phee stared at her. Then huffed. "You sure have a funny way of showing your admiration for my mom."

The woman drew back, then straightened,

looking as if she wanted to say more. But instead, she stuffed the receipt in her purse, her gaze suddenly flighty and even a little . . . fragile. She turned and left the shop without a backward glance.

Phee's first instinct was to call Dad and get to the bottom of this. Why hadn't he told them that he and Karleen had broken things off? Surely, he realized what a relief that would be to all of them. Maybe he would be coming back to Missouri now. And they could take the house off the market. Phee didn't doubt that Dad had business in Florida. He'd been traveling to Orlando off and on with the company as long as she could remember, but he'd always been able to do his work in a few days and then return home.

Phee was preoccupied and grumpy the rest of the day. Thankfully it was a slow afternoon at Langhorne Blooms, so she closed up the shop a few minutes before five thirty and headed to her parents' house.

Britt was there, in jeans and a ratty sweatshirt, ready to work. "I'm thinking of bringing Melvin out to the property with us. Let him get used to the place. Do you care?"

"Fine with me. Maybe he'll get a mouse."

Britt shivered. "I hope not."

"Maybe we should lock him in one of the

small cottages."

Britt shot her a dirty look. "You're just mean."

"I'm not mean. Melvin would probably think that was the greatest adventure ever."

"One step at a time, please. Let's just see how he handles the main cottage first."

"Whatever."

She felt her sister's eyes on her.

"Are you okay, Phee?"

Phee thought for a minute, trying to decide whether to mention her run-in with Karleen. "Guess who came into the shop today."

"I have no clue. Good or bad?"

"Bad." She frowned. "Well, and also maybe good."

Britt rolled her eyes. "Are you going to tell me or not?"

"Karleen Tramberly."

"Whoa! Seriously? I thought she was in Florida. Do you think that means Dad's in town?"

"I don't think so." She relayed her tense exchange with Karleen to Britt.

"Phee! We've got to call Dad. What if something's wrong? Have you talked to him lately?"

"Not since we called to tell him we were buying the property. Have you?"

"No. I've texted him a couple times. His replies were, like, two words."

She nodded. "Mine too."

"What if he's" — she shrugged — "I don't know . . . sick or depressed or something?"

In her surprise-fueled anger, Phee hadn't considered that possibility — and experienced a twinge of guilt. "Maybe we should call him."

Britt frowned. "Maybe we should wait, see if he calls us."

"True. And I really did want to get out to the property before dark." She was grateful Britt was as reluctant to talk to Dad as she was. But how else would they find out the truth? "Okay. We'll wait. Or we can call him another time. Besides, if I talk to him now, I might say something I'll regret."

"You would not."

"I might. I'm so mad at that man right now, I don't even feel like I know him."

Britt sighed. "I know. And then I feel guilty. I just hate this whole thing. It was bad enough we lost Mom. But this . . ."

She gave Britt a quick hug. "Come and help me get that furniture loaded. We'll talk more on the way out there, okay? It'll be dark in an hour."

"I can't believe you managed to stuff all

this in two cars." Britt hefted one end of an old desk, while Phee juggled the other. As Phee remembered, it was a piece Mom had stored in the basement at the house in Cape — something she'd had in her dorm at college. Thirty-some years ago. The desk had never been used in the Cape house that she could remember, but it would be adorable painted a cheery color and distressed. And it made the desk all the more special that it had belonged to Mom. Phee's fixer-upper vibes were kicking into high gear. She wished Jo could have made it, but she had to work late. Again.

The sun slipped behind the naked tree branches shortly after they arrived, and the air turned brisk, but she and Britt were exerting enough energy unloading their cars that Phee was almost grateful for the chilly breeze. They hauled in a couple of side tables, Mom's Persian carpet, and a pair of mid-century chairs upholstered in a muted turquoise fabric — all from Mom's sitting room. Phee rolled out the rug, then placed a chair on either side of the fireplace. She took a few steps back to see the effect.

Behind her, Britt clapped with glee. "That looks perfect. Absolutely perfect."

Phee had to agree. Mom's pieces were just right with the fireplace finish. "The right pillows will make all the difference — and maybe that white faux fur throw I have in my apartment."

"I've got to say, this place is turning out even cuter than I imagined."

"It really is, isn't it?"

"I wish I could envision things the way you do." Britt tilted her head and looked at the arrangement of chairs by the hearth. "I have to see it before I can tell if it works. But wow, sis, this works."

Phee's heart warmed. "I'm going to go get the paintings out of the car. I want to hang a little gallery wall over there" — she pointed to the right of the fireplace — "and then we can pull colors from that for the pillows."

She opened the trunk and pulled the box of paintings toward her. Mom's cherished collection of originals had hung in her sitting room on a wall painted the teal color shared by the carpet and chairs. They would make a perfect gallery wall by the fireplace and pull the whole room together.

But as she headed back into the house lugging the heavy cardboard box, a pang of guilt needled her. First, because she'd taken the paintings from Dad's house, leaving behind a wall of faded rectangles where the paintings had hung in the sitting room.

Although, surely that wouldn't make a difference to a potential buyer. And maybe she'd have time to paint that one wall before the open house next weekend. If the house sold before then, all the better.

But the true source of Phee's guilt was that she was making decorating decisions without Joanna. Britt didn't care as much about this kind of thing, but Jo had strong opinions — and frankly, Phee would be really hurt if the tables were turned and Jo was the one out here arranging furniture and hanging a gallery wall without her.

It had been one of the biggest challenges with the purchase of the cottages — having to be patient and wait on each other's schedules. Having to reach an agreement on what color to paint the bedrooms, what kind of drawer pulls to put on the kitchen cabinets, whether to strip and refinish the hardwood or just install new carpet. So far, they hadn't had any knock-down-drag-outs, and she didn't think any of them felt as if they'd compromised on what they really wanted. Still, it was an exercise in patience.

Like now. She could have these paintings hung in an hour, and oh, what a difference it would make in giving the house some style and the feel of home. And it wasn't as if she was making irreversible changes. They could always rearrange the paintings or move them to another room if Jo didn't like the arrangement. Maybe she could appease Jo by offering to let her take the lead on decorating the bedrooms or the little room behind the French doors that they'd taken to calling "the office," even though one end of it would ultimately hold at least a daybed, so they could rent it out as a bedroom when they got the Airbnb up and running.

Thankfully, their tastes were similar. Jo's style was a bit more minimalist than her own. But they'd always admired each other's apartments, and all three of them — and Mom, before she'd become ill — had often shopped together to furnish their homes.

Phee set the box of paintings near the hearth. "If we were staying all night, I'd light a fire."

"Let's wait and have our first fire the first night we move in. To celebrate." Britt tilted her head. "Do you know how to make a fire? I know Dad taught us, but I'm not sure I remember."

"I think I would. We'll figure it out. The inspector said they had a chimney guy here before they put it on the market, so it should be ready to go."

Britt took a painting from the box and unwound the bubble wrap. "Here, I'll dust them off and you can start working on the layout."

"I'm going to arrange them on the floor first, just to get a feel for —" The needles pricked deeper until she finally couldn't ignore them. "You know . . . Maybe we should wait on Jo before we hang anything."

"Oh." Britt looked deflated, but she conceded. "You're probably right. She'd want to be in on this."

"Where was she tonight anyway?"

"She had some kind of meeting for work."

"Has she been staying with you at Dad's?"

Britt puffed out her chest. "I'll have you know, I have stayed by myself three nights in a row now."

"Way to go, sis. And you're what? Only twenty-six?"

"Very funny. And FYI, I'm twenty-four. You don't even know how old your own sister is?"

"Sorry. I got your age mixed up with Jo's."

"Um . . . if I was twenty-six, that would make Jo twenty-eight."

Phee cringed. "Ouch. She would *not* be happy about that."

"You got that right. She's having enough trouble with twenty-six. Just remember, *I'm* the baby of the family."

"Ha! How could I forget?"

"Even though I act more mature than either of my *much* older sisters."

"Whatever." Phee rolled her eyes, but couldn't help but laugh too. Britt joined in, and it struck Phee that there hadn't been much laughter in their lives since Mom was diagnosed. It felt good. No doubt the credit went to this project of buying and renovating the cottages, which brought hope that there would be more laughter within these walls in the months to come.

CHAPTER 15

Phee moved the box of paintings to the corner of the room. "Let's go work on getting that desk ready to paint. Jo won't mind about that, and we can hang the gallery wall tomorrow night or maybe Saturday."

It was nearly dusk by the time she and Britt finished unloading several smaller pieces of furniture into what would be the master bedroom. With Quinn's help, they'd painted the walls and trim in the two bedrooms, but the floors needed some love before they moved in beds or the larger furniture.

Britt helped her carry the old desk into the office. "It's awfully dark in here. Can we move a lamp in or something?"

"Hang on. I think Quinn left a work light here when we were painting the bedrooms." She hurried down the short hall and found the lamp on the floor in the corner of the smallest bedroom. She carried it into the office and clamped it to the windowsill.

"Much better," Britt declared. "So what color are you going to paint this?"

"I have a little blue and a little green milk paint that I think will mix up a little lighter than the color of Mom's gallery wall."

"So, aqua? Is there any other color in the world?"

"Not for me." Phee grinned, but studied her sister's expression. "Are you not feeling it?"

"Oh, no. I like it. I'm just not surprised."

"I think it'll be nice to have that color carried between the office and the darker teal shade in the living room, since you can see into each room from the other."

"I agree. Did you bring the paint?"

"I brought it the other day. Haven't mixed it yet, but I don't think I want to start on it tonight. I'd rather work on it in the daylight. But we can at least take the hardware off and get the desk cleaned and sanded before we leave."

Together they worked to take out the desk's drawers and remove the metal pulls. If they cleaned up the way Phee thought they would, she'd reuse them.

Britt held out a hand. "I'll go work on those while you sand."

"Hey, help me turn this upside down first,

would you?"

They hefted the desk and stood it on one end, then flipped it onto its top.

"You got it from here?" Britt asked.

"I'm good. Thanks."

Britt disappeared into the kitchen, and Phee gathered sandpaper and rags and set to work. A piece of plywood covered the cavity where the largest drawer had been. The wood was warped and looked as if it had been added as an afterthought. Though for what purpose, Phee couldn't tell. She worked with a claw hammer and screwdriver to pry it from the desk.

Once she'd removed it, she noticed a thin block of wood about the size of a small shoebox lid attached beneath the desktop. At first, she thought it was meant to stabilize the drawer, but on closer inspection, it looked like the piece was hollow. She adjusted the work light and dropped to her knees to see if she could figure out how to open the box.

The whole piece appeared to have been glued to the underside of the desktop. At least she couldn't find any nails or screws holding it in place. It didn't seem to serve any purpose, so Phee tried to pry it off, but the hammer's claw was useless.

"What's all the racket in here?" Britt stood

in the doorway, drying her hands on a rag.

"Look at this." Phee motioned her over and showed her the strange addition.

"What's it for?"

"I have no idea. It's just taking up space and making it so the drawer won't hold as much."

"It won't come off?" Britt hung her rag on the doorknob and held her hand out for the hammer. "Here, let me try."

"Okay, but be careful. I don't want to tear up the desk trying to get it off." Phee handed her the hammer but hovered protectively over the spot where the compartment was.

"Look at this, Phee. It's a box. Like a compartment."

"Let me see." Phee held the light closer.

"This piece is a sliding lid. If I can just get —" She tapped hard on the side of the compartment with the hammer.

"Did you get it? Open it." Curiosity piqued, Phee moved the light closer yet.

"I can't. It's stuck." Britt hammered harder. "You said this was Mom's desk?"

Phee nodded. "I think she said she had it in her dorm at college. Here . . . Hand me that." She took the hammer from Britt and wedged the screwdriver underneath the compartment. "Stand back."

Britt took a few steps back and Phee struck the end of the screwdriver hard with the hammer. The entire box popped off and bounced over the apron of the desk onto the wood floor.

"Got it!" Phee cheered.

"What's inside?"

"Probably nothing, but it's kind of cool. I might try to reattach it. Like a secret compartment." She shook the box. "It doesn't feel like there's anything inside."

"I wonder if Mom even knew this was here?"

Britt lost interest, but Phee worked for another five minutes trying to loosen the sliding lid. It finally gave enough that she could peek inside. "Hey, there *is* something in here! Come here, Britt."

Britt shined the light on the box. "Looks like paper."

Phee worked the lid open further. "It's an envelope."

Britt's eyes widened. "Maybe this is where Mom hid her love letters from Dad."

"No, Dad has those, remember? Mom used to have a stack of them tied with ribbon on her nightstand. Just for decoration."

"Oh, yeah. Dad packed them with that box of Mom's stuff he put in storage."

Phee nodded. "He said we could read

them after he dies."

Britt frowned. "I wish he wouldn't talk like that."

"I don't think he meant anytime soon." She tapped the lid gently with the hammer. It slid a fraction of an inch with each strike. Finally, the opening was wide enough that she could get her fingers inside. She pinched one end of the envelope and carefully withdrew it from the box.

It wasn't only paper. She felt something else, something solid, in the envelope. But the envelope was sealed. Phee turned it over. Nothing written on either side.

"Open it!" Impatience sent Britt's voice up an octave. "What do you think it is?"

"I don't have a clue. Probably extra hinges or hardware to the drawers or something."

Britt's expression fell. "Well, that's not very exciting. If it's just hardware, why would they go to the trouble of hiding it in a secret compartment?"

Phee shrugged. "Do you think we should open it?" For some reason, she didn't feel right about opening the envelope. But if it was something like hardware, what was the harm?

"Duh." Britt ripped the envelope out of her hand.

"Hey. I'm the one who found it!" She

grabbed the envelope back.

Britt didn't fight her for it, but stood watching, waiting for her to do the honors.

Phee took a deep breath, preparing herself to be disappointed when the contents turned out to be nothing more than a couple of rusty old screws and a hinge. It felt more like something metal now that she'd had a chance to feel the outline of the object inside.

She slid the tip of the screwdriver under the flap and carefully sliced it open. A necklace and a plain gold ring fell into her palm. Phee slid the simple gold cross along its delicate chain. "Wow. These must have been Mom's."

"Or maybe Grandma Clayton's. Can I see?" Britt opened her palm.

Phee handed her the jewelry and looked into the envelope again. A scalloped corner of an old photograph poked out. She extracted it. There didn't appear to be anything written on the back. She turned it over to reveal a faded color photo.

"Who is that?"

"I'm not sure." She held the photo up to the light. She frowned. "I think that's Mom. I've never seen this picture of her."

Britt leaned over her shoulder. "But . . . that doesn't look like Dad. Why is she wearing a veil?"

A frisson of alarm went through Phee. She leaned closer to inspect the photo. "Look . . . she's wearing this ring and necklace in the photo." But why was Mom wearing a wedding dress and veil and clutching the arm of a stranger?

"Maybe it was a cousin or something. Or a friend of Dad's. Just someone who wanted his picture taken with her."

Phee shook her head. "Britt, that's not Mom's wedding dress."

"What do you mean?"

"That's not the dress Mom wore when she and Dad got married. Remember? Mom's dress had a high collar. And she didn't wear a veil."

Britt looked closer. "Then . . . what is *this*?"

"I don't know." She studied the photo again, trying to find some clue in the image. "Maybe she was in a play or something?"

"Then it was performed at a real church. Look at the background." The colors were faded, but she could make out an elaborate altar and an arched stained-glass window behind the couple.

"But Mom and Dad didn't get married in a church."

"I know." Her parents had never hidden

the fact that they'd eloped and been married by a justice of the peace in Chicago, where they'd also honeymooned. It was one of the reasons Mom had been so adamant about her daughters having "real" church weddings. And why, as the eldest daughter, Phee had always felt a bit like a failure for not finding a husband before Mom died so her mother could have watched at least one of her daughters walk down the aisle. "But why would Mom save a picture from a play in a . . . secret compartment?"

"Why would she save a picture of herself in a wedding dress with some guy we don't even know?" Britt gave a little gasp and her voice wavered. "You don't think Mom was married before, do you?"

That was exactly what Phee had been thinking, but to hear it voiced aloud made the idea seem ridiculous. Mom had never been one to keep secrets. Certainly not something like this!

Phee stared at her mother's radiant smile. She'd always been able to talk to their parents about anything — same for Jo and Britt — and in the months before Mom's death, their discussions had turned even more intimate and frank. This simply wasn't the kind of thing Mom would have kept from them. Especially if she'd already gone through losing a husband. So . . . how did they explain the photo? And its hiding place?

"Dad?"

"Phee?" Her father sounded groggy. "What time is it?"

"I'm sorry if I woke you. I know it's late there." The clock in her kitchen said ten thirty, but it was five minutes slow. She'd been working up the nerve to call him for the past hour.

"Is everything all right?"

"I have something I need to talk to you about." She took a deep breath, terrified he might cut her off. And if he did, what that might mean for her. For all of them.

"What is it, Phee?" He sounded fully awake now, and the guarded tone she'd heard so often from him recently was back.

She shot up a prayer that this conversation wouldn't end abruptly the way so many of theirs had since Mom's death. "It's a couple of things actually." She gripped the phone tighter. "Karleen came in to the flower shop the other day."

"Oh?" He cleared his throat.

"She asked if you were okay."

"And what did you tell her?"

"I . . . said I hadn't talked to you recently. Did something happen? She sounded like she didn't know how you were. Did you guys . . . break up?"

"I guess you could call it that."

"When were you going to tell us, Dad?" She regretted her caustic timbre as soon as the words were out.

When he didn't respond, she softened her tone. "What happened? With you and Karleen? Are you . . . not getting married now?"

"We're . . . taking a break for a while." Weariness crept into his voice.

"A break? From each other?"

"Yes."

"Is that . . . what you want?"

"It was mutual. And . . . I'm sorry I haven't gotten around to telling you girls yet. If it put you in an awkward position with Karleen, I'm sorry. I didn't realize she'd gone back to Cape."

"I'm not worried about things being awkward. I'm worried about *you,* Dad."

He gave a humorless laugh. "Well, you sure don't need to worry about me. I'm fine."

"Are you coming back here then?"

"I'm not sure. I'll stay in Orlando at least for a while. I'm . . . in the middle of a project. For work."

"I wish you'd come back. We miss you."

"I miss my girls too. I suppose I'll need to

come back for the closing — if we ever get the house sold."

"You wouldn't come back sooner? To see your daughters?" She tried to infuse a smile into her words, but instead, her voice broke.

"We'll see . . . I might be able to get away. I'm not sure."

"Is work" — she struggled for the right word — "swamping you?"

"A little bit. But I'll see what I can do." He cleared his throat again. "You said you had a couple of things to talk about?"

"Oh. Yes. Several, actually. Um . . . I wanted to let you know we closed on the property."

"Quinn told me. Good for you. I'm glad you girls did that. I think it'll be a great investment."

"I sure hope it will." So Dad and Quinn were still in communication. She wondered when they'd talked. And what about.

"So you're a homeowner now? That's great, honey. Quinn said you girls have already started working on the place?"

"Yes, on the bigger house. It could use some remodeling down the road, but we're mostly just painting and cleaning for now. We need to save our renovation money for the smaller cabins."

"Sounds like a wise plan."

"Quinn has been great helping with all the paperwork and the closing and . . ." *All the stuff you should have been here for.*

"Are you moved in yet?"

"Oh, no. But we might be able to before the first of March. I think Ginger, Jo's roommate, found someone to take over her lease. We'd like to not have to pay March rent for our apartments if we can help it."

"Good thinking."

Seconds ticked past, stretching the silence taut, and Phee could feel her nerve slipping. But she wouldn't get a moment's sleep if she didn't ask. "Dad, we moved some furniture out to the cottage today. That old desk of Mom's? The one she had in college, I think . . ."

"I'm not sure I remember it."

"Well, it was in your basement. But . . . we found . . . something in the desk that we can't explain."

"What do you mean?" What sounded to be genuine curiosity colored his tone.

And brought a paralyzing thought: What if the worst was true, and Mom *had* been married but Dad didn't know? That possibility hadn't entered her mind until this moment. But it *couldn't* be. Her parents had never kept secrets from each other. Or so they'd always boasted.

A memory came, something Phee hadn't thought about in years. Freshman year in high school, she'd gotten in trouble for helping another girl cheat on a test. She'd had to get a note signed for the principal. She'd confessed to Mom and begged her not to tell Dad. And Mom's response had been exactly what she expected. "You know better than to ever ask me to keep anything from your father, Phylicia. If you don't want Dad to know something, then you best not tell me."

That rang so true to who her mother was. No way could Mom have kept such a secret from him.

"Are you still there, Phee? You said you found something in a desk?" Dad's voice pulled her back to the present.

"Yes. Some jewelry. A ring and a necklace. And a photograph."

"A photograph?"

Did she detect hesitance in his tone? Or only mild curiosity?

"It was a picture of Mom in a wedding dress. With a man . . . that wasn't you. A stranger. And it's not her wedding dress from your wedding."

"What?" If he was pretending to be surprised, he was doing a great job of it. "You found this in a desk from our house?"

"Yes. That one in the basement. The stuff was in a box glued to the underside of the desk, actually. Sort of like a . . . secret compartment. We never would have found it, except we decided to paint the desk. We found the stuff when we turned the desk upside down and took out the drawer."

"That's strange. I don't know why that would have been there . . ." He let his voice trail off, sounding more cautious now.

"Dad? Was Mom . . . *married* before? To someone else?"

"Phee . . ." His sigh said everything.

"Was she, Dad?" Her heart raced.

"Phylicia, this isn't a discussion . . . for over the phone. When I come home next time, we'll talk then. Okay?"

He'd as good as answered her question. But it *wasn't* okay. Nothing about it would ever be okay.

CHAPTER 16

Phee's breath came in short gasps and she gripped her phone harder, pacing the short length of the kitchen. "She *was,* wasn't she? Mom was married before. No . . . No, I can't believe it." But she *did* believe it. Dad's reaction told her with certainty that it was true. "Why didn't she tell us, Dad? How could she keep something like that a secret? What . . . happened to him?"

"Did your sisters see the photograph? The ring?"

"Britt did. She was with me when I found it tonight. We haven't talked to Jo yet." But she wondered if Britt had called Jo . . . was maybe even talking to her right now. "When were you going to tell us?"

"Phee, I don't know that it was my place to tell you. Your mom didn't want . . ."

"She didn't want what? Didn't want to be honest with her own flesh and blood?" She would have given anything to be able to see

Dad's face right now.

"It's a long story, and it's not really mine to tell. Let's talk about this when —"

"You say it's not your story to tell, but Mom *can't* tell it. This is so unfair! What are we supposed to do with this?"

"You mean . . . what are you supposed to do with the photo? With the jewelry?" He sounded confused.

"No! What are we supposed to do with this *information*? That Mom had this secret life she never told us about?" Was he really that dense that he couldn't see how hurtful this was to her and Britt? And would be to Joanna when she found out. Why would they have kept something like this a secret from their own daughters?

"Phee. You act as if your mother committed murder or something. This isn't some monstrous thing she did. She was a victim. It happened a long time ago and it really has nothing to do with you girls. Your mom only knew the guy for a few weeks before they got married. It was a mistake. One that wasn't even really her fault. She couldn't have known this man wasn't what he pretended to be. It . . . wasn't a good situation. The man was abusive to her. He was a monster, frankly. Thankfully, she was granted an emergency divorce."

"Wait . . . Mom was *divorced*?"

Dad actually laughed. "Well, she couldn't very well have married *me* if she wasn't. The first marriage only lasted a few months. Mom and I got married as soon as her divorce was final, and after that it was . . . almost as if it never happened."

"Almost . . ." The word came out thick with sarcasm, and Phee's mind swirled with confusion. "But then why would she have saved those things? The ring and the photo?"

"I can't answer that, honey. I didn't know she'd saved them. She probably just forgot they were there."

"I just don't understand why she didn't say something. Why she never told us. All those years. And when she knew she . . . wouldn't be around to answer our questions."

"I can't answer for your mother, but if I had to guess, I'd say she was . . . ashamed. No. That's too strong. Embarrassed is more like it. We talked a few times about telling you girls. But Mom didn't want you to know she'd made such a serious mistake. But don't you see, Phee? It doesn't matter now. Your mom never let her mistake drag her down or keep her from being the best wife and mother I've ever known. I don't think you can deny that."

"No. Of course not. I just . . . I don't understand why you would keep this from us."

"There's really nothing to understand. It's just something that happened. Before you were even born, and it doesn't change one thing about how amazing your mother was."

Her stomach churned. Dad was right. She'd judged Mom harshly. But this was a harsh pill to swallow.

"Was there anything else, honey?" Dad's voice was gentle. He sounded more like himself than he had in a very long time. But she could tell he was about to cut her off, to hang up before she was ready to say goodbye. Like he'd done so often since . . . Karleen.

"Just . . . please come home soon. We miss you. We all miss you, Dad." Her voice cracked.

"I'll try. And when you tell your sisters — about Mom — be kind, okay? She would have hated you finding out this way."

"I will. I promise." She swallowed back the lump in her throat. She didn't want to hang up with this conflict between them. "Thanks, Dad. For being honest."

"We'll talk more next time I'm in Cape." The way he said it felt as if he didn't want to own her label of "honest."

"When will that be? When are you coming back?"

"I don't really know. But I'll be in touch."

"Okay. I love you."

"Love you too, honey." The phone went silent on his end.

She laid her phone on the kitchen counter, still trying to absorb news she would never in a thousand lifetimes have suspected. She needed to tell her sisters what Dad had confirmed. But she didn't want Britt to be by herself when she heard that what they'd suspected was true.

Over and over, she replayed her conversation with Dad in her mind, trying to think of how she could tell her sisters in a way that didn't shock them as much as she'd been shocked. Dad had said to be kind. That Mom had made a mistake. *It's just something that happened. Before you were even born . . .*

What did that have to do with it? Dad had laughed a little when Phee expressed shock that Mom had been divorced. *Well, she couldn't very well have married me if she wasn't divorced.*

How soon after Mom divorced this guy had she and Dad gotten married? She didn't think Dad had said.

Their conversation meandered through her brain, circling back on itself, getting all mixed up. Something was strange about the way Dad had worded things. But now she couldn't remember exactly what he'd said. What order he'd said things in. And she sensed that was important.

Something that happened. Before you were even born.

Why had he said it that way? Why hadn't he said, "Before I ever met your mom"? Maybe he hadn't meant anything by it, but he'd clearly been guarding his words. Why had he connected it to *her* birth?

She had pictures in tiny frames on her nightstand. Herself as a newborn in Mom's arms in the hospital, with Dad beside the bed, looking like the quintessential proud new father. Phee had done the math, the way all teenagers did when they realized their parents might not have been pure as the driven snow on their wedding day. Two of her friends had been eight-pound preemies, supposedly born weeks too early. She'd once overheard her parents joke with friends that they'd gotten pregnant on their honeymoon, and she'd felt relieved and a little smug when everything added up as it should. She'd been born May 15, 1987. Mom and Dad's anniversary was August 1,

1986. Close, but not too close.

But now she wondered. She wracked her brain to remember if she'd ever actually seen her parents' marriage certificate. Or her father's name on her birth certificate, for that matter. She thought she would have noticed if anything was amiss. But then it wasn't as if she studied her birth certificate every day. In fact, she couldn't remember the last time she'd looked at it.

She went to the small desk in the corner of her living room and opened the drawer where she kept important papers. She riffled through the folder and found her birth certificate. Dad's name was there, just below her date of birth and Mom's maiden name. Clayton, the same as Phee's grandparents. It all looked official.

She started to file the document away, then remembered an envelope of old photos she'd scanned and copied from family albums several years ago, intending to make a collage to frame. She'd never finished the project, and now she located the envelope at the back of a drawer, spilled the contents onto the desk, and spread them out. Faded family photos taken through the years and black-and-white photos of the grandparents she barely remembered. Finally, she unearthed the picture she was looking for.

Mom and Dad's wedding portrait, presumably taken by someone at the office of the justice of the peace who'd married them.

The faded image was overexposed, causing light from a nearby window to form a halo of light behind Mom. But she was smiling up at Dad with utter adoration, an expression Phee had seen on Mom's face a thousand times.

Her throat swelled, and she ached with longing to see Mom again, to hear her voice one more time.

The photo proved that Phee had remembered correctly. Mom's off-white dress had a high collar, and she wore her hair long and straight, with no veil.

Phee started to tuck the photo in her purse to show her sisters, but something made her study it again. Her parents stood in front of a lectern, Mom clutching a simple bouquet of cream-colored roses in both hands, Dad's arm around her shoulders.

But what made Phee catch her breath was the view outside the bank of windows to their left. The photo was faded and the trees in the image were out of focus, but Phee didn't think either of those things accounted for the appearance of the leaves — unmistakably orange and red and gold.

How could that be . . . *in August*? Could the photo have faded in such a way to give the appearance of autumn outside the windows? She opened her desk drawer and took out a magnifying glass. Behind Mom and Dad in the photo, what looked like a calendar hung on the wall. The photo on the calendar also bore an image of autumn-colored trees and she could just make out the letters *ber* below the calendar photo. Septem*ber*? Octo*ber*? *Not* August. Had they lied about their anniversary too?

Dad said he and Mom got married as soon as her divorce was final. *Soon* was a relative term, but if they hadn't married until the fall before *she* was born, Mom had to have already been pregnant.

Had her parents had an affair while Mom was still married? And lied about it to cover up the pregnancy?

Or — The thought that came next siphoned the air from Phee's lungs. What if Mom had already been pregnant by her first husband? But that would mean — Could it be that Dad wasn't even her real father?

No. It seemed impossible. But then, before today, it seemed impossible that Mom could have had a secret life they knew nothing about.

She pulled several photographs of herself

and her sisters from the envelope and stared at their faces, one by one. Joanna and Britt had often been mistaken for twins when they were little. Even now, they shared very similar features. Thin faces, thin lips, high cheekbones.

Absently, she touched her fingers to her own lips. They were full, her smile wide enough that she sometimes cringed at photos of herself grinning like Lewis Carroll's Cheshire cat. Phee had a higher forehead than her sisters, and rounder cheeks. Their matching blue eyes and brown hair had always flagged the three of them as sisters, but looking at these photos now, she saw the differences more clearly.

She riffled through the photos, looking for the ones of her grandparents. She saw hints of Mom and Dad in their parents, but she didn't see herself, not even in Mom's side of the family. But no one ever really saw themselves in another person, did they? One's own face became too familiar.

She slipped the photographs back into the envelope, her mind churning with possibilities — all of them devastating.

Trembling, she stepped into her boots, threw on a coat, and walked out to the carport. She unlocked the car and slipped behind the wheel. But before heading to her parents' house, she texted Joanna.

Have you talked to Britt? Can you meet me in Langhorne in a few minutes? Sorry so late, but this is important.

She was halfway to Langhorne when her phone pinged Jo's reply. Keeping one eye on the road, she sneaked a peek.

No. What's going on? Everything ok?

She opted to ignore the questions. Apparently, Britt hadn't said anything. Jo would surely come. She might be late, but she'd come.

As she drove on, Phee realized that Britt thought the two of them would be revealing Mom's shocking secret to Jo. But in fact, Phee now had a secret from both of her sisters. She sent up a desperate prayer that her suspicions were unfounded. That there was somehow a logical explanation for everything she was beginning to fear.

The front porch light wasn't on, but a lamp glowed in the dining room window. Britt must still be up. Phee frowned at the real estate sign planted squarely in the front yard as she pulled onto the driveway. If the house sold, they'd need to get beds — and everything else — moved out to the cottage so Britt would have a place to stay. Once they moved everything out, there'd be no reason for Jo and Phee not to move too. It would be nice to get out from under their rent, though she might have trouble getting out of her lease early.

Phee considered waiting in the car until Jo arrived, but if Britt saw her car in the driveway, she'd wonder why she wasn't coming inside. *God, please give me the words to say this right.*

She started to ring the doorbell, then smiled to herself and texted Britt first. *Hey, I'm about to ring your doorbell. Don't call the cops on me.*

Britt opened the door, phone in hand, already rolling her eyes. "Haha. Very funny. Why are you here so late? Is everything okay?"

"Yes . . . and no. I . . . um . . . talked to Dad. About the stuff we found in the desk."

"Seriously?" Britt's eyes went wide. She gestured Phee inside. "So, what's the scoop? Have you already called Jo?"

As Phee stepped through the door, it occurred to her that she should have brought the envelope to show Jo. But she'd put it back in the wooden box and left it on top of the desk.

Phee glanced back toward the driveway. "Jo's on her way over. Let's wait till she gets here so I don't have to say everything twice."

"So . . . is it bad?"

"I don't know for sure. I guess it . . . depends."

"On?"

"Britt, just be patient. I'll tell you everything once Jo gets here."

"Knowing her, that could be hours."

"Exaggerate much?"

Britt threw her a smirk, which quickly turned into a genuine smile. "Do you want some tea?"

Phee nodded. "That would be good."

She followed Britt to the kitchen and put the kettle on to boil while Britt retrieved three cups and matching saucers from Mom's cupboard. For a moment, it dragged her back to the days when Mom had been hovering at death's door and they'd shared a thousand cups of tea while they waited. *With Dad.*

Melvin sauntered into the kitchen and made a beeline for Phee.

"Hey, buddy." She bent to scratch him under the chin. "You haven't had any run-ins with the police lately, have you, buddy?"

"Very funny," Britt singsonged, placing spoons on each saucer.

The teakettle started its high-pitched whistle just as the doorbell rang.

"I've got it." Phee ran to the entryway and

let Joanna in.

"What's going on?"

"Come have some tea, and I'll tell you."

Joanna stripped off her scarf and unbuttoned her coat to reveal pajama bottoms and a fuzzy sweatshirt. She tucked her scarf into the sleeve of her coat and hung it on the hall tree. "This better be good, sister."

"I never claimed it was good."

Her face must have given her away, because Jo looked stricken. "What happened? Is Dad okay?"

"He's okay. In fact, I actually had a good talk with him tonight."

"Then what's up?" Jo preceded Phee into the kitchen, and Melvin greeted her with the same figure-eight dance he'd done around Phee's feet.

"I made tea." Britt held out the kettle. "You want some?"

"Sure. Thanks." She eyed Britt. "Do you know what this is all about?"

"Some of it. I think . . ."

They doctored their tea — Jo and Britt with sugar, Phee with a little milk — and carried their cups and saucers to the table on the other side of the island.

Britt and Jo watched Phee with wary eyes, waiting for her to spill.

■ ■ ■ ■

"So, you seriously think Mom was married before?" Jo looked skeptical.

"Dad admitted it. Why would he lie about something like that?" Phee glanced at the clock on the living room wall. It was after eleven, and she and her sisters were on their second cups of tea. Caffeinated. They'd taken off their shoes and were curled up in their stockinged feet on the love seats. Phee and Britt shared a sofa, and Jo sat across from them with Melvin curled up on her lap, his purr a reassuring cadence.

Jo shook her head. "I just can't believe it."

Phee wasn't surprised her sister was in denial. She had been too, after all. But there was no denying any of it now.

"I had a feeling that's what we were going to find out." Britt seemed to be taking the news in stride. "It just didn't make sense that she would have hidden the ring and the other stuff if it wasn't a *real* wedding picture."

Jo shook her head, her eyes reflecting Phee's confusion. "So, what was his name?"

"Whose name?"

"The guy Mom was married to? Did you try googling it?"

"I didn't even think to ask. And Dad didn't say." She couldn't tell them that she'd been dealing with more startling discoveries.

Joanna fished her phone out of her purse and started typing. "Mom lived in Jeff City when she and Dad met, right?"

"I think so." Phee winced. "If they were telling the truth about *that.*"

"Phee . . ." Britt's voice was scolding.

"Well, how do we know *what* to believe anymore?" If her sisters only knew.

"Oh, wow." Joanna frowned at her phone. "Do you know how many Myra Claytons there are in this world?"

"Did you put in her middle name?" Phee grabbed her own phone and entered Mom's full maiden name.

"Yes, but all that's coming up is Mom's obituary."

"Same here." Phee laid her phone down. She wasn't sure she wanted to know.

"Maybe we can look up the marriage and divorce records at the courthouse and find out something." Joanna was in lawyer mode again.

Phee shook her head. "But wouldn't we have to go to Jefferson City for that? And for all we know, they got married somewhere else. Or eloped in Cancún."

Jo shook her head. "No, Mom and Dad got married in Chicago."

"So they said." Phee huffed. "I mean where Mom's first marriage happened. And the divorce. But how are we supposed to believe anything they ever told us now?" If Joanna went digging for information, what might she uncover? Yet as much as Phee wanted to know the truth, she wasn't ready for her sisters to learn that they might not even share the same father.

"They wouldn't have lied about that. Would they?" Britt twirled a strand of hair through her fingers.

"I don't know." Joanna released a sigh and slumped deeper into the sofa. "Is it getting to you guys that ever since Mom died, it seems like we don't even know who our parents *are* anymore?

"Or who they *were,*" Britt added.

Phee nodded. "It's getting to *me.*" Joanna had no idea how close to home her words hit.

Britt nodded, tearing up.

"It kind of makes you wonder if everything in our childhood was . . . a mirage." Jo looked near tears too. "It just makes me so sad."

"I *wish* it made me sad," Phee admitted. "Right now it just makes me furious. And

afraid of what else we might find out." Her sisters didn't know her worst fears. And she couldn't bring herself to even speak of what she was starting to suspect.

A little sob rose in Britt's throat. "Do you think that's why Dad got with Karleen so soon after Mom . . . ?"

Her sister's tears broke Phee's heart. She scooted closer to put an arm around Britt's shoulders. "What do you mean?"

"Like . . . did he do it out of spite? Toward Mom?"

"No, Britt." Jo could be more of a mother hen than Phee. "It's not like this would hurt Mom."

"I don't think Dad would do that. When we talked on the phone, he just said he and Karleen are 'taking a break' . . . whatever that means."

"Then why doesn't he come home?" Britt's voice rose on the last word.

Joanna shook her head. "And why is he still selling the house? Our house."

"Did Dad say whose idea the breakup was?" Britt's voice went airy like a little girl's.

"He said it was mutual. But . . . I don't know. When I think about how Karleen acted in the flower shop . . . She seemed worried about Dad, and I think it kind of

threw her off when I told her I hadn't talked to him for a while."

"So maybe *he's* the one who broke it off?" Jo's tone turned hopeful.

"I honestly don't know. All he said was that they were taking a break and that it was mutual."

"I'm worried about him." Jo nudged Melvin off her lap, pulled her legs up, and hugged her knees. "It doesn't make sense that he wouldn't come home if she's not in the picture anymore."

Britt's chin trembled. "Do you think he's depressed?"

"He's just lost his wife. And now his . . . *girlfriend.*" Jo said it as if the word had gone sour in her mouth.

Phee shook her head. "He actually sounded better than he has in a while." She didn't want to give false hope, but what she'd said was true.

"Are you sure you didn't just imagine that because *you* were so relieved to hear he and Karleen broke up?" Jo wrinkled her nose. "You know how you sometimes have a tendency to project."

Phee tensed her jaw and prayed for strength to guard her tongue. Her sisters didn't know the possibilities she was wrestling with.

"Guys . . . don't fight." Britt played mediator the way she had when they were teenagers.

"It's okay, sis." And it was. Phee knew Jo didn't mean to attack her or accuse her — even if it felt that way. Joanna was just being her usual thorough, analytical self.

Finally, Phee found words that didn't have the potential to start an argument. "I let Dad know we really want to see him. I practically begged him to come home, even if just for a visit."

"And did he say he would?"

"He said he'd try. At least he didn't hang up on me this time." She gave Jo a sidewise glance. "I really do think he seemed more like himself."

"Okay. I'm glad." Jo's tone held unspoken apology. "It would be nice if he'd call Britt or me and let us know he's alive."

"Don't take it personally. I think I'm supposed to be the spokesperson. Or mediator or whatever. Privilege of the oldest, don't you know. And he asked about you guys." Phee couldn't remember if he actually had. The "old" Dad would have, but she wasn't sure she knew the man she called "Dad" at all anymore.

"I might just give him a call myself." Jo rose from the sofa, yawning.

"You should." Phee stretched. "It's really late, you guys. It's probably not a good idea to be having hard conversations this time of night."

"Good point." Jo straightened the throw pillows and Britt tidied the coffee table.

They started toward the entry hall, and as Jo buttoned up her coat, she regarded Britt. "You okay to stay here tonight? You and Melvin?"

"I've been staying every night." It came out defensive, but she smiled. "I'll be fine. But I will be glad when we all move out to the cottages."

"So, what's stopping us?" Jo said. "Let's do it."

Britt's eyes widened. "Tonight?"

"Huh-uh, not tonight," Phee protested. "I'm going to need toothpicks to prop my eyes open for the drive home."

Britt put a hand on her arm. "Don't you fall asleep."

"I won't. I'm fine."

"This weekend then?" Jo looked from Phee to Britt.

"I thought the open house was this week-end," Britt said. "I better not have done all that cleaning for nothing."

Phee managed a laugh. "Don't worry. It's Sunday afternoon. And I'm going to pick up some flowers at work to take by Dad's house so everything will look perfect. But they don't want us there Sunday anyway. In fact, we'll need to get Melvin out of the house."

Joanna tapped a note into her phone. "Let's plan to move our beds and whatever else we can from our apartments and the house on Saturday."

"The apartments, yes. But remember, the real estate agent wants us to leave the furniture in Dad's house until after the open house."

"Then Sunday night, we can move whatever we still want from this house. Will that work?" Britt looked relieved.

"I don't see why not," Jo said.

"It's a date then," Phee said.

Britt gave a little cheer and reached down to pick up Melvin, who'd followed them to the door. "You hear that, Melvin? We're moving to the country."

Phee felt a strange rush of relief. Moving to the cottages would offer a blessed distraction from the troubling secrets she'd unearthed tonight.

CHAPTER 17

"Pull harder, Jo!"

"I am pulling! What are *you* doing?"

"I'm pushing. Like you told me." Phee set down her end of the box spring and wiped her brow with the sleeve of her jacket — despite the fact that it was only thirty-six degrees outside. Sometimes she hated how out of shape she'd gotten since college. She'd run track in high school and had managed to stay in shape in college, since she had easy access to the university track while she lived on campus. She weighed the same now as she had at twenty, but the toned muscles from those days were a distant memory. She gripped her end of the box spring again. "Why don't they put handles on these things?"

"They do . . . see?" Joanna pulled up a flimsy strip of webbing attached to the side. "But you'd have to be Gumby to get a grip on any two of them at the same time."

A Mozart concerto playing on Phee's laptop swelled to a crescendo as if fortifying them for the task ahead.

Jo gave a little growl. "Can we please turn that music off?"

"I got it!" Britt hustled to close the lid on the laptop.

Phee bit her tongue. They were going to have to make some rules about things like music and noise.

"Why didn't we hire somebody to help?" Jo groaned.

"Because we're cheap, remember?"

"Speak for yourself, sister," Jo shot back.

Phee gripped the edge of the box spring and hoisted her end again. "Ready?"

"As I'll ever be."

"You got the door, Britt?"

"Right here."

"Okay. One, two —"

"Three!" Jo picked up her end and yanked it over the threshold and through the doorway.

A cheer went up from all three of them. Upended, the box spring slid easily on the wood floors until soon they had it in place.

"One down, four to go." Jo blew out a stream of air that ruffled her bangs.

"Thanks for the encouraging words, sis."

"Any time."

They'd borrowed a pickup from a guy Joanna worked with and had moved some of the apartment furniture, along with Phee's beloved bookcases. She'd spent a blissful afternoon yesterday in her little office-bedroom, arranging her ever-growing collection of books and longing for the day when she'd have the time — and focus — to read again.

This morning, they'd managed to load the queen-size beds from Jo's and Phee's apartments as well as the daybed Britt slept on at the house in Langhorne. If they could just get beds set up tonight, they could worry about everything else tomorrow.

But with the beds all here, they were committed to sleeping at the cottage tonight. It was either that or go back to Dad's house and mess up beds and pillows that were all made and fluffed to perfection for the open house tomorrow.

And one glance out the window in the bedroom that would be Jo's told Phee it would be dark in twenty minutes. She did not want to be wrestling mattresses across the rocky driveway and over the porch railing in the dark.

Joanna sighed, apparently feeling Phee's impatience. "Well, here we are."

"Yep, no turning back now." Britt sounded

positively gleeful.

Jo tossed a bed pillow at her. "You're just happy you don't have to stay alone overnight anymore."

"Right. Until you guys run off and get married, and then I'll be staying out here with the mice and the monsters." Britt pulled a face that made her sisters laugh.

Joanna rolled her eyes. "I don't think you have to worry about that anytime soon. We'll probably go down in history as the three old maids of Poplar Brook Road."

"We will *not.*" Phee tossed her head. "Well, *I* might. But you two aren't anywhere near spinsterhood." She winced. *Spinster.* That was Mom's word.

"Twenty-nine isn't exactly headed for the nursing home either, Phee."

She knew that. And it wasn't as if she was desperate to get married or anything, but it *had* broken her heart when Dad told her a few days before Mom had passed away, that one of Mom's biggest regrets was that her illness had made "spinsters" of all her daughters, since they'd put their lives on hold to take care of her. Mom had always dreamed of helping her three girls plan their weddings. Phee had always thought it was because Mom had never had a real wedding of her own. So much for that theory.

Joanna had dated a guy for almost a year before breaking up with him. Ben was a great guy, but he'd told Jo he just wasn't ready to be tied down. But maybe his reasons had more to do with Mom's illness than he admitted. For all three of them — and probably her parents too — as Mom's illness progressed, their friends had drifted away. She understood. People had their own lives to live, and it was depressing being in a house where cancer lived.

Phee brushed away the thoughts, hating it when she turned so introspective. She grabbed two moving boxes they'd emptied and thrust one at each sister. "Let's take these to the truck and get this over with."

As they entered the living room, a light flashed outside the window. Car headlights painted a slow swath of yellow across the trees at the edge of the woods. Phee stopped in her tracks. "Shh. Someone's here."

"Who?" Britt looked alarmed.

"I didn't see the vehicle. Just the headlights. Are you guys expecting anyone?"

Jo and Britt shook their heads.

Without speaking, they abandoned the boxes against a wall and crept into the hallway. Someone knocked quietly, then opened the door to the outer porch.

With her sisters each clutching one of her

arms, Phee peered around the doorway into the living room. She could see a shadow behind the glass. They'd left the front door unlocked and partially ajar, so there was nothing to keep someone from barging in.

"Who is it?" She tried to make her voice assertive.

The door opened a crack, and a man's voice shouted, "Hello? Anyone home?"

"Who is it?" Phee repeated, her heart racing.

"It's me. Quinn." The door went shut with him still on the other side of it.

Phee laughed, relieved to recognize his voice. "Come in, Quinn."

He opened it again and poked his head in, looking sheepish.

Breathing sighs of relief, the sisters congregated around him in the living room.

"A little mouse told me you —"

"Don't say mouse!" Britt squealed.

Quinn laughed. "Sorry. A little *bird* told me you might be moving in this weekend. I went by your dad's to see if you needed any help, but nobody was home, so I thought I'd find you out here. Looks like I'm too late though." He looked around the room. "Looks as if you've lived here forever."

Phee beamed at the compliment. Just last night, the three of them had stayed late decorating the mantel and arranging Mom's paintings on the walls on either side of the fireplace. They'd played with pillows and throws and mirrors and art until they came up with something they unanimously declared perfect.

"Thanks," Joanna told Quinn. "But you are not too late at all. We were just saying we needed some muscle to help us get the mattresses in here. Weren't we, sisters?"

"We were, indeed." Britt winked at Phee.

Quinn flexed a bicep with a comical expression. "I don't know about muscle, but another set of hands and feet is always good when you're moving. Where do we start?"

Phee could have kissed him.

"Follow me." Jo and Phylicia led the way out to the pickup, and Britt stayed behind to hold the doors for them.

Quinn hoped they wouldn't ask him to manhandle an armoire or something that weighed more than he did. But Turner Chandler's daughters had proven they weren't afraid of a little hard work. The real test would come with renovating the smaller cottages, but he still couldn't get over the transformation they'd wrought on this place. He was no expert on decorating, but he'd been in the construction business long enough to know the look of a well-appointed room. The sisters had this living room looking like something straight out of a magazine.

They got the rest of the beds and a box spring moved in and placed on bed frames the girls had already set up. When they brought in the last mattress — a small one for a daybed — he brushed off his hands and watched, amused, as the sisters scurried through the house like the maids on *Downton Abbey.* They shook out sheets and blankets, stuffing pillows into cases like so many sausages, and arguing good-naturedly about who had dibs on which sheets — apparently something called *thread count* was a thing. Who knew?

In the midst of it all, Phylicia and Britt struck a deal that Britt would get one of the bedrooms and Phylicia would take the daybed in what they were calling the "office" off the living room. Judging by Phylicia's smug grin after they shook on the barter, she thought she'd gotten the better end of the deal. But Britt practically skipped back to get settled into her new room.

Phylicia disappeared into the office — now her bedroom — and began scooting furniture around. The French doors were open, and he stuck his head in, clearing his throat to announce his presence. “Phylicia?”

“Oh. Hey, Quinn. Thank you so much for stopping by. We’d still be wrestling with that stupid box spring if you hadn’t showed up.”

“I think you ladies would have found a way without me just fine. The place looks amazing.”

“Thanks. We’re getting there.” She finished stuffing the pillow into its case, smoothing the fabric beneath her hand and tossing it onto a chair. She unfolded a fitted sheet and tucked a top corner of the mattress into it.

He went to the end of the daybed and pulled the sheet over the opposite corner.

“Thanks,” she said again.

They worked in silence until she seemed satisfied that the bedding was free of wrinkles.

She shook out another sheet and situated it on the bed. He reached for the corner at his end of the bed just as she snapped the whole sheet out of his hand like a ship’s sail caught by the wind.

“Sorry. I don’t know what the goal is here.”

She laughed. “That’s okay. I’ve got it from here.”

He stood, arms folded across his chest, watching her work. She tucked the sheets into corners, making the bed look as if it had been neatly gift-wrapped. Then she stuffed pillows into fancy pillowcases. Good grief. How many pillows did one woman need on a little bed? There must have been a dozen of them. Phylicia's hair was pulled back into a clip, and he didn't think she was wearing any makeup. He liked the no-fuss, natural look on her. Even if it did make her look even younger than she was.

She looked up and her eyebrows rose, as if she'd forgotten he was in the room. "You don't have to stay, Quinn. I think we've got it from here."

"You sure?" He cast about the room for an excuse to stay.

"I'm sure. Thanks again . . . for everything."

"So, do I dare assume that you're not mad at me for talking you into buying this place?"

She straightened, but with a bed pillow half in its case still tucked under her chin. "The jury is still out on that."

"Ha! Now you sound like your sister, going all legal eagle on me."

"It will all depend on how the work on the other cottages goes."

He poked one cheek out with his tongue. "I was afraid of that."

"I'm just giving you a hard time. You know

that, right?"

"I don't know. The jury's still out on that."

"Touché." Her grin was the reason he'd come out here tonight.

"So, what does Melvin think of the place?" He cast about the room, searching for the cat.

Phylicia gasped. "Oh, shoot. I forgot! We meant to go get him after we moved the furniture. We can't leave him there, because the agent is coming first thing in the morning to get set up for the open house."

"I can go get him for you . . . if you think he'll come to me."

"Thanks, Quinn, but I wouldn't ask you to do that."

He shrugged. "I've got nothing else to do tonight. Although Mabel might be feeling a little neglected."

"Mabel?"

"My dog."

"Oh, I remember. The cat-eating dog. I thought her name was . . . Hazel."

"What?"

"Never mind. Bad joke."

He frowned. "I don't get it."

"You used to slip up and call Melvin 'Marvin' all the time. I was just giving you a dose of your own medicine."

He laughed, surprised she remembered

that. "Well, if you won't tell Marvin, I won't tell . . . Hazel."

That got a laugh. He liked her laugh . . . and didn't hear it often enough.

"Pinky swear." She stuck out her little finger and wiggled it. "And seriously, Quinn, you've done *more* than enough. You don't have to retrieve our cat too. But thanks for offering." She started to say something, then gave a little shake of her head, as if she'd changed her mind.

"What?"

"It's nothing. Just . . ." She gave the pillow a squeeze. "Can I change my mind? If you really do have time, there are a couple pieces of furniture I'd still love to bring out tonight, but I don't think I can load them by myself."

"Will they fit in the back of my SUV?"

"Oh, easily. It's just a nightstand and a little bookcase. They're not big, but they're heavy."

"Then I'm your man. Just let me know when you're ready to go. And we can bring Melvin back here with us."

"If you're sure."

"No problem at all." He went for his jacket where he'd left it in the living room, then went back to her room to put it on.

"So, this will be your first night to stay here?"

"It will. Although we've practically stayed all night a couple other times. The other night, we just kept saying, 'Let's paint *one* more wall.' When we finally looked at the clock, it was two in the morning!"

"Ouch. That makes for a long day at work the next day."

"Tell me about it." She tossed one last pillow onto the daybed. "Let me tell the girls what we're doing, and then I'm ready to go."

"I'll go crank up the heater. Meet you in the car."

Chapter 18

Phee hadn't thought about the fact that Quinn's offer meant they'd be riding into town together — alone. She'd been so intent on getting those two pieces of furniture for her room moved tonight — and on picking up Melvin too — that she hadn't thought things through.

Now, as she climbed into the dark interior of his SUV, nervous energy made her talkative. Quinn listened politely as she went on and on about the house and their plans for the other cottages. But when the dashboard lights illuminated a hint of a grin on his face, she willed herself to shut up. "I'm sorry. I didn't mean to talk your ear off."

"No, keep going. I've been wanting to hear what you had in mind for the other cottages."

She tilted her head and regarded him. "Then what was that smug smile about?"

"What smug smile?" He looked genuinely

perplexed.

"Never mind. Anyway, we're almost there." It struck her that, except for the supper at McAlister's that she'd ended so abruptly, she hadn't really spent much time alone with Quinn. She wondered why she'd been so nervous with him before.

They drove through town in silence. When they got to her dad's, Quinn backed the car into the driveway and waited while she unlocked the house. Melvin didn't come to greet them the way Phee expected. He'd probably heard Quinn's voice and gone into hiding, although the cat had warmed right up to Quinn the last time he'd been here.

She flipped on the lights as he followed her through the house toward the back bedrooms where the smaller furniture she wanted for her room was. He paused in the living room.

"The house looks really nice. Did you have it professionally staged?"

"Ha! Dad would never spend money on that. We cleaned it, obviously, and put away some of the more personal items, but it's pretty much the way Mom had it decorated." She made a face. "Well, except for the things we've taken out to the cottage. Quite a few, actually. Mom had this house stuffed to the gills with furniture and 'pretties' " — she chalked quotation marks in the air — "as she called them."

He panned the room. "It does actually look bigger than I remember, so maybe taking some stuff out was a good move."

"Yes, let's go with that. Thanks. I don't feel so guilty now."

"Guilty?"

She shrugged. "I know it's our stuff. My parents' . . . Dad's. And he says he doesn't want most of it, but it feels kind of funny taking things from the house when Dad is . . . still living." She stopped and looked at him, debating whether to broach the subject of her father. It was one she was trying to avoid thinking about . . . at least until they got through moving and the open house. "Have you talked to my dad lately?"

Quinn shook his head. "Not since he called about the bank stuff . . . your deposits being made and everything. How's he doing?"

She eyed him. "If you'd asked me that a few days ago, I'd have said I don't have a clue. But I actually had a good talk with him a few days ago . . . Monday, I guess it was. Did you know he and Karleen broke up? Or broke it off . . . whatever you call it when somebody their age is . . . dating."

Quinn's eyebrows went up. "No. I haven't

talked to your dad in quite a while. At least not about anything but business. So . . . he's not getting married after all?"

"Doesn't sound like it. Well, at least not now. They're taking a break." She gave him the abbreviated version of what she'd told her sisters after talking to Dad.

"Well, I guess if it's mutual, that's okay." He touched the sleeve of her jacket briefly. "How do you feel about it? Relieved?"

"I'd feel better if I knew it was permanent. It was just . . . *ridiculous* for him to be dating someone her age, and if she —" She stopped short, sorry she'd made him privy to her snarky thoughts. *But oh, if he only knew.* She was relieved about Karleen, but even more confused and bewildered about what the discovery of Mom's secret might mean for her personally.

"So, tell me how you really feel." Quinn's droll grin said he was being facetious.

She ignored that and answered as if he were really asking how she felt. "I *am* relieved. Except . . . I worry about Dad. I mean, he sounded really good when I talked to him, but he sounded lonely too. I don't understand why he doesn't come back here . . . especially if things are off with Karleen."

"She's not back in Cape for good?"

"Oh . . . I don't know . . . She didn't say." Phee hadn't thought of that possibility.

"Maybe it's just too hard for him to be here, where all his memories of your mom are."

"I guess. Maybe." She desperately wanted to change the subject to something less likely to make her tear up. "Come on back. I'll show you the nightstand I want to take."

She led the way to the bedroom and went to the other side of the oak stand, ready to help, but Quinn picked it up with both hands, as if it were a cardboard box, and started down the hallway with it.

She skirted around him and hurried to open the door. They loaded the bookcase next, and while Quinn secured everything in the back of his SUV, Phee went back in the house to straighten the rooms and do a quick walkthrough to be sure everything was ready for tomorrow's open house.

Quinn appeared in the doorway. "So, where is Melvin? Do we need a carrier for him?"

"Yes, I'll get it. He must be downstairs. That's where his food and litter box are. And sorry, but that stuff has to come too."

"No problem. Just show me where everything is."

She went down and loaded Quinn up with

the bucket of kitty litter, a bag of cat food, and Melvin's empty food and water dishes. The cat was nowhere to be found, but he'd recently been in the litter box, so he had to be here somewhere. While Quinn took a load to the car, she cleaned out the litter box and called for the cat. "Melvin?"

She carried the empty litter pan upstairs and started searching Melvin's usual hiding places. She was starting to worry after looking under the last bed with no sign of the cat, but when she stepped into the hallway off the master bedroom, he trotted out of Britt's room. She hadn't looked there, since they'd moved the daybed — now *her* bed — out to the cottage.

She scooped Melvin up with one arm and put him in the carrier, then tucked the empty litter pan under her other arm. When she picked up his carrier, Melvin wriggled, trying to escape. "Cut it out, Melvin. Don't you know we're going to your new home?" She dropped the litter pan to get a better grip on the carrier. She knelt and put her fingers through the slits of the carrier to scratch him under the chin. Her voice went up an octave into baby-talk mode. "You're gonna love it out there, buddy, with all the mousies and squirrels and skunks and —"

Low laughter made her look up. Quinn

was watching her with a bemused smile.

"Hey, you can laugh all you want." Heat rose to her cheeks. "I was just trying to get him calmed down before I loaded him in your car. You know, so he won't rip your upholstery to shreds . . . or pee on your car seats."

"Hey, did I say anything?" Despite his serious expression, a little snort escaped. "Besides, how is he going to do all that if he's in his carrier?"

"Oh, this one's an escape artist. I could tell you stories." She angled her head toward the litter pan. "Can you grab that . . . and get the door. I think I've got everything else."

He did as she asked, still chuckling under his breath. Quinn loaded Melvin's gear in the back seat, then opened the hatch.

Phee deposited Melvin's carrier inside. "Okay, shut the door."

He lowered the hatch but didn't latch it. "I don't want to crush him."

"You won't." She peered through the back windshield. "He's fine. You can close it."

He gave the door a little shove and the latch caught.

She went around and got in the passenger side. She reached to close her door and was surprised to see him standing there waiting to close it for her. "Thanks again for doing this, Quinn. You don't know how much we —"

"Yes, I do." He put a finger to his lips. "You and your sisters have thanked me about a gazillion times. You're starting to embarrass me."

She laughed. "It won't happen again."

Quinn leaned one arm against the car's doorframe and gave her a look she couldn't read. "I'm happy to help. Anytime." He scuffed at the gravel with the toe of his shoe, looking like he was about to say something. Instead, he closed her door and came around to slip behind the wheel.

He pulled out of the driveway in silence, but as soon as they drove through the neighborhood's entry gates, he turned to look at her briefly. "Phylicia, I'm not helping out just because I'm a nice guy. In case you haven't caught on, I actually enjoy spending time with you."

She eyed him, trying to decide if he was setting up a joke. But that ornery twinkle wasn't in his eyes the way it had been a few minutes ago. "Well, thanks. We enjoy having you around. Especially when you're carrying in heavy furniture and mattresses for us and —"

"I didn't mean your sisters, Phylicia."

"Oh?" She felt pulled in two directions. She liked Quinn. But was she ready for things to move to the next level with him? She scrambled to change the subject. "You might be sorry you ever made that offer to help. Have you seen the other two cottages?" She twisted her mouth, affecting a look of horror far out of proportion to the actual state of the cabins.

He laughed. "You reminded me so much of your dad just then."

"Really?"

"I've seen him make that exact face whenever we took on a project he didn't think we should have."

Quinn had no way of knowing the profound effect his simple observation had on her. Of course, if it was true — if she really had looked like Dad just then — it might merely be the result of being raised by Turner Chandler, of living with him the first nineteen years of her life. It was only natural that she might have picked up some of his mannerisms and facial expressions.

"Well, I have a feeling Dad was making that same horrified face when I talked to him last week. Except we weren't on Skype, so I couldn't actually see him."

"Talking about the cottages?"

"No, something else. I caught him in a lie."

"About what?" Quinn's expression said he was skeptical.

"My dad isn't as perfect as you think he is, Quinn." She looked at her lap. "He's not as perfect as *I* thought he was."

"So, what did he lie about?"

"I guess it's not fair to say I *caught* him in a lie. Actually, it's worse than that."

"What happened?" A deep furrow formed between his eyebrows.

She hadn't meant to step into this with him — or maybe, subconsciously, she had. She needed to talk to somebody, and besides being a good listener, Quinn knew her family and the situation. She wouldn't have to start from the beginning.

She took a deep breath, then blew it out. "I found out my mom was married before."

"What? Before your dad? He told you that?"

"Only because I forced him to." She told Quinn about finding the photo and the jewelry in Mom's desk and about Dad's revelation when she'd confronted him about it.

"Wow, that had to be a stunner. And you had no idea she'd been married before?" It was obvious Quinn was trying to rein in his own shock for her sake.

"No clue. It's weird — in so many ways, we're still trying to grasp that Mom is really gone. That we'll never see her again. In some ways, this is almost anticlimactic." Of course, she hadn't told him the real shocker. And she wouldn't. She wasn't ready to voice her suspicions — her *fears* — out loud yet. Not to her sisters and certainly not to him.

"If you call *that* anticlimactic, it says a lot about how hard it was — *is* — to lose your mom. I remember how that felt . . ." His voice trailed off.

Her breath caught. "I'm sorry. I kind of forgot you'd lost your mom . . . and your father too." She remembered Dad talking about how Quinn had lost both of his parents a few years back — their deaths coming quite close together, if she recalled correctly. It made her realize that Quinn understood firsthand what she was going through. Considering that, she didn't feel quite so bad for spilling everything to him.

"Honestly, Phylicia, I grieved when I heard your mom had died almost as much as I grieved my own mom. I hope that doesn't sound weird. I guess . . . seeing how much your dad loved her . . . I felt for him. Everybody at the office felt her loss, even though some of them had never even met her."

"Wow. That means so much, Quinn." She struggled to speak over the lump in her throat. "I guess I never thought about how everyone at the company empathized with Dad. With us." She remembered how hard her coworkers at the flower shop had taken her mom's death. But she'd never connected that it was probably even more so at Langhorne Construction, given that Dad had been there so much longer and even more people there had known and loved Mom.

"That's true. I think people took her death very personally. I know I did."

She tilted her head. "Personally?"

"I don't know if you knew . . ." He bit his lower lip and groaned softly. "This gets complicated. And maybe it's not even . . . relevant."

"No. Please go on." He had her curious now.

"I don't mean it to take the focus off of your mom . . . of what you lost. But I don't know if you knew that my brother had cancer."

She shook her head, scrambling to remember if Dad had ever mentioned this. "No, I don't think I knew that. Is he okay?"

"Markus is a cancer survivor. Over twenty-five years now. He was nineteen when he was first diagnosed. Melanoma. But it had already spread to the lymph nodes. The survival rates were pretty dismal. But he beat the odds. And after three years, the cancer was gone. Completely gone. The doctors flat-out called it a miracle, and my parents attributed it to the prayers of hundreds of people. I was a teenager at the time, but it was maybe the first glimpse I got of how . . . *personal* God is."

"Wow. I didn't know any of that, Quinn. That's amazing! And wonderful."

"It is. Except, it gets a little complicated. First, Markus doesn't acknowledge God's work in his life. I think he believes in *a* God, but he doesn't live like he believes. He's pretty caught up in material things. In being the boss of his own life. There's been some . . . tough stuff between us. Not just because of that. I'll just leave it at that."

"I'm sorry." She didn't know what else to say. He'd made her curious, but it seemed clear he didn't want to elaborate.

"I'm sorry too." He frowned. "But when your mom died, it just made me angry that God would heal a man who pretty much turned around and threw it back in His face. And then refuse to heal a wonderful

Christian woman like your mom. Where's the fairness in that?"

"I don't know." Her mind reeled at his revelation. But mostly at the fact that Quinn had been so deeply affected by her mom's death. It touched her in a way she didn't quite understand. But a thought came to her, and she risked voicing it. "Maybe God knew Markus needed time . . . to come to faith in Christ. My mom had lived out her faith for years. She was closer to God than anyone I know. And hard as it is to not have her with us, we *know* where she is. And that we'll see her again." Just speaking those words brought healing — a much-needed reminder of a truth that had somehow gotten lost in her grief.

He thought for a moment. "I guess I never thought of it that way. That actually makes a lot of sense."

The turnoff for the property was just ahead. They rode in silence while Quinn navigated the narrow lane, seeming to ponder what she'd said. The porch light had been turned on, but only one dim light shone from the back of the house.

"Looks like the girls went to bed." She frowned. "We were going to celebrate by lighting a fire our first night."

"Do you have wood? I could help you get

a fire going."

"We do, but I don't want to wake them up. And they'd be pretty unhappy with me if I made our first fire without them. Although, I guess it would serve them right since they left me to deal with Melvin." She turned in her seat and craned her neck, trying to look into the back.

"He's been awfully quiet. You sure he's okay?"

"He's fine. He never likes to be put in the carrier, but he usually settles down once he's in there. Dad used to take him for drives *without* a carrier. Melvin loves that."

Quinn put the SUV in Park but left the engine running. He angled his body, propping his right arm on the armrest. "I feel like I hijacked your conversation earlier. I didn't mean to cut you off or change the subject. You were talking about your mom . . . and everything you've found out."

"No, I'm glad you told me about your brother. And I think I said everything I wanted to about Mom. I'm just not sure what to do with the things I know now." And the things she hadn't told him . . . *couldn't* tell him.

"What do you mean? Why do you have to *do* anything with it? Besides just absorb it?" He winced. "I didn't mean that to sound as callous as it came out."

"No. It's okay. It's a fair question. It just makes me wonder what else I don't know about her. And now she's not here to answer my questions."

"I would guess that every parent in the history of the world has a few secrets their kids don't know. And never will know." He cocked his head. "Granted, this is a pretty big one, but it really doesn't change anything about who your mom was. To you. Myra's — your *mother's* — faith was strong, and it stayed strong to the end from what your dad and you have said. That's all that's really important. I sure wouldn't want anyone to judge me by the mistakes I made when I was younger . . . not that I don't still make plenty."

She nodded. "No, you're right. But . . . she carried a lie to the grave with her, Quinn."

"It doesn't seem fair to call that a lie. An omission, maybe. But —"

"She never did tell me and my sisters the truth."

"But she didn't actually tell you a lie either, right?" His words were gentle and comforting.

But she could only shrug in reply.

He sat silent for a long minute, then held

up a hand. "Not meaning to put salt in a wound, but just asking . . . Do you think you'll tell your kids everything about your life before they came along?"

"Um, in case you haven't noticed, I don't have any kids."

He made a face at her. "You know what I mean. Your future kids."

"Well, it's not as if I have a secret marriage to hide from them, if that's what you mean."

"Not yet, you don't."

"Haha." She didn't appreciate his efforts to humor her out of her funk.

"I'm not saying you have *any* big secrets, but . . . I guess what I mean is, do you really think parents owe their children all the details of their lives before said children were even born?"

She hadn't thought about it that way. She shrugged. "I'm not sure. But I think the really big stuff . . . yes. I don't think secrets like that should be kept from your kids."

"Um, in case you haven't noticed, I don't have any kids." He grinned.

"Haha, very funny."

"Unless you count Hazel . . . I mean Mabel. That's my dog."

She tried to keep a straight face. "You are just a barrel of laughs." It irked her that his ploy to get her in a better mood was working.

"Sorry. Couldn't resist. But in all seriousness, your mom's secret really didn't have anything to do with you. It was before she met your dad. And she told *him.* That's what's important."

"I suppose." She reached for the door handle. "I'm sorry. I really didn't mean to make you play counselor."

"You mean on top of moving man and cab driver? Don't worry," he said. "I'll send you a big fat bill."

She cringed, but his grin wouldn't let her feel guilty. She returned his smile, grateful for some levity to end the evening with. She opened her passenger-side door and the dome light flickered, casting a yellow glow across his face. In the light, he looked younger and even more handsome than she'd noticed before. She wondered, not for the first time, why Quinn had never married. Or maybe he had and was keeping his own secrets. The thought turned her smile wry.

"What was that for?"

She tilted her head. "What was what for?"

"That look? That little smirk, like you're zinging me in your mind. And now I don't even have a chance to come up with a clever comeback."

She laughed. "Exactly. I always get the last word that way."

"No fair. One could even say you're keeping secrets." He winced, as if he was afraid he'd crossed a line with that comment.

"You're not my kid, so apples to oranges, in case you were trying to make a point."

"Point taken." Grinning, he opened his door. "I'll help you with Melvin's stuff."

"Ka-ching, ka-ching. That's the sound of my bill racking up, in case you couldn't tell."

"That's exactly what it sounded like." He bobbed his chin. "Good sound."

Rolling her eyes, but a little charmed too, she went around to retrieve Melvin from the back of the vehicle.

CHAPTER 19

It was almost ten when Quinn got home from delivering Melvin. He collected three days' worth of mail from the box at the end of his drive. Maybe if he ever got anything exciting, he'd remember to check the box more often.

He unlocked his front door, and the smell of fresh paint and tile adhesive greeted him. Almost as good as a pot of stew simmering on the stove. *Almost.* Mabel galloped from the back bedroom to meet him. He squeezed through the unframed doorway with the mutt jumping for joy even as she sidestepped toward the mudroom where her food dish was.

Stepping over a pile of baseboard and trim that still needed to be installed, he dropped the mail on the kitchen counter and went to the mudroom to scoop dog food. He was halfway back to the kitchen when his phone buzzed from his pocket. He glanced at the caller ID. *T. Chandler.*

Interesting. Except for a couple of brief business email exchanges, he hadn't talked to Turner for over a week — which was rather unusual. Before Turner had left for Florida, they'd talked on a daily basis, even when Turner was working in the Langhorne office. It had actually crossed Quinn's mind that his boss might be on his honeymoon. Until Phylicia had told him tonight that her dad and that woman had broken things off.

He quickly shrugged out of his jacket and pressed Accept. "Hey, there. How are things in the Sunshine State?"

"Sunny. At least it was a few hours ago. I hope I'm not calling too late. Am I catching you at a bad time?"

"Not at all. I just came from your daughters' place, actually."

"Is that so? Which daughter?"

"Oh, no," he corrected quickly. "I meant *daughters,* plural. The cottages."

"Oh? How are things going out there?"

"Good. They got the beds moved in tonight, so this will be their first night to sleep there. They have it looking really nice."

"That's good to hear."

"Phylicia and I took Melvin out there just a little bit ago."

"How's ol' Melvin doing?"

"I'm not much of a cat person, but it seems like he's doing okay. I didn't hang around to see how he took to the new house, but he handled the car ride out there okay."

"He was strange like that. Never did mind riding in the car, as long he wasn't caged. Stupid cat. Myra was crazy about him."

"Well, I know he'll be well taken care of out there. I think the girls were going to let him have a go at the smaller cabins as soon as he settles in. We saw a mouse in one of them the first time they looked at the place, so they were anxious to put Melvin to work." He smiled to himself at the memory.

Turner chuckled. "Oh, I bet that caused a ruckus."

"And then some."

Turner laughed harder at that, but still not the familiar belly laugh that had always characterized the man. He'd changed. Quinn understood Phylicia's sadness a little better, realizing how different Turner had been since Myra's death . . . and even before that, when she'd been so ill.

Quinn wondered if his boss was struggling with his faith. The whole community had prayed for the Chandlers after they revealed Myra's grave diagnosis. And they'd been outspoken about their faith in God's goodness — whether He chose to heal Myra or not. But maybe the reality was different now that Myra was gone. Shoot, like he'd told Phylicia, *he* had questions about why God would take a woman like her at such a young age. It stood to reason Myra's husband and daughters would have even tougher questions.

"Listen, Quinn, this is kind of short notice." Turner cleared his throat loudly. "But I wonder if I could ask a favor."

"Sure."

"You know our . . . *my* open house is tomorrow. I wondered if you might just stop by there for a few minutes, see how things are going. I know the girls won't want to be there, and I don't expect them to. They've done enough getting the house ready to show."

"It looks really nice too. I went in with Phylicia when we went to get Melvin earlier. Your daughters have everything looking really sharp."

"That's good to hear. This is hard for them, all three of them . . . selling the house they grew up in."

"I'm sure. And I'd be glad to drop by and check on things. It's two to five, right?"

"I'm not even sure. I can find the listing and shoot you a —"

"No, I can look it up. No biggie. You have it listed with the best realty company in town, and it's a good house."

Mabel trotted out to the kitchen, her face dripping from a dunk in the water bowl. Quinn wiped the dog's chin with his bare hand, then dried his hand on Mabel's brindle coat. He silently motioned the dog toward her blanket draped over the sagging sofa in the living room. She went obediently. "I'm honestly a little surprised your place hasn't sold yet."

"Yes, I am too." Turner paused. "I was hoping to get that all over with before now. Kind of like ripping off a Band-Aid, you know?"

Quinn winced at the apt analogy and paced between the kitchen and the adjoining living room. "I can see that. Hopefully it isn't too painful. For all of you."

"I think this property the girls bought will help take their minds off things. Do you . . . get the sense they're doing okay?"

He hesitated. "I do. They're still grieving, of course. It's only been a few weeks. They —"

"Three months. It's been three months, Quinn."

Quinn hadn't meant his words to come off as an accusation — well, maybe he had

— but Turner was on the defensive. Quinn scrambled for something to smooth things over but came up blank. "They miss you a lot . . . your daughters. Any idea when you'll be back here next?"

"Not for sure. And the girls have each other. That gives me a lot of peace. Which reminds me, I've been hearing your name quite a bit when I talk to my girls. One in particular."

He was a little surprised to hear that. He assumed Turner meant Phylicia and wanted to press for details.

But before he could think of a nonchalant way to inquire, Turner blurted, "Did Phee tell you about finding the ring?"

"Yes. Well, she told me a little."

"I guess I always figured the time would come when this would come out. Myra and I, at first anyway, had every intention of telling the girls about her first marriage — when they were old enough to understand. But time got away from us, and suddenly Phee was a teenager and we still hadn't said anything. And then Myra didn't want to. She was afraid the girls might think less of her if they knew she'd been divorced. Even that it might affect our daughters' dating relationships and eventually their own marriages." Quinn could almost see the wry smile Turner's voice held. "Ironic that, except for Jo, the girls haven't dated much at all. That really bothered Myra. She blamed herself for so much. As if she could have helped getting cancer. But she was devastated that she didn't get to see any of her daughters walk down the aisle or meet her future grandbabies."

Quinn nodded, remembering the selfless woman Myra had been.

Turner cleared his throat. "Anyway, bottom line, we never did tell the girls about Myra's other marriage. It was a mutual decision. I agreed that her first marriage really didn't have anything to do with our daughters. By the time Phee left home, we'd kind of become comfortable with just . . . letting that be in the past."

"But then they found the photo?"

Turner was silent for a few long seconds. "Yes. But I had no idea that photo even existed. Or why she would have saved it. I still don't get it . . . The man was abusive to her. In the worst sort of ways. She was desperate to get out of the marriage. But he was a public figure — older, rich — so of course, he called all the shots. He had her in a financial stranglehold."

Quinn had a hard time picturing the self-confident Myra Chandler he'd known as the woman Turner was describing. He guessed it was the same for Phylicia.

"Do you think . . . Is Phee taking it okay?" Turner's voice broke into his thoughts.

"I think she's doing okay. But I really couldn't say for sure. She's talked about it a little, but not so much her feelings. More just . . . the facts." He couldn't bring himself to reveal how angry and disappointed Phylicia had been with Turner over his marriage announcement.

"Has she said anything about . . . the possibility that I'm not her father?"

"What?" What was he talking about? Quinn had to back-pedal through his thoughts to even make sense of the question.

"If I know Phee, she's been digging into things. I don't know what Myra might have said to her, but . . . there's a chance Phee may have questioned whether or not I'm her biological father."

"No. She hasn't said anything like that to me." Quinn went to the sofa and sat down next to Mabel. The dog looked up at him as if checking to be sure he was okay. Seeming satisfied, she curled up with her head on Quinn's lap. "Why would Phylicia think that?" He wasn't sure he wanted to know the answer.

"You knew Myra, Quinn. You know what a good heart she had."

"Yes. Of course." *What did that have to do with his first question?* He didn't like where he feared this conversation was going. He'd been Turner's confidant on a lot of things, but never anything this personal — or profound.

A heavy sigh came over the line. "I may as well get this out of the way first. Myra was still married to Bill —" He stopped abruptly. "We've never told anyone his name. And I won't. I don't want the girls to know who he was. Do you understand?"

"Of course. I wouldn't say anything." *Be careful what you promise.*

"Not that the girls would recognize his name. He was quite a bit older than Myra, and he's been out of the public arena for years now. Retired, I think. Shoot, he may be dead for all I know. For a while, I kept track of him, just to be sure he didn't come anywhere near Myra. But after a while, I just wanted to pretend the lousy —" He caught himself, as he always did. "I just wanted to pretend he didn't exist."

Turner was not one to use profanity, but Quinn could fill in the blanks. His thoughts churned. If this Bill Whatever-his-name-was had retired, he was likely in his mid-sixties now, maybe older.

"Anyway, Myra and I worked together in Jeff City. There was nothing between us — we had feelings for each other, obviously, but I mean we didn't act on them. Not until after her divorce. But I knew she was in trouble. In danger. Even without her coming out and saying anything."

Phylicia hadn't told him any of this. Not that she necessarily would have. She seemed reluctant to talk about any of it. "But . . . why would Phylicia think you're *not* her biological father? You *are,* aren't you?"

Another sigh. "Quinn, I honestly don't know if I am or not."

"And if you're not?" He let the question hang in the air. How could a man not know such a thing? He and Myra would have had to marry very quickly after her divorce for what Turner suspected to be true. Or else Myra was sleeping with both men before her divorce — which Turner had denied, and Quinn found difficult to believe.

As if Turner had read his mind, he explained. "Myra finally came to me, desperate and terrified of what he might do. The abuse had escalated. The man was vicious. Criminal even. Making her do . . . things against her will." The pain — and anger — in Turner's voice were palpable.

Quinn couldn't imagine how helpless Turner must have felt. Yet probably reluctant to get involved on behalf of a married woman.

"It got so bad, I finally enlisted the help of another woman we worked with," Turner continued. "After we threatened to turn him in, we were able to get her away from the man. She quit her job and hid out until he finally agreed to a divorce — as long as Myra promised to keep her mouth shut about the abuse. He had connections and pulled some strings, arranged for an emergency divorce. He had their divorce records sealed, so none of it would come back to haunt him. The guy had political aspirations, I think."

"I can't even imagine. I never knew . . ."

"No. No one did. Myra never wanted anyone to know. But for a few months, he still made threats, tried to shake Myra up. That's why we moved to Langhorne after Phee was born. We wanted to be sure he stayed far away from Myra and the girls. And it's why we were so reluctant to tell the girls. At least when they were younger."

"But why does that make you unsure whether you're Phylicia's father — biological father?"

Another heavy sigh. "Myra was in a desperate financial situation — the guy saw to that . . . it's how he controlled her . . . so we married right away. As soon as her divorce was final. We were young, but by then I knew I loved her, and she loved me. A month after we got married, Myra discovered she was pregnant. We joked in public that it happened on our honeymoon, but" — he cleared his throat — "neither one of us were walking with the Lord back then, and . . . let's just say it could have happened before we were legally married. I hope you don't find that disappointing. Like I said, we were young and we weren't where we should have been spiritually."

"Hey . . ." Quinn held up a hand, even though he was aware Turner couldn't see the gesture. Mabel struggled to her haunches, watching him closely as if she sensed his tension. "I'm sure not going to stand in judgment." He let his voice trail off, hoping Turner wouldn't guess how little right he had to judge.

"Anyway, it could have happened a few weeks before our wedding. And . . . it could have happened before she was divorced. That monster forced himself on her on numerous occasions, especially after he knew she was trying to leave the marriage."

Quinn blew out a long breath. "I'm so sorry."

"Even the doctors were never sure about Myra's due date — tests for that kind of stuff weren't quite as precise as they are now, and her cycles weren't regular. But then . . . Phee came five weeks early — that is, five weeks if Myra got pregnant our first time. And the baby — Phee — weighed almost seven pounds. I forget exactly now. But . . . well, the math doesn't quite add up." He gave a frustrated grunt. "I suppose it's *possible* a baby born that early could be that big, but it's not probable. And there are . . . other things . . . that make me question whether Phee is mine."

"Wow. But you don't know for *sure*? You never had DNA tests or genetic testing done?" Trying to put himself in Turner's place, he found it hard to believe Turner wouldn't have pursued answers. *He* would have been asking a whole lot of questions.

"I think . . . I didn't *want* to know . . . if I wasn't her father. Myra and I made the decision to, um, *alter* our wedding date. The date we told people we'd eloped — the date we always celebrated as our anniversary — was actually the day Myra's divorce became final. And we *did* elope. That part was true, and the girls have always known about it. But the day her divorce was final — that was the day we considered ourselves married in God's eyes. With . . . all the privileges of marriage." He gave a humorless laugh. "I'm not saying we were right. A man will tell himself strange things to justify sin."

Quinn blew out another audible stream of air. He knew all too much about that. And it was another reason his breakup with Heather had been so agonizing. If they hadn't given in to temptation, the whole fiasco with Heather wouldn't have been nearly as complicated then — or nearly as awkward now.

He shook off the thoughts. This wasn't the time. Turner was waiting for a response. "So, you and Myra never talked about it? About the possibility that Phylicia wasn't yours?"

"Of course she's mine. It's my name on her birth certificate. I'm the one who was in that delivery room holding Myra's hand. Shoot, I even cut Phee's cord." His voice lost a little steam and he cleared his throat. "Not that I get why that's such a big deal. Kind of gross, if you want to know the truth. But I'm the one who brought her and Myra home from the hospital. I've been her father in every way. From day one."

"Of course. I didn't mean to imply —"

"No. I'm sorry. And I didn't mean to lash out at *you*. This mess isn't your fault."

Quinn took a deep breath. "So, what you're saying is that you and Myra never talked about the possibility that her first husband could be Phylicia's father?"

"After Phee was born, we never talked about the man. About any of it. It was as if that part of Myra's life had never happened. It was odd, really, because there wasn't anything else we couldn't talk about. But then . . ." His voice took on a faraway quality. "At the very end . . . just a few days before Myra became unable to speak, she told me some things. And even then, it wasn't a confession by any means. But she said some things that opened the door to the possibility that I might not be Phee's father — it was more than she'd ever hinted at before."

"Wow. That had to be hard." Quinn hung on every word, even as he wished Turner would shut up. He didn't want to know the things the man was saddling him with.

"Honestly, Quinn, I couldn't even think about it. It was all I could handle — still is — to face losing my sweet Myra. But when Phee told me about the photo and the ring . . . I wonder now if maybe Myra felt like she needed to tell Phee. I still don't know if she said anything to her or not. I don't think she did." He gave a shuddering sigh. "I didn't know Myra had saved that stuff, but the only reason I can think of that she *would* save it was in case Phee needed some kind of proof someday."

"Proof?"

"I don't know . . . to obtain her medical history maybe? Or . . . maybe Myra thought Phee should have an inheritance from him or something? The guy was wealthy. I honestly don't know what she had in mind. And I'll never know. That's why I hate that Phylicia even found that stuff."

"I'm sorry. I wish I knew what to say." Quinn had to wonder if Myra had another reason for keeping that photo. He knew if it were him, his imagination would be going berserk.

"You don't need to say anything. I really didn't intend to lay this all on you. And please . . . keep it on the down-low. In case Phee hasn't thought about the possibilities yet."

"You're going to tell her though? I assume."

"I don't know. I'm not sure I should. I think she has enough on her plate right now with losing her mother, and buying the property, and now finding out about Myra's first marriage. Not to mention the mess *I've* made of things."

"You?"

"Moving to Florida. Jumping the gun with Karleen. I at least should have stuck around and told them face-to-face. About Karleen."

Quinn couldn't disagree, so he remained silent, scratching Mabel under her chin.

After an overlong pause, Turner asked, "Did the girls tell you we broke it off? Karleen and I?"

"Phylicia said something about it."

"I think it was for the best." He let out a short huff. "I need to let myself grieve. And I need to get my head on straight before I do anything as drastic as marriage."

"Yes, that's probably wise. For anybody." He attempted a laugh.

"Wish you would have told me that a few months ago." Turner's voice held a smile.

"I don't recall you asking." Quinn tried to keep levity in his own voice, relieved that they seemed to be back on even footing. But he couldn't feel relieved at all about the information he now had in his possession. Turner had told him way too much — the man was obviously getting things off his chest.

But now the weight of these secrets and lies were on *his* chest. And Quinn wasn't sure what to do with that. Especially if he wanted something beyond friendship with

Phylicia Chandler.

And he *did.* He most definitely did.

CHAPTER 20

Meow.

Phee sat up in bed, forgetting for a minute where she was.

Meow. The cry came again and a white-tipped black tail swished past the closed French doors of Phee's new room. She reached for her phone and glanced at the time. Apparently, the daybed was plenty comfortable, because it was almost eight o'clock.

She eased her legs over the side of the mattress and stretched. Barefoot, she padded out to the living room, Melvin shadowing her every step. The house was chilly, so she turned the furnace up a notch, glancing longingly at the fireplace. Living in an apartment, she'd missed having a fireplace. Dad had taught each of them the art of building a good fire before they left home, but they hadn't wanted to risk a fire when they were leaving the cottage overnight. Maybe some weekend when they planned to be here all day, they'd give it a try.

Instead, she lit the grouping of candles they'd placed in the firebox and went into the kitchen for coffee. The morning sun streamed through the windows, but the aroma of coffee brewing was absent, as was any sign of life from her sisters. They must have slept soundly too. Either that or they woke early and went to church without her.

She tiptoed into the hallway and peeked into her sisters' bedrooms. Both still sawing logs. And their doors were open. She picked Melvin up and carried him into the living room and set him down. "Silly cat. *My* door was closed. You couldn't choose one of the open doors?"

He chirped in reply, cocking his head and giving her what Mom had always called his sad puppy dog face. It *was* hard to resist. "You hungry? Come here, buddy." She went to the tiny back porch off the kitchen where she'd set up his area last night after Quinn left. Melvin had left a little "gift" in the litter box beside the washing machine. "Good boy. Tell you what. I'll feed you, and we'll let one of the sleepyheads clean out the litter box." They hadn't discussed how Melvin duties would be divvied up, but she laughed to herself imagining how that conversation would go down.

She looked at the clock on the coffee-maker. If they were going to make it to the nine o'clock church service, she'd better get in the shower. She rummaged in the boxes they had yet to unpack and located a towel and some shampoo. They'd washed out paint brushes and cleaning rags in the tub and it could stand a good cleaning, but that would have to wait for another day. It would do for now.

Twenty minutes later, someone pounded on the door. She quickly rinsed the last of the conditioner out of her hair and turned off the water. "It's open."

"I need to get in there." Britt knocked again.

"The door is open, Britt. I'm in the shower."

The door handle rattled. "It's locked."

"No, it's not."

"Yes, it is."

She gave a little growl. She knew she hadn't locked the door. For exactly this reason. "Hang on. I'm just about out." She shoved the shower curtain aside and stepped over the side of the tub. She grabbed the towel and, wrapping it around her, went to open the door.

The doorknob jiggled but wouldn't turn.

She bent to inspect the lock mechanism. The vintage lock was about as simple as they came, but it wouldn't budge either way.

"Hurry up, Phee! I've gotta go."

"You must have locked it from the outside, because I can't get it open."

"What?"

"I can't get the door open from this side."

"Well, I sure can't get it open from this side, or I would have been in there five minutes ago."

"Hang on." She dried her hands and tried the lock again. "It won't budge. Did you check if there's a way to turn the lock from that side?"

"There's not. And besides, who would be stupid enough to put a lock on the *outside* of a bathroom door?"

"Well, you're going to have to figure something out. I can't get it from this side, and it's not like I have a toolbox in here."

"What's going on?" Joanna's groggy voice joined Britt's on the other side of the door.

"Phee locked me out."

"I did *not* lock this door."

"Did you see what time it is? We're going to be late for church," Jo said.

"That will be the least of our problems if somebody doesn't open this door." Britt sounded desperate.

"Go outside," Phee hollered through the door.

"How will that help?"

"No, I mean *go* outside. In the bushes."

"Are you crazy?"

"Do you have a better idea?"

Britt growled and then heavy footsteps headed down the hall and the back door slammed. Phee couldn't help but laugh. But she was still stuck in this four-by-six-foot bathroom. "Jo? You still there?"

"I'm here, but what am I supposed to do?"

"You're sure there's not a place for a key on that side?"

"Not that I can see. Do you have a nail file in there? Something you can jiggle around in the keyhole?"

"You make it sound like a jailbreak."

Joanna giggled. "There's a pretty good gap under the door. Maybe I can fit an ice pick or . . . something under the door to you."

Phee heard the back door slam and Britt jabbering, sounding out of breath.

"What is wrong with you?" Joanna didn't sound too sympathetic.

"Somebody just pulled in the driveway. Thanks to you, I came *this* close to being caught with my pants —"

"Who is it?" Jo asked.

"I don't know. It's an SUV."

"Hang on a sec, Phee. Somebody's here."

"Wait! Don't leave me locked in here . . . Jo?"

Scuffling footsteps, then silence.

Phee sat on the edge of the tub. The 1940s muddy-pink tile was something she'd thought they could live with — maybe tone it down with white paint and white shower curtain. But if she had to sit here surrounded by it for even two more minutes, she might start ripping off tiles with her bare hands.

She moved to the window, but she couldn't see past the corner of the house, so she went back to the door and hollered for her sisters. After what seemed like an eternity, she heard the front door open and multiple footsteps. "Jo? Britt?"

"We brought help." Jo sounded positively gleeful.

"You hanging in there, Phylicia?" Quinn's voice boomed through the crack in the door. "We'll have you out of there in a few minutes."

What was he doing here? She stole a glance in the mirror and her breath caught. "Hang on! Wait a minute . . ." She cast about the room, then grabbed her flannel pajamas off the hook by the shower and scrambled to put them on. Thank goodness she'd slept in something halfway decent last night, not knowing how warm her new room would be.

She ripped the towel off her head and tried in vain to untangle her wet hair, then decided a little blush and lip gloss would be a more noticeable improvement. But she'd left her makeup in her room since the three of them were sharing the small bathroom.

She gave a longing glance toward the window, wishing it were big enough to crawl out of. This was beyond embarrassing! And what was Quinn doing here anyway? He hadn't told her last night that he was coming back. In fact, he'd mentioned going to the early service at his church in Cape.

"Here, Joanna, can you hold this pin while I grab a screwdriver?" Quinn sounded all business, and on the other side of the door, scraping and hammering and muffled conversation ensued.

Peering into the bathroom mirror, with a cautious eye on the door, Phee gave up on her makeup and hurriedly pinned her hair — as much as it would cooperate while still damp — into a messy bun.

The scrape of metal against metal made her cringe, but the door shuddered, then lifted.

"You decent in there? This door's coming

off . . ." The humor in Quinn's voice made her want to smack him.

The door, with Quinn's tanned fingers gripping either side, slid to create an opening.

Not meeting his eye, Phee slipped through sideways into the hall. "Thank you," she muttered.

One eyebrow rose and he chuckled. "Thanks for tearing your door off?"

"Better than spending the weekend in the bathroom." She tucked a wayward strand of hair back into the bun on top of her head.

"Hey," Britt said, "it's better than being locked *out* of our bathroom all weekend."

Joanna laughed. "You came in the nick of time, Quinn. Britt was — *ahem* — exploring the great outdoors about the time you —"

"Hush!" Britt gave Jo a sisterly shove. "You don't need to tell every little thing you know."

Phee shot a sideways glance at Quinn, who looked befuddled by the whole conversation. For the first time, she noticed he was wearing dress pants and a button-down shirt. A tweed suit jacket was lopped over a bench at the other end of the short hall.

"Don't pay any attention to them. Thank you for the rescue." She studied the door, now leaning against the wall outside the bathroom. "You couldn't get it unlocked either, huh?"

"I think a little WD-40 will take care of it, but I didn't happen to bring any with me. I might have to take the whole doorknob assembly out to get at it."

"I think there's a can in a box somewhere around here. In the kitchen maybe? But Quinn, you don't have to do that."

He shrugged. "It's no big deal. It won't take long."

"So, Quinn . . ." Britt stifled a giggle. "Did you hear Phee yelling all the way from Langhorne? Or were you just passing by?"

He glanced at Phee as if she might fill in some missing blanks for him. When she didn't, he shrugged again. "Actually, I was on my way to church, but I wanted to drop off the stuff you left in my car last night."

"I left something?"

"Well, Melvin did, actually." He motioned toward the front door. "I left it out on the porch. The bag of cat food and whatever was in that brown paper bag."

"Oh, his brushes and vitamins. I forgot all about those. But you didn't need to make an extra trip."

"No big deal. It was right on the way."

That was a bit of an exaggeration, but she

wasn't going to belabor the point. Not when she was standing safely on the *outside* of the bathroom door.

She glanced at the clock Jo and Britt had hung in the dining room last night. "If that time is right, you're going to be late for church, Quinn."

"And we flat-out missed church," Joanna said. "But I'm thinking God will understand this once."

"Yeah, that's what you said *last* week." Britt grinned.

A corner of Quinn's mouth quirked. "Surely God will count this good deed as my 'church' for the week."

Phee laughed. "If by good deed, you mean replacing our bathroom door — the door someone ripped clean off its hinges, I might add — then yes, I think the Lord will understand."

Quinn winked. "Yes, but what excuse are *you* three going to give Him?"

Chapter 21

"There. All done." Quinn tucked the hammer and screwdriver in his back pocket and stepped out of the way so the sisters could admire his handiwork. It had taken the better part of an hour to fix the lock and replace the door, but everything seemed to be working correctly now. He inhaled deeply, breathing in air that smelled of shampoo and baby powder and perfume, and a host of other intoxicating womanly scents.

Phylicia reached for the handle and tried the door. "Looks good."

Quinn looked from Phylicia to each of her sisters, then back to her again, studying each of their features, trying not to appear too obvious. But with his conversation with Turner last night at the forefront of his thoughts, he couldn't help but look at the sisters in a different light.

All three sisters had the same crystal blue

eyes and honey-brown hair, like their mother's, but Joanna and Britt did look the most like each other. Phylicia's mouth was fuller and her forehead higher than her sisters'. Of course, Quinn had always thought they all looked like their mother, which actually might lend even more credence to Turner's suspicions.

"The real test" — Joanna's teasing voice drew him out of his musings — "is if you can get out again after you lock yourself in."

Britt gave her oldest sister a nudge. "Go on, Phee. Why don't you test it?"

"How dumb do you think I am?" Phylicia nudged her back.

"What?" Quinn affected a pout. "You don't trust my handyman skills?"

"I'll test it if you promise to let me out" — Phylicia threw him a sideways glance — "just in case you didn't quite get it fixed."

While he tried to think of a comeback that would earn him a smile, she stepped into the bathroom and turned the lock. A second later, the door handle rattled, and she hollered. "Hey! Somebody let me out."

Deflated, he reached for the doorknob. But before he could turn it, the door flew open and she emerged wearing an ornery grin. "Just kidding."

Not quite the smile he'd been aiming for, but he'd take it.

Meanwhile, her sisters cackled like farmyard hens.

"Very funny." He shot her a stern look, then turned it on Joanna and Britt. "You're all just a barrel of laughs. But seriously, if I were you, I'd give that lock another shot of this stuff" — he held up the blue and yellow spray can he'd used to loosen the stuck lock — "maybe every month or so until you're sure it's not going to stick anymore." He'd shown Phylicia earlier how to use the straw taped to the can to target the lubricant into the key mechanism.

"Thanks again for coming to the rescue, Quinn."

He gave a little salute. "Well . . . let me bring in Melvin's stuff from the porch, and I'll get out of your hair. Where *is* the infamous cat, by the way? How'd he do last night?"

"I never heard him until he started meowing at my door first thing this morning. But I haven't seen him since before my ill-fated shower."

"I think he's sleeping on my bed." Britt went to the door down the hall from the bathroom and poked her head inside. "Yep," she whispered. "He's sawing logs on my bed. You'd never know he hadn't lived here all his life."

"Well, don't let him get too comfortable. He has work to do in the other two cabins, remember."

"Not yet." Britt moved to stand in front of the doorway to her room, as if she were a Buckingham Palace guard. Or a bouncer.

Laughing, Quinn glanced around the room for a clock. Ten thirty. He took a deep breath, thinking for only a split-second before he took the risk. "We could still make the eleven o'clock service at my church. Anybody want to come with me?"

"No way." Britt scrubbed at her face, then added quickly, "Thanks for the invite and everything, but I haven't even showered yet. There's no way I could get ready in time."

"Sorry, me neither." Joanna smirked. "Especially if I should happen to get stuck in the bathroom."

His odds of a yes were dwindling quickly, but he turned to Phylicia anyway. "How about you? Since you've already washed your hair and everything." He tried for a cool smirk but it merely felt nerdy.

He was so busy feeling stupid that he almost missed her matter-of-fact reply.

"Sure, why not? Just give me a minute to get dressed."

■ ■ ■ ■

Phee and Quinn were halfway to his church when it struck her that this was the second time in two days that she'd agreed to go somewhere with him by herself. Either she was getting comfortable with the idea of being friends with one of her dad's friends or something else was going on in her peabrain . . . something she didn't dare explore right now. She'd always prided herself on her analytical nature, on knowing her own motives and intentions well. She couldn't — or didn't want to — explain this one.

"What's so funny over there?"

She turned to see Quinn smiling at her, a question in his eyes. His hands gripped the steering wheel at exactly ten and two, his shirt cuffs peeking out from the sleeves of his suit coat. Usually a suit made guys look older and more mature, but somehow Quinn's tweed made him look younger. More carefree.

She gave a self-conscious laugh. "Sorry. Just . . . you had to be there, I guess."

"And apparently I wasn't? There?"

She waved him off. "It's nothing. It's just kind of been a crazy morning. I'd given up on making it to church after about fifteen minutes stuck in that bathroom, and now here I am going to a whole different church."

"I almost waited until after church to stop by, but I thought Melvin might not appreciate having to wait that long for his breakfast."

"Oh, the bag I left in your car was just for refills. I brought in his bucket of food last night. But I'm sure glad you changed your mind and stopped before church."

He chuckled. "I'll bet. Otherwise, you might still be stuck."

"Excuse me, but I'd like to think my sisters and I would have come up with some brilliant means of escape by now."

"You mean like taking the door hinges off?"

"Yeah, yeah . . . I'll give you that. That was pretty brilliant."

"That's all I wanted to hear: Quinn Mitchell is brilliant." He gave her a sidewise glance. "And handsome? Care to add that?"

She rolled her eyes. He did look handsome, but the repartee was getting a little too snappy for her comfort, so she sat hugging the passenger-side door in silence the rest of the way in to Cape.

When they pulled into the church parking lot, Phee realized she'd been here before.

"One of my high school friends got married in this church. Mandy Franklin."

"Sure, I know the Franklins. So you were at the wedding?"

"I was a bridesmaid." She regretted telling him that as soon as the words were out. She would have bet one of the cottages what was going through his mind right now: *Always a bridesmaid, never a —*

"Always a bridesmaid, never a bride, huh?"

"Are you kidding me?" She stared at him. "How did you do that?"

"Do what?"

"Read my mind."

"Seriously? So you were thinking that too? Always a bridesmaid, never a bride?"

"No, I was thinking that *you* were probably thinking that . . . about me. Sorry, but I've heard that infernal little trope too many times recently — usually from busybodies who come into the flower shop —" She decided against finishing her sentence with *trying to hook me up with their loser sons.* At his age, Quinn had probably heard whatever the male equivalent of that trope was often enough.

But the way he'd said it didn't seem to carry an ounce of meanness. In fact, she'd never seen anything unkind in him. Maybe that was why she liked Quinn so much. That, and the fact that her parents had always thought the world of him. "One of the good guys," Mom had declared once, when Dad was talking about an issue at work that Quinn was dealing with.

"Actually . . ." His grin was contagious. "I *was* wondering why a great girl . . . a great woman like you has never been married."

She wasn't sure how to respond. Or what he even meant by that.

He dropped his head briefly, then looked up. "I apologize. That was probably worse than the bridesmaid deal . . . not to mention a really sexist thing to say."

She held up a hand. "Hey, that's not me. Not that I don't think women should be respected and all, but I'm not one to get riled up over stupid things that weren't even intended to be offensive."

"I appreciate that. I think. Sorry if it was stupid."

"No." Laughing, she shook her head. "That's not what I meant. And to answer your question, I've just never met the right guy. This might sound strange in light of a recent conversation you and I had, but . . . before Mom got sick, I always thought my parents had the best marriage of anyone I knew. I never wanted to settle for anything less than what they had. But . . . I guess . . . things weren't quite as rosy as I always imagined." She folded her hands in her lap and dropped her head.

"Why do you say that? Just because your dad met someone so soon after your mom passed away, doesn't mean that they —"

"He met her *before* Mom died, Quinn."

"But . . . you don't really think there was anything going on between them before, do you? That doesn't sound like your dad. Not the man I know anyway. Your parents had a great marriage. And I've always thought that people who marry again after losing a spouse are proving that they saw marriage as a real blessing."

"Maybe. But he's changed, Quinn. Dad is different since Mom died." They'd had this conversation before and she didn't want to rehash it. She reached for her door handle. "I'm sorry. I didn't mean to start that whole thing again. And I'll feel really bad if I make you miss church *twice* in one day."

His smile held sympathy, but he reached for his door as well. "Okay. To be continued after church."

The feather-light touch of his hand at the small of her back, as they entered the church and she preceded him into the sanctuary, was comforting — and a little unsettling at the same time.

CHAPTER 22

"Now to him who is able to keep you from stumbling and to present you blameless before the presence of his glory with great joy, to the only God our Savior, through Jesus Christ our Lord, be glory, majesty, dominion, and authority, before all time and now and forever. Amen." The church service ended with Pastor Franklin's usual blessing from the book of Jude, followed by an invitation for the congregation to meet for a brief time of fellowship in the adjacent hospitality room.

Quinn gave Phylicia a sidewise glance, torn between wanting to show her off at the gathering and not wanting to be forced to make awkward introductions when he had no clue how she saw him. *Dad's coworker? Friend? Potential more-than-a-friend?* Besides, selfishly, he wanted her to himself the rest of the afternoon.

They slipped into the aisle, shuffling

among the crowd to the back of the sanctuary. "Shall we go grab something to eat?" he whispered behind her.

She looked over her shoulder at him, crinkling her nose. "I should probably get back and make sure my sisters aren't stuck in the bathroom."

He laughed. "I'm pretty sure that WD-40 did the trick."

"Maybe we could stop and get a couple of pizzas . . . take it out to our place to eat? The girls wanted to try to finish getting all our rooms put together this afternoon, and if I want help with my room, I'd better be there to help with theirs."

"Sure. And I can help if you need to move anything heavy. Or whatever. As long as it doesn't involve decorating anything."

She laughed. "If you're sure you don't mind. I hope you're keeping track of your hours."

He waved her off.

"No, I'm serious, Quinn. We had an agreement that we'd *hire* you guys . . . and we have a budget for it. Not a very big one, but still . . ."

"That's fine. Once you're ready to start on the other cottages, I'll start racking up a bill for you. But this one I'm just doing as a friend."

She looked up at him. "Are you sure, Quinn?"

He was growing to love the sound of his own name when it came from her lips. "I'm positive. I've actually enjoyed it. You three can be pretty entertaining."

She lifted one eyebrow. "Oh, we've been on our best behavior. You haven't seen entertaining yet. Just wait till we cut loose a little."

He laughed, wondering if she realized that she'd actually — just in that moment — cut loose a little. It was a side of her he hadn't seen since she was younger and still living at home with her parents. And he was more elated about catching a glimpse of *that* Phylicia than he would ever admit to her.

They finally made their way through the crush of people, and when they emerged through the doorway, they both gave a little gasp. It was pouring rain outside the tall windows in the foyer.

"Wow. I didn't even know that was in the forecast." Phylicia opened her purse and rummaged through it. "I used to have an umbrella in here, but I must have left it somewhere."

"I have one in the car." He cringed. "A lot of good that'll do us, huh? Wait here. I'll go get the car and pick you up under the overhang." He pointed to a covered side entry at the end of the corridor.

"I don't mind going out in it. We'll run."

"You sure? It's a downpour."

She nodded and started for the main entrance they'd come in.

He followed her through the doors, but once outside, she ducked her head and sprinted to the parking lot. Despite his longer legs, he had to jog to catch up. He'd forgotten the girl ran track in school.

He fumbled for his keys and had the car unlocked before she reached the passenger door. They climbed in and slammed their doors shut. Turning to look at each other, they cracked up.

Phylicia combed her fingers through her dripping hair. "Do I look as much like a drowned rat as you do?"

He craned to catch his reflection in the rearview mirror. "Believe me, it's a much better look on you."

She swabbed at her face with a tissue. "Good day to stay huddled by the fireplace. But this won't be good for Dad's open house."

Quinn frowned. "Probably not. Maybe it will let up before then."

"I hope they put down plastic for people to walk on."

"I would think they would, but I can give them a call and request it. I told your dad I'd stop by the open house and see how things were going."

"Oh . . . You talked to Dad? Recently?"

He froze. He hadn't really meant to let that slip. It exposed too many doors that could *not* be opened. Not by him anyway. "Yes. He called last night, actually. To ask if I'd stop by the house. In Langhorne. So you girls wouldn't have to. Sorry, I should have let you know I'd talked to him."

"Did Dad . . . sound okay to you?"

Quinn hesitated, pre-examining his answer for the potential to let any cats out of the bag. He hated the invisible wall that had gone up between them with this newfound knowledge. "He sounded good. Actually seemed more like himself than he has in a while."

Her shoulders relaxed visibly. "I'm so glad. I thought the same thing last time we talked. Monday, I guess it was. I just wish he would come home. Even for a visit. Did he say anything to you about when he might be back?"

"Not really."

"I thought for sure he'd want to be here for the open house."

"They don't want the owners to be present for those things. Only the agent. They would have just asked him to leave anyway."

"I know that, but to help get the house ready and everything."

"I'm sure he trusted you girls to do a good job on that. And you did, from what I saw last night." He leaned forward and turned the key in the ignition. Turner Chandler owed him. He hoped the man appreciated all the times he'd come to his defense.

"Shall I call ahead for the pizza? Do you care where?"

"Your call. I never met a pizza I didn't like."

She dialed, and he heard her order three large pizzas. When his brow went up in surprise, she laughed and looked at him over her phone. "We like leftovers," she whispered. "You can take some home too."

He gave a big thumbs-up.

A few minutes later, they were headed out to the cottages, his SUV filled with the aromas of hot pizza and cold rain. As soon as they came around the curve of the cottage lane, they saw that Phylicia's car was the only one there.

"Hmmm. The lights are off. I hope the electricity isn't out." Looking puzzled, she twisted in her seat to take in a one-eighty view of the property. "They must have gone to church after all."

Disappointment flooded him, but he knew he needed to offer. "I can just go on home."

"Without eating pizza?"

"I wasn't sure you'd be comfortable if it's . . . just the two of us."

Her laughter sounded more like the nervous kind. "Quinn, we just spent the entire morning 'just the two of us.' I'm fine with you coming in for —" She stopped midsentence. "Oh. Unless you have a policy or something."

"About being alone with a woman?"

"About *not* being alone, actually . . . Dad always had that policy. That he'd never be alone with a woman who wasn't his wife. You know . . . just to avoid temptation."

He nodded, trying to ignore the fact that she'd seemed clueless that such a policy might apply to him. With her. What did he have to do for her to see how he felt about her?

He curbed a smile, wondering how she'd respond if she knew what he was thinking. "I've always admired your dad for that. It's inconvenient sometimes to have to rearrange things so he's not alone with a woman . . . office doors open and traveling in separate vehicles. And he gets razzed for it sometimes."

"Really? I never knew that."

"It's good-natured — for the most part. But I'll tell you this: several of the guys at the office have adopted similar policies because of your dad."

Her face fell.

"What? Doesn't that make you proud?"

She huffed. "I guess there needed to be a policy about hospice nurses."

"Phylicia . . ." He wasn't sure why he was so reluctant to let her vent about her suspicions about her father. Except that he'd always felt a strong loyalty toward his boss. His friend. He'd never dreamed that loyalty might pit him against the woman he was . . . *just admit it, Mitchell . . .* falling in love with.

But it tore him up to see her turn against Turner this way. Especially given what he knew about her father now. The man didn't need any more strikes against him. "Has your dad come out and admitted that things started with this nurse *before* your mom passed away?"

"No. He hasn't. But even if it started after Mom died, it's just a little too soon for comfort." She shook her head. "I'm sorry I said anything. I didn't want to go there again."

"I really don't mean to lecture you, but I know your dad pretty well. Differently than you do. I just don't believe he would do anything that wasn't appropriate."

"So you *believe* it's appropriate to get engaged two months after your wife dies? Because that's a fact. I heard it from the horse's mouth." She seemed surprised by the bitterness of her own words and hung her head. "Again, I'm sorry. I should keep my mouth shut. None of this is your fault."

"Can you at least withhold judgment until you know for sure how it all happened?"

"I'll try." She gave a wan smile and tapped the pizza boxes stacked on the console between them. "Now about that policy. Is it going to keep you from sharing this pizza with me?"

"I seem to recall your dad had a policy for his daughters too."

"Oh, he did. Not that I ever needed it while I was living under his roof."

"I remember him telling about Joanna violating the rule once."

That made her laugh. "Oh, she got in so much trouble! Mom and Dad came home and found a boy in the house . . . in Jo's room, no less. I honestly think that might be when Jo decided to become a lawyer, because Dad basically grounded her for the rest of her known life. Yet, somehow she managed to weasel out of it. Britt and I were so mad. It was totally unfair." Her wistful expression made him think her thoughts had carried her back to happier times.

Outside, the rain had let up a little. He turned off the ignition, sorry to break her reverie but not wanting to get drenched again either. "Hey, let's make a run for it while we can."

She looked through the windshield. "Good idea. I'm starving."

He handed her the umbrella he'd retrieved from the glove compartment and reached for the pizza boxes. "Can you get everything else?"

She held up her purse. "This is it. But don't you think the guy with the pizza should have the umbrella?" She opened her car door and stuck the umbrella out far enough to open it. "Stay there . . . I'll come around."

He did as she ordered, and she came around to share the umbrella with him. And with the pizzas, of course. Close enough to smell her heady perfume, he hunkered shoulder-to-shoulder with her, heads together, laughing and jostling each other as they climbed the steps to the porch.

She unlocked the door and they shed their coats on the covered porch. The house was chilly and he offered to light a fire.

"We haven't had a fire yet, but you could light those candles if you want. In case the electricity goes out."

"Oh . . . sure. I'm kind of surprised it hasn't yet. That speaks well of the wiring in this old house."

He lit the candles with the wand lying on the mantel. The effect was charming . . . and romantic. Though he didn't dare voice that thought.

They both jumped when thunder shook the cottage. A few seconds later, lightning flashed outside the windows.

Phylicia poured iced tea, set out plates and napkins, and opened the pizza boxes.

"Mmm . . ." He inhaled. "Smells good!"

"Help yourself." She handed him a plate. "I'm going to call my sisters and make sure everything's okay."

He put three slices on his plate and carried them to the table by the window in what they called the breakfast nook. He didn't start eating, waiting for her.

She'd carried her phone around the corner into the living room, but he overheard most of her end of the conversation. It sounded as if her sisters had gone to Joanna's to finish moving her things out, but when the rain started, they decided to do a little shopping instead.

When Phylicia came back, she loaded her own plate with two slices and joined him at the table. "My crazy sisters are out shopping in this deluge."

"I gathered that." He pointed toward the living room. "Heard your end of the conversation. I . . . really wasn't trying to eavesdrop."

"No problem." She took a few steps into the living room and looked out through the enclosed porch at the rain. "I sure hope the cabins don't have any leaks."

"I didn't see any water damage when we walked through, did you?"

"No, but it's been a long time since it rained this hard."

"Do you want to go check on them? I'll come with you."

"Maybe we should. But let's eat first before our pizza gets cold."

She returned to the table and for the next twenty minutes they laughed and talked. About this morning's sermon, about growing up in an all-girl family, and about Quinn's opposite experience of having just one brother. An older brother.

"Older, huh? So, he must be like, my dad's age?" She worked to keep a poker face.

"You had *better* be kidding."

She laughed at his appalled expression.

But it created an opening to ask something she'd been wondering about more and more since Quinn had told her how his brother had been healed of cancer. "How old is Markus?"

"He's . . . I guess he'd be forty-eight now. Wow. That *is* old."

Really old. Why did that bother her so much?

"But hey, don't lump me in with him," Quinn added quickly. "Markus was almost seven when I was born."

That meant Quinn was forty-one. Maybe forty-two. Still . . . she was in her twenties, he was in his forties — two whole decades. Funny, he didn't seem that old to her anymore.

"Does your brother live around here?"

"No. He's in Austin. Married, with a baby girl, a dog . . . the whole enchilada."

"Ah, so you're an uncle." She could easily picture him with a couple of giggling toddlers slung over his shoulders.

"I am, but . . . I don't see my brother's family."

"Ever?"

"Not since he got married."

"You haven't even met your niece?"

He shook his head.

"Really? Why, you don't like kids?" Maybe

that was why he'd never married.

"I like kids fine. It's not that."

She frowned. "I'm sorry. You said you and your brother have some issues?" Her questions sounded too forward now that the words were out, especially given how he'd clammed up last night.

But he didn't flinch. "It's not that I don't love him. We just . . . aren't close. Physical distance is part of it. And we were so far apart in age. And the whole faith thing. But . . ." He shook his head. "It's complicated. Let's just leave it at that."

Despite her heightened curiosity, the pain in his expression kept her from pushing him. "I don't know what I'd do if my sisters moved away." That was even more true now that Mom was gone. She didn't want to go there and sought something to lighten the moment. "Of course, I might not feel the same after we've all lived together in this little cottage for a few more weeks."

He laughed. "It won't be so bad when the cabins are done and you each have your own place."

"Except when we rent the cabins out and all end up here together again."

"Still, if you're doing things the way you first planned, you'll at least each have your own place to get away most of the time."

Phee admitted that she was getting excited about the possibilities. And even about renting the cabins out as an Airbnb. "It's a lot easier to be excited about the renovations now that we're living here." She looked around the small, open cottage. "There's still a lot I'd love to do to this place, but it's already more charming than my apartment ever was. I never cared that much about the apartment. How it was decorated."

"That's because it wasn't yours. It makes a difference when you own a place and the stamp you put on it is at least somewhat permanent."

"True." She didn't correct him. Even though she was beginning to feel as if she could talk to Quinn about anything, he didn't need to know her reasons for never bothering to fix up her apartment — that it would have felt as if she were settling for being single. And Quinn *was* right that ownership made a difference in how she viewed this place and in how much she was willing to invest of her time, money, and affection. "And getting this cottage fixed up has given us ideas for what we want to do with the cabins."

"Speaking of the cabins" — he wadded up his napkin — "shall we go see if they're staying high and dry?"

"Sure." She closed the lids on the pizza boxes and blew out the candles Quinn had lit earlier. As the smoke curled up toward the ceiling, her stomach clenched at the realization that Quinn might have taken the candles as a romantic overture.

The knot tightened when she realized that she wouldn't have minded at all if he had.

CHAPTER 23

The rain had let up a little, and Quinn held the door as Phylicia made a dash across the property sans umbrella. She didn't seem to mind if she got wet now that she'd changed into jeans and a hoodie. He'd hated to end their conversation over pizza. As long as they kept on neutral territory, he loved talking to her.

At the same time, he'd been a little on edge, worried that the conversation would turn to her dad, and then he'd have to clam up to avoid revealing his secrets.

"I didn't mean to rush lunch, but I promised your dad I'd look in on the open house, and I didn't want to leave here until we checked on the cabins."

"I really appreciate that, Quinn." She unlocked the door to the first cabin, but stepped back and motioned for him to go in first. "Just in case that mouse is still here."

"That mouse and his twenty-seven brothers."

She shuddered. "I can't even go there."

He laughed at the goofy face she made and entered the darkened cabin, flipping on lights as he went through the rooms. The place smelled mustier than he remembered, but given this rain and the heavy air, that was to be expected. Together, they walked through to the back of the house.

"Oh, wow . . . Look out here." She opened the back door and stepped onto the little stoop that overlooked what had been a mostly dry creek only yesterday. Now, muddy brown water flowed through in a steady stream.

The stoop was open, barely covered by the narrow eaves, so he stood behind her, just inside the door, looking over her shoulder. "Looks like you're getting that waterfront property after all."

"I just hope we don't get houseboats!" She looked genuinely concerned.

"The water still has a ways to go before it reaches the walls. I don't think you have anything to worry about." These rock walls were likely built to afford some protection from flooding, but they were crumbling in places now, and Quinn doubted they would hold if the water actually rose that high. Of course, he wasn't about to tell Phylicia that. And unless the rain kept up for days, the chances of the tributary suddenly flooding its banks were pretty slim. But he was a little surprised how close to the banks these cabins had been built.

Phylicia turned to come back inside, and he took a couple of steps backward to let her pass. She smelled faintly of baby powder and something citrusy, and her nearness was disconcerting in a most pleasant way.

"I'll check the back bedroom for leaks, but so far, so good."

She didn't reply, but started opening cupboards and closets, cautiously peering inside as if she expected a mouse to jump out at her at any moment.

Assured this cabin was weathering the rain well, they ran to the other one and repeated the check.

"Uh-oh," Phylicia called from the kitchen.

He stepped into the small room to see her pointing at the ceiling above the stove. He flipped on the light under the stove's vent, but the bulb was burned out. Using his phone's flashlight, he located the water spot on the ceiling. He climbed up onto the counter and wiggled a stained tile. "I'm going to pop this out and see if I can figure out where the water's coming in."

"Do what you need to. I don't know anything about it. Shall I run and get something for the water to drip into?"

"That would be good. A plastic tub, or the biggest cooking pot you have should keep it contained overnight. You might want to empty it before you go to bed. Just to be sure."

"I'll let my sisters do that when they get home." She gave a little laugh and headed for the front door. It slammed behind her, and a few minutes later she appeared with two empty plastic ice-cream pails and a roll of paper towels in hand.

"That'll work." He placed one of the containers on the stove and made sure it was situated to catch the drips. "The ceiling tiles will need replacing, but I'll leave this one on the counter just in case."

Together they mopped up the rainwater that had splashed onto the old floors, then checked the rest of the rooms, relieved when they appeared to be leak-free.

"You're going to want to get that roof fixed as soon as possible. You want to save these wood floors, and even if you're not planning to keep the ceiling, you don't want to let the sub-roof get soggy. Not to mention moldy."

She sighed. "I guess we have to start in

sometime. We figured new roofs for these two houses into the budget, but it's going to take a huge chunk of it."

"Assuming you still want Langhorne Construction to do the work, we can get you scheduled. And hopefully get started as soon as it stops raining."

"I'll talk to my sisters, but I'm sure they'll say yes. It needs to be done." She looked up at him. "I must admit, it's kind of exciting to actually be diving in. I'm even getting kind of pumped about having guests in the cabins."

"That's when the investment will really start to pay off. Your dad gave you quite a gift when he found this property —"

"And coerced you to push it off on us." There wasn't a trace of antagonism in her voice.

"The man *can* be persuasive."

"Oh, don't I know it."

"I wouldn't be too critical. I happen to know that at least one of his daughters takes after him in that regard."

A wry smile came to her face. "I'm sure you're not talking about *moi.*"

"*Especially* you." The minute the words left his mouth, he realized the subject of what traits she'd inherited from her father could be dangerous territory. It almost felt as if he'd just told her a calculated lie. He wanted to throttle Turner for saddling him with all the disturbing secrets he had. Even if they weren't true, even the possibility would devastate Phylicia when she found out. *If* she found out.

Apparently oblivious to his thoughts, she threw him that wry smile again and held up the keys. "You ready?"

"I am. And I'd probably better get going if I'm going to make the open house before it's over."

They walked side by side across to the cottage, the rain falling a little harder now.

"Would you mind giving me a call and letting me know how it went?"

"Sure. I'd be glad to."

At the porch, he stopped. "I guess I don't have anything inside. I'll just go from here."

"Do you want a towel to dry off? You look like a drowned rat."

"As do you." He grinned. "But no, I'm fine. I'll give you a call." He turned to leave, wishing he hadn't promised Turner about the open house.

"Oh, wait! Pizza! You need to take some of this home." She ran back into the house and returned with a pizza box.

"You're sure? I don't want the Chandler girls mad at me."

"Hey, you snooze, you lose. They know the rules. Besides, there's plenty for everybody. I told you that's why we get extra."

"Right. Leftovers." He gave a little salute and took the box from her. "Good policy. I'll have to remember that." He risked touching her arm briefly. "Thanks for coming to church with me. And for lunch. I really enjoyed the day."

"I did too, Quinn." Something about the way she spoke his name made him feel as if he might have finally gotten through to her. Or maybe it was only wishful thinking.

"I'll call."

"Bye." She stood on the porch, arms crossed.

He waved and jogged to his SUV.

He backed around, then headed down the lane, watching her in his rearview mirror. She was still standing there on the porch when he rounded the curve and the cottages disappeared in the trees.

It was a sight he could get used to. And it was a sight he wouldn't mind coming home to each night.

Phee went inside and changed into dry clothes. Her phone was vibrating on the coffee table when she returned to the living room.

She grabbed it, cringing when she saw half a dozen texts and voicemail messages in her notifications. She tapped Accept. "Britt? Hey, what's up?"

"Finally! Didn't you get our messages?" Britt couldn't veil the frustration in her voice. "We've been calling you for two hours. Both of us!"

"Sorry. I must've forgotten to turn my ringer back on after church. Where are you guys? Is everything okay?"

"We're at Jo's apartment. Are you back at the cottage?"

"Yes. Quinn just left a little bit ago to go to the open house. We've got a leak in one of the cabins, but he helped me take care of it."

"Is it bad?"

"Nothing a gallon pail can't handle for now, but Quinn is going to have Langhorne get started on the roofs of the cabins as soon as it quits raining."

"Yeah, I guess we need to." Britt sounded distracted. "Hey, listen, do you mind staying there tonight?"

"By myself? Why?"

"Joanna wants me to help her pack up the rest of her apartment. She may be able to get out of her lease early if she can get moved out in time."

"Sure. I guess that's okay." Dread inched its way up her spine. She would have to brave the cabin in the dark, by herself, to empty the ice-cream pail before she went to bed. She and Quinn hadn't actually seen any mice there a few minutes ago, and it wasn't as if she was a total wuss. But she was already dreading it. "I'll be fine."

"Okay. Jo has to work early tomorrow, but I'll be home before you leave for work. I thought I'd paint the ceiling in my bedroom tomorrow while you guys are at work."

"Okay. I'll see you tomorrow then. You haven't heard anything about the open house, have you?"

"No. We drove by there about three thirty and there were only a couple of cars in front of the house. But other than that, I don't know anything. I figure that's Dad's problem."

Quinn's number appeared on the screen. "Okay, Britt. Gotta run. I'll see you in the morning." She didn't wait for a reply, but clicked off, then quickly answered Quinn's call. "Hey, thanks for getting back to me."

"Well, I wish I had better news for you."

"Uh-oh. It didn't go well?"

"The agent didn't think so. I guess only seven people signed the register, and he seemed to think they were all looky-loos."

"What's that?"

"Looky-loo? You've never heard of a looky-loo?"

"Not old enough, I guess. Must be one of those terms you elderly people use."

"Would you cut that out? I was just quoting the agent. And besides, this guy was younger than me."

"That's actually not saying a lot."

"Watch it!" But he was laughing.

She had no idea what had gotten into her, but she was teasing . . . *flirting.* And she liked that she'd made him laugh. He had a nice laugh.

A few minutes later, after they'd hung up, she walked past the mirror over the fireplace and was surprised to catch her own smile in the reflection.

She was still smiling when she went to bed that night. She'd survived the trip to the cabin in the dark, and the pail had collected only about three inches of water, so it would easily last until morning.

Tucked in the comfy daybed in her cozy room, with the doors locked and double-checked and a few small lamps lit throughout the house, Phee replayed the memories of her day with Quinn. Those memories helped her ignore the rain that pelted the roof of the cottage and the gusts of wind that dashed branches against her windows. She and her sisters were starting to grow used to the litany of groans and creaks the cottage produced, but the downpour outside — and being alone in the house — magnified every squeak and tap.

For the first time, she had more sympathy for Britt's seemingly unreasonable fears. She'd never been afraid in her apartment, because she knew she was surrounded by people who would hear her cries if she was in trouble. And she thought she would feel the same when the day came that her sisters — or even complete strangers — were sleeping in the cabins across the lane.

Curled up on the end of her bed, Melvin snored as if he hadn't a care in the world. Phee rolled onto her back, watching rainwater run down the window panes. When the clock on her nightstand flipped to midnight, she yawned, finally growing drowsy.

CHAPTER 24

Phee sat straight up in bed, wide awake as a second crack of lightning hit. Melvin yowled and scampered beneath the daybed. Heart pounding, she threw off the covers and went to the window to see if the lightning had hit something. The rain fell in sheets and it sounded as if the lightning and thunder were hitting simultaneously. The storm must be right on top of them.

It was almost six a.m., but the sky was pitch black outside. She could hear the wind blowing through the trees, though it must have died down a little because the branches were no longer thrashing at her bedroom windows.

She went to the covered porch and peered into the darkness. What if the rain, now that it was coming down this hard, had overflowed the bucket at the cabin? She didn't dare go out with lightning hitting so close, but if it let up at all, she would make a run for it.

She flipped on some lights and went to the kitchen to start a pot of coffee. Twenty minutes later, the rain showed no signs of letting up, but then, lightning hadn't struck for several minutes either. She decided to risk it. Better than waiting and discovering the cabin was flooded and the beautiful wood floors ruined. If they were going to spend most of their budget on new roofs, they couldn't be replacing the floors too.

She put on a jacket over her pajamas and went to the porch, where she slipped into her muddy tennis shoes from last night. She waited a few minutes, watching the inky sky, hoping the rain would let up. When it didn't, she made a mad dash across the lane to the leaky cabin.

The water had only filled the bucket about halfway. Definitely more than last time she'd checked but not alarming. She turned off the lights and went to the kitchen windows that looked out over the little walled-in yard. She could hear water trickling behind the house, but it was hard to tell if it was just running off the gutters or if the creek now had enough water in it to flow. That seemed impossible considering the dry gully it had been only a couple of days earlier.

Thunder rumbled low, sounding farther away than before, so when the crack of lightning came a few seconds later, she gasped. At first she didn't believe what she was seeing, but another flash of lightning left no doubt. The water was mere feet — maybe inches — from the stone walls. Surely her eyes were playing tricks on her, but it looked as if the water was flowing, even lapping at the foot of the walls by the other cabin. She squinted into the darkness, waiting for another flash of lightning, terrified of what it might reveal.

The rain had let up a little, and as she jogged back toward the cottage, she punched Dad's number into her phone. Thankfully it was seven a.m. in Florida.

"Hey, early bird. What are you doing up at this hour?"

"I think we've got trouble, Dad. I don't know what you can do from Florida, but I didn't know what else to do!" Her voice rose an octave and she slowed her steps, panting and trying to catch her breath.

"Calm down, honey. What's wrong?"

"I'm at the cottages and the water is rising fast. It's almost —"

"Water? *Where* are you?"

"At our property. That creek that was dry when we bought the place is filling up fast.

And . . . it's too dark to tell for sure, but it looks like the water is about to reach the walls! You know . . . those stone walls around the smaller cabins?" She'd forgotten he'd only seen the place once and likely didn't remember the lay of the land. She strained to look between the two cabins, but it was still too dark to see anything.

"You're not in harm's way, are you? Right now?"

"No, I'm walking back to the cottage where we're all living. Until we get the cabins ready. The water isn't anywhere near our cottage, but if it gets any higher, the two smaller cabins will flood for sure. What do we do, Dad?"

"Okay, listen, can you tell where the water's coming from? Is it just rainwater, or is it coming from upstream?"

"It's too dark to tell. I wouldn't have even seen it if a flash of lightning hadn't come just when I looked out."

"Well, thank the good Lord for that! You just keep an eye on the water level and get out of there if it looks like you're in trouble. Do you need to move your cars to higher ground? Where are your sisters?"

"They stayed in town last night. At Jo's place."

"What? You're there by yourself?"

"I'm a big girl, Dad. And my car is fine. The water's not anywhere near where we park."

"Okay. Just so you're safe. I'm going to make some calls and get some help out there. Is there other flooding around you? Have you seen anything on the news?"

"I don't know. I haven't listened to the news. But it's been raining all night — and most of yesterday. I didn't see any flood warnings though. Oh, Dad, if we lose the cabins, everything we invested . . . Mom's inheritance will be totally wasted."

"Don't even go there, Phee. You're not going to lose the cabins. And you're sure not going to lose the property." He paused, waiting. "Now, you listen . . . I'm sending help, but meanwhile, you be careful. Don't you go near the water. I'll get back to you as soon as I can."

She inhaled deeply, then blew her breath out in a steady stream. He needed to hear strength in her voice. "Okay, Dad. Thanks."

"And while you're waiting, pray!"

"Don't worry, I already am. This is freaking me out!" She couldn't seem to catch her breath.

"Just stay calm . . . Phee? Are you there?"

"Yes, I'm here. I'm fine."

"Okay. I'll call you as soon as I can. You

keep your phone close."

"I will. Thanks, Dad." She hung up, surprised at the rush of feelings that came over her. The old, familiar assurance of utter safety. And the childlike faith that her dad would take care of her. How she'd missed that security. And her dad.

She ran the rest of the way to the cottage, slipped her shoes off on the porch, and once inside, dialed Joanna.

"What time is it?" Her sister's voice was croaky with sleep.

"I'm not sure. About six thirty, I think, but you guys have got to get out here!"

"Why? What's wrong?" She sounded wide awake now.

"You need to come. The water is rising, and it's already almost up by the stone walls at the cabins."

"What? Are you sure?"

"Of course, I'm sure!" She gave a little growl. "Dad said he'd send some help out here. I don't know what can be done at this point . . . maybe sandbag it?"

"It seems like it's too late for that. You're not *in* the cabin, are you?"

"No. I'm back at the cottage. But . . . could you guys please come out here? And be careful on the roads. I don't know if it's just us flooded or if it's widespread."

"Okay. I'll wake Britt up and we'll get there as soon as we can."

Phee clicked off and went to pull on jeans and a sweatshirt. For the next half hour, she paced the cottage, waiting for the sky to turn from black to gray, going from window to window. Even in perfect weather, the cottage had only a sliver of a view of the creek, if you looked between the two cabins. The clouds must have been thick today, because though the rain had nearly stopped, it was still unusually dark for almost seven o'clock.

She would wait another ten minutes, and if Jo and Britt weren't here by then, she'd go check on the leak and get a better look at the rising water.

She'd just zipped up her jacket and stepped onto the porch when headlights appeared around the curve of the lane. But it wasn't either of the girls' cars. The headlights got closer and she could make out a pickup — and another one behind it.

The first truck pulled up and parked beside the cottage. The other vehicle continued slowly up the lane between the cottage and the cabins, then maneuvered to shine its headlights toward the water.

The beds of both pickups were covered with tarps. Her phone rang and she lifted it. Dad. "Wow, that was fast!"

"What do you mean?"

"Your guys are already here."

"Oh, good. That's why I was calling. Let me talk to Quinn."

"Oh. Is he coming? The trucks just pulled in. I haven't talked to anyone yet."

"How's the water situation?"

"It's just now getting light enough to see anything." Across the way, she saw Quinn climb out of the pickup that had parked by the cottage.

He jogged across the lane looking serious, but he lifted a hand in a perfunctory wave as he reached the front porch.

"Hi." She held out her phone. "My dad's on the phone."

He nodded and took the phone from her. "Hey, Turner." He listened for a moment. "Not sure. We just got here . . ."

Quinn looked at her and gave a little smile, then spoke into the phone again. "She's fine. She's standing right here." Another pause. "Well, we'll do what we can. We were able to get hold of about three hundred sandbags, but I don't know what we're dealing with yet. We'll just hope it's enough."

Her dad and Quinn spoke for another minute before he handed Phee's phone back to her. "Tell him we'll keep him posted. I'm going to see what it looks like down there."

He hurried back to the pickup and drove down to where the other truck had parked. Phee told her dad goodbye and jogged down to see what was going on.

By the time she got there, Quinn and two other men had pulled back the tarps and were unloading sandbags from the back of the other truck. She recognized one of the men from Dad's office, but she didn't know the other one, and they were all too intent on their work to make introductions.

"What can I do?"

"If you can lift these sandbags, you can get in the 'bucket brigade.' It'll go faster, and we need to hurry."

She looked past him to the creek. For the first time since it had gotten light enough to see anything, she got a good look at their situation. The water was lapping against the stone wall of the cabin farthest from their cottage, and it was flowing quickly, judging by the violent thrashing of limbs and leaves caught in its wake.

She watched the men for a few seconds, to get a feel for the rhythm, and then grabbed a sandbag from the truck. "Is this even going to help?"

"It's our best bet. The rock walls are actually in pretty good shape, except for a few places. We'll shore those up best we can, and then we'll sandbag to make the wall higher. If the water doesn't come up much more, I think the other cabin will be fine."

"I wasn't even watching the news. Should I have been doing this last night? Oh, Quinn, if those cabins wash away . . ." She couldn't finish verbalizing that thought. But if that happened, everything they'd sunk their inheritance into would be totally wasted. And if she and her sisters were stuck — all three of them — living out here in this little cottage together, with no place to rent out for income and no options . . . She couldn't let her mind go there.

Quinn didn't reply, but took the sandbag from her and placed it back on the truck. "Here . . . Come down to the middle of the brigade so you don't have to pull the bags down from the truck. This is hard on backs." He put a hand at her back, as if that might strengthen her, and guided her to a spot between the two other men. "Guys, this is Phylicia."

"Hi." She lifted a hand. "Thanks so much for coming. I don't know what I would have done without you guys."

Quinn went back to the truck, and within a few seconds they had a rhythm going again. Quinn tossed sandbags off the truck to one guy, who passed them to her, then she lugged them to the other guy, who placed the bags strategically on or around the wall.

A few minutes later, her sisters appeared from behind the truck. Phee had been so intent on the task at hand, she hadn't even heard them drive in.

Quinn jumped down from the pickup and worked Jo and Britt into the brigade line, but he pulled Phee out. "You need to take a break. Those things weigh forty pounds or more. You're going to be sore tomorrow."

"I'm fine," she protested.

"How about you go start a pot of coffee? We're all going to be cold and exhausted when this is done. And call your dad while you're at it. He's probably going crazy wondering what's happening."

She'd forgotten about Dad in all the excitement. Her gaze followed the water's route down the tributary. "Is it still rising?"

Quinn looked up and down the stream, then at the sky, which for now had quit dumping rain on them. "I'm afraid it is. But not as fast as it was when we got here."

"We can't lose these cabins, Quinn. We can't."

He looked her hard in the eyes. "You are

not going to lose *anything.*" He turned away and rejoined the brigade.

Chapter 25

Standing on the open tailgate of the pickup, Quinn removed his cap and wiped his forehead with his sleeve. "Well, that's the end of the bags. We've done what we can. Now let's just pray the Lord sees fit to reward our efforts."

He didn't speak those words lightly. He couldn't remember when he'd last prayed so hard about something — at least not for someone else's sake. And he *was* praying in the interest of the Chandler sisters, but he had a pony in the race too, given that they'd bought this place, in part, on his recommendation.

He jumped down from the tailgate and shook his coworker's hand. "Thanks, Duane." Duane Parker had recruited a friend, and the three of them had rounded up the sandbags from one of Langhorne Construction's sites that had remained high and dry. "Phylicia has coffee brewing up at the cottage."

The guys waved him off in unison. "Thanks, man, but we're gonna grab breakfast in town. You want to come?"

"No. I'm good." Quinn had sent Joanna and Britt up to the cottage half an hour ago, and he thought he smelled bacon frying. He would invite himself to breakfast if they didn't offer.

He let himself heave a sigh that released a taut band of tension. There had been some frightening moments as the water continued to rise and their supply of sandbags dwindled in direct proportion. He'd sweat blood wondering how things could possibly be redeemed if Phylicia and her sisters lost even one of the cabins. And they still weren't completely in the clear. But as he'd told Duane, it was out of their hands now.

The guys gathered up gloves and tools and loaded their pickup. As Duane climbed behind the wheel, Quinn hollered after him, "You guys can mail me your chiropractor bills."

They laughed and waved back at him as they drove away. Quinn walked around behind the cabins to check on their handiwork again. The rain was no more than a fine mist now, and the backyard stone fence around the far cabin had been built up two feet with sandbag "bricks." The water hadn't receded, but neither had it risen. If a dam broke upstream, or if it started raining again, there was nothing else to do. He shot up a prayer that the wall would hold and the cabins would survive. "And if not, Lord," he whispered, "please let Phee and her sisters see your purpose in whatever happens."

It startled him a little to hear himself refer to her as "Phee." But after being around Phylicia's sisters, who never called her anything else, he'd come to think of her by that nickname. Thoughts of her were almost constant now. And he wasn't sure what to do about that.

He finished loading his pickup and drove the short distance back up to the cottage. Maybe he should just leave. They hadn't invited him to breakfast, and they were surely exhausted. But the enticing aromas of bacon and coffee were more than he could resist. He put the truck in Park and went to knock on the door.

Britt opened it almost before he could finish knocking. "Come in. Breakfast is ready."

"I was hoping you'd invite me to stay."

"Are you kidding? Of course you're invited." She looked over his shoulder to the lane. "Where are the other guys?"

"They went into town."

Joanna appeared in the arched doorway of the breakfast nook, hands on hips. "Then you'd better be ready to eat about forty-two pancakes."

"And a pound of bacon!" Phylicia's voice floated from the kitchen.

He laughed and hollered back, "I think I just might be able to manage that." He worked his boots off and set them by the porch door. "I need to wash up."

"Help yourself." Phylicia came through the kitchen wearing an impish grin. "You know where the bathroom is. But you might not want to lock the door."

"Seriously? Is that still giving you trouble?"

"I'm just kidding." Phee looked much as she had that morning he'd rescued her. She'd changed into clean clothes, and her hair was damp, burnished a darker shade of honey-brown than usual. "The door seems to be working fine. If you ever need a new career, you might consider locksmithing."

"I would if I hadn't already decided to go into dam-building." He nodded toward the infamous door and went to wash up.

Her laughter behind him made him thankful he hadn't chickened out on inviting himself to breakfast.

■ ■ ■ ■

Phylicia flipped another pancake and looked over at the kitchen table where Quinn sat across from her sisters.

"I saw you go off that tailgate, Quinn!" Britt's giggles were contagious. "I thought for sure you were going to break your neck!"

"You should have seen it, Phee." Jo spoke over a bite of pancake. "We're talking Olympic-quality swan dive."

"Well, what did you expect?" Quinn affected an offended tone. "I told you it was intentional."

"Ha!" Britt pointed at him. "Funny. You were nowhere near the water when you took that nosedive."

He cleared his throat. "*Swan* dive. Please. Get it right."

Joanna and Britt weren't buying it, having witnessed the whole thing, and had been giving him all kinds of grief, which Quinn was taking with his usual good nature.

Laughing with them — and a little jealous that she hadn't been there — Phee flipped the last of the pancakes and turned off the stove. "Last call for pancakes. Who wants another one?"

They all groaned, and Quinn puffed out

his belly and patted it. "I had my forty-two. I've done my duty."

She moved the griddle to a cool burner before rejoining them at the table. Her sisters' teasing laughter mingled with Quinn's. The friendly scene around the kitchen table made this morning's drama seem like a forgotten nightmare.

Thankfully, the rain seemed to have stopped altogether. A few minutes ago, the sun had even peeked out for a short while. Still, Quinn had warned them they weren't completely out of the woods yet. While they'd done everything they could to shore up the rock walls, there was no guarantee their makeshift dam would withstand a rising river.

Joanna rose, collected the plates sticky with maple syrup, and deposited them on the counter beside the sink. "I really need to shower and get to work."

"I need to get to work too." Britt pushed her chair back.

Quinn looked surprised. "Where are you working, Britt? I didn't realize you'd started a job."

Britt blushed. "Oh, I haven't. I just meant at Dad's house. Now that the open house is over, I'm going to pack up the rest of my things to move out here."

Phee shot her sister a look. "Oh, sure. Leave me with the dishes just because I got the day off."

Quinn scooted back his chair. "I'll help with the dishes."

"Oh, no. You don't need to do that, Quinn. I was just giving my sisters a hard time."

He gathered the syrup bottle and the butter dish and carried them to the counter. "It's the least I can do to thank you for that amazing breakfast."

"Are you kidding? That breakfast was the least we could do to thank you for you saving our cabins."

"I think you give me a little more credit than I deserve." He unbuttoned his cuffs and rolled up his shirtsleeves. "Point me to a dishrag and I'll get started."

"Thanks for everything, Quinn." Britt started gathering up her belongings.

"Yes, thank you. I need to hit the shower." Joanna waved and ducked into the hallway.

"You guys be careful on the roads." Quinn checked his phone and followed Britt to the front door.

Phee listened from the sink. "I don't see any warnings on the news, but with all this rain, there could be water over the road in spots."

"I'll be careful. Thanks."

The front door slammed, and Quinn came back to the kitchen.

Phee moved dirty dishes aimlessly around the counter, suddenly nervous to be alone with him. And yet, she didn't want him to go either. She grabbed a fresh dishrag from the drawer and tossed it to him, then turned on the hot water to fill the sink. "Sorry, but this place doesn't have the luxury of a dish-washer."

"What? No dishwasher?" He put a hand to his chest, feigning shock. "Who talked you into buying a place that didn't even have a basic appliance like a dishwasher? That's just crazy!"

She swatted at him with a dish towel. "Very funny."

He rolled his eyes. "If I wasn't kidding, I'd be a hypocrite, since I have a dishwasher in my kitchen but never use it."

"I didn't use mine in the apartment much either. When I did, there was never a clean dish in the cupboards because it took me a week to fill that thing up."

"I get that. Besides, I grew up without one and it didn't kill me." He gave a little laugh. "Well, my mom always said she had two dishwashers — a Markus brand and a Quinn brand."

"My mom said the same thing." Phee

laughed, memories flooding back. "Well, of course her brands were different than yours. Must be a mom joke, because my sisters and I did *not* think it was very funny."

"We didn't either. Especially when she bought a dishwasher the minute I left for college."

"My parents did that too! What is the deal with that?"

He rinsed a plate under running water and handed it to her to dry. "Must be a conspiracy."

It felt good to remember her mom from better, more ordinary days. Her nervousness had vanished, and she was suddenly very thankful the cottage *didn't* have a dishwasher . . . well, except for the "Quinn brand" standing beside her.

They worked in companionable silence while, in the hallway on the other side of the kitchen wall, they could hear Joanna rattling between her bedroom and the bathroom. A few minutes later, Jo poked her head in the kitchen. "Gotta run. Thanks again, Quinn."

The door slammed and they were alone again. Really alone this time.

Quinn handed Phee the last dish and dried his hands on the corner of her towel. "I'm going to drive down and check on our sandbags. See what the water level looks like by now."

"Mind if I go with you?"

He started to say something, then shook his head as if he'd changed his mind. Finally, he looked at her with what she could only describe as . . . *tenderness* in his eyes. "I'd like that a lot."

His simple words filled her with an emotion she couldn't name — an exhilarating brew of joy and terror and *hope.*

Chapter 26

March

Phee leaned over the front porch railing and looked up to the wooded hills above the cottage. A thousand daffodils waved their yellow heads in the greening vegetation along the lane, and there must have been at least as many birds singing their hearts out on this bright Sunday morning. In the rumpled flowerbed below the porch, a baby bunny nibbled a weed.

It was hard to believe that only three weeks ago they'd been frantically hauling sandbags in the cold winter rain, trying to save the cabins. Now, in the woods above the cottage, a faint mist of green quivered on the trees, and the hopeful scent of spring was thick in the air. She and her sisters had walked up to the clearing in the woods yesterday and discovered redbud and serviceberry, and even dogwood blooms on the verge of opening.

Thanks to "springing ahead" for Daylight Savings, they'd had an extra hour of daylight each day this week, and tomorrow it would be officially spring.

Through the open window, she could hear Jo and Britt bickering over the bathroom. Phee and Joanna had both moved out of their apartments the week after the floods to avoid paying March's rent. They were stuck now — all three of them — in this cottage. And charming though it was, this one-bathroom, three-sisters situation bordered on dire. Phee was thankful she'd claimed first dibs this morning, so she'd have time to dry her hair and do something besides throw it in a messy bun on top of her head — a style she'd pretty much lived in since they'd moved out to the property.

The three of them were meeting Quinn for breakfast, and they'd agreed to go to church with him afterward. Quinn was probably sick of seeing her with her hair like that. She'd been a hot mess for the past two weeks, while they cleaned up the debris from the flooding, dumped sandbags, and cleared out the cabins for renovation. Despite the protests of Phee and her sisters, Quinn had shown up every evening after work and stayed until it was too dark to do more.

It was hard, dirty work — and Phee had been putting in full hours at the flower shop besides — yet she'd never felt so fulfilled in a task. She was so grateful for the extra hour of daylight they had now. And not just because it meant they got more work done.

Taking a sip from her steaming mug of coffee before setting it back on the porch rail, she laughed to herself. If Quinn had simply waited to show them this springtime view of the property, he would have saved himself a lot of grief. This peaceful spot on the edge of Langhorne had won her over long before this morning, but if this had been her first view of the cottage and cabins, she was pretty sure she would have signed on the dotted line without a second thought.

She sobered thinking how much they owed Quinn Mitchell, though the man was loathe to take an ounce of credit for saving the cabins from flooding. He'd insisted that her dad's orchestrations from afar, the generosity of his coworkers, and the manual labor of all of them combined were the reason the cabins had withstood the flood-waters.

Phee hadn't realized on that frightening morning what an almost-miracle it was that Quinn had been able to get the sandbags from his construction site on such short notice. She shuddered to think what they might be dealing with had things gone differently. As it was, the roofers were due to start on the two cabins bright and early tomorrow morning, and Quinn had put together a crew from Langhorne to start interior work the following week.

He hadn't said for sure, but she hoped — and suspected — that he would be the one to head up that crew. Mary had graciously given her next week off from the flower shop, and Phee had a whole list of things she hoped to accomplish before she had to go back to work.

She was thankful for the distractions. Even the flood that had almost spelled disaster kept her from obsessing about the whole thing with her dad. And with Mom. She'd talked to Dad a couple of times since the flood but only about surface things. And while he sounded more himself, he always seemed eager to end their calls just when she thought she might be able to ask him some questions. He hadn't mentioned Karleen, yet for some reason, Phee wondered if Dad was back with the woman. How strange that now she almost hoped that was the reason her father seemed to be avoiding her, rather than something more personal.

It was little comfort to learn that Joanna and Britt had talked to Dad on Friday afternoon while Phee was at work. They were bubbling when they told her about it, because, as Britt put it, "I feel like I have my daddy back!"

"Phee!" Britt's voice drifted through the open window as if summoned by Phee's thoughts.

Sighing, Phee tossed the dregs of her coffee over the rail and went inside.

"Oh, there you are." Britt pulled a sweater over her shirt. "Can I borrow your tan boots? Pretty please?"

"No, Britt. I was going to wear them." She'd actually decided not to wear her favorite boots given the muddy mess the yard still was. But she would be more careful with them than Britt would, so she'd take her chances.

"Then I guess I'll have to change clothes, because I don't have one pair of shoes that goes with this outfit."

"It's supposed to be warm today anyway. I don't think you're going to want a sweater."

"I will in church. You know how cold they keep that sanctuary."

"That's so you won't fall asleep."

"Whatever." She gave a little growl. "Phee,

may I *please* borrow your boots?"

When Phee didn't respond, Britt huffed and made a show of shrugging out of her sweater. Seeing that Phee wasn't going to weaken, her sister stomped back to her bedroom like a petulant seventh grader.

Phee laughed and went to dry her hair, praying she and her sisters would still be friends by the time they got the cabins finished and each had a space to call their own. Yet even as the whispered prayers left her lips, a disturbing question nagged at her. Were her sisters even actually her true sisters? And if she discovered they weren't, could anything ever be the same between them?

Quinn waited in the church foyer across the hall from the women's restroom, feeling awkward while the three Chandler sisters did whatever it was women did when they went to the restroom in packs.

He was already squirming from the subject of this morning's sermon, especially worrying that Phylicia might think he'd purposely invited her here to hear Pastor Franklin expound on the different types of love the Bible spoke of. The truth was, if he'd known what the topic was, he probably would have waited a week or two to issue that invitation.

Instead, he'd sat with Phylicia on one side of him and Britt on the other, while the pastor spoke about *phileo,* or brotherly love, and *agape,* the sacrificial love Christ had for His church and that the church was to have for one another. But Pastor Franklin had also spoken quite frankly of *eros* love.

Quinn was certain his emotions sat on his sleeve for all to see. *No.* For *Phylicia* to see. And there was no doubt in his mind that the love he felt for Phylicia — more and more every time they were together — had grown beyond brotherly love, beyond *agape* love. His feelings toward her were passionate. Not inappropriately so — at least not yet. But he couldn't go on pretending to her that she was just one of the sisters, just one of three gals he enjoyed being around. It already felt dishonest that he hadn't declared his feelings for her.

And if by some miracle Phylicia ever returned his love, he wasn't looking forward to the day when he would have to confess to her that he had selfishly abused that *eros* kind of love with Heather. Granted, he hadn't been walking close to the Lord back then. And no matter how much he regretted it, no matter how certain he was that

God had forgiven him for going too far in his relationship with Heather, still, his actions would carry consequences.

And those consequences would affect Phylicia if they ever had the relationship he desired with her. Worse, the consequences might be that he never even had a chance with her. He didn't know how she felt about such things, how easily she might forgive.

The sisters finally emerged from the restroom, startling him from his introspection. The three looked no more or no less beautiful than they had when they'd gone through the bathroom door a full — he glanced at his watch — *six* minutes ago.

"Did you think we'd ditched you?" Britt nudged his arm playfully.

He shook his head, struggling to match her lighthearted mood. "I was just trying to figure out exactly why it is women can't seem to go to the restroom alone. Does it always have to be a group activity?"

Joanna started to say something, but Phylicia shook a finger at her. "Huh-uh. Sorry, Quinn, but that will just have to remain one of the great mysteries of life."

He shook his head, attempting to look more exasperated than he felt. "Along with the mysteries of why women take so long to get ready and why they have to own fifty pairs of shoes when a man can get by with five, at most?"

Phylicia gave a little growl. "Now you're treading on dangerous territory, buddy."

Britt giggled. "Yes, and don't think those two mysteries aren't connected either."

"Right. Nice outfit, by the way, Britt." Phylicia gave her youngest sister a teasing shove, apparently sharing some private joke. They giggled in that annoying yet somehow charming way the sisters had with each other.

As so often happened when he was with the three of them, he was on the outside looking in. Not that he really had a desire to know why any female would need fifty pairs of shoes. Unless she was a centipede. He chuckled to himself, ignoring their curious stares. Men could have their secrets too. The flippant thought sobered him instantly. The secret he'd been harboring — Phylicia's secret — was no laughing matter.

"I'm starving," Britt said.

"I'll buy pizza." He pulled his wallet from his pocket. "We can take it out to your place — if that's okay." Warm memories of that day three weeks ago were still fresh.

"Hey, maybe we can have a picnic!" Britt looked out at the sky, shading her eyes against the sunlight streaming through the large windows in the foyer. "It's going to be a beautiful day."

"We could take a picnic up to the clearing?" He made it a question, since he hadn't officially been invited yet.

Phylicia cringed. "*Clearing* may be an oxymoron. I haven't been up there since you took us up, but if things are growing there like they are everywhere else, we may need a machete to get in."

He cocked his head trying to decide if she was making excuses not to have lunch with him. But she didn't seem to be holding him at arm's length as she too often did.

"Put your wallet away, Quinn. We have sandwich stuff in the fridge." Joanna frowned. "Well, if you don't mind bologna and egg salad?"

"Oh, please come, Quinn." Britt looked like an eager child.

He would have rather the invitation came from Phylicia, but she nodded along with Britt, and he didn't give her a chance to change her mind. "I'd love to, if you're sure you don't mind."

"Of course not. And in case you wondered, Joanna didn't mean bologna and egg salad in the same sandwich." Phylicia gave a little laugh. "Unless you like it that way."

"I'll take it however you make it." He

stopped short of asking if Phylicia wanted to ride out to their place with him. He was already in danger of being the over-eager puppy dog.

Chapter 27

The air was still a bit chilly when they headed up the hill to the little amphitheater in the clearing, and Quinn wished he'd brought a heavier jacket. The sisters had changed out of their church clothes back at the house, and now they were bundled up as if it was the dead of winter.

Phylicia had seemed quiet since they got home from church. She walked ahead of the rest, carrying the picnic basket they'd packed.

Quinn hefted a cooler of drinks, wishing it was a Thermos of coffee instead. Joanna and Britt each clutched thick quilts in their arms.

The girls gasped when they reached the top of the old stairway, then exclaimed in glee. Quinn didn't have to guess why. English ivy and woodland ferns, punctuated by clumps of wild daffodils, blanketed the ground under the canopy, but the look was anything but overgrown.

"Look!" Phylicia set down the wicker basket and bent to inspect something growing in a crevice at the base of one of the log benches. "This is sweet william! Growing wild!"

Quinn suspected someone had carefully managed the natural greenery and bulbs that bloomed under the tree branches in the clearing. He wondered what other surprises the space might hold as summer unfolded. He felt unaccountably proud of the space, though he wouldn't pretend he'd had a clue it was here when he was trying to convince the sisters to buy the property.

Quinn picked up the wicker basket and carried it to the bench, where the sunlight was brightest, then he set the basket on the ground and took the quilt Joanna offered. "Ground or bench?"

"Bench." Phylicia shivered. "Too cold for the ground."

"Yes, but it won't be long before we'll be sunbathing up here." Britt tipped her face to catch the sun's rays.

Quinn shook his head. "Don't wait too long. This will be shady and sunless in another month. But you'll be glad for a cool place to relax in the evenings."

Phylicia spread the second quilt on the

bench and frowned. "I don't think there's going to be any relaxing going on around here for the foreseeable future."

"Don't say that," Quinn chided. "You can't work all the time, or you'll burn out." He dragged the other log bench over to face the one where the sisters were setting out a spread that looked like a lot more than egg salad and bologna.

But Phylicia made a face. "There's still a lot to do before we can get this place earning some money with the rentals."

Joanna poured lemonade into red Solo cups. "Don't forget how much money it's already saved us in apartment rent though."

"Good point," Phylicia conceded. "It was really nice not to have to write that rent check when March first came around."

"That's for sure." Britt made googly eyes at her sisters.

"Ha!" Joanna gave Britt a good-natured punch in the arm. "You wouldn't know a rent check if it bit you on the backside."

Phylicia laughed at Britt's fake cries of *ouch*! "Maybe we should start *charging* you rent, little sister. Just to educate you about real life."

It was good to see Phylicia loosen up a little. Quinn had gotten used to the sisters' antics and found it one of his favorite things about spending time with the Chandlers — even if he didn't always get their girly jokes. It was something he remembered from spending time with Turner's family in the early days of his employment with Langhorne Construction. But even now, as adults, the sisters remained playful with one another. Maybe it was the fact that they were so close in age. The seven years between him and his brother had created an emotional distance in addition to the physical distance created when Markus left home for college.

But if there'd ever been this kind of merriment in his own home growing up, Quinn couldn't remember it. Heather had introduced that element into his life. It was one of the things that had attracted him to her when they worked together in the cafeteria their freshman year of college.

Heather had also drawn Markus in to the fun the first time they met. Quinn hadn't given it a thought. In fact, he'd been glad they got along so well. But it wasn't long before Quinn started feeling like a fifth wheel whenever his brother joined Heather and him. And after that, nothing was ever fun again.

Until now.

■ ■ ■ ■

The sun had grown warmer, so after they finished lunch, Phee shed her coat and scarf. Her sisters and Quinn followed suit. It had been a perfect Sunday afternoon, and she wished it wasn't almost over.

The four of them had talked about everything from this morning's sermon, to the recent flood, to the work slated to begin tomorrow morning on the two cabins' roofs.

They packed up the picnic basket and carried the quilts to the edge of the clearing, then spread them on the ground overlooking the cottages and the river.

"Pretty amazing . . ." Quinn stood at the far edge of the clearing, his gaze trailing past the cottages to the river. "You almost lost the cabins to the flood, and instead, you ended up with a waterfront property. I don't know if I've ever met three luckier women."

Phee shook her head. "Not lucky. Blessed."

"That's for sure." Quinn looked apologetic. "And you know, I don't really believe in luck. Well, except maybe when you three are playing double solitaire. Now *that* was pure luck."

The sisters laughed, remembering the night the three of them had ganged up to shut Quinn out of a single win during an impromptu card game after a long day of painting.

Still smiling, Phylicia looked up at him from her perch on the quilt. "Speaking of luck, once we get listed as an Airbnb — if things go really well — don't you think there'd be room to build another small cabin at that far end of the lane?" Phee pointed to a spot down the rocky hill.

Quinn followed her line of sight. "I don't see why not. If you keep it a simple one- or two-bedroom floor plan, all on one level, you could do it pretty cheaply too."

"There wouldn't be any zoning restrictions out here, would there, Quinn?" Joanna asked.

He scratched his chin. "You'd have to check on that, but I doubt it."

Phee loved the way Quinn let them dream without reminding them of worst-case scenarios or forcing their feet back to solid ground. The way Dad had always been with them. She pushed a strand of sadness away as if it were a sticky spiderweb and forced herself back to the conversation. "Maybe we could add a room onto the cottage too — a master suite, so we'd have more room when all the cabins are rented out."

"You just don't want to share a bathroom with anyone," Britt accused.

"I never said the suite would be for *me.*"

"But you wouldn't turn it down, right?" Joanna sing-songed, teasing.

"Fine, if you insist, I'll take the new suite." Phee folded her arms, looking smug.

Quinn laughed. "You haven't even drawn up the plans, and you're already bickering over it. You ladies are something else."

Joanna unfolded her lanky frame and rose. "Speaking of something else . . ." She yanked on the quilt she and Britt had been sitting on.

"Hey, cut it out." Britt tumbled off the edge of the quilt but laughed as she scrambled to her feet.

"Sorry, sis, but I've got some stuff I have to do before work tomorrow."

"I need to go too." Britt helped Jo fold the blanket. "Here . . . I'll help you carry stuff down."

Not ready for the day to end, but trying to keep the disappointment from her voice, Phee stood and folded her quilt. "I'll get the basket." She started toward the bench where the remainders of their picnic sat.

Joanna held up a hand. "We've got it. You guys stay a while."

"Don't worry . . ." Britt winked. "The dishes will still be waiting when you get back."

"Dishes?" Quinn feigned confusion. "I've heard of thrifty, but you guys wash your paper plates?"

"Just kidding, Quinn." Joanna turned to Phee, and the look she gave her seemed to say, *We've got this covered. You stay.*

Phee shrugged. "Thanks, guys. I'll be down soon."

Jo and Britt hurriedly gathered things up and disappeared down the wooden stairs cut into the side of the hill.

Quinn watched them go as if he were eager for them to disappear from sight. Phee was beginning to wonder if he'd conspired with her sisters to get some time alone with her.

A frisson of anticipation went up her spine. But why did that little thrill always have to be followed by uncertainty? She pushed the nerves away, determined to just enjoy being with Quinn. "This was a really fun day." She sat on one end of the bench, arms beside her, gripping the edge.

"It was," Quinn agreed. He took a seat at the other end, his body angled toward her. Looking toward the stairs Jo and Britt had descended, he gave a low chuckle. "I just love your sisters." He turned to her and added quickly, "The *agape* kind of love, I mean."

She laughed. "I just love my sisters too. But hey, what am *I,* chopped liver?"

"Chopped liver?" He made a face. "What even *is* that?"

"You've never heard that expression?"

His eyebrows went up. "Sounds like something an old lady would say."

She gave his arm a slug. "Watch it. But don't you just *agape* me too?" She was flirting, forcing things. And she suddenly didn't care.

But Quinn's expression turned serious. "I . . . *agape* you too, Phylicia. But surely you know by now that it's more than that. So much more."

She swallowed hard. "You're . . . making me nervous."

He laughed, but the music of his laughter quickly faltered. "I'm making me nervous too. But I have something I need to say. I can't do this anymore if I don't know where you stand."

"You can't do *what* anymore?"

He studied her, not speaking.

"And . . . where I stand on *what*?" Why was she playing dumb? She knew the answers to both of those questions. Knew them very well. But the timing seemed all wrong for this discussion. There were so many things she was struggling with right now, so many things she was confused about. She didn't want grief and the conflict with her father and the chaos of renovating the property to keep her from having a clear mind where Quinn was concerned.

And yet, in so many ways, she felt as if she'd waited her whole life to have *exactly* this discussion.

CHAPTER 28

The silence between them went on for what seemed an eternity. Quinn rose from the bench where they sat, feeling like a man about to propose to a woman who might not say yes. But he'd been on the fence too long, waiting for her to respond to his cues.

He had to declare his feelings for her before he drove away from here today. Because if she was not interested in him the way he was in her, he needed to figure out a way to extricate himself from the Chandler sisters' project. It was already torture being around her and not having a clue how she felt toward him.

But was she so blind she couldn't see how *he* felt toward her? Why was she making him work so hard for this?

Surely, she wasn't so oblivious that she couldn't see how his eyes lit up the minute he spotted her, or sense how his heart sped up at the sound of her voice. But if she was aware of those things, she was evidently not taking any chances that she might be wrong. Either she was waiting for him to make the first move or she had zero interest in pursuing anything beyond casual friendship with him.

He was not interested in casual friendship with her. He'd tried that, and it was pure torture. So, what did he have to lose? If she felt nothing for him, better to know it now than to fall one more day in love with her.

He turned to face her, strangely moved by the innocence in her face as she looked up at him. "Phylicia, in case you haven't figured it out yet, I'm going to lay things on the line. Yes, I really like your sisters. But you aren't part of a package with Jo and Britt. They're sweet, and you guys are immensely entertaining together." He let a smile come. "But what I feel for you — *you* alone, Phylicia — is so much more than the *agape* kind of love Pastor Franklin talked about this morning. I don't know why it's taken me so long to get off my duff and say something to you. I guess —"

"Quinn —"

"No. Let me finish. Please." He held up a hand, resisting the desire to take her in his arms. But he knew better. He had to take it slow with her. She looked like a frightened bird, wanting to take the seed from his hand, but ready to dart away at any false move too. "Phylicia, I thought I was giving pretty big hints. But I don't want there to be any doubt. I really like you. I'm falling for you. I want to see where our friendship might go, and I have high hopes for us. You and me." He pointed between them as if she might still be confused about his intentions.

"Quinn . . ." Her eyes never left his face. "Oh, Quinn. I'm sorry, but . . . you're . . . *I'm* only in my twenties. Don't you realize that? It's a *big* gap. In age and —"

"Seriously?" He shook his head. "You make it sound like I'm ancient! How old do you think I am anyway?"

She tilted her head. "How old *are* you?"

"Barely in my forties."

A tiny smile came. "Let me rephrase that. *Exactly* how old are you?"

"Just turned forty-two." His hopes notched up a little with his own declaration. Maybe all along she'd thought he was much older.

"Forty-two?"

"And I hate to tell you, but if I have my math right, your days of being in your twenties are numbered."

"Please . . . don't remind me. I'd like to

remain blissfully ignorant for as long as possible." Her words were teasing, but the hint of a shadow that crossed her countenance made him wonder if she was struggling with this milestone birthday.

He made a note to tread lightly. "Am I right though? Won't you turn thirty soon?"

"Sadly."

"It's not sad. And it's not such a big age difference. Between us, I mean. Twelve years. It'd be different if you were sweet sixteen." He cringed inwardly, wishing he hadn't said that, given that he'd been attracted to her when she was exactly that age. But she'd always been mature for her age. And of course, he'd never acted on his attraction for her when she was so young. "We're both adults, Phylicia. We share our faith in God. Those are the things that should matter."

"You're a Gen Xer. I'm a Millennial."

"Oh, come on. You don't really put any stock in those labels, do you? What does that even mean?"

She shrugged. "I'm just saying . . . there's a gap. I can't exactly freak out about the age difference between Dad and Karleen, and then start hanging out with someone *your* age."

He gave a short laugh. "So quit freaking

out about your dad. Besides, I thought they broke up."

"They did. But I have a feeling if it's not her, it will be someone else. Soon enough. Dad's not the type to live the rest of his life alone."

"Would you want him to?"

She thought for a moment, her eyes saying more than she likely intended. "I want him to be happy. But why does that have to mean being with someone?"

"Someone besides your mom, you mean." He was careful to make his voice gentle, even as frustration welled that she'd managed to completely change the subject. Still, he knew this couldn't be easy for her to think about.

"Yes." She dropped her head. "I know that sounds stupid and selfish. But why can't he just wait a while?"

"Maybe he is waiting. Maybe that's why he broke up with her."

"Then why isn't he here? In Missouri? Why is he still hiding out in Florida?"

"I don't know the answer to that, Phylicia. But I think you have to give your dad a break. He's just been through the most difficult thing a man could ever experience. Maybe —"

"The most difficult thing?" She scoffed.

"He sure has a funny way of showing it."

"Sometimes grief makes you do strange things." If she only knew how well he knew that. "Phylicia, maybe your dad just needs some time away. Alone."

"What about us? We *need* him, Quinn. And he just *left.* At the worst time."

"I know." Again, it was all he could do to resist putting a comforting arm around her shoulders. But this wasn't the time.

"I'm sorry." She bowed her head. "I didn't mean to go off on a tangent."

"No. It's okay. I know this has been really hard for you."

"Everything is just so confusing right now. I . . . I like you too, Quinn. I really do. Maybe" — she gave him an impish grin — "even more than *agape.* But I'm still figuring things out. I'm not sure —"

"Phylicia . . . Phee . . ." He sat down beside her and took her hand, aware that he'd called her by her nickname. Not even sure what that meant, but savoring the feel of her small hand in his.

But it seemed to get her attention. She sat silently, not trying to pull away, simply waiting for him to go on.

"I don't mean to rush you. I'm not trying to force you to say something you don't mean. But please don't give me hope if there isn't any. If you don't feel the same about me, I need to know that. And maybe I need to" — he shrugged — "I don't know . . . leave town?"

"Stop." She gave a little laugh. But her expression turned serious again. "You're not really kidding, are you?"

"About falling in love with you? I wouldn't kid about something like that." He hadn't meant to use the word *love.* Not yet. But there it was. And he wasn't sorry. "About wanting to leave town if you don't feel the same about me? Maybe that's a bit of an exaggeration. But can you tell me where I stand with you? If I even have a chance?"

It wasn't really fair for him to ask her such a question when he was holding back some incredibly iffy cards. Heather, yes. But more than that, the things he knew about her that she didn't even know herself. The things Turner had told him.

"I can't make any promises, Quinn, but I'm glad you're in my life. I'd hate it if you left town. If I didn't see you again."

He smiled, hope soaring again. "Well, that's . . . something, I guess."

"Can we take it slow? Just be friends for now?"

Hope dipped and nearly crashed. "Just be friends? That's what nice girls say to guys who don't have a prayer. To keep from hurting their feelings."

"I promise I'm not just trying to let you down easy." She looked at their hands clasped between them. "Quinn, I'm twenty-nine years old and I've never even had a serious boyfriend. I can count the number of dates I've had on one-and-a-half hands. I've always held out this . . . *dream.* That I would wait for someone like my dad. Mom always called him her knight in shining armor. But . . . that armor is tarnished now. *So* tarnished . . . I don't know if I even believe in knights anymore."

He squeezed her hand. "Phylicia . . . Your dad is still a knight. Yes, he's human, and he's going through a tough time. He's probably made some mistakes in his lifetime, but he's a good man. I've known him most of my adult life, and I think you can believe in him — and believe that other men like him exist." Quinn wanted to be a man like that for her. Wanted to prove to her that there were still good men in this world.

Phylicia pulled her hand away and rose, turning her back to him.

Her shoulders shook, and Quinn was shocked to realize she was weeping. "Phylicia, what's wrong? What did I say?"

She whirled to face him, anger in her reddened eyes. “Believe in him? How can you say I can *believe* in my dad, Quinn? I don’t even know if Turner Chandler is my real father.”

Chapter 29

"What?" Quinn stared at Phylicia, hating that he felt the need to feign surprise, yet he was determined not to lie to her. That would only make things worse than they already were.

The air in the clearing took on a chill as the afternoon sun faded. Quinn felt his courage wane with it.

Phylicia looked up at him, her eyelashes beaded with tears. "Did you hear what I said? I'm not sure if Dad —" She dropped her head. "If the man who raised me is my real father."

"But . . . I don't understand." So much for not lying to her. He understood all too well. He shot up a desperate one-word prayer. *Help!*

"I'm sorry. You don't want to hear all my woes." She shook her head and waved her hands in front of her face as if she could erase the words.

"No, Phylicia. Please tell me what's going on." Was it lying to pretend you didn't already know what someone was about to reveal? It was at least deceitful. There was no doubt about that. How could Turner have put him in this position?

She looked up at him. "Are you sure?"

"Of course. Sit down." He put his hand at the small of her back and guided her back to the bench. He wished Jo and Britt hadn't taken the quilts down to the cottage with them.

Long seconds passed before Phylicia finally let out a deep sigh. "I told you about Mom being married before, but there's more."

Weighing every possible response, Quinn opted to stay silent, hoping she would continue without prompting.

"Some of the things Dad told me make me wonder if he is even my real father. My birth father, I mean." Her suspicions — including almost everything Turner had already confessed to him — poured from Phylicia as if she were sloughing a great weight from her shoulders.

"Wow. You've been bottling all this up? Why didn't you say something? Do you really think the man your mom was married to before might actually be your father?"

"I don't know what to think, Quinn. That's the hardest part — *not* knowing."

If Quinn hadn't talked to Turner, his natural response would have been, *Are you sure? Maybe you're wrong!* But saying that would have been the worst of lies, because he *was* sure. At least, as sure as Turner was. Quinn didn't want to play games with her. And he had to admit, the conclusions Turner had drawn seemed pretty persuasive. As they obviously had to Phylicia.

Tension coiled in Quinn's gut. "Have you *asked* your dad?"

"Even if I could ask Dad, how could I ever trust him to tell me the truth? He — and Mom too — lied to me my whole life. How can I ever believe anything they told me? If they didn't tell me about Mom's first marriage and divorce, who knows what else they're keeping from me. Everything was a lie. My parents' marriage. My family . . ."

"That's not true, Phylicia. Your parents had a great marriage. You know they —"

"But if Dad isn't even my real father, it was all based on lies. Oh, Quinn, for all I know my sisters aren't even really my sisters!"

"Of course they are! And what your parents had was real. Their marriage, their love for you and your sisters. Anyone who worked at Langhorne Construction would tell you that. I witnessed it with my own eyes. Even if what you fear is true, Phylicia, it doesn't change the truth of your family. You can't fake *love* for an entire lifetime. What's on your birth certificate is only a name."

"Oh, it's Dad's name on there. I checked." She dipped her head as if she should be ashamed for investigating.

"Then that should settle it. Could your dad have adopted you?" He was getting in way too deep. And Turner's name on the birth certificate didn't settle anything. Quinn knew the truth.

The deeper he dug this pit of deceit, the more reason Phylicia would have for not trusting *him,* for doubting his love for her, his worthiness to be the kind of man she'd waited for her whole life.

She took a shuddering breath. "Dad's name on my birth certificate doesn't mean anything. Apparently, you can put any name you want in the space that says 'Father.' I was always told I weighed just under seven pounds at birth, but what if that was a lie too? What if I weighed nine pounds?"

His face must have revealed his confusion.

"Don't you see? If Mom was already pregnant by her first husband, then I could have come along full-term only a few months after they got married. They would have had to lie and say I was a preemie or . . . lie about when they got married." Her jaw went slack, and her tone said she'd only now thought of that possibility — one Turner had confirmed to Quinn was exactly the case.

He scrambled to think of a response. "Isn't . . . a baby's weight on the birth certificate?"

"I don't think they put that on birth certificates. At least not in Cole County, Missouri. I was born in Jefferson City. At least that's what my parents told me. But how do I know if any of that is true? If what they showed me is even my actual birth certificate?" She scrubbed her face with the palms of her hands.

"Phylicia, you wouldn't even have gotten into college without a *legal* birth certificate. Just because your parents didn't tell you the truth about your birth father —" He stopped short. He was digging his own grave. "What I mean is . . . your mom being married before doesn't mean they've lied about everything since."

She stared at him. "Why did you say that?"

He willed himself to meet her gaze. "Say what?"

"Do you know something, Quinn? You just said, 'the truth about your birth father.' Why would you say that?"

"That's what *you* said."

She cocked her head and the sting of betrayal in her voice told him he needed to come clean. Now. But how could he, when he was in danger of losing the trust he'd worked so hard to gain? If he was straight with her, he was equally in danger of causing a rift between her and her father. Far worse than the one that was already there.

Not to mention the wedge it would put between *him* and Turner if he betrayed his boss's confidence.

What a mess! He raked a hand through his hair. He should have stopped Turner before all that spilled out, but it had happened within a matter of minutes. And he'd had no way of knowing the overwhelming details that were going to come out. Or the profound ramifications those details would have toward the woman he loved.

Yes, he *loved* her. He knew that now without a doubt.

And Turner's revelation may have ruined any chance Quinn had of ever winning Phylicia over. His jaw tensed. This conversation was not going at *all* the way he'd planned.

■ ■ ■ ■

Phee stared into Quinn's brown eyes, his gaze intense in a way that didn't give her any comfort. "What is going on?"

He looked away. "Phylicia . . ."

"What did you start to say, Quinn?" The minute the words were out, she knew they were the wrong ones. She'd hijacked his declaration of his feelings for her. But she had to sort out this mess with Dad before she could think straight about her feelings for Quinn.

"What were you trying to say just now?" she asked again. "And I don't mean earlier . . . about us. Is there something you know? Something about Dad that you're not telling me?"

His eyes filled with pain she didn't understand. "You need to talk to your dad, Phylicia. It's not my place to even answer your question. I . . . you just need to talk to your dad." His Adam's apple worked up and down. "And I need to go."

He rose and took two long strides.

She ran after him and grabbed his arm. "Quinn, what is going on? What are you not telling me?" She couldn't even fathom why Quinn would know something he couldn't talk to her about. Something she was supposed to talk to Dad about. "Have you talked to my dad about this?"

He gently but firmly removed her hand from his arm. "I'm really sorry, but I need to go. I know it feels cruel for me to just leave like this, but I don't have a choice. You call your dad. Talk to him. And then we'll talk. I promise."

She called after him, but only heard the scuff of his boots as he quickly descended the steps. And then the roar of his pickup. She ran to the steps in time to see his truck disappear down the lane in a cloud of dust.

It was almost dark now, as the sun gradually slipped behind the trees. She descended the steps slowly, feeling dazed. She replayed their conversation, trying to figure out how they'd gotten from Quinn telling her he cared for her — loved her, even — to the disturbing questions he'd raised about Dad. She couldn't trace the path of their conversation, but she had a sinking feeling that her questions *had* been answered. By Quinn's refusal to speak about it with her. What else could it mean?

She didn't feel like talking to Jo and Britt, so she slipped into the house and grabbed her keys and phone and went out to her car. She dialed Dad's number, but it rang four times, then went to voicemail.

She bent over the steering wheel. "God, I'm so confused! Everything is hitting at once. I can't talk to my sisters about this without betraying Mom and Dad, and now I feel like I can't even talk to my best friend about it." She took in a short breath.

Was Quinn her best friend? She hadn't consciously thought of him in that way before. But of all the people left in her world, he was the one she wanted to talk to now, when everything seemed dark and perplexing. He was the one whose shoulder she wanted to lean on, cry on. But just like Dad, Quinn had shut her out. And she didn't even know why.

And why had she rejected *him*? It couldn't have been easy for Quinn to confess his feelings for her. And though she honestly couldn't remember how the conversation had veered so far afield, she knew she'd rejected him. Why? If she thought of him as her best friend, *why*? She thought the world of Quinn.

But Dad's strange actions had made her leery. And weary. If she couldn't trust her own father — or was it her *own father*? Did she even know that man?

She didn't know who she could trust anymore.

She scrubbed at her face, as if she could wash the confusion away. She should go inside so her sisters wouldn't worry about her, thinking she was still up at the clearing after dark. Ordinarily, Jo and Britt were the first ones she would have gone to when life didn't make sense. Especially as her childhood friends had begun to marry and move away. But if she told her sisters about her suspicions now, they would be devastated. And angry at Dad. And that wouldn't help anyone.

She dialed Dad again. Again, it rang a few times before going to voicemail. Was he purposely ignoring her calls? Or had something happened? Now she was worried about him, thinking of Britt's fears that Dad might be going through a depression or some kind of breakdown.

The tears came, and she took deep breaths, forcing herself to calm down, to go for help to the One who was never confused. The One who'd loved her since before the day she was born, who knew every detail of her life and loved her regardless.

She bowed her head, and though her whispers seemed garbled to her own ears, she knew that God understood perfectly.

A tentative peace finally came. Not a peace that came from having all her questions answered. Far from it. But a sense of calm blanketed her, one she knew would carry her through the night. God's mercies would be new tomorrow and tomorrow and every tomorrow to come, until she finally had the answers she needed.

CHAPTER 30

"Quinn? You're up awfully early." Nine hundred miles away in Orlando, Turner sounded like he hadn't a care in the world.

But Quinn wasn't in the mood for pleasantries. "I've been trying to reach you since last night."

"Why? Is everything okay?" Now alarm tinged Turner's voice.

"You need to talk to your daughter."

"What's going on? Has something happened with the girls?"

"The girls are fine, but you need to talk to your daughter," Quinn said again. He'd made up his mind on the drive home from the cottages last night that he was going to be frank with Phylicia's father, and he didn't care if it meant losing his job or forfeiting his friendship with Turner.

An overlong moment of silence on Turner's end. "My daughter? I assume you mean Phee?"

"Yes. You need to tell her everything you told me. She already suspects most of it, and she's confused and feeling like she's lost you, along with her mother."

"Lost me? She told you that?"

"Yes, and why wouldn't she feel that way?" He braced himself. What the man had done wasn't right, and Turner needed to know how it was hurting his daughters. Phylicia especially. None of this should have been any of Quinn's business, but Turner had made it Quinn's business when he'd confided in him and then kept those same secrets from Phylicia. "Your daughter is an intelligent woman. An adult. Surely you can understand that the things her imagination is conjuring up are far worse than the truth. You need to tell her what you know. What you told me."

Turner blew a sigh into the phone. "The truth is going to hit her pretty hard."

"Maybe. But she already suspects the truth. She needs to know what you know. And she needs to hear it from you. And I don't mind telling you that I don't appreciate you putting me in the position you did. Having this secret and needing to protect your confidence and —"

"Hey, now. I never asked you to get involved."

"Actually, yes you did. When you asked me to put your house on the market. When you had me show your daughters the property. Either way, like it or not, I am involved. How did you think I could *not* be involved after everything you told me? And while we're at it, I don't know what you're doing hiding out in Florida, but your daughters need you. They are hurting here."

His heart was racing like a speeding train. But he was determined not to hang up until he said what needed saying. He took a deep breath. "I've always admired you, Turner, but unless there's something I don't understand, you're blowing it big-time right now."

Turner sighed. "I'm not sure I'm . . . strong enough right now."

"Your daughters don't care if you're strong enough. They just want you in their lives. You've left them to grieve alone, to sell your house for you, to figure out how to keep you happy and buy the property you wanted them to have. Don't get me wrong, I was glad to help with some of that . . ." He forced his voice down a few decibels. He was being pretty hard on a man who was obviously struggling. "I truly was glad to help, Turner, but I can only do so much. And it's not me they're aching for." How he wished it *was* him that Phylicia longed for.

But right now, despite the fact that she would soon turn thirty, she needed her dad. And if it was the last thing Quinn was allowed to do for her, he would see to it that Turner got his butt in gear and made things right with his daughters. And made amends for bailing on them at the worst possible time.

"I'm struggling, Quinn. This whole grief thing isn't for the faint of heart. I told myself if I got out of the way, my girls would learn to lean on each other." Turner sounded cowed. It wasn't a tone Quinn had ever heard from his boss. "It was an excuse, and I know it, but I really did think it would be better for them if I got out of the way. Given the shape I was in . . ."

"I don't know where you got that crazy idea. Your daughters need you, man! I don't know everything that's going on with you, but you need to get your act together long enough to be a father to your daughters. If you don't want to lose them."

"I'm struggling here, Quinn. I've blown it. I know that. But . . . I think maybe it's best if I stay out of the way."

"Whatever you've done, your daughters will forgive you. But you've got to make things right. And not just with a phone call."

Silence.

Quinn sighed. "I'm sorry if I've overstepped my bounds, but I have some pretty important things at stake here too."

"Meaning?"

"Meaning, I'm in love with your daughter." There. He'd said it. "I love Phylicia, but she's too confused and heartbroken right now to think about anything other than what she's lost. I don't mind telling you you're ticking me off." He tried to let Turner hear a smile in his voice. But there was too much truth in his words, and he didn't really feel like smiling.

And no doubt tomorrow, when he got his pink slip, he'd feel even less like it.

"She's a smart girl, Quinn. She'll come around. And I can't think of anyone I'd rather have her end up with."

"Well, I appreciate that, sir. But the ball's in your court right now." He didn't really think Turner would fire him for the things he'd said, but he might have damaged their friendship beyond repair. And his friendship with Turner Chandler was more important than ever, now that Quinn was in love with his daughter.

"Well, then, I'll see what I can do." Turner gave a little chuckle . . . one that made Quinn sigh with relief. The man just might be coming around.

■ ■ ■ ■

Phylicia hadn't expected Quinn to show up with the roofing crew Monday morning, but there he was, as if nothing had happened yesterday. She watched him from the kitchen window of the cottage, waving his arms around, telling everybody what they should be doing and how.

He reminded her of Dad on the job. Of course, Quinn had learned from her father.

Her father. Her heart grew heavy at the thought. But she couldn't let her mind go there right now.

She knew she should go out and talk to Quinn, but he would only wonder what she was trying to accomplish. He'd told her to talk to her father. Well, she'd tried. She'd tried to call Dad again this morning — twice — and had still gotten only his voice-mail message.

She could at least tell Quinn that. That she'd tried.

She checked her reflection in the mirror. The dark circles under her eyes testified to her lack of sleep, but no amount of makeup could hide that. She finger-combed her hair and put it back into a messy bun, then headed outside before she lost her nerve.

Two other trucks were in the driveway now, and a crew of men unloaded unwieldy packages of shingles and tarpaper. A couple of the men looked up as she walked toward Quinn, but he had his back to her and seemed unaware of her approach.

"Quinn?"

He turned, and a spontaneous smile bloomed on his face. But then, she could almost see him remembering their conversation from yesterday, and the smile faded as quickly as it had come.

He gave a short wave to the roofing crew and motioned her out of their hearing to the side of the far cabin — the same spot where they'd unloaded sandbags the night of the floods. It seemed like a lifetime ago.

With a questioning look, he removed his cap and waited for her to speak.

She dipped her head before looking back up at him. "I just . . . wanted to let you know that I'm trying to reach my dad. I tried last night and again this morning, but he's not answering. I'm starting to get a little worried about him."

She thought she detected surprise in Quinn's eyes. "I'm not sure why he's not answering. But just so you don't worry . . . I talked to him last night. I think he's . . . okay."

"Just *okay*? Why did you hesitate?"

He slapped his cap against one knee. "Phylicia, I *hate* this wall that's risen between us. But until you talk to your dad, there's really nothing else I can say."

"What if he *won't* talk to me? Apparently, he's ignoring me."

"I think he'll call you. I really do. But if he doesn't, keep trying. You *need* to talk to him."

"You're scaring me."

"That's not my intention. I promise you, it's not." He bit his lower lip, as if trying to decide whether to say something. Letting out a long, low sigh, he looked at her. "As I'm sure you've guessed, your dad told me some things he probably shouldn't have. In his defense, he didn't know . . . how I feel about you. He was just getting some things off his chest." He shook his head. "No, that didn't come out right. What I mean is, he was just talking to me as a friend, the way we used to talk before everything happened with your mom. I really do think he's okay. But, like I said, we talked about things that — Your dad didn't know what was at stake for me."

"You will talk to me about it though? After I've talked to Dad?"

One side of his mouth rose in a wry smile.

"I just hope you'll talk to *me.*"

"I will, Quinn. I know I kind of derailed your . . . *speech* last night. I feel bad about that."

"Yeah, well . . . not as bad as I feel."

She smiled. "If it's any consolation, I've thought a lot about things. I'm . . . I'm really confused right now, Quinn. And . . . I can't even remember how our conversation took the turn it did. I admit, I'm concerned about what Dad is going to tell me. But Quinn, I meant what I said to you last night. I wasn't giving you the brush-off when I said that about . . . just being friends. I can see how you might have thought that, but I promise I wasn't."

One eyebrow went up. "I'll hold you to that."

She hoped she wasn't giving him false hope. But she meant what she'd said. She did want to talk to him, to continue the conversation he'd opened up. If they could take it slow, if he would be patient with her, she was starting to think maybe God had a reason for putting Quinn Mitchell in her life right now. A good reason.

"I need to get to the office — and I know you probably need to get to work too — but can you come to the truck for a minute?" He pointed to where his company vehicle was parked a ways down the lane. "There's someone I want you to meet."

She gave him a questioning look. She hadn't seen anyone in the vehicle with him when he'd driven in earlier.

Without waiting for her to reply, he started toward the truck. She followed.

He opened the passenger-side door, squatted down, and patted his knee. "Come, girl. Come on . . ." He gave a low whistle, and a medium-sized, brindle-colored dog shot out of the truck and bounded for Quinn, almost knocking him over.

Phee couldn't help but laugh. "This must be Hazel."

"Very funny." Quinn grinned up at her, clearly getting her joke. "Mabel, meet Phylicia."

"Hey, Mabel." She put out a flat hand and took a step toward the dog.

But Quinn held out his palm in warning. "She won't bite, but you might not want to get too close. She's in desperate need of a bath. I'm dropping her off at the groomer before I go in to the office. But I thought since I had her with me, it'd be a good chance for you two to meet."

Phee felt like she'd been offered an olive branch. And she didn't take it lightly. "I'm not afraid of a little dog stink." She knelt on one knee and took the dog's large head between her hands.

Mabel wriggled with pleasure, her tail wagging.

"She's marked so pretty. What breed is she?"

"Pure mutt. The vet thinks she has some Labrador in her. And maybe a little pit bull." He looked at Phee as if he thought that might scare her. "Don't worry. She wouldn't hurt a flea."

Phee moved one hand to stroke Mabel's coat. "Her hair looks like mine."

Quinn looked askance at her.

"She has flecks of paint in her fur." Touching her own hair, Phee laughed. "It's the going style apparently."

Quinn smiled. "She's been helping me paint. At my house."

Phee pulled a tiny chip of paint from the dog's hair and inspected it. "Great color. Sea salt?"

His eyes went wide. "Exactly. Sherwin Williams. How'd you know?"

"It was one of Mom's favorite paint colors. We're using it in all the bedrooms in the cottage. In fact, that's probably what's in my hair." She bent her head toward him, but straightened quickly, feeling awkward.

"Well, good job, Mabel. Way to pick 'em."

He patted her flank, as if Mabel had selected the paint color herself.

Phee laughed, heartened by his response. After yesterday, she'd been so afraid things would be forever awkward between them, but meeting Mabel had broken the ice. She wondered if that had been Quinn's intent all along.

He straightened and pulled the passenger door all the way open. "Okay, Mabel. Back inside, girl."

The dog looked like she might balk, but walked to the side of the truck and reluctantly climbed in.

"Wow. You have her well trained. Melvin might need to take a lesson or two from Mabel."

Quinn chuckled. "I thought about asking if Melvin might want to meet Mabel —"

"What?" She feigned distress. "Your cat-eating dog? I don't think so." She couldn't quell the grin that came.

He shook his head. "Don't worry. I thought better of it." His grin matched hers.

But there was something about his demeanor that disturbed her.

He checked his watch. "I really need to get going. I think I've got the roofers squared away for the day."

"How long do you think it will take?"

He glanced up at the sky. "A couple of days if this weather holds. Maybe three. Long days. They'll probably still be here when you get home from work tonight."

"Actually, I took today off." She frowned. "To call my dad, for one thing. Plus, I wasn't sure if the roofing guys might need me for anything. I thought I could take some cookies out to them later."

"You don't have to do that."

"I know I don't have to. But my mom always did that whenever we had people working on the house." She forced a smile and swallowed over the lump in her throat.

"I remember. I was the recipient of her fresh-from-the-oven cookies more than once. That's really sweet of you, Phylicia."

"It's no big deal. Things have been pretty quiet at the flower shop anyway." Phylicia had been thankful for Mary's flexible scheduling since they'd moved to the cottage. And without a rent payment to make, she didn't feel the dent in her paycheck quite so much.

"Well, that's good then." Quinn's mouth tipped into a half-smile. "I would have assigned myself to this crew if I'd known about the cookies."

She laughed, mostly at the relief this whole conversation had offered. "Maybe I'll save you one."

Mabel barked from the cab, and Quinn tipped his hat at her and took a couple of backward steps toward the truck. "That's my signal. Gotta run."

She waved, still smiling. But as his truck disappeared around the bend, doubts assailed her again. She might be back on friendly terms with Quinn for now, but whatever he knew about her dad was serious, and Quinn had hinted that it might have repercussions for *their* relationship too. Such as it was.

Sighing, she walked back up to the house and steeled herself for a difficult conversation with Dad.

If she could ever get the man to answer his phone.

CHAPTER 31

Phee tipped open the oven door and checked on the last pan of chocolate chip cookies. They were still a little gooey, so she set the timer for two more minutes.

She smiled at the memories of her mother that came with the heavenly aroma of chocolate and warm sugar. Mom would have loved the way the roofing crew had snarfed down two dozen cookies in less than five minutes. Phee had almost grown embarrassed at the men's effusive thanks — even while she understood why Mom had found sharing cookies so rewarding.

This last pan was for her sisters. And maybe a couple for Quinn, in case he showed up again tomorrow morning to get the crew started.

The warm memories were crowded out by the reminder that she needed to try to reach Dad again. If it wasn't for the fact that his phone was ringing before going to voicemail, she would have suspected he'd changed his number or gotten a new phone. Surely, he would be worried if he saw that she'd tried to call him repeatedly. But he'd been anything but predictable since Mom's death.

While she waited for the timer, she washed the last of the dishes and set them to dry on a clean dish towel. The timer dinged and, at the same instant, the doorbell rang.

Phee removed the hot cookie sheet and set it on top of the stove. She turned off the oven, then quickly ran to see who was at the door.

Bending to peek through the living room window to the enclosed porch, her breath caught. "Dad?" Trembling, she fumbled with the doorknob and crossed the porch to open the outer door. "Dad?" All those unanswered calls — and now here he stood in the flesh? She almost couldn't believe her own eyes. "What are you doing here?"

"Hi, honey." He motioned behind him where the roofers were cleaning up the day's debris. "Pretty nice place you've got here."

"Dad . . . Come in!"

He opened his arms to her, and she fell into his embrace, forgetting all the angry feelings she'd harbored toward him, simply glad to have her father's arms around her.

He gave her one more squeeze, then held her at arm's length. "You're a sight for sore eyes."

Her insides trembled as she studied him, still unable to believe he was really here.

He'd lost weight, and his jeans hung loose on him. And despite the Florida tan that leathered his skin, beneath it, he looked wan and exhausted. Yet at the same time, he looked . . . *sweet.* The softer appearance of the loving father she'd grown up with. The edge of bitterness she'd sensed in him recently was gone. But he did not look defeated. He looked like a man who had fought a hard battle — and won.

"Something smells mighty good." He slipped the baseball cap from his head. His hair was longer than he usually wore it, curling around his ears and at his collar.

"Come in . . . please. How long have you been here?"

He gave a little chuckle. "Just got into town. I flew into St. Louis last night."

"What? You must be exhausted. Have you been to the house yet? Your house, I mean? Have you seen the girls?"

"Not yet. There will be time for all of that. I came to see you, sweet Phee."

Her throat filled with emotion at the endearment from her childhood — a play on *sweet pea.* She'd almost forgotten.

He stepped into the living room and looked slowly around, taking it all in. Phee tried to see the house through his eyes — and was pleased with what she saw. The cottage was at its best this time of day, with sunlight slanting through the windows on the west side and painting patches of saffron on the wood floors. Jo had fluffed the sofa pillows before leaving for work this morning, and the bouquet of wildflowers Britt had gathered from the creek's edge last night starred on the mantel.

A slow smile came over Dad's face. "Quinn said you had the place looking like something out of *Fixer Upper.* I've never watched the show . . . but I guess now I don't need to. Looks great, honey. You've done a super job."

"Thanks. It's been a joint effort for sure. I don't know how we could have done it without all of us working together."

Dad's smile widened.

"We still have a lot to do. Don't be too impressed until you've seen the other two cabins." She gave a little laugh. "We've been calling this one a cottage. The other two got demoted to *cabins* the first day we saw them. They're pretty rough. But you probably saw they're getting new roofs this week.

Then we're ripping up carpet and getting the walls ready to paint."

"Well, if you work the same magic as you did in here, you'll soon have three *cottages.*" He studied her. "No regrets?"

"For buying the place?" She wanted to be sure they were talking about the same thing.

He nodded.

"No regrets. It's been hard, but it's been good. And . . . I think Mom would have approved."

"I know she would have." He angled his head toward the gallery of paintings on the fireplace wall. "This would have made her happy for sure."

"It makes *me* happy too. Mom's sitting room was always one of my favorite rooms in the house." Tears welled behind her eyelids, but Phee was surprised to find they weren't mournful tears.

Melvin sauntered in from the hallway and practically pranced over to where Dad stood, curling his tail around Dad's leg.

"Well, look who's here." He bent and scooped Melvin into his arms. "So what do you think of the new place, Melvin?"

Melvin answered with a loud purr.

She'd never seen Dad be so affectionate with Mom's cat.

"Do you want something to drink? Some

cookies?"

"Maybe later."

"Well, come and sit down for a minute."

Dad carried Melvin over to the love seat in front of the fireplace. He started to sit down, then turned to Phee. "Is he allowed on the couch?"

She laughed. "He's pretty much allowed wherever he feels like going. Britt spoils that cat rotten."

"She learned that from Mom."

"I know. It's the only reason I tolerate it." It did her heart good that Dad had mentioned Mom at least twice in the space of a few minutes. And the truth was, Phee spoiled that crazy cat as much as Britt or Mom ever had.

"So, you haven't been by your house yet? Any offers?"

"Not last I heard. Is everything still turned on there? Thought I'd stay there tonight."

"We haven't turned the utilities off, if that's what you mean. But there's no food at your house. Why don't you stay here, Dad?" She could sleep in one of the queen beds with a sister and give Dad her bed. "Jo and Britt are going to be so excited that you're here."

"I hope you girls aren't too upset with me for putting the house on the market."

She looked at the floor. "I know you . . . needed to do it. And it's not like any of us were going to live there. It's just . . . hard. Just feels like one more thing we've lost. We always thought that even after Mom was gone, at least you'd be there at the house. For us." She didn't mean to put a guilt trip on him, but at the same time, it felt good to be honest with him.

"I'm sorry, Phee. I wish it could be different. We've all got to figure out a new normal. None of this is what any of us would have chosen, but it's what we have to work with."

"I know. I really do. And it'll be okay. Eventually."

He eyed her and shook his head slowly. "You are so like your mother sometimes."

"Really?" She wondered if he ever saw *himself* in her. His candid appraisal made her risk asking. "Do you ever think I'm like *you,* Dad?"

He cocked his head and studied her. "In what way?"

"*Any* way. I just wonder if you see *yourself* in me the way you see Mom in me . . ." She swallowed hard, bracing for an answer she dreaded. Even though she remembered the night Quinn had told her how much she reminded him of Dad.

Dad shrugged. "I don't know, honey. I

don't think we ever really see ourselves as we actually are, and you're so much like Mom, it's hard to say if —"

"Dad." The lump that came to her throat almost rendered her speechless, but she couldn't stop now. "I'm trying to ask you . . . are you my father? I know you're my *dad.* And nothing will ever change that. I couldn't love you more. I couldn't have had a better childhood. But, ever since we found that photo of Mom . . ." She put a hand to her mouth, fighting to compose herself. "I've been trying to put two and two together, and I'm not always coming up with four."

"Oh, Phee . . ." He shook his head. "I didn't ever want to have this conversation." He stroked a hand down the length of Melvin's back, eliciting another purr.

"Are you my father? My biological father?" She repeated her question, suddenly unemotional. Just needing an answer.

"Did your mom say something to you?"

So it must be true. Her heart felt leaden. "No! Mom never said *anything.* About being married before. About whether or not you were really my father." She swallowed back the bitter taste in her mouth. "Is it true then? You're not my father?"

Dad closed his eyes and rubbed the bridge

of his nose before he met her gaze. "If you want the truth, honey, I don't know. I suspect . . . it's possible I'm not. But your mom never told me otherwise. And I never asked."

"What do you mean Mom never told you? Did she lie to you too? About something that important?"

Dad paused for a long minute as if weighing his words carefully. "I don't think your mother ever told me a lie in her life. Unless it was a lie of omission. But . . . toward the end, Mom said some things that made me wonder if" — he scrubbed a hand over his face — "if she was trying to . . . leave another possibility open. I thought maybe she'd talked to you too."

"No. What did she say?" She couldn't seem to stop her hands from shaking. She folded them and slid them between her knees, not wanting Dad to see.

He shook his head. "It would feel funny to tell you."

"Why?" She waited, pleading with her eyes.

"You know your mom. She was trying to encourage me . . . trying to say goodbye." His voice broke and he put his head down, collecting his emotions. "She was telling me I'd been a good dad and that —"

"You were a good dad. You *are,*" Phee added quickly. Seeing him, being with him, had made the truth of that so much more clear. "Please tell me what she said, Dad. Every word. I need to know."

He bit his lip, his face a mask of pain. Phee almost wanted to stop him. Anything to keep him from the agony he wore on his countenance. But her need to know the truth was stronger than her compassion for her father. So she waited in silence.

"Mom told me . . ." He swallowed hard. "Her exact words were, 'Phylicia — all our girls — could not have had a better father than you were to her. Don't ever think otherwise, Turner Chandler.' " Speaking his own name brought emotion again, as if Dad were hearing Mom say those things for the first time. When he'd recovered his voice, he continued. "I could be wrong, but the way she said it . . . the fact that she singled you out. Something about the . . . pleading in her eyes. I don't think Mom knew for sure herself, but I think she did the same math you and I did and knew that it was possible I wasn't your father. I think maybe she was reassuring me that even if I suspected the same, that it . . . didn't matter."

Phee was surprised to find that she didn't feel angry or even shocked at what was surely the final evidence she needed. She'd suspected as much for a while now, in those moments when she allowed herself to think about it.

Instead, the emotion that filled her now was gratitude. And a realization that Mom was right. It didn't really matter. Not in the whole scheme of things. What Mom had told Dad was a larger truth than anything else. He *had* been a wonderful, loving father.

A thought teased at the corner of her mind and made her breath catch. Had Dad treated her with love because, for most of her life, he'd thought she was his own? Would things have been different if he'd known for sure she *wasn't* his? Would she have been the Cinderella of the family, the despised stepdaughter?

She dared to broach the question, even though she wasn't sure she was strong enough to hear the answer. "What if you'd known for sure, Dad? What if you'd known for certain, from the very beginning, that I wasn't yours?"

"Oh, Phee . . ." He toppled Melvin off his lap and scooted over on the sofa, putting an arm around her, pressing her head to his shoulder. "I think maybe I *did* suspect the possibility. From the very beginning. It's why I never pressed Mom for answers. It's why I never looked for proof, one way or the other."

So he had considered the possibility that she wasn't his biological daughter. Since she was a baby. Or even before she was born. And still, with his suspicions, he'd been the same kind of dad to her that he'd been to Joanna and Britt — his for-sure biological daughters.

The profound and simple reality of that knowledge brought a flood of tears. Dad handed her a tissue from a box on the side table and took one for himself.

He cleared his throat and squeezed her shoulders tighter. "I couldn't have loved you more, Phee — whatever the truth is. I don't have the answers you're looking for, but . . . if you feel like you need to know for certain . . . if you want to do a DNA test or whatever they do these days to figure all that stuff out, I completely understand. And I'll do anything you need me to. So you'll know as much of the truth as there is to know. But whatever we find out, it won't change that I have always loved you as my own. I hope you can believe that."

"I don't have to believe it, Dad. I *know* you did."

She had a thousand questions for him, and she knew that some of them would be painful and some would likely never be answered. But for now, one thing was settled in her heart: Dad was — and always had been — her father in every way that mattered. And nothing she learned would change that fact.

They sat in silence together on the sofa for a few minutes, both too emotional to speak.

But Phee didn't want to waste an opportunity when Dad was being so open and willing to share. She scooted over and curled up in the corner of the love seat, angling herself toward him. "I tried to call you a dozen times. It kept going to voicemail. Did you get a new phone or something?"

He sighed. "I'm sorry about that. I owe your sisters an apology too. A lot of people have been trying to call me. Except for work, I've kind of been . . . laying low."

Melvin jumped up and settled in the space between them, prompting laughter from both of them. But Phee quickly turned serious, not wanting to lose the opportunity. "Are you okay, Dad?"

He thought for a minute, a faraway look coming to his eyes. "I'm going to be okay. I need to tell you some things, but I want your sisters to hear too." He gave a low harrumph. "I don't think I have the gumption to say everything twice."

"Is it about . . . Karleen?"

Again, he paused, seeming to weigh his answer before he spoke. "Not really. I think, in truth, it's more about your mom. And me and God. I promise I'll explain everything. As much as I understand it myself."

"Okay." A frisson of fear went through her. She wanted to ask him outright if he'd had an affair with Karleen. But she was afraid that would shut down their conversation. And if she was wrong, she would feel terrible for making such an accusation.

Chapter 32

"Do you want another sandwich, Dad?" Phee lifted a platter that held two soggy leftover grilled cheese sandwiches.

"Or some more soup?" Joanna looked like she was offering him a pot of gold. "There's plenty."

"I'm good, ladies. But thanks. That hit the spot." He winked at Phee. "Now, I might be persuaded to eat another one of those amazing chocolate chip cookies you made."

"Sure!" Pleased at his compliment, Phee pushed back her chair and went for the plate of cookies.

"I still can't believe you're here, Daddy." Britt laid her head on Dad's shoulder, looking like she was twelve again. On his other side, Joanna leaned as close to Dad as their chairs would allow.

"Well, pinch me if you need to, Miss Britt." Dad gave her shoulders a squeeze. "I'm really here. You have Quinn to thank for that, by the way."

Phee stopped, wondering what he meant by that, then returned to her chair directly across from her dad. She looked from Britt to Jo, then back at Dad between them. He already had more color in his cheeks than he'd had just a couple of hours ago. But as relieved as Phee was to have him here, something about the scene at their table made her feel lost.

No, made her feel like a misfit.

She pushed away the unwanted emotions. This was Jo and Britt's turn with Dad. She'd had her moment with him this afternoon, and he'd reassured her — several times — of his love for her.

Still, the unanswered questions assailed her. If Dad wasn't her father, who was that man? What was he like? Was he still alive? Could it even be someone she knew?

That day they'd found the photo and the ring in Mom's desk, Dad had explained that Mom's first husband had been abusive to her. Dad hadn't gone into detail, but Phee assumed it was only emotional abuse. But maybe it was worse than that. Maybe her birth father had physically abused Mom. The thought made her sick to her stomach.

She dreaded what Dad might reveal when he talked to all three of them later. She had a feeling they weren't going to like what he told them.

"What did you mean when you said we had Quinn to thank for you being here?"

Dad shook his head slowly and gave a little laugh. "That man can be pretty persuasive."

"What do you mean?" Phee repeated, narrowing her eyes. "Quinn made you come?"

Dad met her gaze head-on. "No, I came because it seemed like maybe my daughters needed me — and truth be told, I needed them." He swallowed hard, but a smile came quickly. "And yes, Quinn informed me that I had put a wedge between you and him. Apparently, I owe you both an apology. I didn't realize there was something brewing between you two."

Joanna and Britt exchanged glances.

"I *told* you!" Britt pointed an accusing finger at Jo. "For someone who supposedly has lawyerly investigative skills, you missed that one big-time, sister."

Joanna shook her head. "I didn't deny it. I just didn't have enough evidence to convict."

"Excuse me!" Phee cleared her throat. "I'm sitting right here. And Quinn and I are . . . friends."

Dad winced. "Just friends? Are you sure?

Quinn seems to think it's a little more than that."

"What did he say?" Her cheeks felt like they were on fire.

"That's for him to say. But, honey . . . if he's misunderstood, you need to let him know. I think the man has it bad for you."

"Anyone with eyes could see that." Britt aimed the comment at Joanna.

Joanna leveled her gaze at Phee. "Don't you dare lead him on if you don't have any intention of —"

"Would everybody cut it out? This is between me and Quinn. We're . . . *talking.* And okay, there might be something *brewing,* as you say, Dad."

Her sisters cheered.

"Stop! And don't you dare say anything to Quinn about this."

Britt put her hands on her hips. "Well, *somebody* needs to say something to Quinn. At the rate you two are going, I'll be sixty before I get to walk down the aisle as your bridesmaid."

"Bridesmaid? We haven't even had a date yet. And we've only known each other for two months."

Dad shot her a skeptical look. "You've known each other practically your whole life."

"I hardly think that counts, Dad. I was sixteen when we met." *Yes, and Quinn was twenty-eight.* She still struggled a bit with their age difference. Especially since she'd made such a big deal about the age difference between Dad and Karleen.

"I think it counts for plenty." Dad gave a bob of his chin. "And I've known Quinn even longer. And think the world of him. You certainly have my blessing."

"Would you guys please quit talking like we're engaged already?"

Britt gave her a cheesy grin. "You soon will be. I'd bet money on it."

"If you *had* any money." Joanna ducked out of her little sister's reach.

Dad pushed his plate away and rose from the table. "Why don't you girls show me around this property before it gets too dark." He scooted his empty chair up to the table. "And then we need to talk. The four of us."

The sisters exchanged worried glances, and Phee knew they were all wondering the same thing: Had Dad and Karleen gotten back together?

"Why don't we light a fire in that fireplace? Don't you girls think it's a little chilly in here?" Dad rubbed his hands over the hearth as if there were already a fire blazing.

Britt clapped her hands. "Finally! We were going to celebrate our first night here with a fire, and we just never have gotten around to it. This is perfect to have you here for it, Dad!"

"Did I see some wood out on the porch?" He pointed toward the covered porch.

Joanna nodded. "That was here when we moved in, but it should still be okay, shouldn't it?"

"As long as it's dry."

Jo and Britt went to bring in wood, while Phee searched for matches and some newspaper for kindling. Dad arranged the logs in the fire and fiddled with the flue. Before long, there was a cozy fire crackling.

Sitting with her sisters and the warm, loving version of their dad, Phee almost wanted to request that Dad save his news or speech — or whatever it was — for another time. If only they could have had their dad with them through the whole process of buying the property and fixing it up. What a difference that would have made.

Phee willed the thoughts away, not wanting to ruin whatever time they did have with Dad.

It had been fun to give him the tour of

their property this evening. Of course, he'd seen the land, with Quinn, before they bought it, but he'd been appropriately impressed with even the little they'd done to improve the place.

The roofers were still working and had greeted Dad with surprise. They weren't all employees of Langhorne Construction, but Phee gathered that most of them had worked on one of Dad's crews at one time or another. Dad joked with them, and they promised him both cabins would have new roofs by noon on Wednesday, as long as the weather held.

She'd forgotten how much Dad's workers seemed to respect and admire him. It made her feel proud to be his daughter.

The thought brought her up short, and she wondered if, for the rest of her life, she would have to amend every thought, reminding herself she likely was not his daughter by birth. It shouldn't matter, but for some reason, tonight it felt like it mattered a lot.

The girls all grabbed comfy spots on the sofa and chairs gathered around the fireplace. Dad poked at the kindling and rearranged the logs until he was satisfied with the flames. Finally, he took a seat in one of the teal chairs that had been in Mom's sitting room at the house.

Joanna leaned forward in her corner of the sofa. "So what did you want to talk to us about, Dad?"

Phee flinched. Why did Jo have to turn every gathering into a tribunal? Couldn't they just enjoy having their dad back for an hour before they had to have a *proceeding*? Or a "family meeting," as Dad had started calling it whenever there was a difficult decision to be made about Mom's care. It seemed like their lives had been relegated to one big family meeting over the last three years.

But Dad didn't flinch. He leaned forward and put his elbows on his knees. "I guess we may as well get it over with."

Britt bit her bottom lip and coiled a strand of hair around her finger. Phee knew how she felt.

They waited while Dad took several deep breaths and repositioned himself in the chair. Phee didn't remember ever seeing him look so uncomfortable. Or nervous.

But when Dad finally spoke, his voice didn't waver. "First of all, I owe all three of you an apology. I hope you'll believe me when I tell you that I had the best of intentions. But then you all know what the road to hell is paved with." He gave a little chuckle.

But Phee and her sisters sat silent.

"My intention — originally anyway — was to spare you girls having to witness my grief. I thought I was handling losing your mom pretty well. But the truth is . . . I sort of fell apart. It wasn't a pretty picture, and I didn't want you to have to see me like that."

"Fell apart? What do you mean by that, Daddy?" Britt twisted the coil of hair tighter.

"It's hard to define, sweetheart. Maybe the best way to say it is that I had a crisis of faith. For so long, right up to the end, I was secretly convinced — as sure as I've ever been about anything in my life — that your mom was going to beat this thing. I know what the doctors said. And I know you girls were being more realistic about it than I was. But she survived so much longer than they said she would, and I just *knew* that she'd amaze all the doctors and be miraculously healed . . ." He bent his head, his voice showing the first signs of emotion. "I wanted it *so* bad. I thought I knew it in my bones — that God had promised it. That He owed me, even. When it didn't happen, I was just mad. Mad at everybody and everything. Mad at God. Even mad at you girls."

Phee knew her own eyes had gone as wide

as her sisters' at Dad's confession.

He gave a sad smile. "Don't worry. You didn't do a thing wrong. Not one of you. In fact, you girls were all that kept me going during those days. My anger wasn't rational or right. It didn't even make sense. But I couldn't seem to control how I felt. I felt as if God had betrayed me. Betrayed our whole family. And betrayed your sweet mom, above all."

"But, Dad. Why didn't you tell us?" Joanna's voice remained steady. "We would have understood."

"I couldn't, honey. I wasn't thinking straight. It was almost like I was under the influence of some crazy drug. My counselor says grief is kind of like a drug."

Phee and her sisters exchanged surreptitious glances. They hadn't known Dad was seeing a counselor.

Dad didn't seem to notice their surprised expressions. "I look back now, and I realize how irrational my thinking was. But then, I just wanted everything to be fixed. To go back to the way it was before cancer entered our lives. When . . . when I realized that nothing would ever be the same, I flipped out a little."

Phee and her sisters waited, none of them daring to interrupt. Phee couldn't remember Dad ever being so vulnerable with them. She couldn't decide how she felt about it.

"I was at least rational enough to know that I didn't want you girls to have to deal with my . . . *crisis,* so I asked the head office if I could work in Florida for a while."

"So . . . Florida really was about work?" Phee fought to not jump to conclusions.

Dad closed his eyes. "It was partly about work. But —" He opened his eyes and looked at each one of them in turn. "I need to explain about Karleen."

CHAPTER 33

Dad rose from his chair and put another log on the fire. He sat back down heavily, sighing for the tenth time. "Karleen was part of my reason for going to Florida. A pretty big part, I guess. If I'm honest."

"Are you back together with her?" Britt squeaked.

"No, honey. I can't say for sure, but I doubt we ever will be."

"When did things . . . start with you two?" Phee had to know.

He hesitated. "Karleen kind of played counselor from the beginning. For Mom *and* for me. But then after Mom passed away, she really helped *me* begin to process everything. She lost her husband just two years ago, and she understood what I was feeling, offered a listening ear. We grew very close and one thing led to another and then —" He stopped and looked up at Phee, as if a realization had just hit him. "You didn't think there was ever anything going on between us *before* Mom died, did you?"

Her face must have told the truth, because Dad gave a low moan. "Girls . . . Oh, my girls, I would never have done that to your mom. Surely you know that . . ."

"We *didn't* know, Dad. We didn't know anything." The words poured out of Phee, and she couldn't seem to stop them. "You were acting so weird, and it seemed like you were so eager to get away from us. Then the next thing we know, you're engaged. What were we *supposed* to think?"

"Phee, I am so sorry if I ever made you fear for one minute that I wasn't totally devoted to Mom. Until the very last minute of her life. I know things happened quickly with Karleen. Too quickly. I should have reassured you. It just never crossed my mind that you would believe something like that of me." He held up a hand, as if anticipating that they'd interrupt. "In hindsight, I understand why you might have. Especially after you found the photograph and Mom's . . . other ring."

Phee looked from Joanna to Britt. After supper, she and Dad had filled her sisters in briefly about the new details Dad had revealed concerning Mom's first marriage, but she still hadn't had a chance to talk with

Jo and Britt privately about the possibility that Dad wasn't Phee's birth father. She knew that would rock her sisters' worlds. And she wanted time to process things herself before adding her sisters' emotions to the mix.

She wasn't sure she could even explain to them how she felt, but she did know that Dad's words just now offered immense relief.

"Let me say again, girls . . . I was never disloyal to your mother a day in my life. But . . . I made a mistake in becoming so close to Karleen. Even though we never did anything . . . inappropriate, I shouldn't have allowed myself to become so close to her, either before or after Mom's death. But I was drawn to her because she knew Mom and loved her. She understood what I'd lost. And she knew *who* I'd lost."

"We did too, Dad." Phee swallowed back tears.

"Of course you did, honey. But Karleen . . . being a widow herself, she understood that part of it. And she helped me feel like Mom was still . . . close. Karleen listened without judging my wavering faith. I could tell her things I couldn't tell anyone else. Not even my beautiful daughters."

He offered a wan smile, then swallowed

hard. "It was a mistake, but . . . well, one thing led to another, and I got confused and off track. I hurt you all — and maybe Karleen most of all — in the process. She put her job at risk to come back to Florida to be with me. She's a lovely woman, and I'm grateful for her help, but the truth is, I was — I *am* — still in love with your mother. It's going to take some time." He shook his head, emotion thick in his voice.

Phee let the tears come and found surprising comfort in sitting here weeping with her sisters and with Dad.

After a few minutes, Dad chuckled softly and went for a box of tissues. "We're going to keep the tissue companies in business." He passed the box to each of them, then waited for them to dry their eyes before he went on.

"I won't bore you with the details. There's nothing to be gained by that. But the bottom line is that Karleen and I both realized we'd made a mistake. She is back here in Cape for a while —" He looked between Joanna and Britt. "Phee probably told you Karleen came in to the flower shop. Anyway, I think as long as she's here, it's best for me to continue working in Florida."

"But Daddy —" Britt's eyes pled with him.

Again, he held up a hand. "It's just for a while, baby girl. Karleen's job moves her around quite a bit, and by the time she's settled somewhere else, I'll probably get transferred back to Langhorne." He flashed a sheepish grin that took them all in. "Don't think you can get rid of your old man so easily."

A chorus of feminine murmurs went up — mostly of relief and affirmation that they wanted Dad home in Langhorne as soon as possible — and a new round of tears flowed.

Dad looked relieved too. And Phee hoped the worst of his confessions were over.

He got up to tend the fire again, then sat on the raised hearth and steepled his hands, elbows on his knees. "I don't want to give you girls any false hope. I'll still need to sell the house."

"Couldn't you rent it out or something . . . until you're ready to come back?"

Phee could almost see Joanna's legal mind sorting the options.

"It's not just financial, honey. There are just too many memories there. Good ones, of course. But a few hard, sad years were spent in that house too. I need to make a new start."

Phee guessed that the disappointed expressions on her sisters' faces mirrored her own.

"But Dad . . ." Joanna's brow furrowed. "Is it good for you to be there, in Florida, all alone?"

"I'm not alone, honey. That's one thing I know for certain. God has been with me every step of the way. Even when I couldn't feel Him there. And I know He's with each of you girls too. I've been going to a good church in Tampa, and" — he bit his lip — "I'm getting some counseling, from one of the pastors at the church, actually. I'm doing fine. It's going to take some time, but I'll be fine."

"So you're still selling the house?" Britt looked near tears.

"I have to, honey. For lots of reasons. Besides, I don't need to be rattling around in a house that big. But don't you worry, I'll find an apartment when . . . *if* the time comes to move back. Meanwhile, I'll come visit now and again. I promise. And when I am in town, maybe I can just book an Airbnb reservation." He winked. "I happen to know of a really cute one on the edge of town that's just about to open."

Phee carried her lunch to the screened porch, grateful Mary had let her leave work early since the roofers had promised to finish around noon. She watched the crew gather up stray shingles and nails and pack their gear into the two trucks. She trained her gaze on the lane, willing Quinn's vehicle to round the curve. She'd spoken with him briefly this morning when he'd come to check on the roofers.

Things had been cordial between them — even friendly, the way they'd been Monday morning — but she could tell he felt the same sense of unfinished business that she did.

The foreman of the roofing crew was headed toward the cottage, and Phee stepped off the porch stairs to greet him. "All finished?"

"Yes, ma'am."

"It looks really good. Thanks, Rick."

Rick tipped his baseball cap. "Our pleasure. Those roofs ought to last you for a long time to come."

"That's good to know."

"Anything else we can do for you before we head back to town?" He dusted the knees of his jeans with his cap.

"I don't think so." She craned her neck and looked up the lane again. "I was hoping Quinn would come by before you were finished. He knows a lot more about what to look for than I do."

Rick shot her a crooked smile. "Don't worry, ma'am, he'll keep us honest. If he doesn't make it before we leave, just tell him to give me a call if he sees any problems. We'll get right out and take care of it."

"Well, they look good. I doubt there are any problems. I'd just feel better if Quinn —"

The roar of an engine made them both turn.

Rick chuckled. "Speak of the devil."

Quinn parked the company vehicle and climbed out. He waved at them, which prompted Rick to jog across the lane to talk to him.

Phee retreated to the screened porch, watching them, loving the timbre of Quinn's voice as he discussed the project with the foreman. She couldn't make out everything they were saying, but there was a lot of laughter and kidding around, and she got the impression that Quinn was satisfied with the job the crew had done.

Though dressed for the office, Quinn donned work gloves and helped the crew finish cleaning up. As they drove away, he followed along, walking a ways down the lane. As he headed toward his truck, Phee was afraid he was going to leave without coming to talk to her, but after tossing his gloves into the vehicle, he turned and walked toward the cottage.

Phee stepped onto the outer porch and waved.

The smile he gave her held something she couldn't quite define. Even so, that smile made her insides do funny things.

He crossed the lane but stopped at the bottom of the steps. He looked up at her, concern in his eyes. "Are you okay? A little bird told me you got to talk to your dad."

"In person. Did you know he was here?"

"I suspected he was on his way."

"Well, whatever you did to get him back here —" She choked up unexpectedly and swallowed hard, composing herself. "Thank you."

"Does that mean your talk with him went well?"

"He told me some . . . Well, you know what he told me. I can't say I was surprised." And yet, she still felt a little stunned at the suspicions Dad hadn't been able to deny — the very things she'd feared.

Quinn studied her. "Do you have some time to talk?"

She nodded. "Do you want to come in?"

He shook his head. "Could we sit out here?"

Remembering their conversation about how Dad would never be alone with another woman, she led the way to the lawn chairs on the open porch. "Do you want something to drink?"

He waved her offer away. "I'm good."

She sat down.

Quinn chose a chair beside hers, angling it so they were almost facing each other. "Could you — in a nutshell — tell me what your dad told you? Just so I don't stick my foot in my mouth again?"

She began at the beginning, surprised that rehashing Dad's confession to Quinn wasn't more emotional for her. She was thankful. The last thing she wanted was to sit here and blubber like a baby in front of him. "That's pretty much it. Is . . . is Dad still holding out on me?"

"If he is, he's holding out on me too. Not that he owes me anything," he added quickly. "So, are you willing to talk to me now? Or . . . do you need some time? To process everything."

"No, I'd love to get this over with." She grinned, but saw too late that he took her comment wrong. "I didn't mean that the way it sounded."

He cocked his head. "Then how do you mean it?"

"Honestly, Quinn?"

"Of course."

"I've hated this wall between you and me. I'm glad we can talk about everything now." She regarded him. "Even that certain topic you tried to bring up Sunday night."

He reached and touched her arm briefly. Testing, she thought. She leaned toward him, overcome by a yearning for him that grew undeniably deeper each day.

"I don't want to rush you, Phylicia."

"Can I talk to you about some things with my dad first? As a friend?"

He grinned. "Ah, so we're back to just being friends now?"

"I hope we'll always be friends. Best friends. But more on that later." She offered him her best smile.

"So, tell me how you're feeling about everything with your dad. Are you going to try to find out if he is your birth father . . . with testing or whatever?"

"I don't know. Part of me feels like I need to. I've talked some about it with my sisters, but I'm just not sure what purpose it would serve." A gust of wind blew through the porch. Shivering, she pulled her legs up into the chair and hugged her knees. "Dad agreed to do DNA testing if I wanted, but part of me is terrified of what I might discover."

"Let's just say you *do* find out that your dad isn't your biological father. Does that make him any less of a good father to you? Does that negate all the times he sat up with you in the middle of the night when you were sick? Does that undo him teaching you how to ride a bike? Or him helping you with your algebra?"

Phee couldn't help but laugh at that. "Oh, he had to be such a patient man to get through that year."

Quinn laughed. "At the risk of sounding really old, I actually remember that. Your dad about pulled his hair out trying to figure out how to help you pass that stupid class! You'd probably be surprised how much your dad talked about his daughters at work." He looked across the lane to the cabins with their tidy new roofs, a faraway look in his eyes. "Maybe that's why I was so crazy about you when you were barely a teenager. Your dad was always bragging on you. All of you girls. But you first, Phee. You were his firstborn. However it all came about, he's loved you the longest."

Phee swallowed back tears. She'd never considered that, even though she might not share Dad's genes, he'd been her father even longer than he'd been Jo and Britt's.

And it would always be so.

"Thank you for that, Quinn." She took in a breath. "I told them everything yesterday."

"Your sisters? How'd they take it?"

"About like I expected. They've been so sweet to me ever since, it makes me want to cry."

"Did you expect any less from those two?"

"I shouldn't have." She stopped, overcome with emotion. "All of this . . . You were right, Quinn. It doesn't really change anything. And you know, even if I decided to do the DNA tests to find out if this other guy was actually my father, it's not like I would look him up or try to have a relationship with him. Not at all. Dad said this man was abusive to Mom. Did he tell you they got an emergency divorce? The man may not have ever known — if Mom *was* already pregnant with me before she married Dad."

Quinn nodded. "It sounded like your Dad didn't think your mom even knew for sure. And like your dad told me, *he's* the one who held your mom's hand in the delivery room. And cut your cord. And brought you home from the hospital —"

"Dad cut my cord? Really?"

Quinn nodded, looking like he might have slipped and said something he shouldn't have. "That's what he told me."

"I never knew that." It was such a simple, primal thing. But to her, that image of her father in the delivery room, cutting her umbilical cord, felt profound — a symbol of how fully and completely Dad *was* her father in every way that counted. From her first moments of life. Her very first breath.

She sighed and relaxed back into the lawn chair. That thought somehow settled everything for her. "I don't think I need to know. I don't need to know anything about that man." She heard the awe in her own voice. "I already know my father." She stood and went to the edge of the porch, leaning over the rail to watch a glowing sun that promised to put on a show later.

Quinn rose and came to stand beside her. "That's so true, Phee. And you got a good father."

It was such a simple statement, yet somehow those words seemed to set everything right. About Mom. About Dad. But even more, about Quinn.

Why had it taken her so long to see that this man standing beside her was . . . well, pretty much perfect? She turned to him. "Thank you for being so patient with me, Quinn. For helping me see my dad through your eyes. For being a good friend."

He gave her what her sisters called the

stink-eye, his shoulders slumping. "And there it is. We're back to being just friends."

"Now don't put words in my mouth." A slow smile started. "I never said *just* friends."

His eyebrows arched. "In that case, will you go out with me Friday night? A real, honest-to-goodness date?"

He laughed at the surprised look she gave him. And with brown eyes twinkling, he turned to put his hands on her shoulders and leaned in to plant a soft kiss on her cheekbone. His kisses traced a path to her lips, but he kept his touch light and gentle.

Heart soaring, she let him kiss her. But tempted as she was to let his kisses deepen, she took a step back, unable to stop her smile from fully blooming. "Wow. So much for taking it slow."

"Hey, when you're as old as I am, you can't waste a minute!" With that, he winked and turned on his heel. He headed for his car but called over his shoulder to her. "See you Friday. I'll call you."

Phee stood there, fingers to her mouth, not wanting to forget the gentle pressure of his lips on hers. She watched him drive away, pretty sure her own eyes were twinkling too.

Chapter 34

"So, this is it." Quinn cut the engine and turned in his seat to watch Phylicia's reaction. He wasn't disappointed. "Oh, Quinn! What a gorgeous piece of property. And the house looks like it was designed to sit right on this spot. It's perfect!"

He laughed softly. "You might want to withhold judgment. You haven't seen the inside yet."

"Well? Are you going to give me the tour?"

"I will. But I want you to know that Mabel is our chaperone for the evening, and she absolutely will not put up with any hanky-panky."

She gave him a look. "Well, don't look at me. I'm the one who gave a lecture about taking it slow and then *you* —"

"Shhh . . ." He put a finger to her mouth, wishing it was his lips. "We're not going to talk about that. And I promise we'll only stay for a few minutes, and then I'll take you out to eat as promised."

He hopped out of the car, then jogged around to open Phylicia's door. He held out an arm to escort her.

She climbed out and looped her hand through the crook of his elbow, grinning up at him.

He had to let loose to unlock the front door but was happy when she voluntarily took his arm again as they stepped into the foyer. It was new to have her so close, not a bit skittish the way she'd been with him until the night he'd first kissed her. He liked the fact that this was a woman who would take some wooing.

"Now before we go any farther, I just want to remind you that this is a work in progress. I'm doing all the interior work myself, and I'd be a lot further along if I hadn't had to stop working to help these three crazy chicks with some Airbnb scheme they came up with."

She laughed and gave his arm a gentle slug. "Crazy chicks? Excuse me?"

He flipped on the lights as they entered the great room and kitchen. "This is probably the most finished space . . ."

Her eyes widened. "Quinn, this is gorgeous! You've done this all yourself?"

"Mostly. The inside. I had some help with

the plumbing and electric, but I'm trying to do the finish work myself. Like I said, there's a long way to go still."

"Maybe, but I can see what it's going to be. You've been working on this for four years?"

He nodded.

"That's dedication. But what a great home you'll have when it's all done."

"Actually, I'll probably list it for sale the minute it's finished. In fact, if you know anyone who'd want to buy it as-is —"

"What? Why?"

He looked at the floor littered with wood shavings and dog hair, despite the fact that he'd swept just yesterday. "I didn't really want to get into this before dinner, but maybe it'd be good to get it out of the way . . . so we can enjoy dinner."

Her expression was a mix of curiosity and . . . was it fear?

"This house started out as a project for . . . a girlfriend. We weren't engaged or anything, and Heather never knew how much I'd invested — emotionally — into this place. For her. That whole thing . . . didn't work out. And I've kind of lost my enthusiasm for finishing it."

"Her name was Heather?"

He nodded. "The story is . . . complicated.

And it doesn't have a very happy ending. But I'd like you to know it."

"I'm listening."

He pulled out a stool from the kitchen bar and motioned for Phylicia to have a seat.

Before taking the stool beside her, he looked around for Mabel. Their chaperone seemed to have walked off the job. He gave a low whistle and patted his knee. "Mabel? Here, girl . . ." The dog trotted in from the hallway that led to the bedrooms. Quinn knelt and rubbed behind her silky ears. "Sit, girl. Right here."

Mabel obeyed. Quinn held out his palm and feigned a stern tone. "Now, *stay.* Some chaperone you are." He looked up at Phylicia with a smile, trying to inject some humor into what had the potential to be a heavy conversation.

She rewarded him with a smile.

He straddled the stool and leaned one elbow on the high bar counter. "To make a long and boring story short, Heather had the decency to break up with me — and wait a whole month and a half — before she and my brother started dating."

"Markus?" He couldn't miss the empathy in her eyes. "Oh, Quinn. I'm so sorry." She briefly touched his arm.

"Yeah. Slightly painful. Three months

later, she and Markus were engaged. And now they are happily married — as far as I know — with a little girl. They live in Austin. I don't see my brother often, for obvious reasons."

"That must be so hard. I'm sorry."

"It was beyond hard for a while. I know it sounds a little childish now to say this — especially after what you've just been through — but at the time, I wasn't sure I'd survive the whole mess. The rejection." He hung his head, feeling the shame afresh. "But worse, I felt like I'd lost my brother too. Not just Heather." He reached for her hand. It felt like the most natural thing in the world to entwine his fingers with hers.

She must have felt so too, because she didn't withdraw her hand. "It doesn't sound childish, Quinn. It sounds human."

"Thanks for that." He squeezed her hand. "My parents kind of took a just-get-over-it-and-move-on attitude. Which hurt too."

"I'm so sorry."

"What I didn't understand back then is that they *couldn't* take sides. Or even defend me. Heather was going to be their daughter-in-law. The mother of their grandchildren — well, if they'd lived long enough to meet them. So they couldn't take sides. In some ways, it put them in a more impossible situation than mine. They risked alienating all of us. And I'm sure it broke their hearts to know that my brother and I were at odds."

"Well, that explains why things are so strained between you. I've wondered. Do you think you'll ever see him again? Ever meet your niece?"

He thought for a moment, wanting to be honest with her. "I've forgiven Markus. We've talked about it a little. I can't say it doesn't still hurt. I *can* say I'm not ready to fly to Austin and face Heather. Not yet."

"I totally get that."

"I think the day will come when I'll be able to be with them without it hurting so much." He didn't tell her that *she* was making that day seem more and more possible. "But I don't have any illusions about us someday being one big, happy family the way my mom always hoped." He met her gaze. "Mom got one thing right though."

Phylicia gave him a questioning look.

"She said God must have something better in mind for me."

Phylicia gave a little smile, as if she hoped, but wasn't sure, he was referring to her.

He put his hand over hers on the counter. "That includes you, Phylicia. And God definitely had something better in mind. I believed in God at that time, but I wasn't walking with Him. As much as I wish I didn't have confessions to make, I want to be sure you know my history before you decide if you really are willing to be more than just a friend."

"Thank you for telling me, Quinn. For trusting me with the hard things you've been through and —"

He removed his hand from hers and held it palm out to stop her. He needed to get this out before she thought this was only about him gaining her sympathy. He steeled himself with a deep breath. "Part of the reason the whole thing with Heather was so difficult was because we . . . shared things we shouldn't have shared with each other — physically. Obviously, without benefit of marriage. Maybe that doesn't surprise you, but I —"

"I understand what you're saying, Quinn. I don't need details. And . . . I know you're different now."

"I am. I hope you believe that. As much as I wish I could go back and . . . change things, I can't. It's my biggest regret. I know some people would think that sounds crazy, given how this culture has cheapened sex. And . . . I want you to know there was never anyone else — before or after Heather. And there never will be until that woman is my wife. I just never understood how much a physical relationship bonds you to someone — as God intended it to — in a way that is . . . excruciating when that bond is broken."

Phylicia nodded. And for a minute, Quinn wondered if she had a similar confession to make. From things she'd said, he didn't think she'd ever had a serious boyfriend . . . not that "seriousness" made a difference to some people. But he didn't think she was like that. He was pretty sure her faith had been strong from childhood.

In truth, he would be disillusioned and sad if he learned she'd given herself to another man in that way. But he couldn't very well ask forgiveness for his own sins if he wasn't willing to offer her the same. "Is that . . . a deal-breaker for you, Phylicia?"

She studied the counter for a long minute before looking up at him. "I'd be lying if I said I wasn't disappointed. But you said you weren't walking with God then. I know that makes a difference in how you would . . . *behave* now." She smiled down at his dog. "I'd say Mabel's presence here today is proof of your intentions."

His relief came out in laughter. "Score one for Mabel."

She laughed with him, but quickly turned

serious again. "So, no, it's not a deal-breaker. As long as you know that I have the same goal. To be pure before God and to save that part of love for marriage."

"So when I kissed you the other night . . . did that offend you?"

Her smile was pure joy. "No, it did not. In fact," — her blue eyes shone — "I thought maybe you missed." She tapped her cheekbone where he'd landed the first kiss.

He laughed. "I'd love another shot at it." He winked. "They say these things take practice."

She tilted her head, as if daring him.

"Do you know how bad I want to kiss you right now? Properly." He slipped from the stool and edged closer. But he didn't want to take any risks. Not after the conversation they'd just had.

But she didn't flinch. "If Mabel approves — and if you promise not to *miss* this time." She tapped a finger to her lips, marking the spot.

He looked down at the dog. "What do you think, Mabel?"

His dog gave him a look that said, *What are you waiting for, dummy?*

Phylicia must have read Mabel's expression the same way because she giggled — and slid from her own stool.

Quinn took her in his arms and kissed her forehead, breathing in the intoxicating scent of her. He took a small step back and cupped her beautiful face gently between his palms. He tilted her chin up and kissed the space between her eyebrows.

She looked up and met his gaze, all hesitance gone. She stroked a finger down his cheek.

He kissed each eyelid, then — with a knowing smile — the spot on her cheekbone where he'd kissed her that night on her porch.

"You're getting warm," she whispered.

Heart swelling, he touched a finger to her lips. She kissed his fingertips, and he captured her hands in his own and held them to his chest, then bent to match his lips to hers. He wondered if she could feel his heart hammering.

Mabel's dog tags jingled as she rose and moved closer with a little whimper.

Quinn broke the kiss with great reluctance and looked down at his dog. "Yeah, yeah, I know. Time to go."

Phylicia's laughter was music, and Quinn joined in the song while Mabel's tail wagged in double time.

Chapter 35

April

Phee trailed behind Mary as her boss picked up a vase of freshly arranged flowers and carried it to the walk-in cooler at the back of the shop. "Mary, are you *sure* about this? I've already taken so much time off — when Mom was sick and then when we were moving out to the property." She studied her boss. "Are you sure?"

"Phylicia, if you ask me that one more time, I'm going to change my mind! I wouldn't have offered you the time off if I didn't mean it. I figure with your dad's house selling and the work on your cabins, you have plenty of other things to do." Mary rested a hand on Phee's arm, letting it linger, her eyes full of concern. "How are you feeling about that — your house selling?"

The gesture was so like one that Mom would have made. That choked her up more than the thought of the house she'd grown up in, the house where Mom had spent her last days, now belonging to someone else. The closing had happened last week, and it hadn't hit Phee as hard as she'd thought it might. Britt took it a little harder, having lived there more recently, but they were all resigned.

"I know it had to happen," she told Mary. "It's kind of sad, but I guess it's not as sad as having the house sit empty. I drove by yesterday, and there were already bicycles parked on the driveway. That kind of made my heart happy."

"Then it makes my heart happy too." Mary smiled and tucked a strand of graying hair behind her ear. "I'm serious about the time off. Now, if you decide you need the hours, I can always find things for you to do, but in case you hadn't noticed, it's been pretty dead around here. So if you'd like the time off, please take it."

"That would be amazing."

"I'll want you back here regular hours in time for Mother's Day, of course —" A look of chagrin shadowed Mary's lined face. "That was thoughtless. I'm sorry. I know that will be a hard season for you. I remember my first Mother's Day without my mama."

Tears pressed heavy behind Phee's eyelids, as they so often did whenever people offered sympathy. She prayed the tears wouldn't fall. "It'll be a hard weekend whether I'm working or not. But thank you so much for the time off. That would be wonderful. There's so much we want to get done on the cottages, but there just aren't enough hours."

Mary patted her shoulder. "You take the time you need. All I ask in return is a tour of your place once everything is done. It sounds amazing!"

"We'd love to have you as a guest anytime. Our compliments, of course! Thanks again, Mary."

The phone rang in stereo at the cashier's desk and in the back office.

"I'll get it." Phee gave her boss a quick hug before hurrying to the front to pick up. The relief that washed over her took her by surprise. And was instantly replaced by excitement and a flood of ideas for the projects she wanted to complete on the cabins and, especially, on the landscaping.

She picked up the phone. "Langhorne Blooms. How may I help you?"

"Oh, Phee. I was hoping you'd answer."

"Hey, Jo. What's up?"

"We have a problem."

Phee frowned. "What kind of problem?"

"Um . . . the really big kind."

"What? What happened?"

Joanna blew a sigh into the phone, then breathed in. "Remember the other night when I had you and Britt test our Airbnb listing?"

"Yes."

"Well, remember I had to make the site live before you guys could test it?"

"Yes. Get to the point, Jo."

"Um . . . apparently I forgot to take it offline, and it's been live all this time."

"So just take it offline now. Why is that a problem?"

Another deep breath. "It's not. Unless somebody books."

"So?"

"Somebody booked. Three nights next weekend."

"What? No way are we ready for guests! No. Way. Can't you just tell them our calendar is full for those dates?"

"But it *wasn't* full for those dates. That's the problem. When the client went to the site, the calendar was wide open. I hadn't blocked any dates out. I thought we were just testing."

"Well —" She raked a hand through her hair. "The client will surely understand, won't they?"

"They might. But what if they don't? We could start off with the worst review ever and never book another night the rest of our lives."

Phee tapped a pencil on the cash register, frustration mounting. "So . . . what were the dates again?"

"I told you. Next weekend. It's just one couple. Checking in Friday afternoon, checking out Monday morning."

"No. No way, Jo. For starters, I have a date Friday night."

"Again? You two aren't wasting any time, are you?"

It was true. Since that day at his house, she and Quinn had talked almost every day and spent several magical evenings together, walking the wooded trails in Cape Girardeau's parks and sitting in a cozy coffee shop near campus talking for hours. They'd even taken turns helping each other with projects at the cottage and at his house. Always with her sisters — or Mabel — playing chaperone. Despite the underlying sadness at Mom's death and Dad being so far away, Phee couldn't remember being happier.

"Phee? Please hear me out. I really think we can make this work."

"I'm listening." *But not with an open mind.* Joanna was asking the impossible.

"Okay, here's the deal." Jo spoke slowly and clearly as if speaking to a child. "When I took our listing live for you and Britt to test out, I was just plugging in numbers because I had to put some amount in. But I priced the place at two hundred fifty dollars a night. And this couple *still* booked, Phee! That's seven hundred fifty dollars! We can't turn that down."

"We don't have a choice but to turn it down."

"Yes, we do. We can get the cottage ready. I know we can."

She blew out a sigh. "I guess we can put the guests in the master with use of the bathroom. And we can all pile in Britt's room and just pee in the woods and bathe in the river." She paused. "I hope you're catching my sarcasm, Jo."

"Oh, I'm catching it all right. But you don't understand, Phee. This couple rented the whole cottage. That's what we advertised. Remember?"

They'd had such fun the night they created the listing. They'd named their property *The Cottage on Poplar Brook Road* and posted photos that Jo had taken on a perfect spring morning, with the sun splashing patches of light on the hardwood floors. That night, it had all seemed so romantic and ideal. Now, not so much.

"Phee. Are you there? We have to vacate. To honor what we advertised."

"We? *We* did not advertise." She huffed. "So where are we supposed to go?"

"We could stay in one of the cabins."

"No, we couldn't. Remember, they're coming Monday to start on the sheet rock and painting. I had enough trouble getting on their schedule. We can't cancel. And the guy said it would probably take a week to ten days to finish, and they didn't recommend sleeping there until we've aired it out for a few days. Not to mention, it won't be anywhere near ready to sleep in for another month."

Jo sighed. "Too bad Dad's house sold."

"Yeah. Very bad timing. I guess we could get a hotel in town." How could Jo have forgotten to turn off the listing? "Wait . . . Please don't tell me you promised them breakfast too?"

Silence.

"Jo!"

"Settle down, Phee. I have an idea."

"I'm listening." She tapped the pencil harder.

"Dad has a tent in storage. We could go

get it from his unit and camp up in the clearing. It'd be fun! We could even have a campfire in the evening."

"I am *not* camping in the clearing."

"Why not? The weather is supposed to be great — high in the seventies — and who knows, our guests might even enjoy doing s'mores around the fire."

"Right, and you can bring your guitar, and we can all sing *'Kumbaya.'* It'll be perfect." She hoped Jo could "hear" her rolling her eyes.

But her sister only laughed. "Please think about it, Phee. That's a chunk of change. Money we can put into decorating the cabins. Please?"

"Have you asked Britt?" She blew out a hard breath. "Never mind. She'll be all over camping out."

"See? It's perfect!"

"It is not perfect. But . . . that *is* a lot of money."

"So, you're in?"

"Lucky for you, Mary just gave me all next week off. If you promise to help Britt and me, we can probably make the cottage presentable by Friday. But just so you know, I'm not canceling my date Friday night, so you and Britt are on your own greeting our guests and setting up the tent."

"Guests let themselves in. We just tell them where the key is. That's how it works. And no problem with the tent. Britt and I have got this under control."

"I thought you said you hadn't talked to her yet."

"I haven't, but she'll be fine with it." The excitement in Jo's voice was palpable. "You won't be sorry, Phee. This will be a blast."

Phee shook her head. *Famous last words.*

CHAPTER 36

"Is that everything?" Britt tossed a Target bag onto the kitchen counter.

"It'd better be." Phee surveyed the mountain of shopping bags they'd just carried into the cottage. "Jo, did you fail to calculate that it would take almost half of our profits from this first booking just to get the place ready?"

"Don't look at it that way, Phee. This was all stuff we were eventually going to need for the cabins anyway."

"I guess that's true." She shrugged and started unpacking the shopping bags. "Well, let's get a move on. This isn't exactly how I wanted to spend my week off."

Britt shot her a dirty look. "You know, for being in love, you sure have been cranky lately."

"I have not." She stopped short. "Have I?"

"A little." Jo agreed.

"Sorry, guys. I'm just nervous about this gig. Especially since I won't be here to let our guests in tomorrow night." The couple who'd booked the cottage were driving in from Chicago and wouldn't be arriving until six p.m. — an hour after Quinn was to pick her up for dinner and a concert at the Show Me Center arena on campus afterward.

Joanna shook her head. "I told you, Phee, we don't even have to meet them if we don't want to. A lot of people prefer to check themselves in. I've been in close communication with this couple the whole time, and they know where to find the key."

"Everything is under control, sis." Britt gave her a playful shove. "Just chill, will you?"

"I'll try." She unwrapped a new set of sheets and went to put them in the washing machine.

For the next four hours, the three of them worked together getting everything ready except for the bedding. In the morning, they'd put fresh sheets on the beds, hang new towels, and put everything out for coffee and breakfast.

Phee baked cranberry pecan muffins to go with fresh fruit, coffee, and orange juice, and the whole house smelled delicious. She'd enjoyed being in the kitchen —

admittedly because it gave her time to daydream about a day she might share housekeeping and muffin-baking duties with a certain brown-eyed man.

She hadn't said anything to her sisters yet, but she was starting to worry a little about how the plans for the property might change if things got serious between her and Quinn. She smiled to herself. As far as she was concerned, they were already serious. And she thought Quinn felt the same.

She tried not to think too far into the future, but sometimes she couldn't help herself. And as much as she liked the house Quinn was building, she wasn't crazy about the idea of moving into "Heather's house." But husbands hadn't figured into the plans when she and her sisters had talked about doing this Airbnb thing.

Since they'd moved into the cottage, Britt had been doing most of the cooking, cleaning, and grocery shopping, since she still wasn't working. And they'd all agreed it made sense for her not to look for work, at least until the cottages were finished, since so often, someone needed to be here for the work crews and delivery trucks.

Jo brought a load of clean laundry to the kitchen table to fold. "Man, it's a challenge to have guests when you're sleeping in their beds the night before."

"Tell me about it." Britt wiped down the countertops. "I'll be glad when the cabins are finished and we can make those our main rentals."

"Yes, but I doubt we can get two hundred fifty dollars a night for them."

Phee laughed. "I still can't believe you were able to get that much, Jo."

"Maybe we should make the *cottage* our main rental and just stay in the cabins ourselves. Once they're done, I mean." Britt took a pretty dish towel Jo had just folded and hung it over the oven door handle. "Don't anybody use this towel. Under threat of death."

"Oooh, now who's cranky?" Phee smiled even though she was still stinging a little from Britt's comment earlier. "We can figure out all the details later. Let's just get through this weekend first. You got the tent out of storage, right, Jo?"

"It's on my to-do list for tomorrow. And Britt, you'll help me set it up?"

"I'll be here."

Melvin sauntered in from his usual perch on the hearth in the living room. "Oh! I forgot about Melvin. Jo, you're *positive* the couple is okay with Melvin being here in the cottage?"

"Positive. The woman sounded delighted. Remember Melvin was in one of the photos on the website? Apparently, this woman had a tuxedo cat that looked just like him when she was a little girl."

"Aw, that's sweet." Britt chucked Melvin under the chin. "You be a good kitty, you hear, buddy?"

He meowed in response.

"Okay then." Phee stood and stretched. "I think we're good to go. I'm heading to bed."

Phee did one last walk-through, trying to see the cottage the way guests might. It wasn't perfect, but it had plenty of charm about it, and Phee thought their guests would find it quaint and comfortable.

The dogwood had just started blooming, and she cut a bouquet of branches for the mantel. She straightened a couple of pictures on the gallery wall by the fireplace and declared the place guest-ready. Quinn would be here to pick her up in a few minutes.

Jo and Britt were already at the clearing, setting up camp. They'd decided to use the bathroom in the closest cabin in lieu of a chamber pot. Hopefully the fumes wouldn't kill them if they didn't stay any longer than it took to brush their teeth or take a quick shower. It was going to be the height of inconvenience, but she was actually a little excited about it too.

The weather had cooperated beautifully. It was still in the upper sixties and trees were flowering all over the property, with a riot of wildflowers waving their heads among the grasses at the river's edge and the daffodils having their last hurrah.

It struck Phee that if a real estate agent had been showing this property now, it would have been purchased in a bidding war — for far more than she and her sisters paid. She'd grown ever more grateful for Dad's — and Quinn's — insistence that they buy this place.

But more than that, over these past few weeks, for the first time, this cottage and these pretty-beyond-words acres were truly beginning to feel like home. She couldn't help but wonder how much her budding relationship with Quinn had to do with that fact.

Hearing his SUV rolling up the lane, a smile came. Since she'd given herself permission to . . . *fall in love* with Quinn, she felt a little like Jasmine on her magic carpet ride with Aladdin. It truly had opened up a whole new world. Why had she resisted her attraction to Quinn in the beginning? Maybe

God knew she'd needed all her emotional energy to grieve Mom and to process the things she'd learned about her parents. Or maybe she'd just been stubborn and stupid.

Quinn parked in front of the cottage and got out to open her door for her. It might be a little old-fashioned, but she loved his thoughtfulness.

As they drove up the lane, Phee turned in her seat to look up toward the clearing. "Pray for my sisters, would you?"

Quinn turned to her, looking mildly alarmed. "Is everything okay?"

"It's doubtful. They're up in the clearing, pitching a tent as we speak."

Chuckling, Quinn pulled the SUV to the edge of the lane, put it in Park, and bowed dramatically over the steering wheel. "Lord, if ever we've needed you, we need you now . . ."

They both lost it. Phee giggled all the way into town. But she also whispered her own — rather more sincere — prayer that this night wouldn't end in disaster.

CHAPTER 37

It was after ten o'clock when Quinn and Phylicia exited the arena, carried along with an eclectic crowd that ranged from rowdy college students to families with children to a gray-haired couple holding hands. Quinn pointed them out and whispered in her ear, "That'll be us someday."

"Ha! That's you *now,*" she teased.

"Cut it out." He put an arm around her and squeezed her tight enough to make her squeal. "You're going to give me a complex with all the 'old' jokes."

"I've decided I actually *like* older men. So you're safe."

He squeezed tighter, happy for an excuse to do so. The woman had come out of her shell in the last few weeks and had become a consummate flirt, at least with him. She made him laugh. She gave him hope. He liked the man he was when he was with her.

It had been twilight when the concert

began, and now they both looked up at the night sky, obscured somewhat by the campus streetlights.

"Almost a full moon tonight." Quinn pointed, and she followed his line of vision.

"That'll be helpful. For our little camping adventure tonight."

He grinned. "I wonder how Jo and Britt are doing."

Their eyes met, and they burst into laughter, remembering Quinn's roadside prayer. He loved the fact that after only a few short weeks of knowing each other — as more than friends — they had a whole arsenal of private jokes between them. And sometimes it felt as if they were reading each other's minds.

As they made their way to the parking lot, the crowd thinned out. Phylicia fished her phone from a side pocket of her purse. "If you don't mind, I'm going to call Jo and check —" Her phone pinged a dozen times and she gave a little gasp. "What is going on? Look at all these texts."

He looked over her shoulder. "Your sisters?"

She nodded, looking worried.

He steered her out of the flow of the remaining concert-goers to a spot between two parked cars. "You'd better call and see what's going on."

She fumbled with her phone. Jo's photo appeared on the screen, but her call went to voicemail. Phylicia dialed Britt. It rang several times, but finally Britt picked up. Phylicia clicked the speaker icon.

The roar of cars leaving the parking lot and the usual noise of the nighttime campus made it hard for Quinn to hear, but from what he could gather, the crisis involved Melvin.

"Just hurry up and get home, Phee." That from Jo, who was usually the most cool, calm, and collected of the sisters.

"We're just leaving campus. We'll be there as quick as we can." She hung up and started jogging toward where they'd parked.

He had to hustle to catch up with her. "Something happened to Melvin? I couldn't make out everything Britt said."

"I couldn't either, but apparently they decided to take Melvin up to the clearing — something about our guest being allergic to cats — and now he's lost up there." She frowned. "How could that be? That woman *agreed* to having Melvin stay in the cottage. She sounded excited about it. Did she not know she's allergic? I don't get it."

He shrugged. "Maybe her husband wasn't quite so enthusiastic."

"I'm sorry. I know you had your heart set on a milkshake, but I really need to get home."

"Don't worry about it. There'll be plenty of time for ice cream some other day."

As soon as they rounded the curve in the lane, Quinn could see the flashlights arcing through the trees up in the clearing. He pointed them out to Phylicia.

"They must not have found him yet. You can just let me out here, Quinn. I'm sorry about cutting the evening short."

"Don't be ridiculous. I'll help you look." He parked the SUV and turned off the ignition, then reached across her to open the glove compartment. "There should be a decent flashlight in here . . . There it is. Come on."

They jogged to the end of the lane, Quinn holding the flashlight high as they navigated the wide board steps up to the clearing. Phylicia was barely winded, and he was beginning to regret dating a high-school track star. "Have you ever been up here after dark?"

"Never. It's . . . kind of a different place at night." She looked up at him. "I'm really glad you didn't just drop me off."

He stopped and cupped his hands around

his mouth to call Jo and Britt.

But Phylicia tugged on his shirt. “Shhh. Wait till we get to the top of the stairway. I don’t want to make a commotion and upset our very first Airbnb guests.”

They climbed on to the top and, in unison, called out to her sisters. “Jo? Britt?”

After they’d waded a few yards through dense trees and brush, the clearing opened up. The tent was pitched between two of the long log benches and glowed from within, thanks to lanterns. Phylicia called to her sisters again.

From the corner of his eye, Quinn spotted movement. “There they are!” He pointed to the far side of the clearing, where two flashlight beams flitted up and down.

They trudged across the clearing, calling again.

Jo and Britt shined their lights directly at them. Then seeing who it was, they dashed across the clearing. Britt stumbled, but caught herself.

When she reached them, she rambled on at ninety miles an hour, her voice wavering. “That stupid woman decided at nine o’clock that she didn’t want Melvin sleeping in the house with them.”

Phylicia put a hand on Britt’s arm. “Calm down, sis. Why didn’t they want him there?”

"She wouldn't say. I think she just probably didn't want to get any cat hair on her precious cashmere sweater."

"Britt . . ." Phylicia went into a mother-hen mode that Quinn rarely saw.

Joanna shined her flashlight down the hill. "He must have gone off the property, because we have covered every square inch of this clearing with no sign of him."

Quinn pointed his flashlight in the same direction. "Melvin's not declawed, is he?"

Britt shook her head. "No. Why?"

"Then I really think he'll be fine. Cats can defend themselves in a lot of ways. And the worst he'd run into up here is a coyote, or maybe a raccoon bigger than he is. But I think he could outrun either one."

Jo wrinkled her nose. "I'm more worried about him cozying up to a skunk."

Quinn resisted mentioning that Melvin looked quite a bit like a skunk himself. "He's probably just taking advantage of his freedom and exploring the big, wide world." Quinn was probably in danger of being accused of lacking compassion, but he felt sure the cat would come back as soon as it got hungry.

But Britt was near tears. "If anything happens to him, I'll never forgive myself."

He'd forgotten until now that Melvin had

been Myra's cat. Suddenly it seemed more important to find him than it had a few minutes ago. "Do you have any of his food up here?"

Britt nodded. "In his carrier."

"Canned food or dry?"

"Both." Britt sounded defensive.

Joanna gave a little snort. "She wanted to bring the litter box up here too. Until I pointed out that this entire property is one big litter box as far as Melvin is concerned."

For Britt's sake, Quinn swallowed back his laughter. "Maybe if we open the can of cat food, that'll get him up here. It has a much stronger smell than dry food. When was the last time Melvin ate?"

"I don't know. His bowl was empty, so probably pretty recently."

Phylicia put an arm around her sister. "It'll be all right, Britt. He'll be fine." Quinn thought he detected a thread of worry in Phylicia's voice too.

For the next hour, they circled the woods with a can of stinky cat food, calling Melvin, rustling bushes, and turning over logs and even leaves. Quinn made them stop several times to listen, but once the crickets started their nightly chirping, it was hard to hear anything else.

They'd first split up, going four different

directions. But Quinn argued that tactic might confuse Melvin, so the four of them searched together. The term "herding cats" came to Quinn's thoughts several times. He still thought it would be best if they sat in the clearing and waited for Melvin to come to them.

"Maybe we should be looking up," Phylicia said, craning her neck toward the treetops.

"Melvin has never climbed a tree in his life." But Britt looked up too.

"There's always a first time." Joanna followed their line of vision. "He's never had a chance to climb a tree. But you know he'd give it a try if he could."

Quinn shined his flashlight back and forth on the trees overhead. "Wouldn't it be funny if this whole time, he's been up there watching us search?"

Silence from the sisters. Apparently, there wasn't much funny about Melvin being missing. Quinn made a note to self: *Just shut up and search.*

Joanna walked a few feet from the group and looked up. "I wonder if he would come down if we —" A muffled ring came from her coat pocket. She fished the phone out. "This is Joanna . . ."

She listened for a few seconds, then strode

purposefully over to the three of them, waving her free hand. "You guys! He's down at the house!"

Britt pounced on Joanna's phone, but Jo turned away from her, speaking into the phone. "Yes, we'll come right away. I'm so sorry for the disturbance."

"Someone found him?" Britt's eyes were bright with hope.

Joanna hung up, muttering something about "that witch staying in the cottage," then turned to explain to the waiting search party. "Apparently, 'that cat' is howling outside the back door of the cottage, and could we please do something about it?"

"Oh, we'll do something about it all right." Britt clenched her fists and paced the floor of the clearing. "I vote we kick her sorry self out and tell her to never come back."

"Britt! We can't do that." Phylicia spoke softly. "These people are counting on having a place to say. And they're paying us good money."

Joanna laughed. "That's not what you were saying when I was trying to convince you not to cancel the reservation."

"I didn't say" — Phylicia huffed — "oh, never mind."

"Come on, Britt. Let's go get him." Joanna

started for the stairs. "You bring the carrier. And make sure it's latched this time."

"It was latched!" Britt grabbed the carrier from the tent and hurried after her sister.

"And be nice!" Phylicia called after them.

"I know, I know," Britt grumbled. "These people are paying us good money."

"Hey, listen . . ." Quinn waited for the sisters to come back close enough to hear him. "You guys would be more than welcome to come out to my place and stay if you want. I don't have beds in the guest rooms yet, but you could bring your sleeping bags. At least you'd have a roof over your heads. And a bathroom."

Phee looked hopefully at her sisters, but she knew better.

Joanna zipped her coat up to her chin. "Thanks for the offer, Quinn, but we're kind of excited about having this little initiation for our woods."

"Yeah, thanks, Quinn." Britt hefted the cat carrier. "That's thoughtful of you, but you can't really expect us to bring Melvin to a house with a cat-eating dog."

Quinn smirked and turned to Phylicia. "That's something we might have to talk about at some point."

Britt tossed her head. "There's nothing to discuss."

Shaking his head, Quinn stepped out of the way and tried not to laugh, still mystified by the world of women. And sisters. These three in particular.

Chapter 38

Quinn held up a hand and cocked his head, listening. "Sounds like all's quiet on the western front."

"Yep. I think they're all asleep, except maybe Melvin." Phee laughed softly and leaned her head back against Quinn's knees, trying to get comfortable on their perch on the wooden steps below the clearing.

Above them, all was quiet in the tent where her sisters slept. The crickets had ceased their noise, and now the only sounds were the distant lapping of the river behind the cabins, the occasional hoot of an owl, or a plaintive cry from Melvin, who was safely crated and zipped into the tent with Jo and Britt for good measure.

It was after midnight, but Phee and Quinn had sat here on the steps and talked about everything . . . and about nothing. And she'd loved every minute with him.

She looked into the night sky, the moon

high over the trees now, and a myriad of stars twinkling down on them.

Quinn chuckled.

"What's so funny?"

"I've got to say, that was not the evening I was expecting."

"Better than a milkshake though, right?"

"Almost. Not quite. I could go for a milkshake about now."

She laughed. "I'd go down to the cottage and make you one if there wasn't a witch staying there right now."

"Your sisters are something else."

"I know, but what would I do without them?" She tipped her head back and smiled up at him, but turned serious when she realized he was watching her with an expression she couldn't decipher. "What?"

"You are such an enigma."

"I am?"

"I honestly do not know how you escaped marriage."

"What are you talking about? Escaped?"

"Phylicia, you should have a thousand guys beating your door down."

"Stop." She hoped he couldn't see that she was blushing.

"I'm serious. There is no way that you should have been here . . . available . . . when I was finally ready to find you. I'm just going to chalk it up to God saving you for me."

"That goes both ways, you know."

"And thank the good Lord for that." He brushed a strand of hair away from her face.

"To be honest" — she wrapped her arms around herself — "I've worried sometimes. That something might be wrong with me . . . that I never found anyone I liked enough to go out with more than once or twice, let alone *marry.* I did have a *few* show interest." She nudged him, grinning so he wouldn't worry that he'd hurt her feelings.

"I remember. You could count them on one-and-a-half hands. That's what you told me."

"You remember that?"

"I remember everything about you, Phylicia."

"It wasn't that I didn't want to be married. I just always wanted a marriage like my parents had. The kind of love that gives you a reason to live, a reason to breathe. But after I thought Dad had betrayed Mom — and vice versa — I wondered if any such marriage had ever existed. I even started to feel *grateful* I hadn't wasted any more time on boyfriends. And so when you started to show an interest, of course, I . . . rejected you almost immediately."

He frowned. "So I noticed."

"It's funny. I was thinking about that earlier this evening, while I waited for you to pick me up." That seemed like a lifetime ago. "I don't think any of my . . . *reluctance* was about *you* at all, Quinn. It was about the whole idea of loving someone. Really loving them, sacrificially and unselfishly. Like I know now, my parents *did.* So few people have that kind of love."

He shrugged. "I know. It's a little scary. And scarier the older I get. Because it's so rare. Shoot, I know people my age who are already on their second marriages."

"That's so sad. But I kind of get it. I mean, I thought Dad had proved there was no such thing as a good man. And who could I trust if I couldn't trust my own father?" She looked up at him, feeling sheepish. "Not fair, I know. To you *or* Dad. I'm just telling you how it was in my mind."

"I understand that. I really do." In the dim light of the hovering moon, Quinn's face had a bluish glow. "I wish I'd understood better . . . when I was working so hard to woo you."

She grinned. "Well, it didn't help that you were trying to sell me that money pit at the same time you were trying to woo me." She pointed down to where a few dim lights flickered from the cottage. She could imagine their guests — likely very nice people who just didn't want to share their little getaway with a strange cat — curled up on the sofa, enjoying their time at The Cottage on Poplar Brook Road. And none the wiser to the mayhem that had gone on up here in the clearing.

"Money pit?" Quinn scooted down to sit on the step beside her. He leaned back and studied her, as if trying to be sure she was teasing. "You don't regret it, do you? Buying the property?"

"Oh, Quinn, no." She gazed up into the canopy of stars sparkling overhead. "This place . . . all of it . . . is possibly the best thing that ever happened to me."

"Whoa! Wait . . . what am I? Chopped liver?"

Giggling, she gave him a little punch. "Watch it, old man." But she let her smile fade, not ever wanting him to doubt. "Quinn, the only thing that would make this place more perfect would be to share it with you. To have you here always."

That infernal spark came to Quinn's eyes. "That sounds like a proposal to me."

"Well, if it does, then please say yes."

He cocked his head, his eyes never leaving hers. "I'm not teasing, Phylicia."

"I'm not either." Her pulse beat erratically. What had made her so bold? But she knew the answer — *hope.*

"I don't know . . . Are you going to be okay if this is our story? Forever after?"

"What do you mean?"

"That *you* proposed to *me*?" The twinkle was still in those brown eyes of his, but there was an earnestness behind it now. "I've always thought you were kind of a traditional girl."

"I guess I am."

At that, Quinn took her hand in his and took a knee on the step beside her.

Tears flooded her throat. "Yes."

He laughed down at her, but put a finger over his lips. "You can say yes, but I'm still going to ask the question. Just so I can say I did." Now he pulled her closer. "Phylicia Beth Chandler . . . *Phee* . . . I love you with everything that is in me. Will you marry me?"

Her heart swelled. "Oh, Quinn. *Yes.* I . . . I love you too. I don't know what took me so long to come around."

He made a goofy face. "I don't either, because we elderly don't have all the time in the world, you know."

"There *isn't* enough time in the world." It came out in a whisper, and sadness threatened to overwhelm the joy she was feeling — that Mom hadn't lived long enough to share this joy. That she and Quinn were getting a late start. That she'd wasted too much of her life worrying about things that didn't really matter.

A tear escaped and rolled down her cheek. Quinn wiped it away with his thumb and pressed a kiss to her lips before pulling her to sit back on the step beside him. "Don't cry, Phee. We're going to pack a whole lot of living into however many years God gives us. I promise."

She smiled through the tears. Believing him completely. But thrown by a tiny detail. She looked up at him, stroked his cheek, loving its roughness beneath her palm. "You called me Phee. Have you *ever* called me by my nickname?"

He grinned. "I wondered if you'd notice. Do you know why I didn't like it . . . at first . . . your nickname?"

She shook her head, trying to remember if he'd ever told her, but drawing a blank.

"Nobody likes paying a fee for something. I never liked thinking of you that way. Besides" — he traced his finger along the bridge of her nose — "Phylicia is such a pretty name. I've always thought so."

"So, why did you call me Phee just now?"

"Because I'd pay any price to make you mine."

"Oh, Quinn." She didn't want to cry. Not now.

Seeming to sense that, he winked. "And because it cost me a small fortune to finally win you over."

She giggled. "Well, it might take a while, but I'll try to make it worth your time."

He kissed her again, long and slow. "You already have, sweet woman. You already have."

A NOTE FROM DEB

Dear reader,

Thank you for choosing the first book in my Chandler Sisters Novels series! I don't think readers ever fully understand how very much we authors treasure you and value your opinion. I always say that hearing from a reader is like fuel to my writer's engine. You are the very reason I write!

When I set out to write a series about three sisters, I couldn't help but think of my own sisters. As I said in my dedication, Vicky, Kim, and Beverly were the first friends I knew, and while Kim has been in heaven for many years now (tragically killed in a car accident as a twenty-one-year-old newlywed), Vicky and Bev remain my dearest of friends. We've been blessed to live in the same town for most of the past six years, and my sisters would be in my Top Five list for any road trip or girls' night out.

I knew writing about sisters might be

fraught with tension as I did my best to not make my Chandler sisters too much like my real-life sisters. I was not successful! Let's just say that any lovely and winsome qualities in Phylicia, Joanna, and Britt Chandler came straight from my own sisters. And any of the annoying or frustrating qualities of the Chandler sisters are purely inventions of my imagination (or perhaps those traits spring from my own personality? After all, I was the bossy eldest.)

All jesting aside, I hope this novel ultimately shows sisterhood in the beautiful, loving light I've known it to shine. Those we shared our childhood home with understand and know us like no one else can. And — hopefully — they love us despite our many flaws. In short, sisters are a gift from God and a blessing beyond words. (And brothers too! My dear, longsuffering brother Brad managed to grow up unscathed, despite being the lone brother of four sisters. Poor guy!)

My deepest thanks goes out to the many people who made this book possible. My agent, Steve Laube; my editors at Gilead, Becky Philpott, Karli Jackson, along with Lynne Everett; my beloved critique partner and friend, Tamera Alexander, and others who read my manuscript and offered suggestions and corrections — especially my dear friend Terry Stucky and my sister Vicky Miller. Last and most of all, thanks to my best friend and love of my life, my husband Ken Raney, without whom none of this would be any fun at all, and with whom life has been more amazing than I ever dreamed possible. God is good, and I am blessed beyond words.

Deborah Raney
July 24, 2018

BOOK CLUB DISCUSSION GUIDE

SPOILER ALERT: These discussion questions contain spoilers that may give away elements of the plot.

1. In Reason to Breathe, the Chander sisters have become even closer to one another because of the recent death of their mother from cancer. Why do you think adversity often brings siblings — and perhaps especially sisters — closer together? Does it always work that way? If adversity brings division, what might be the reason? What has your personal experience been?

2. The three Chandler sisters choose to buy property together with their shared inheritance from their mother. In essence, because of the Airbnb possibility, they choose to go into business together. Do you believe this was a good idea? Why or

why not? What pitfalls might they face, especially as the years go by?

3. The sisters are stunned to learn that their father, Turner Chandler, plans to remarry only two months after their mother's death. How much input do you think adult children should have in such a decision for widowed parents? Were the sisters justified in their concerns over their father having a new relationship so quickly?

4. Some might say that Turner Chandler did most of his grieving during the three years that his wife was dying from cancer. Do you think that's a valid conclusion? Is it possible to grieve someone before they actually pass away? What is a reasonable time frame for a person to "move on" to a new chapter of life after the death of a spouse?

5. Phylicia, the oldest sister, has been attracted to her father's colleague as a young woman, but now that he seems interested in her, she is shunning his attention, and worried about their twelve-year age gap. What do you think about age gaps larger than ten years between couples? Does is

make a difference when both parties are older?

6. Given their ages (Phylicia 29 and Quinn 42), what are some of the age-related issues they might face when their friendship turns romantic? How might their age difference affect their relationship when they are older, say 49 and 62? Or 59 and 72?

7. To their shock, the three sisters learn that their mother had been married (and divorced) before she married their father. They feel betrayed to learn this news after their mother's death. But Quinn asks Phylicia, "Do you really think parents owe their children all the details of their lives before said children were even born?" What do you think? Why or why not?

8. Phylicia also discovers evidence that Turner Chandler may not actually be her biological father, even though he has assumed the role of father to her even before her birth. Do you think her response to this news is justified? How would you respond to such news? Would it change the way you viewed the man who'd raised you as his own?

9. Phylicia's mother, Myra, either wasn't sure about who had fathered Phylicia, or she chose not to reveal the truth, even to her husband. But Turner suspected the truth and never confronted his wife or discussed it with Phylicia. Why might each of them have made the choices they did about telling the truth? Is refraining from revealing a truth as serious as out-and-out lying about something?

10. For a time, Phylicia feels that her whole life has been a lie. How can she forgive her mother for keeping this secret when Myra is no longer there to discuss it with her? If the secret is true, does it change the happy childhood Phylicia thought she had? Does it negate the happy marriage Turner and Myra shared?

11. The secret of Phylicia's paternity isn't the only secret in the novel. Quinn is holding a secret about his relationship with Heather. How do you decide how soon to reveal secrets with the person you're falling in love with? Is there a danger in revealing a secret too soon? Is there a danger of waiting too long? Is it possible to have a solid relationship with someone when there is a significant, profound

secret that one person is keeping from the other?

12. By the end of the novel, Phylicia has decided not to pursue testing to find out for sure which man is her father. Given her circumstances and reasons, do you think you would make the same choice in her shoes? Or would you feel compelled to find out the truth? If so, why? And how would knowing the truth change your attitude or your circumstances? How might knowing the truth change Phylicia's relationship with the man she has always called "Dad"?

13. Do you have a sister or sisters? If so, what is your relationship with each other? If you have more than one sister, are you closer to one than the others? What factors do you think affect that dynamic? How has your relationship to your sisters (or siblings) changed from when you were children? Do you expect the relationship you now have as adults to change again as the years go by? How might it change? What might cause those changes?

ABOUT THE AUTHOR

Deborah Raney dreamed of writing a book since the summer she read Laura Ingalls Wilder's Little House books and discovered that a Kansas farm girl could, indeed, grow up to be a writer. Her more than 35 books have garnered multiple industry awards including the RITA Award, HOLT Medallion, National Readers' Choice Award, Carol Award, Silver Angel from Excellence in Media, and have three times been Christy Award finalists.

Her first novel, *A Vow to Cherish,* shed light on the ravages of Alzheimer's disease. The novel inspired the highly acclaimed World Wide Pictures film of the same title and continues to be a tool for Alzheimer's families and caregivers. Deborah is on faculty for several national writers' conferences and serves on the advisory board of the 2700-member American Christian Fiction Writers organization.

She and her husband, Ken Raney, traded small-town life in Kansas — the setting of many of Deb's novels — for life in the city of Wichita. They have four children and a growing brood of precious grandchildren who all live much too far away.

Website: deborahraney.com
Facebook Group: Deborah Raney Readers Page
Instagram: @deborahraney
Twitter: @AuthorDebRaney
Pinterest: @deborahraney

The employees of Thorndike Press hope you have enjoyed this Large Print book. All our Thorndike, Wheeler, and Kennebec Large Print titles are designed for easy reading, and all our books are made to last. Other Thorndike Press Large Print books are available at your library, through selected bookstores, or directly from us.

For information about titles, please call:
(800) 223-1244

or visit our website at:
gale.com/thorndike

To share your comments, please write:
Publisher
Thorndike Press
10 Water St., Suite 310
Waterville, ME 04901

COUNTY LIBRARY
TILLAMOOK, ORE.